About the authors

Heidi McLaughlin is a *New York Times* and *USA Today* best-selling author of The Beaumont Series, *The Boys of Summer*, and *The Archers*. Originally from the Pacific Northwest, she now lives in picturesque Vermont with her husband, two daughters, and their three dogs. In 2012, Heidi turned her passion for reading into a full-fledged literary career, writing over twenty novels, including the acclaimed *Forever My Girl*, which has been adapted into a film starring Alex Roe and Jessica Rothe. When writing isn't occupying her time, you can find her sitting courtside at either of her daughters' basketball games.

New York Times and *USA Today* bestselling author **L. P. Dover** is a Southern belle living in North Carolina with her husband and two beautiful girls. Before she began her literary journey she worked in periodontics, enjoying the wonderment of dental surgeries. She loves to write, but she also loves to play golf, go on mountain hikes and white-water rafting, and has a passion for singing. Her two youngest fans expect a concert each and every night before bedtime, usually Christmas carols. Dover has written countless novels in several different genres, but she has found a new passion in romantic comedy, especially involving sexy golfers. Who knew the sport could be so dirty and fun to write about.

Cindi Madsen is a *USA Today* bestselling author of contemporary romance and young adult novels. She sits at her computer every chance she gets, plotting, revising, and falling in love with her characters. Sometimes it makes her a crazy person. Without it, she'd be even crazier. She has way too many shoes but can always find a reason to buy a new pretty pair, especially if they're sparkly, colorful, or super tall. She loves music, dancing, and wishes summer lasted all year long. She lives in Colorado (where summer is most definitely NOT all year long) with her husband and three children.

USA Today bestselling author **R. J. Prescott** was born in Cardiff, South Wales, and studied law at the University of Bristol, England. Four weeks before graduation, she fell in love with a crazy firefighter and stayed in Bristol. Ten years later, she convinced her husband to move back to Cardiff, where they now live with their two sons. Juggling work, writing, and family doesn't leave a lot of time, but curling up on the sofa with a cup of tea and a bar of chocolate for family movie night is definitely the best part of her week.

Amy Briggs is a Texas-based writer. Formerly a firefighter and EMT in New Jersey living next to a military base, Amy was initially drawn to creating stories around emergency services and the military and draws on her experiences to show the depth and emotional side of the lifestyle. Her love of fairy tales carries through each of her novels, and she hopes to inspire readers to fall in love with love.

Christmas With You

Heidi McLaughlin,
L. P. Dover, Cindi Madsen,
R. J. Prescott, Amy Briggs

piatkus

PIATKUS

First published in the US in 2018 by Grand Central Publishing,
a division of Hachette Book Group USA Inc.

First published in Great Britain in 2018 by Piatkus

13 5 7 9 10 8 6 4 2

A CIP catalogue record for this book is available from the British Library.

ISBN 978-0-349-42166-7

Typeset in Caslon by M Rules
Printed and bound in Great Britain by Clays Ltd, Elcograf S.p.A.

Papers used by Piatkus are from well-managed forests
and other responsible sources.

MIX
Paper from
responsible sources
FSC® C104740

Piatkus
An imprint of
Little, Brown Book Group
Carmelite House
50 Victoria Embankment
London EC4Y 0DZ

An Hachette UK Company
www.hachette.co.uk

www.littlebrown.co.uk

Contents

Snowflake Lane Inn

L. P. DOVER

*This book is dedicated to everyone
who loves Christmas just as
much as I do.*

Chapter One

Colin

"Looks like everything's ready to go," I said, walking through the house one last time. The place was spotless. But was it good enough for a diva like Layla Aberdeen? Let's hope so because she has rented it for the next year.

My sister, Brianna, walked in with a basket full of goodies and set it on the table. She was thirteen years younger than me. Sometimes it felt like I was her father instead of her brother. For the past ten years, I guess you could say I was. Our father died of lung cancer, and I was the one who had to help take care of her.

Her dark brown hair was in curls down her back, and she was dressed up as if she was going to a dance club. I looked at her like she'd lost her mind. "What are you doing?"

Grinning sheepishly, she rearranged the chocolates and the bottle of wine. "It's a basket for Layla." Brianna was a twenty-three-year-old college student who loved anything about fashion, even though she was going to school to be a nurse.

Guess it didn't really surprise me that she wanted to make an impression on Layla Aberdeen.

"Since when do we do that?" I asked.

She waved me off. "Since now. One of the top designers in the world is coming to stay here. I can't wait to meet her. What time did she say she was coming into town?"

I hadn't personally spoken to Layla, but my real estate agent had. "Jane told me two o'clock. She's going to meet Ms. Aberdeen then. Is that why you're all dressed like . . . " I waved my hand down her body. "Like that?" She had on a silver sparkly top that hung off her shoulders along with a pair of jeans and heels. Not exactly something you see a lot of people wearing in the winter.

Brianna looked down at her clothes and then glared at me. "Seriously? You're so clueless. These are Layla's designs." She bounced on her feet. "I wish I could be here to welcome her. Think I can maybe hang around and casually stop by when she shows up?"

Grabbing the keys off the counter, I nodded toward the door. "That's a bad idea. You're bound to see her around town. Just don't get your hopes up. She looks like she'd be a . . . "

"Colin," she shrieked, "you don't know her."

I shrugged and followed her out the door, walking close so I could catch her if she slipped on the snow. The air was cold and crisp, a perfect December day with clear blue skies. It wouldn't be that way for long. We had a snowstorm brewing that'd hit us by the end of the night. "She's probably like every other Hollywood celebrity. Full of herself and obsessed with money."

Brianna shook her head. "I don't think Layla's like that. She was devastated when her last line didn't do well. Honestly, I think it's a good idea she's coming here. She has to be under a lot of pressure."

We got in my truck and headed down the road. "Maybe so, but I don't want you bothering her, Bri."

She huffed and focused her attention at the window. "Fine. But you're shattering my dreams, brother."

I burst out laughing. "You'll get over it. I'm going to go ahead and drop you off at the inn. Mom's waiting for you. I have some things I need to pick up in town."

"Okay."

The Snowflake Lane Inn was one of the top-rated inns in all of Friendship. After my grandmother died, she left it to me in her will. It was supposed to go to my father, but since he died before she did, she passed it down to me. I intended to keep her legacy alive by keeping it the way she always wanted it. We turned onto Snowflake Lane, the gravel kicking up underneath my truck. The road was lined with magnolia trees, all decked out in soft white lights, and the white fence was draped in garland. It was exactly how it'd been decorated for decades at Christmastime.

Our mother was on the front porch with the town mayor, George Lingerfelt, when we pulled up. Brianna hopped out of the truck and said hello to George as he made his way down to me. I lowered my window and held out my hand. "Mayor Lingerfelt," I said as he shook my hand, "what brings you by this morning?"

"I came to see you. Is everything ready for the tree lighting tomorrow?" George was in his late forties, short and a little plump in the middle, with salt and pepper hair.

I nodded. "I wired everything up first thing this morning. You should be good to go."

His smile widened. "Excellent. Will I see you there?"

"Of course, I wouldn't miss it. But right now, I need to run into town. I'll see you tomorrow." I waved at my mother and headed back down the road. Everywhere you looked, everything was decorated for Christmas. We had tourists who came up here just to experience the lights. It was what kept Snowflake Inn one of the best places to stay during the holidays. We get booked a year in advance.

Once I reached Main Street, I parked behind the general store and walked around to the front. The best coffee shop in town was right beside it, and sitting on the bench out front was a man I'd never seen before. By the old, filthy clothes and skin, I'd almost say he was homeless, not exactly something that was common in our little town. We all knew each other, but I didn't recognize him at all.

"Good morning," I called out, approaching him slowly. The man looked up at me and smiled, his face slightly wrinkled and smudged with dirt. His dark brown hair was hidden underneath a black cap and he had crystal blue eyes. He stood, and I shook his hand. "It's a little chilly this morning, don't you think?"

He blew out a breath and rubbed his hands together. "It is. I smell snow too. I think we're going to get some tonight."

"The news this morning said we have a storm coming in, at least six inches of snow." Which, obviously, wouldn't do him any good if he had nowhere to go. "I'm Colin Jennings," I said, keeping the conversation going. "Are you new in town? I don't think I've seen you around before."

His lips pulled back into a kind smile. "Yes, I'm new to this quaint town. The name's Gabe. I rode a bus in from Boston. I didn't know where it was going to drop me off at, but I like this place."

The thought of him being alone in the impending snow didn't sit well with me. "Do you have a place to stay tonight?" I asked him. Gabe focused back on me, almost like he was studying me curiously. Clearing my throat quickly, I held up a hand. "Not that I'm assuming you have nowhere to go, but if you don't, I know a place where you can stay."

His lips pulled back into a smile. "That's very kind of you. I haven't run into too many people willing to help an old man like me."

"It's no trouble at all," I said. "I have an extra room at the Snowflake Lane Inn that I always keep open." It was a small room with a twin bed, but it'd give him a warm place to stay.

Gabe placed a hand on my shoulder. "Thank you for your generosity, but I'll be fine. I appreciate the offer."

"Are you sure? You could always help me around the inn. There's always something needing fixing."

He chuckled, and it sounded so carefree. His hand slipped off my shoulder, and he waved me off. "I'm sure. Thank you again. I know where to find you if things change."

I held out my hand, and he shook it again. "Sounds good, Gabe. You take care of yourself." I nodded at the door to the café. "Want anything to eat? They have awesome blueberry muffins in there."

Gabe shook his head. "Don't trouble yourself with that. You've already done enough for me as it is by offering me a place to stay."

I patted his shoulder. "Just trying to help."

He smiled again. "I appreciate that."

A part of me wondered if he was just being polite in not accepting my hospitality. Pride was a huge thing for me, and I could see myself doing the same thing if the situation were reversed. Then again, maybe he did have somewhere to go, and I shouldn't assume he was homeless by the way he looked. There were days I was covered in dirt after doing the landscaping at the inn.

The bell jingled on the door as I walked into the café. It was warm, a definite contrast from the chilly air outside. I was accustomed to the cold, especially since I'd been living in crazy winter weather my whole life.

Jill waved from behind the counter and placed a cup of coffee and a blueberry muffin onto the counter. "You know me well," I said, laughing.

She shrugged. "It's what you've ordered for the past two years. When I saw you outside with that man, I figured I'd get it ready for you."

I gave her the money and smiled. "Thanks. You're the best."

"Anytime."

Peering out the window, I saw that Gabe was still there, watching people walk by with a smile on his face. Not many people acknowledged him, and others hurried to get away. It was obvious the people of Friendship weren't accustomed to seeing a strange man dressed in shabby clothes and roaming the streets.

"Jill," I called out. I glanced at her over my shoulder and nodded at Gabe. "Do you mind fixing another coffee and grabbing another muffin for me?"

A sad smile spread across her face. "Of course."

Grabbing the extra coffee and muffin, I took it all outside. Gabe was still sitting on the bench, so I set his coffee and muffin down beside him. With a heavy sigh, he looked at it and then up at me. "You are a miracle, son."

Chapter Two

Layla

When I decided to rent the house in Friendship, I knew it was going to be in the middle of nowhere, but I didn't realize how far away it was from the main town. There was a dusting of snow on the ground, and it terrified me to drive on it. As long as I was in my house before the snowstorm hit tonight, I'd be fine. It wasn't that I was scared of how people would drive around me, it was the fact that I was afraid for them given the way I drove in the snow. I'd end up in a ditch somewhere, stranded in the freezing cold.

I was used to the bustling streets of big cities. I'd lived in New York for a while during college and then moved back to my hometown of Charleston, South Carolina. I already missed the smell of the ocean and the feeling of the warm breeze dancing around me. Moving to a place as desolate as Friendship really put in perspective how sad my life had become. Luckily, in a small town, there was a ninety-nine percent chance no one would know who I was.

I pulled into the driveway and looked up at the house. The place was small, just three bedrooms and two baths, with dark blue siding and a burgundy front door. It wasn't what I was used to, but it was quaint and by the river with not a neighbor in sight. All I wanted was some peace and quiet to rejuvenate my mind. My career depended on it.

A woman walked out of the house, dressed in a navy pantsuit with her brown hair in a bun. She waved as I got out of the car. "Good afternoon, Ms. Aberdeen. I'm so glad you made it safely."

"Me too," I said with a laugh. I walked toward her and held out my hand. "You must be Jane?"

She nodded and shook my hand. "I am. I wanted to welcome you to Friendship and make sure you got settled before I leave. My husband and I are spending the holidays in Bermuda. We wanted a change of scenery this year."

"Nice. It's amazing down there. You'll love it." I'd been a couple of times over the years.

Jane held up the keys and dangled them in the air. "Here are the house keys." She pointed at the second key. "This one opens the back door."

"Thanks," I said, taking them from her. "How is cell service around here?"

She waved me off. "You're not that far from everything. Cell service can be pretty spotty out here though. The closest supermarket is fifteen minutes away, and so is our downtown square. We have tons of shops and an amazing bakery. We're also having a tree lighting tomorrow night. Might be a good way for you to meet some of the locals."

It sounded exciting, but I didn't know if I was ready to be around the public. "I'll think about it. I still need to get settled in."

We walked into the house, and it smelled like cinnamon apples. I breathed it in and smiled. It made me feel like I was at my cabin in the Appalachian Mountains. Unfortunately, I had to sell it when my business started to tank. I followed Jane into the living room, and there was an amazing view of the river. The furniture was made of brown leather, and the whole place had a warm, yet rustic feel.

"Does everything look okay?" Jane asked.

"Yes," I said, turning to face her. "This house is amazing."

A wide grin spread across her face. "Great. I hope you enjoy it here. Friendship is an amazing little town. I've lived here all my life."

I shook her hand again. "Thanks, Jane. I'm sure I'll love it here as long as I have cell service. Have fun in Bermuda."

"Oh, I will. Take care of yourself, Ms. Aberdeen."

She walked out, and I stood at the door, breathing in the clean, frosty air. The sun shone across the snow, making it glitter and shine. It was breathtaking.

Once Jane was gone, I brought in my suitcases and unpacked. Since I had no food in the refrigerator, I left to find a grocery store. Jane was right, the cell phone service wasn't that great, so I drove around and finally got good reception when I reached downtown Friendship. It was like I stepped into a Hallmark movie. I parked on the street and got out. The wind had picked up, so I buttoned my jacket. I definitely wasn't used to the cold.

The general store was up ahead, so I decided to check it out. I always loved the ones in the mountains back home. It was a place you were for sure going to run into some nice people. That was what I loved about small towns. I walked in and looked around at all the provisions. I grabbed a few jars of homemade apple butter and pickled vegetables. My grandmother used to make them both on her own until she passed away. My favorite was her pickled beets.

Arms full of goodies, I walked up to the front and set them on the counter. The man at the register looked at me, his face wrinkled with age and his snow-white hair combed over. I smiled, only he didn't smile back. In fact, he looked uninterested in talking to me at all. "It's cold out there today, isn't it?" I said, hoping to strike up a conversation.

He snorted. "It's December. What'd you expect?"

There were other people in the store, staring at me, clearly not welcoming either. Was it my Southern accent? It was obvious I was an outsider. Clearing my throat, I paid for my things and hurried out of the store, only to run right into someone.

"Oh my goodness, I'm so sorry," I shrieked. The man had fallen to his knees, and I grabbed his arm to help him up. "Please forgive me. I came out of the store too fast."

The man grunted as I pulled him upright. "It's okay, miss. I know you didn't do it on purpose." He was taller than me with dark brown, shaggy hair and a beard. By the looks of the tattered clothes, old boots, and dirty skin, it made me wonder if he was homeless. His bright blue eyes stared right into mine, and then he looked down at the paper bag hanging on my arm. "It's a good thing you didn't drop your glass jars."

Taking a deep breath, I nodded. "True."

His brows lifted. "You sure you're okay? You walked out in a hurry."

I glanced into the window of the general store and shrugged. "They weren't exactly nice to me in there. I wanted to get out of there as fast as I could. Guess I thought a small town like this would be a little more welcoming."

The man chuckled and looked around. "From what I can

tell, the people around here don't like change. You're different. I think it's the clothes that make you stand out." I looked down at my designer outfit and high-heeled boots.

"I thought it was my accent," I replied with a laugh.

He held out his hand. "That too. Don't worry, though, they'll come around. So far, I've met several nice people. Don't give up on them just yet. My name's Gabe."

I shook his hand. "Layla. I moved here from Charleston."

"It's nice to meet you, Layla," he said, letting my hand go. "What brings you to Friendship?"

"Lots of things, I guess." I turned my gaze to the Christmas lights, twinkling in the trees. Every single building was decorated with garland and ribbons. "My career took a major hit, so I thought it best to move away for a while. Maybe find some inspiration."

Gabe smiled when I looked at him. "You'll definitely find that here. I have no doubt." He stepped back and moved out of the way. "I'm sure you have to get going. It was nice meeting you, Layla. I'm certain I'll see you around town again."

"It was nice meeting you, too, Gabe." I walked past him to my car. When I turned around, he was nowhere to be found.

Chapter Three

Layla

All through the night, I dreamed about my new fashion line and how it skyrocketed across the globe. Imagine my disappointment when I woke up to find it wasn't real ... and that it was ice cold in my house. The three quilts piled on top of me weren't enough.

"What in the world?" I griped, teeth chattering. I slid out of bed and slung one of the quilts over my shoulders. When I got to the thermostat, it said it was fifty-eight degrees. I turned it off and then on again, hoping it just needed to be reset. Nope. It was dead. "This can't be happening to me." What made it worse was that it was snowing outside. I looked out at the tiny specks of white, falling from the sky. "Wouldn't that make for some great news ... *Designing diva freezes to death as she escapes scrutiny from the fashion world*."

Grabbing my phone, my fingers trembled as I punched in Jane's number. I knew she was leaving for vacation, but I was hoping to catch her. The line rang and rang, the reception going in and out. I didn't know anything else to do besides drive into town.

I dressed quickly into a pair of jeans and a double layer of sweaters. If it was freezing inside my house, it had to be even worse outside. However, when I got out there, it wasn't nearly as cold as it was inside. My house was colder than a meat locker.

When I got into town, I dreaded going to the general store. There was a bank close by, but it was Sunday and they were closed. The only other place was the coffee shop. It just so happened that a familiar face was right outside, sitting alone at one of the tables, his head resting on his arm. I parked and walked up to his table, silently taking the seat beside him. He slowly lifted his head and sat up quickly when he noticed me. "Miss Layla, what brings you out so early in the morning?"

"My icebox of a house. It's much warmer out here than it is there. I came into town to see if someone could help me."

Gabe's brows furrowed. "What can I help you with?"

"Do you know of anyone who does heating and air? My heater died on me sometime last night, and it's so cold. I don't know who to contact."

He patted my hand. "Don't worry, I know just the guy. His name's Colin Jennings." He pointed at the street. "If you go up that way and take a right, all you have to do is follow that road until you get to Snowflake Lane. The Snowflake Lane Inn will be at the end. He'll be able to help you."

"Thanks," I replied, feeling ever so grateful. "He's not like the people in the general store, is he?"

Gabe chuckled. "Not in the least. Colin's a good man. You'll like him."

Squeezing his arm, I stood. "Thanks again." I turned to

leave but then stopped and glanced at him over my shoulder. "Gabe, forgive me if I'm being too nosy, and you can tell me to mind my own business, but . . ." I paused for a second and glanced around to make sure no one heard me. "Do you have a home to go to?"

A sad smile spread across his face. "Friendship is my home, Layla. Whether it be sleeping at this table or in a box behind the bank, this is where I belong for now."

My heart broke for him. Reaching into my purse, I pulled out a fifty-dollar bill. It was all I had on me. "Take this," I told him.

He shook his head. "I'm not taking your money, young lady."

"Please," I begged, setting it in front of him. "You don't take me as the kind of man to beg for money, but I want you to take it. You've helped me, and I want to return the favor."

With a heavy sigh, he held the money in his hands. "Thank you, child. This means a lot."

"You're welcome. Stay warm out here."

He chuckled again. "You too."

Getting in my car, I followed his directions to Snowflake Lane and down to the Snowflake Lane Inn. The second I saw the large, yellow house all decked out for Christmas, I gasped. It was exquisite, and more beautiful than any house I'd ever seen. There was garland draped with white lights everywhere, and red ribbons at the top of each fence post. It was something you'd see on a postcard.

I pulled up, and there was a man on a ladder, cleaning out the gutters . . . in the snow. It wasn't like Charleston here. When it snowed back home, everything would shut down, and people would seclude themselves inside where it was warm. Not here, apparently. All I wanted to do was grab a good book and drink hot chocolate.

When I got out of the car, the man on the ladder looked down at me. Even from the distance, I could see his eyes were a bright shade of green, almost magical. His dark brown hair was mussed like he had just ran a hand through it, and he had on a pair of jeans and a flannel shirt that no doubt hid his muscular arms beneath.

"Can I help you?" he asked, slowly making his way down the ladder.

I cleared my throat. "Gabe sent me here. He told me to find Colin Jennings."

The man smiled and approached me. "He did, did he? I guess you came to the right place then, Miss Aberdeen."

My breath caught. "You know who I am?"

He snorted. "I think everyone in this town does."

Groaning, I ran a hand over my face. "That must be why I got a cold greeting at the general store."

His smile faded. "I'm sorry to hear that. Some people in this town aren't too fond of outsiders, even if they are famous."

"That's not the way I imagined it would be here," I said softly. "Besides, I'm not famous anymore."

The man shook his head and waved it off. "Give it time. So why did you come to see Colin?"

I pulled my jacket in tighter. I was freezing, and he was outside in the snow with just a flannel shirt on. "The heat died in the house I'm renting. I didn't know who to call to come and fix it, but a man in town told me to come here. I was hoping Mr. Jennings could either help with the heater or help me get in touch with the owner. The real estate agent is the only one I know who has his number, but she's on vacation."

The man chuckled. "You're in luck. I know just how to contact him."

"Great. If you give me his number, I'll call him up."

Pulling a set of keys out of his pocket, he backed up toward the big, red truck in the driveway. "No need. I'll head over there now."

"You don't have to do that. Let me call the owner."

He opened his truck door and smiled. "I am the owner. I'm Colin Jennings."

Chapter Four

Colin

Layla wasn't anything like I expected her to be. She was much more beautiful in person. She followed behind me to her house, and I had to slow down several times to make sure she caught up. It was obvious she wasn't used to driving through the snow.

I pulled into her driveway first and grabbed my toolbox out of the back. The snow had slowed down, but we'd gotten the six inches the weatherman had predicted.

Layla rushed out of her car and ran over to the door. "I don't know why I'm hurrying. It's probably warmer out here."

That I found hard to believe ... that was until I stepped through the door. It was unnaturally cold. The sound of her chattering teeth grew louder. Arms crossed over her chest, she bounced on her feet. "Told you it was cold."

Setting my toolbox down, I blew into my hands. "You're telling me." I walked over to the thermostat to see if there was something wrong, but it looked normal. "I'm going to take a look at the heating unit outside. I just replaced it last summer. I don't see how there could be problems."

She followed me out the door and into the snow. "I wonder what's going on with it then. I only turned the heat up to seventy."

When we got around to the side of the house, that was when I saw the issue. "Wow," I said, dropping my toolbox. "I think we know what's wrong."

Her eyes widened. "That is crazy. It's frozen solid."

The unit was nothing but a large ice cube. I'd never seen anything like it before. "Yes, it is. It's a first for me."

Layla sighed. "Think you can fix it?"

I picked up my toolbox, but there was nothing I could do. "I can, but it won't be today. I'll have to get another unit and install it tomorrow."

She looked terrified. "You're kidding me, right? How am I supposed to stay here without freezing to death?"

Growing up, there were many nights we had to deal without heat or power, but I'd never felt it that cold before. There was no explanation for how frigid it was inside her house. I couldn't let her stay there alone.

Taking a deep breath, I placed my toolbox back into my truck. "You can always stay at my inn," I suggested. I turned around to face her. "There's a small bedroom that's vacant."

Holding a hand over her heart, she breathed a sigh of relief. "That would be awesome. I'm going to take you up on that."

I thought she'd yell and complain about the house, but that wasn't what I got. She surprised me. Guess I thought she'd be full of herself and demanding. "Great," I replied. "It's the least I can do for you. I've never had problems like this with the heat before."

"It's okay. I'm just glad I have somewhere to stay. If I didn't, I don't know what I'd do."

Her lips pulled back into a gracious smile, and I couldn't help but smile back. "I'll call my sister to get the room ready for you. She'll be thrilled to know you're staying. I think she's your biggest fan. The gift basket was her idea."

There was a twinkle in her eyes. "I'll be sure to tell her thank you."

I opened my truck door. "As soon as you're ready, just come on over to the inn. I know you'll want to pack some things."

"Yes," she breathed, turning her attention to the house. "Hopefully, I won't freeze during that time."

Chuckling, I hopped in my truck. "See you in a few, Layla." She waved and disappeared into the house.

Once I was out on the main road, I called Brianna. "Hey," she answered.

"Think you can get the small bedroom ready really quick?"

The sound of her typing away on the computer stilled in the background. "Of course. I'll have it ready in twenty minutes."

"Good. Because it just so happens it's for Layla Aberdeen." The line went silent. "Brianna?"

She sucked in a breath. "Are you seriously telling me that Layla Aberdeen is staying at the inn tonight?"

"Yep. Just left our old house. The heater is frozen solid. I can't leave her there all night."

"You can't leave her in the small bedroom either," she gasped incredulously. "Layla is fashion royalty. The Rose bedroom will be like putting her in a broom closet."

Leave it to Brianna to be dramatic. The Rose bedroom was small, but it wasn't *that* small. "It's a place to stay, Bri. We don't have anywhere else to put her."

"She can stay with me and Mom. Our guest room is way bigger than the one at the inn."

An exasperated chuckle escaped my lips. "Not going to happen, Bri. I know what you're trying to do here." She just wanted the bragging rights of having someone like Layla in her house.

"Seriously, Colin, I'm not trying to do anything. Sticking Layla in that tiny bedroom is not the kind of publicity we need. We need to impress her. Just think about all the good things she'll say about the inn. We'll be booked up year-round."

She had a point, and unfortunately, I had an idea. It wasn't exactly to my favor, but it'd be all for the inn. "Fine. I know just what to do."

Brianna squealed. "This is so exciting. I can't believe I'm about to meet Layla Aberdeen."

"Bye, Brianna. When she arrives, bring her back to the cottage." I hung up just as she squealed again. She knew what my plan was going to be. Don't get me wrong, I was a nice guy, but I really didn't want to kiss up to the fashion diva just to get good ratings on the inn. Then again, it was a sacrifice I was going to make.

Chapter Five

Layla

There was literally nothing as breathtaking as driving down Snowflake Lane. The amount of work that was put in with all the Christmas decorations was phenomenal. It didn't take me long to pack up a few things at my freezing house. It took longer driving to the inn with all the snow. Granted, I had a four-wheel-drive Jeep, but I still felt unsure on the slippery roads. Hopefully, I'd get used to it. I wanted a drastic change from my current lifestyle, and I got it.

Pulling up to the Snowflake Lane Inn, I couldn't help but smile at its beauty. I parked behind Colin's truck and stepped out, breathing in the cool, crisp air. The door to the inn opened and a young woman rushed out, her smile radiant.

"I really thought I could control myself and act cool with you being here, but I don't think it's possible. I love your designs." She ran down the steps and held out her hand. "I'm Brianna, Colin's sister."

They had the same dark brown hair and green eyes. "Yes, I

can see that," I replied. "It's nice to meet you." She seemed like a nice girl, probably in her early twenties. What I loved most was the top she had on. It was one of my designs.

I grabbed my bag out of the backseat, and Brianna took it. "It's such a pleasure to meet *you*, Layla. When I found out you were moving to Friendship, I couldn't believe it."

A laugh escaped my lips. "Neither could I. Although I am happy to see that someone around here likes me."

Brows furrowed, Brianna nodded toward the house. "Colin didn't make you feel unwelcome, did he? If he did, I'll slap him upside the head."

"No." I laughed. "He was very friendly. However, the man at the general store didn't seem too thrilled to be around me."

She scoffed. "That's just Earl. He's a grumpy old man. Don't let him sway your opinion of our town. The people of Friendship all stick together. We're like family."

I followed her down the walkway and around the back of the inn, where a quaint little cottage sat by a small, frozen lake. A gazebo sat at the water's edge, covered with bright white Christmas lights and red bows. The stone path leading up to it reminded me of something you'd see in a storybook. "From the front, I didn't even know this place was back here," I murmured.

Brianna glanced at me over her shoulder with a big smile on her face. "This is where you'll be staying. I can't believe the heater froze up on the house. It never did that when I was growing up there. Although it has been colder this winter."

It was colder than what I'd ever experienced. "Thank you for the gift basket. Colin said it was your idea."

We stopped at the cottage door. "You're welcome. I'm one of your biggest fans. Not many people around here care about fashion though."

I sighed. "But they know who I am, don't they?"

She snorted. "Everyone knows who you are. Did you think a small town like ours wouldn't know who you were?"

"Kind of," I replied with a shrug. "Was that naive of me?"

She burst out laughing. "Yup. You can't escape who you are, especially when the world already knows you."

The door to the cottage opened, and Colin stepped out with a duffel bag draped over his shoulder. He nodded toward the door. "It's all yours. The guest bedroom is up the stairs on the right. Feel free to use whatever you want in the kitchen."

"What?" I gasped, glancing at them both. I looked at Colin's bag and then into his striking, emerald eyes. "Is this your home?" The last thing I wanted to do was inconvenience him.

He nodded. "It's yours tonight."

I shook my head. "Definitely not. I don't want you giving up your place for me."

"It was either that or the tiny twin bedroom in the inn," Brianna cut in. "I figured you'd want more space."

"I'm fine with the smaller room." She had a hold of my bag, and I reached out for it pleadingly. "Seriously, I don't mind. I'm just grateful I won't be freezing to death."

Brianna handed me my bag, her gaze curious. It was obvious they had misconceptions about me. Hopefully, I'd be able to change that.

Brianna and Colin stared at each other, but Colin spoke first, his lips tilting up in a small smile. "Take the cottage, Ms. Aberdeen. The whole inn is my home. You're not putting me out."

"Are you sure? I feel bad."

"Don't," he said, setting his bag on the porch. He reached for mine and picked it up. "Come on, I'll show you around."

Grinning wide, Brianna backed away. "I'll leave you both to

it. Oh, and Layla?" She winked. "My mother and I make the best breakfast in town. Just come in through the back door, and you'll be right in the kitchen. If you need me, I'll be just inside."

"Thanks. I'll be sure to do that." I really liked Brianna. As she walked toward the inn, I couldn't help but notice how amazing she'd be on a runway. She had the perfect height, a pretty face, and amazing silky hair. If only I had designs to put on a runway.

Colin cleared his throat. "You okay?"

I jerked my attention back to him. "Oh yeah. Just lost in my thoughts for a second."

He opened the door, and it smelled exactly like the other house—cinnamon apples and crisp snow—mixed in with Colin's cologne. I breathed it in and smiled. The walls were a light yellow, very homey and inviting, and most of the furniture was Victorian antiques. Not exactly what I'd imagine a man like Colin to live in. He looked so rugged on the outside with his flannel shirt and jeans and five o'clock shadow.

A giggle escaped my lips, and I held my breath when he turned to me, clearly having heard me. "Something funny?"

"No," I announced quickly. I looked around the living room, loving how beautiful it was. Antiques were my favorite, and the room was filled with various vases and paintings. "It's just . . . I'm a little shocked. It doesn't look like a man lives here."

His gaze narrowed, but I could tell he wanted to smile. "Are you questioning my masculinity?"

Cheeks burning, I held up my hands. "Oh my God, no. That totally came out wrong."

He burst out laughing. "I'm just messing with you." He pointed at some of the antiques, and his gaze turned sad. "My grandmother decorated all of this. It was her dream to keep the inn and this place as close to her heart as possible."

He walked over to the fireplace mantel and picked up a picture. It was an old black-and- white photo of a young couple. "When my grandparents left this place to me, they made me promise not to change a thing." He set the picture back down and turned to me. "Even if I didn't promise, I wouldn't have changed a thing. I have too many wonderful memories here."

"I don't blame you," I agreed. "It's a beautiful place." In a way, I was envious of his memories. I would've loved to have ones like he had.

"Thanks," he said as he nodded toward the stairs. "Your room's up here. Mine is the one on the left." I followed him up the stairs to the first room on the right. Colin opened the door, and the room was absolutely breathtaking. The walls were a light purple with a hint of gray. It complimented perfectly with the silver and light purple comforter and canopy that draped over the bed. "This used to be my grandmother's antique storage room before I changed it to a bedroom for Bri. She likes staying here sometimes, especially during the busy season at the inn. It's much easier and quicker to get over there."

He set my bag down, and I walked over to the window. I had a perfect view of the small pond. "So your grandparents left all of this to you and not her or your mother?"

I could see his reflection in the window. He looked down at the floor and sighed. "My grandparents knew that, when the time came, Brianna would leave Friendship for bigger and better things. And as for my mother, she's been sick for a while, a rare disease called Addison's. Basically, her adrenal glands don't function properly."

"Oh no," I gasped, turning to him. "I'm so sorry. I've never even heard of that before."

He met my gaze. "Not many people have, and not that many

medical professionals know how to treat her. After my father died, she had an adrenal crisis. The stress of his death put too much strain on her body. I was afraid we were going to lose her, too, but she made it through." With a heavy sigh, he averted his attention to the window. "She knew she couldn't handle this place on her own, so she asked my grandparents to leave it to me."

My heart hurt for him, even though I couldn't relate. I didn't know what to say. My parents were healthy and traveling the world. I used to do the same thing until my latest line tanked. I wanted to hold on to the money I had saved.

Colin cleared his throat and stepped out into the hall. "I guess I'll let you get settled in. If you need anything, I'll be inside the inn."

I nodded. "Sounds good. Thank you."

He turned to walk away and stopped, leaning his body against the door frame. "I don't know if you know or not, but the Christmas tree lighting ceremony is tonight. If you want to go, you can ride with me."

My heart skipped a beat. There was a time when Christmas used to fill my heart with joy, but I'd forgotten what all of that felt like. "I'd love to," I answered.

His grin made my heart skip another beat. "Good." Then he glanced down at my clothes. "But you might want to wear something warmer. It'll be cold out tonight."

My breath stilled as he made his way down the stairs and out the front door. I watched him walk toward his truck and drive away down the long, decorated driveway. Heart racing, I hurried out of the house to the back door of the inn. The snow seeped through my designer boots, and I hissed. I was *not* prepared for rural life. The kitchen was immaculate with fresh baked breads on the counter and chocolate chip cookies in an antique-looking glass bowl. Across the way was a library, and Brianna was on the window seat, reading a book. She jumped up when she saw me.

"Layla, you okay?"

I shook my head. "Your brother just invited me to the town Christmas tree lighting tonight."

She squealed. "That's freaking awesome. Is it a date?"

I shook my head and gasped. "No, of course not. We just met."

"I'm just kidding, silly. Then again, he's good looking and single. What's not to like?"

"That's not it," I claimed in all honesty. "Colin is very hot, and he makes me nervous, but that's not my problem right now."

"Then what is?" she asked, clearly confused.

I glanced down at my clothes. "I have nothing to wear."

Brianna burst out laughing and tossed her book onto the old oak table. "Who would've thought a fashion designer wouldn't have the right clothes?"

"Exactly," I agreed. "I didn't realize how cold it was going to be up here."

She nodded toward the hallway. "Let me get my keys, and I'll take you to my house. My mom and I live just down the road from here. I'm sure we can find you something to wear." An amused smile lit up her face. "I'll make you look like a local in no time."

I followed her to the kitchen and watched her grab her purse off the counter. "I'm surprised you don't live here in the inn," I said.

Shrugging, she pulled out her car keys. "I could if I wanted to, but it gives us more space to accept guests. Also, my mom didn't want to sell our house. She has too many memories there of my dad. It helps her feel close to him." I could see the sadness on her face at the mention of her father, but I didn't want to pry into her life. Grabbing my arm, she plastered on a smile and pulled me toward the door. "Enough sad talk. It's time to get you fixed up."

Brianna and I wore the same size, so it didn't take long to find something that would fit. What intrigued me most about her closet was the amount of my designs she had, only she'd told me she couldn't afford the ones from my expensive label. I was going to have to change that. Looking in the mirror, I barely recognized myself. I loved the skinny jeans and the thick, cream-colored sweater. Brianna even put my hair up in a messy bun so I could wear her cream-colored ear warmers.

My phone rang, and I stared at it, watching it light up on my bed. I'd gotten so many calls from the media requesting inter-views, but I refused to do any after my last fashion line bit the dust. My humiliation wasn't for the world to see. All I wanted was to regroup and get my head together before I even attempted to put out a new line. Unfortunately, privacy wasn't a luxury I had. With everyone in Friendship knowing who I was, it was only a matter of time before my semblance of a normal life would be cut short. Someone would eventually post a picture, and I'd be found.

Sighing, I walked over to my phone, and luckily, it wasn't anyone from the media. It was my parents. "Hey," I answered.

"Hey, honey," my mother replied. "How are you?"

I shrugged and looked at myself in the mirror again. "Not too bad. Getting ready to go to a tree lighting ceremony." I certainly wasn't going to tell her about the heating issue at my house. My parents already thought I was insane for moving to a town in the middle of nowhere. The last thing I wanted to hear was *I told you so*.

"That sounds fun. How are you liking your little country town?"

Turning away from the mirror, I looked out the window at all the snow. Colin's truck was parked in front of the inn. "I like it, Mom. I've met some really nice people. In fact, I'm riding to the tree lighting with the guy I'm renting the house from."

"I see. You need to be careful, Layla. Remember what happened with the last guy you got mixed up with?"

"Colin's not like that," I replied, my gut clenching with the memories.

My mother scoffed. "Don't let them fool you, honey. You're beautiful and successful."

The last guy I dated was an up-and-coming actor. He'd landed his first major role when we were together. However, when my business profits took a dip, he split. The embarrassment of my failure wasn't something he wanted connected to him. It was another reason why I wanted to disappear for a while.

"The people here are different," I said. At least, that was what I hoped. I was about to meet a lot of them for the first time tonight.

"For your sake, I hope not." She blew out a sigh. "Your father and I are getting ready to get back on the boat. We're in Rome right now. Figured it was a good time to call. We'll make sure to get in touch with you again to wish you a Merry Christmas."

"Sounds good, Mom. Be careful out there. Tell Dad I said hello."

"I will." She blew a kiss through the phone. "Love you."

"I love you too." We hung up, and my heart felt heavy. I wished they were going to be home for Christmas. I'd always had friends to spend the holidays with, but this year, I was alone.

My eyes burned, but I sucked the tears back and joined Brianna in the living room. She jumped up from the couch and clapped her hands together. "I know you're probably getting tired of me acting like an idiot, but this is seriously a surreal moment in my life. I'm hanging out with Layla Aberdeen, and she's wearing my clothes."

Laughing, I ran my hand down the soft, fluffy sweater. "Pretend I'm just like everyone else ... because you know what, I am."

Brianna looked out the window. "It's killing me not taking pictures of us together so I can share them with my friends."

"Why haven't you?" I asked curiously. It hadn't escaped my notice how she hadn't pulled out her phone at all since we'd been together.

Her gaze saddened, and she shrugged. "I know you're here to escape. I'm not about to ruin that for you by sharing pictures on my social media." She held up her hands. "Now, I'm not saying I have a huge following, but if word were to get out, it might leak to the wrong people."

I nodded. "You're right, it possibly could." I didn't know Brianna that well yet, but I could see us being close. I pulled her in for a hug. "Thank you for that. You have no idea how nervous I've been about the media finding me. All I want is to be normal."

She locked her arms around me and patted my back. "But you're not. Although I do think you'll be surprised by our town. A lot of people know why you're here, and they respect that. They're not going to exploit you."

I let her go, wishing I could believe that. "Guess we'll see."

There was a knock on the door, and she opened it to Colin. He'd changed clothes from earlier. He had traded his plaid button down for a nice gray sweater, covered with a gray wool coat. Even his face was freshly shaven. My heart skipped a beat, and I smiled. He looked so different.

Colin's brows furrowed when he saw Brianna. "Still here?" he asked her.

Brianna opened the door all the way, and that was when he saw me. "I was just leaving," Brianna replied. "Layla needed my help."

Colin stepped inside and cleared his throat, his attention solely on me. "Wow, you look ..."

"Beautiful?" Brianna added, winking slyly at me. "Yes, she does."

Colin rubbed the back of his neck, a trait I'd noticed when men were nervous. "Actually, I was going to say different, but definitely beautiful as well."

My cheeks burned. "I could say the same about you," I said.

Brianna snickered and stepped outside onto the porch. "All right, you two, I'm heading out. I'll see you at the ceremony."

Colin turned to face her. "You don't want to ride with us?"

With a twinkle in her eyes, she shook her head. "Nah. I'm riding with Mom. See you there." She winked at him and took off for the inn.

Colin glanced at me over his shoulder. "I think she's up to something."

I chuckled. "I'd say so." And we both knew what it was.

"Are you ready to go?" he asked.

"I am." Brianna had let me borrow one of her coats, so I slipped it on and stuffed some money and my phone into one of the pockets. Colin locked the door behind us, and we walked slowly to his truck. The smell of snow lingered in the air as it crunched beneath our feet. Brianna's boots kept my feet warm, not like my designer heels.

We stopped at his truck, and he opened the passenger-side door for me. I held up my hands. "So, what do you think? Could I pass for a local?"

Colin's smile made my heart melt. "You could, actually. Sometimes it's hard imagining a celebrity like you being normal."

"But I am," I murmured. "I'm hoping you'll see that."

He smiled again. "Working on it. You're doing a good job making me believe it, especially with how nice you've been to Brianna. She looks up to you."

"And I admire her. She's been nothing but kind to me. I owe her big time for the clothes. I'm going to see if she'll do a trade-off with me. My clothes for hers."

He burst out laughing and helped me into his truck. "You won't have to twist her arm for that. Half of her closet is nothing but your designs."

"I know," I said with a giggle. "She said it's all she wears when she's away at college." I hopped in the truck, and he shut the door. My palms were sweaty, and my heart raced. It'd been so long since I'd gone out with someone who didn't want anything from me, but yet, deep down, I wanted something from him, something real.

It was so magical driving down Snowflake Lane and looking at all the twinkling lights. I felt like a kid at Christmas, mesmerized by the beauty of it. "I bet every Christmas was amazing for you as a kid, wasn't it?" I asked.

Colin glanced out his truck windows and then over at me. "For the most part. It takes a lot of work to keep all those Christmas lights going. When I was young, my grandparents would make me replace all the burned-out bulbs."

"I wish my parents would've decorated the outside of our house. I used to be so jealous of our neighbors. They always had such cute Christmas displays."

We turned off of Snowflake Lane and onto the darkened street. I wasn't used to seeing everything around me pitch-black. Living in a big city, pretty much everywhere you went was lit up with some kind of streetlight. If your headlights didn't work here, you'd be in some serious trouble.

"Why didn't your parents ever decorate?" he asked.

I shrugged. "Probably because we were never home. They love to travel. Guess they thought taking me places all the time was what I wanted."

"What did you want?"

Sighing, I looked out the window, and more decorated homes came into view. "I wanted to be a normal kid and wake up in my own bed Christmas morning. To smell our freshly cut Christmas tree that I helped decorate while I opened up my presents." I looked over at him. "It's not that I'm ungrateful. I know you probably think I have nothing to complain about since I got to see the world."

He shook his head. "That's not what I'm thinking at all. Traveling the world wouldn't have made me happy. Being here and having my family traditions was what I enjoyed most."

"And that's exactly what I wanted," I murmured. I'd seen so many Christmas movies and how amazing they made the holidays seem. I would never forget the memories and adventures I had with my parents over the holidays, but it wasn't what I wanted to pass down to my family if I ever had one of my own. I wanted normal Christmas traditions with Santa Claus and a gazillion presents underneath the tree my kids helped me decorate.

We slowly approached downtown Friendship, and it looked like a winter wonderland. Wrought iron light poles lined the street, all wrapped in garland and white lights with red ribbons. A group of men and women—dressed in old-fashioned clothes—strolled up and down the street, caroling. I rolled my window down so I could hear them.

"We're almost there," Colin said. He pointed down one of the side streets. "There's also a pond down that way where everyone goes to ice-skate. If you want, I can take you there. It'll give you a chance to meet new people."

I gasped. "Definitely not. I haven't ice-skated in years. The last thing I want to do is make a fool of myself."

He burst out laughing. "No worries. If you don't want anyone watching you, you can ice-skate on the pond at the inn. Some of our guests enjoy the privacy of it."

That sounded like a better idea. I didn't want pictures of me falling on my butt all over the internet. "The only way I'm going out there is if I have someone to help me. Maybe Brianna will do it with me. I'd love to try it again." I glanced at him quickly and then turned my attention to the road, silently hoping.

"If she can't skate with you, I'll be happy to do it. I don't want you breaking any bones."

Mission accomplished. Grinning wide, I turned to him. "Perfect." We arrived at the center of downtown, which was a park with a large fountain in the middle. There were people everywhere, surrounding a very large Christmas tree.

Colin parked, and I slowly opened the door, trying not to stare at everyone else gawking at us curiously. Colin shut my door, and I cleared my throat. "I'm not going to be making any of these women mad, am I?"

Colin glanced around and smiled. "You're good. My last girlfriend left town to pursue bigger things. She didn't want a small-town life." He said it so flippantly, but I could see from his face that it hurt deeper than he wanted to admit.

"I'm sorry, Colin. Believe it or not, I know what it feels like to be dumped."

He nodded. "I know. I remember Brianna talking about your breakup after she read it in the tabloids." Groaning, I closed my eyes and he squeezed my wrist. "Hey, it's okay. There's nothing to be embarrassed about. Your ex was an idiot. To this day, I haven't watched any of the movies he's been in."

Opening my eyes, I breathed a sigh of relief. "Thanks. That actually makes me feel better."

He nodded toward one of the booths. "Good. Now how about we get some hot chocolate?"

He held out his arm, and I linked it with mine, loving how comfortable I felt with him. It was like we'd known each other for years. "Sounds yummy."

We walked over to the booth, and an older lady with short, white hair beamed. "There you are, young man. I've been wondering when I was going to see your sweet face here." She hurried around the counter and hugged him.

Chuckling, Colin hugged her back and kept his arm around her shoulders. "Mrs. Mable, I'd like you to meet Layla. She just moved into town. I'm showing her around."

Mrs. Mable held out her hand. "It's nice to meet you."

I shook her hand. "Likewise."

She patted Colin's arm. "I used to teach this one at the elementary school. One of my favorite students."

Colin squeezed her and let go. "And she used to be my favorite teacher."

"Thank you, dearie." Mrs. Mable walked back around to the other side of the booth and handed us both a hot cup of cocoa with marshmallows. "Seems like forever and a day ago. You kids grow up so fast."

Colin held out his arm and I took it, my stomach fluttering the entire time.

"Take care of yourself, Mrs. Mable," Colin said with a wave. "Tell that grandson of yours I said hello."

She winked. "Will do."

We walked away, and he leaned in close. "I grew up with her grandson. I haven't seen him since he moved to Maine last year."

I shivered just thinking about it. "Maine, yikes. I'm sure it's colder there than here."

"Just a little, but not much," he replied, laughing. He nodded toward the stage that stood in front of the massive Christmas tree. "Come on, let's see if we can get a good spot."

Arm in arm, we strolled over to a vacant area by one of the wrought iron streetlamps. People stared at us in passing, but it was obvious they were trying to be discreet. I blew the steam off my cocoa and took a sip; it was heaven.

"What do you think?" Colin asked. When I looked up at him, he scanned the crowd. "About our town. Think you'll be happy here?"

I took another sip of my cocoa. "Possibly. It does have its charms." He was one of them. "I do love it here." His gaze met mine, and I smiled. "Things seem to move a lot slower here. When I was traveling from place to place, it was hard to catch a breath."

He looked at me as if he understood. "Are you going to continue designing, or are you giving it up for good?"

My heart ached just thinking about giving up. "I'm definitely not quitting. I just need to find some inspiration."

"Or try something new," he replied, finishing off his cocoa.

I did the same. "New . . . like what?"

With a shrug of his shoulders, he threw our cups away and gestured a hand at everything going on around us. "Breathe in the air and take a look around at everything going on. Listen to the sounds of laughter and watch the way the snow falls down from the sky. How does it make you feel?"

I glared at him like he'd lost his mind. "It's cold. It makes me feel cold."

He burst out laughing. "Think deeper than that. Do you know how many artists have found their passion for painting here?" I shook my head. "Lots," he added. "I know you don't paint, but it's basically the same thing. You don't need to see the inspiration. You just need to feel it. Find somewhere that inspires you. When you do, I have no doubt you'll find what you're looking for."

Mouth gaping, I couldn't take my eyes off of him. He smiled down at me again. "Why are you looking at me like you're shocked?"

"I guess because I am. I wasn't expecting you to say something like that."

He smiled and shrugged it off. "There's a lot you don't know about me. Just like there's a lot I don't know about you, well, other than what the tabloids say." I groaned, and he held up a hand. "Don't worry. I don't believe any of that mess they publish."

"Good," I replied, breathing a sigh of relief. "Recently, it's been hard to deal with. My failure has been published for the world to see." Colin nodded in understanding, but I knew he had no clue what it was really like, how suffocating being part of the media's attention could actually be. Granted, I loved the spotlight and seeing my designs on celebrities, but there was a darker side of fame I could live without.

"What happened anyway?" he asked. "You were on top of the world, and then one day you weren't."

I stared into his emerald eyes and could feel myself getting lost in them. Why was it so easy to talk to him? With Colin, I could see and feel his sincerity.

"Greed can make people do despicable things." Gaze

narrowed, Colin waited for me to continue. I hadn't spoken of what happened to anyone. "There's another designer who I thought was my friend. We shared our ideas with each other. That was how much I trusted her. At least, I did until she stole my ideas."

Colin growled low. "Seriously? What happened after that?"

I shrugged. "Her career took off, and I was left crushed with nowhere to turn. It was her word against mine, but she had made sure to get her collection on sale before I could. I had no way to prove that my designs were created first."

"I'm sorry, Layla."

Breathing in the cool, crisp air, I let it out slowly, watching the fog of my breath move in the wind. My eyes burned, so I turned away from him and focused on the crowd of people. They all seemed so happy with their carefree, genuine smiles. I wanted to be like that. "After that, I was heartbroken, and I tried coming up with a new line, but as you know, it didn't do well. When I realized how vindictive the world really is, I had to take a step away for my own sanity."

Colin stepped closer, and I could feel his warmth behind me. "That part of your world might be harsh and cruel, but it's not like that here." I wanted to believe that more than anything.

"Layla!" Brianna shouted.

Quickly, I wiped my eyes and turned toward the sound of her voice. She waved and rushed through the crowd with a woman behind her. I knew who she was just by looking at her face. Plus, I recognized her from the pictures in Colin's cottage. Colin resembled his father while Brianna shared a lot of the same features with their mother: same build, curly brown hair, and smile.

She grabbed her mother's arm and pulled her closer. "Mom, this is Layla. Layla this is our mother, Theresa."

I held out my hand. "It's so nice to meet you. Colin and Brianna have been a tremendous help to me since I arrived in town."

Theresa smiled radiantly at me. "It's an honor to meet you too. I don't think I've ever met anyone famous before." She winked over at Colin and Brianna. "My daughter's done nothing but say good things about you."

Brianna clutched my arm. "That's because she's awesome."

Mrs. Mable called out Theresa's name, grabbing her attention. Theresa let my hand go and sighed. "Sorry to cut this short. Make sure to come into the inn in the morning for breakfast. I can't wait to learn more about you."

"Sounds good."

She hurried off toward Mrs. Mable's booth, while Brianna backed away with a sly grin on her face. "You two have fun. I'll catch you later."

Colin and I glanced at each other. "She's not very subtle, is she?"

Shaking my head, I focused on the stage, knowing my cheeks were burning. A group of what appeared to be a middle school band congregated around the stage. "Not at all."

The mayor walked up onstage and welcomed everyone. He led the crowd in song, and I watched as the people sang a Christmas carol. After that, the band played "Silent Night," and then the crowd counted down until the mayor flipped the switch that lit the tree. Suddenly, the park sparkled. Lights twinkled all around the tree, making the multicolored ornaments glitter in the night.

"It's so beautiful," I whispered. Something fell on my cheek, and I looked up at the sky to see giant snowflakes cascading down. The crowd cheered in delight, and I smiled. It was a perfect night, and I knew exactly what I was going to do the second I got back to Colin's cottage.

Chapter Six

Colin

I'd installed the new heater at Layla's house, and it worked like a champ. When I got back to the inn, I found her in the gazebo, completely transfixed by her sketchpad and bundled in my grandmother's quilt. Her hands moved delicately over the pages, but I couldn't see what she drew.

As I approached, she could hear my steps on the wood, and she looked up. As much as I wanted to deny it, she'd grown on me. "Hey," she called out.

Joining her in the gazebo, I smiled and glanced down at her sketchpad. "Hey yourself. Looks like you've been working hard."

Her eyes brightened. "Have I ever. Take a look." She moved closer, and I could smell her raspberry-scented perfume as she flipped through the pages.

Women's fashion didn't interest me whatsoever, but to see her excitement and to actually feel it made me think otherwise. She handed me her drawings, and I slowly skimmed through them. It had to have taken her hours.

"What do you think?" she asked, sounding nervous.

Closing the sketchpad, I set it down between us. "I think they're amazing. How long have you been out here?"

She yawned and leaned back against the bench. "All night. After you dropped me off, I came out here and couldn't stop." Her tired smile spread wider as she looked around the pond. "I don't know what came over me. It was like everything came to me after the tree lighting ceremony. Being out here just inspired me even more."

"Just know, you're more than welcome to come here anytime you want." I held up her house keys. "But your new heater has been installed. You can go home."

Her eyes widened, and then a hint of disappointment flashed in them briefly. She reached for her keys, and our fingers touched. "Thank you. I know you're probably ready for me to be out of your house."

I shook my head. "I kind of like you being around. Makes things more interesting here."

Grabbing her sketchpad, she clutched it to her chest. "I like being here too," she replied. "And you promise I can come here anytime I want?"

"Anytime." I rubbed the back of my neck. "So what do you say I show you around town this afternoon?"

Her cheeks reddened just a tiny bit. Hopefully, it was a good sign. "I think that sounds awesome," she said, yawning again, "but I should probably get home and get a couple hours of sleep first. I didn't realize how tired I was."

She stood and swayed on her feet, but I caught her. "Whoa. I think you're right. Do you want me to drive you home?"

Her eyes grew heavier by the second, and she yawned again. "Actually, that might not be a bad idea. Do you mind?"

I put my arm around her, steadying her. "Not at all. Let's get your things, and I'll take you."

Once her belongings were packed up in her bag, I loaded up the truck and helped her in. Leaning her head against the window, she fell asleep the second we left Snowflake Lane.

Chapter Seven

Layla

The last thing I remembered was packing up my stuff and getting into Colin's truck. After that, it was all a blur. I woke up in my bed, wrapped in Colin's quilt and feeling toasty warm, with a note on my bedside table.

> *Call me when you wake up. We'll head into town if you're up for it.*
>
> *~Colin*

I was definitely up for it. Now I just hoped I didn't snore while he was driving me home. Talk about embarrassing. After taking a quick shower and changing into a clean pair of jeans and one of Brianna's sweaters, I called him.

"Hey," he answered.

My heart skipped a beat. "Hey. I'm sorry I didn't get a chance to say thank you earlier for bringing me home. Hopefully, you didn't break your back carrying me to my room." I folded up his quilt and carried it downstairs.

He burst out laughing. "Piece of cake. I'm assuming the heat is still working?"

I sat down on the couch, sighing with relief. "It is." The quilt was so soft as I rubbed my hand over it. "When you're ready, I'm free to go into town."

"Give me about twenty minutes, and I'll be right there."

Silently, I sucked in a breath and grinned triumphantly. "Perfect. See you then." We hung up, and my pulse raced while I waited for him to show up. He made me more nervous than one of my runway shows.

He arrived in twenty minutes on the dot, and I met him outside just as he got out of his truck. Like a gentleman, he opened the passenger side door for me. "Thank you," I replied sweetly.

"Of course," he answered back, giving me that dashing smile of his. It was freezing outside, but my palms were sweaty. The inside of his truck smelled like his cologne, and I breathed it in. Once he slid inside, we were on our way. "What do you want to do in town today?"

"I want to go into some of the stores to see if I can find some Christmas presents."

"Speaking of Christmas, you know you're more than welcome to spend it with my family at the inn. I know your parents are out of town."

Just the thought of not being with my family on the holidays made my chest ache. With everything going on in my life, it would've been nice to have my parents around, but they'd had their vacation planned before the fiasco with my fashion line, so I couldn't blame them for still being gone. Actually, I could, but I didn't want to spend Christmas being bitter.

Releasing a heavy sigh, I turned to Colin. "Sure you don't mind?"

"Not at all. You already know my mother and sister love you." He winked. "My mom is a good judge of character, so if she likes you, it's a good sign." That was great to hear, but what I really wanted to know was what *he* thought about me.

When we arrived in downtown Friendship, there was a handful of people walking up and down the streets, and looking in the shop windows. But one man caught my attention, sitting on the same bench I'd seen him on a couple days ago. I nodded toward him. "That's the man who told me where to find you."

Colin followed my line of sight as we pulled into the parking lot behind the general store. "His name's Gabe. I tried to get him to stay at the inn, but he wouldn't agree to it."

We got out of the truck and walked up the street. "I gave him some money. Hopefully, he has somewhere to go. I can't imagine being on the street in this kind of weather."

Colin's gaze saddened, and I could tell he was genuinely concerned for the man. It was obvious a place like Friendship wasn't accustomed to homelessness. Gabe seemed to have faith in the people, especially when he told me to give the town a chance after my run-in with the crabby general store owner.

Gabe sat on the bench, still wearing the same dirty clothes and reading a newspaper when we approached him. There was a half-eaten sandwich sitting beside him on a napkin. He lowered the paper and smiled. "Good afternoon. I see you two found each other." He folded up the newspaper and set it down on the bench.

"Yes," I replied thankfully. "Colin was able to fix my heater this morning."

Colin held out his hand, and Gabe shook it. "I knew he was the right man for the job."

"How are you?" Colin asked him.

Gabe shrugged. "Can't complain." He nodded down at his sandwich. "Just finishing up an early dinner."

I glanced over at Colin, and he sighed as he took a seat next to Gabe. "Please forgive me if I'm overstepping, but are you sure you don't need somewhere to stay?"

Gabe shook his head. "I'm fine, son. Really, I am."

Colin patted his shoulder and stood. "Okay. You know where to find me if you need anything."

"And me," I added. "If it wasn't for you, I'd be frozen to death."

Chuckling, Gabe reached for his newspaper, eyes twinkling. "True. Keep a watch on those heaters. They're finicky this time of year. It wouldn't surprise me if it froze over again."

I grabbed my chest. "I hope not."

"If it does, I know how to fix it," Colin said.

Gabe's grin widened. "That's what I like to hear. Hope you two have a lovely evening."

"You too, Gabe. Take care."

Colin and I left him to stroll down the sidewalk. I glanced back at Gabe, and there was a look on his face like he knew something we didn't. "Why do you think he turns down your help?" I asked, turning back to Colin.

He shrugged. "Pride, maybe. If I ever found myself in a situation where I had nowhere to go, I'd probably deny help too." Sighing, he glanced back at Gabe. "I'd want to do it on my own. At least he seems to be content."

"He does," I agreed. "Kind of gives you a new perspective on life, if you think about it. As long as you're happy, anything's possible. I thought my career would end after what happened with my last line. I lost all hope until last night. Even if I don't do anything with my designs, I know that I still have what it takes."

He stopped and turned to me. "You have to take a chance."

I'd never experienced the fear of rejection before. It was one of the worst feelings in the world, and I didn't want to experience it again. "Maybe I will one day. For now, I'm keeping my new designs under wraps."

He nodded in understanding, and we continued our way down the sidewalk to the shops. There was a bookstore, a bank, a clothing store, and a diner that smelled heavenly as we walked past.

Colin heard my stomach growl and laughed. "Want to get something to eat?"

I was about to take him up on the offer, when a woman called his name as she stepped out of what appeared to be a small art gallery. She looked to be in her mid-fifties with graying auburn hair, dressed in a white apron with paint splattered on it.

Colin waved. "Mrs. Denton."

She stopped in front of us. "Sorry to interrupt your conversation, but when I saw you walking up this way, I wanted to catch you." She took in a breath and blew it out. "My nephew and his wife are coming in after Christmas for their anniversary, and they're staying at the inn. I wanted to see if you'd let me surprise them by putting their present in their room before they arrive."

"Of course," Colin agreed.

Mrs. Denton smiled at me. "I took one of their wedding photos and painted it on canvas."

Colin gently bumped me, grabbing my attention. "Mrs. Denton is one of our famous artists. Her work is in art museums all over the country."

I gazed past her into the gallery where her work was on the walls. Art was something I'd always been fascinated by. I held out my hand. "It's a pleasure to meet you, Mrs. Denton. I'm Layla."

She shook my hand. "I know. You have a lot of talent, young lady."

"So do you." I pointed to her work. "How long does it take you to make a painting?"

She shrugged. "Not long. When I'm in the spirit, I can get one done in a couple of days. And on rare occasions, I can pull a Bob Ross and get one finished in a day." I used to watch Bob Ross episodes on television every Saturday morning as a child.

An idea popped in my head and I smiled. "Think you can paint something for me before Christmas? I'll pay whatever amount you want."

Her grin widened. "Come inside, and we'll work something out."

I started to follow her, and Colin chuckled. "What are you up to?"

I winked up at him. "It's a surprise."

After I finished with Mrs. Denton at the art gallery, Colin and I ate dinner at the Wallflower Diner. I'd consumed a huge bowl of banana pudding for dessert. It was some of the best down-home country food I'd ever had. "I'm going to have to run ten miles to burn off everything I ate," I said as we drove down the road toward Colin's cottage so that I could retrieve my car.

Colin burst out laughing. "So am I. We could always skate around the pond. That'll work some of it off."

I didn't want the night to end, so I nodded. "But I don't have any skates."

He waved me off. "We have several sizes for our guests. I'm sure we'll find ones that fit."

We arrived at the inn, and the twinkling lights around the gazebo lit up the pond. Colin glanced down at my feet. "What size are you?"

I lifted my foot slightly off the ground. "I'm an eleven. I have big feet."

"Yes, you do," he teased. He took off inside the inn and came back out with two pairs of skates. He handed me a pair. "Try these. They should work."

He sat beside me on the bench, underneath the snow-covered tree, as we put on our skates. They felt heavy on my ankles. I tried to stand and wobbled on my feet. Colin took my hand to steady me. My breath hitched as electricity sparked between us. Judging by the look in his eyes, he felt it too.

"I won't let you fall," he murmured. I smiled up at him, and he winked. "You might sue me."

I smacked his arm. "Seriously? You know I'm not like that."

Grinning wide, he dragged me out onto the ice. I squeezed his hand so hard I could barely feel my fingers. I'd forgotten how hard it was to ice-skate.

"I know, Layla. I'm just giving you a hard time."

Slowly but surely, I glided across the ice beside him, enjoying the serenity of it all. Everything in Friendship moved a lot slower than I was used to, but I loved it. It was time the hectic part of my life took a break. I needed to concentrate on myself. So far, the outcome looked rather promising.

My grip on Colin's hand loosened, but he didn't let go. "I had a good time with you today," he said. "I want to do it again."

Heart racing, I tried to hide my smile and failed. "I'm good with that."

He started to slow down, but my feet didn't know how. Instead, I tripped over myself, and he caught me, pulling me against his body. I held on to him for dear life. A deep chuckle escaped his lips. "I like being around you, Layla. I'm hoping you feel the same way. It's been a long time since I've felt like this about anyone."

Looking into his emerald eyes, I couldn't help but melt against him. "Same," I confessed. "I guess the question is ... what are we going to do about it?"

He leaned in closer. "I have some ideas."

Closing my eyes, I waited for the kiss to come, but a car door slammed and broke me out of the trance. Colin and I glanced over at the inn, where some of his guests were headed inside. Cheeks burning, I reluctantly let him go.

"It's getting late. I should probably get home."

His grin made my heart jump. "Okay, but you owe me a kiss." That was something I definitely looked forward to.

Chapter Eight

Layla

I went to bed all cozy warm until first thing that morning, but when the heat clicked off, I knew something was wrong. Wrapped up in Colin's quilt, I hurried outside to the back of the house, only to see the frozen heater.

"You have got to be kidding me." Hurrying inside, I grabbed my phone and called Colin.

"Good morning," he answered.

"I wish I could say it was, but it's freezing over here. The heater's frozen solid."

"What?" He sighed. "I don't understand."

"I know. That's what's crazy. Think you can come over and take a look?"

I could already hear him starting his truck. "Be there in a sec."

When he arrived at the house, he appeared to be more baffled than I was as he studied the frozen heater. Rubbing the back of his neck, he stared at it. "I don't understand. I've never seen this happen before."

"Neither have I. We never really needed a heater much in Charleston."

Sighing, he stopped beside me, still looking at the heater. "Until I figure this out, you might want to come back to the inn. You can have my cottage again."

Excitement bubbled in my chest. I hated not being at my house, but I loved being at his cottage. "I'll grab some of my things and my sketchpad and head right over."

He turned away from the heater, still baffled as we walked around to the front of the house. "I'll contact one of my buddies and see if he knows what to do. It might take a while to figure it out."

"No worries," I replied, trying to hide my glee. "I just feel bad for kicking you out of your cottage." Which I did, but his home gave me so much inspiration.

We walked to the front door, and he got ready to leave. "It's fine. Brianna's there now. Maybe you could show her your new designs?"

I nodded. "I think I will."

Once I had a few things packed, I made my way to the inn. Brianna was sitting on the front porch swing, talking to Colin while he fixed one of the window wreaths. Brianna jumped up and raced down the stairs. I opened my car door, and she was right there. "Is it true?"

Colin grinned at me from the porch and continued messing with the wreath. "Is what true?" I countered.

Her gaze landed on the sketchpad, sitting on the passenger's seat. "Uh ... your designs. I need to see them, like, yesterday."

Giggling, I reached in and fetched them for her. She carefully held the sketchpad as if afraid it'd break apart. Eyes wide, she slowly looked through the designs. By now, Colin had joined us and peered at them over her shoulder.

"These are absolutely perfect," she gasped, handing the sketchpad back to me. "When you get them on the runway, I'll be one of your models." She said it flippantly, but she couldn't have been more right. Her body and height were perfect, and her walk was great for the runway.

I stared at her, and her eyes widened. "Why are you looking at me like that?"

I held the pad against my chest. "Because I think you just found yourself a job."

Grabbing her heart, she swayed on her feet. "You can't be serious? Me ... a model?"

I waved a hand up and down her body. "You have all the qualifications. Now all I have to do is put together a full fashion line and find the courage to share it."

She bounced up and down and hugged Colin. "This is like a dream come true. I can't wait to tell Mom." Letting him go, she hurried inside the inn.

Colin shook his head and laughed. "You do realize what you've done, right? She's going to have a big head now."

I shrugged. "She's beautiful. I'd love to have her model my designs." Smile fading, I sighed. "That's if I ever do anything with them. I've never been so scared in my life."

Colin placed his hands on my shoulders, the warmth of them seeping into my skin. He looked into my eyes, all serious and determined. "I know we're just getting to know each other, but I have faith in you. You can do this."

"Thanks," I murmured. My gaze focused on the gazebo, and I nodded toward it. "Guess I better head to my office and get busy."

Colin chuckled. "Go. Have fun."

Turning on my heel, my feet crunched through the snow as I headed for the gazebo.

"Layla," Colin called. I glanced at him over my shoulder, and he smiled. "How about dinner tonight? There's a couple of steaks in my refrigerator that I need to grill."

My heart did that crazy flutter thing it always did when he was around. Grinning wide, I continued on my way. "Guess it's a date then."

Chapter Nine

Colin

"I'm so stuffed right now."

Layla handed me the last pot, and I dried it off. "I take it you enjoyed dinner?"

She patted her stomach. "Definitely. I didn't know you could cook."

I handed her a glass of wine and grabbed my beer. "My grand-mother taught me lots of things."

She followed me to the couch and sat beside me, curling her legs underneath her. "Hopefully, I'll get to experience more of your cooking since I'll be here for a while?"

I nodded. "Until we figure out what's going on at your house, you're more than welcome to stay right here. With businesses being closed around Christmas, it'll probably be after the holi-days before I can get anything done." She didn't seem to mind, and neither did I. "Besides," I added, "didn't you mention earlier that you can make a killer chicken pot pie?"

She beamed. "I did." But then her expression saddened, and

she glanced down into her wine. "It's my great-grandmother's recipe passed down. My dad's parents died when I was young, so I don't remember them, but my mom's mother made up for it all." She looked up at me and smiled, her eyes glistening. "I learned how to draw from her. Then it turned into a love for fashion. At least, she got to see my first fashion line take off before passing away." A tear fell down her cheek, but she quickly wiped it away. I knew what it felt like to lose someone so close to me.

"When your next line does the same, do you think you'll move back to the city?" I asked, really not ready to hear the answer. I knew she had her house rented for the next year, but that didn't mean she'd stay. I didn't want her to leave. Before I even knew her, I didn't think she'd fit in with our small-town lifestyle, but I couldn't have been more wrong.

Blowing out a sigh, she took a sip of her wine. "Not sure. I might. Saying it'll take off is being really optimistic." She snorted and laughed it off, clearly underestimating herself.

Finishing off her wine, she set her glass down on the coffee table, grinning mischievously. "Okay, enough about fashion. You, Mr. Jennings, have some explaining to do."

"Oh yeah?" I said, laughing. "What about?"

She waved a hand about the room. "Your living room. Why is there no Christmas tree? It's almost Christmas, and you have nothing." Crossing her arms over her chest, she stuck her head up, chin jutting out defiantly. "If you don't get one, I will. I'll be here until after Christmas, and I can't spend the holidays without one." It was the first time I'd seen the holiday spirit twinkle in her eyes.

"All right," I said. "We'll pick one out tomorrow."

Chapter Ten

Layla

It was strange how certain events in life could lead you down different paths. As I stared down at my sketchpad, I looked at what I hoped to be a huge milestone in my career. I never would've gotten the inspiration to finish a complete fashion line if I hadn't been in this magical spot.

Brianna slammed her car door, and I waved to catch her attention. She waved back. "Hey, Layla!" She zipped up her coat and joined me in the gazebo. "It's early. What are you doing out here?"

I smiled as I handed her my sketchpad. "I finished my designs."

Excited, she sat beside me and flipped through all the pages. "I am so happy for you. What do you do now?"

I shrugged. "Usually, I'd show them to Miriam Parrish. She was the one who discovered me to begin with."

Her eyes widened. "The fashion editor for *Runway*? She's amazing. I didn't realize that was how you got started."

The memories came flooding back to me. "Yep. It's crazy,

really. I was living in New York at the time, working as a hostess at this high-end restaurant while in college. One day, I was sitting on a bench in Central Park, sketching some designs, not realizing she was right behind me."

Brianna grabbed her chest. "I bet you freaked out."

I laughed. "You have no idea. It was so embarrassing. She scheduled a meeting with me the next day, and then everything took off." At least, until she looked at my last line and refused to recommend them.

"Does she know that your original designs were stolen?"

"No," I said, shaking my head. "As much as I wanted to tell her, it would've been a PR nightmare."

Brianna tapped my sketchpad. "You're going to send these to Miriam, right?"

Holding the sketchpad to my chest did nothing to stop my racing heart. "I might. I think I'll wait until after Christmas."

By the look on her face, she didn't like my answer, but I didn't want to tell her how afraid I was. I hadn't spoken to Miriam in months.

The back door of the inn opened, and Colin stepped out, waving when he noticed us.

Brianna snickered and shook her head. "In a million years, I never would've thought my brother would be dating a famous designer."

"We're not dating," I replied regretfully. "We haven't had that talk yet. I don't know what we are."

She glanced over at Colin, who had started toward us. "He's into you, Layla. Anybody can see that. All you have to do is ask him."

"Hey, you two," Colin called out.

We both stood, and I smiled at him. "Hey."

Brianna patted him on the shoulder. "I'm going inside to help Mom with breakfast. You two have fun today." She winked at me and hurried off to the inn.

Gaze narrowed, Colin watched her walk away. "Something going on I should know about?"

"Nope," I said quickly. "It's just Brianna being Brianna."

"I understand that. You about ready to pick out a tree?"

Excitement bubbled in my veins. "More than ready." We hopped in his truck, and I set my sketchpad in the backseat. "Are you sure you don't mind if I buy a tree for your cottage?"

"I'm sure," he said, grinning over at me. "It gives me a reason to break out the ornaments. They haven't been used in a long time." The way he said it made me curious. There was a sadness in his tone.

"Why not?"

Clearing his throat, he turned his attention back to the road. "Guess I never really had a reason to have a tree for myself. The last time I got one was when I was still with my ex."

"I see," I murmured. "Mine never wanted a real tree because he thought they'd make a mess."

His gaze met mine. "Looks like we're better off without them."

"Can't argue with you there."

We pulled up across the street from the Christmas tree lot. This close to Christmas, I knew there wouldn't be many trees left. Colin and I got out of the truck, and he pointed over at a white-haired man, wearing overalls underneath his heavy-duty jacket. "That's Tom. He cuts down each one of these trees from his tree farm and brings them here to sell."

"Wow. That has to be a lot of work."

Colin agreed with a nod. "It is. He always saves his biggest and best ones for the inn." He leaned in close. "I think it's to impress my mother."

"Has she dated at all since your father passed?"

A sad expression crossed his face, and he shook his head. "No. I wouldn't mind if she did. All she does now is focus on the inn."

I linked my arm with his. "Maybe one day she'll be able to love again," I murmured. "You never know."

Smiling at me, he pulled me closer. "How about we find a tree?"

We crossed the street, and I still kept hold of his arm. It felt good to be close to him.

There were only a few trees left, some short, some tall, ranging from full to slim. There was even a Charlie Brown tree for good measure. A red ball hung from the top, making it slump over.

We walked up and down the rows, and it wasn't until we got to the last one, where the perfect tree stuck out at me. However, there was a man I knew standing right in front of it, still dressed in the same dirty clothes from before. He stared at the tree with utter delight on his face.

"Hi, Gabe," I called out.

He turned to us and took off his black cap. "Good morning, you two. Out Christmas tree shopping?"

Chuckling, Colin nodded down at me. "She couldn't live without one. With her heater still on the fritz, we're setting it up at my place."

Letting him go, I smacked him on the arm. "Hey, I just thought your cottage could use a little Christmas spirit. Besides, I need a tree to put presents under."

Gabe's eyes twinkled mischievously. "I'm happy to see things working out for you two." His gaze landed on mine. "Aren't you glad you gave this place a chance? You might've missed out on where you were meant to be."

Cheeks burning, I took a quick side glance at Colin. "I am. Turns out I found my inspiration again."

He nodded. "Hopefully, that means more fashion designs?"

That caught me off guard. "How did you know that?"

His grin widened. "I know a lot of things, Ms. Aberdeen. With your newfound inspiration, don't be afraid to take a chance." Slipping on his black cap, he took a couple steps back. "That goes for both of you."

Colin and I looked at each other skeptically, and when we turned back to Gabe, he was gone. It was the strangest thing. "He hurried off rather quickly," I pointed out.

Agreeing with a nod, Colin searched around, but Gabe was nowhere to be seen. "That he did."

He was, but I had no explanation. "What does he mean by *you* taking a chance?" I asked.

Colin shrugged, and I could see the uncertainty on his face. "Not sure."

Tom came around the corner, catching our attention. He waved toward the tree. "It's a beauty."

Before Colin could pull out his wallet, I already had my money in hand. "Yes, it is," I said. "We'll take it." Tom took my cash, and I grinned wide at Colin. "Too slow."

He burst out laughing and stood back. "You're too much. I have to say, you surprise me every day I'm with you. I bet you have the paparazzi following you around everywhere, don't you?"

For the longest time in New York, I did. That was why I moved back to Charleston, to hopefully enjoy a somewhat normal life. I thought being back in my hometown would help, but it didn't. "It's not all it's cracked up to be," I confessed truthfully. "I never knew who genuinely liked me or if they wanted to be around me because of who I was."

With a heavy sigh, he closed the distance between us, brushing his fingers against my cheek as he pushed a strand of hair away from my face. "Hopefully, you don't feel that way here."

I shook my head. "I don't."

The corner of his lips lifted slightly. "What if . . ."

Heart racing, I waited for him to finish his sentence, but Tom cleared his throat. "Your tree is all ready for you."

I looked back at him and smiled. "Thank you." When I turned back to Colin, I raised my brows. "What were you going to say?"

Colin brushed it off. "Nothing." He picked up one end of the tree, and Tom took the other end. "It's time to decorate."

Chapter Eleven

Colin

"You seriously haven't made a move on her?" Brianna asked incredulously. "You've been around her all week."

I brushed off the snow that'd accumulated on the new house heater. Everything looked good with it, but it still wasn't working. I had no clue what to do to fix it. "I don't know, Bri. She's not like any other woman I've been around. She . . ."

Brianna giggled. "Makes you nervous? Intimidates you? I get it. She's famous, and you're not."

I got to my feet. "That's not it." Then it hit me, maybe the latter part was it. What would Layla want with a guy like me? I wasn't an A-list celebrity who had a mansion and a ton of money.

Brianna's smile faded when she saw my face. "You're worried you're not good enough for her, aren't you?"

She followed me around to the front of the house. "I don't know. What's going to happen when her new line takes off?

There's no way she'll stay if it does." We walked inside, and it was still an icebox. "She's definitely not going to stay if I can't get her heater fixed."

"Or she could just stay where she's at," Brianna said, grinning wide.

"Yeah, right."

"You'd be surprised. I know she likes you, Colin. Anybody can see it. I don't know how you haven't."

Sighing, I locked the door behind us. "I'm not the kind of guy she's going to want on the red carpet with her. I mean, come on," he said, turning to me, "can you see me in a suit and smiling at all the cameras?"

Brianna stared up at me, her expression serious. "Actually, I can. You're amazingly handsome, more so than ninety-nine percent of the actors on TV. You have a cuter smile than anyone I know, and you're a great guy. The complete package. People will be seeking you out once they see you."

I scoffed. "Whatever, Bri," I said, not believing her for a second. "Come on. Let's get back. We have to get ready for the Christmas party."

She hopped in my truck, and we started on our way. "Is Layla going with you?"

I shrugged. "We haven't discussed that part, but I know she wants to go. I'll ask her when we get home."

Brianna patted my arm. "Awesome. Just so you know, it might be a good time to tell her how you feel. That way, when things do look up for her, she'll stay."

The way she said it gave me pause. I, especially, didn't like the sheepish look on her face. "What did you do?"

Clasping her hands together, she popped her knuckles like she always did when she was nervous. "Well ... I can't really explain too much right now. All I can say is that things are about to change."

Groaning, I ran a hand over my face. "A good change or bad?"

She shrugged. "I don't know, but we're going to find out soon."

That was not what I wanted to hear.

Chapter Twelve

Layla

I'd wondered if Colin and I were going to the community Christmas party together, and luckily, he asked if I'd go with him. We'd spent tons of time together this past week, but I still had no clue what was happening between us. It was maddening.

On a brighter note, I had talked to my parents. They promised to never leave again over the holidays.

I was all ready to go when a knock sounded on the front door. I looked at myself one more time in the mirror. It was crazy how so many things had changed. Usually, I'd be dressed in a fancy gown and going to lavish parties. Now I was wearing sweaters, jeans, and boots and going to community Christmas parties. It excited me more than anything.

I hurried downstairs and opened the door. Colin greeted me with that handsomely devilish smile of his and handed me a cup of hot chocolate. "Ready to go?"

The cocoa scent made my mouth water. "I am."

His grin widened. "Great. Because I have a surprise for you. You'll need your thick coat."

I grabbed my other coat and slipped it on. "Is this party outside?" I asked, hoping it wasn't. Small flakes of snow had already begun to fall, and the temperatures had dropped now that the sun had gone down.

Colin chuckled as we walked to the front of the inn. "No, it's not outside. You'll see why in a second."

When we turned the corner, I gasped in surprise. There was a huge sleigh, decorated in white sparkly lights and garland, sitting behind two midnight-colored horses. Tom, the owner of the Christmas tree farm, waved from the driver's seat. "Wow. Are we going to the party in that?"

"We are." Taking my hand, he led me over to the sleigh and helped me in, taking care not to spill my hot chocolate. "Tom just bought the sleigh a few weeks ago and wanted to test it out."

Tom glanced back at me and smiled. "People have been telling me to do this for years."

Colin sat beside me, and I moved closer to him. "I couldn't agree more," I said. "People who visit will love to take rides in it. Could be a huge moneymaker in the winter."

Tom nodded and focused back on the horses. "That's what I'm hoping."

He clucked his tongue, and the horses took off at a gentle trot. "I swear, it feels like we're in a Hallmark movie right now," I said, fascinated by it all. There was nothing more magical than riding into the snow-covered town and looking at all the twinkling lights.

"Does it make you want to stay?" Colin asked, his voice serious.

I met his gaze. "It does, but I can't stay hidden forever. I'm shocked I've been able to for this long. From what I can tell, the media doesn't know where I am."

He nodded. "And they won't. Everyone here knows how important that is to you."

"Why is it like that? No one really knows me around here."

Tom pulled up at the community center, and Colin helped me out of the carriage. "But they want to, Layla. There are a lot of people here who want you to stay."

Music and laughter buzzed from inside the center. We stopped at the door, and I figured it was now or never. "What about you? Do you want me to stay?"

He stared at me, those emerald eyes of his boring into mine. It took my breath away. I waited for his answer, but before he could open his mouth, a group of kids charged outside and into the snow. Colin's mother saw us and waved for us to come inside. There were people dancing and eating tons of food.

Taking my hand, he nodded toward the crowd. "Come on. We should go in before she comes out to get us."

For the whole week, he'd dodged every single question I asked regarding what we were to each other. Every single time, it hurt my heart further. Maybe he didn't see me as anything more than a friend.

"Okay," I said, hoping he couldn't hear the sadness in my tone. "Let's go."

Chapter Thirteen

Layla

The Christmas party was fun, but once we were around everyone, I never had any more alone time with Colin. Brianna and his mother rode back with us in the sleigh when it was all over. I had a great time getting to know more of the townspeople. They really helped me feel at home.

Taking a deep breath, I gathered up the Christmas presents underneath the tree. Colin's family was having a Christmas Eve dinner at the inn, and they had invited me. I didn't want to go empty-handed. It just so happened the most important present for Colin was finished just this morning. I'd dropped off Brianna's present earlier since it was a huge box. I couldn't wait to see her face when she opened it. Most importantly, I couldn't wait to see the look on Colin's face when he opened his.

I walked over to the inn and snuck in through the back door, heading straight to the foyer to put my gifts under the tree. The smell of ham, potatoes, and homemade biscuits filled the air. The dining room was across the hall, and I gasped when I got a look at all the food. It looked like a Christmas magazine cover.

Theresa turned around and opened her arms. "There you are."

I hugged her hard and smiled. "Thank you so much for inviting me. The food smells amazing."

Across the hall in the library, Colin met my gaze. He smiled and joined us in the living room, including Brianna who had joined us from the kitchen with her mouth full. She hurried over to me and threw her arms around my shoulders. "Merry Christmas, Layla. You have no idea how honored I am for you to be here."

I giggled. "I'm just glad you all invited me."

She stepped back and smiled. "Hopefully, you'll like what I got you. It was hard trying to find something for someone who has everything."

I shook my head. "I don't have everything, Brianna. But thank you. I'm sure I'll love whatever it is."

"All right, you guys, let's eat," Theresa called out.

Brianna grabbed her plate and dug in while I stood back and let Theresa get her food first. Colin stepped up beside me, his arm brushing against mine. "I'm sorry your family's not here to celebrate with you."

I shrugged. "It's okay. I'm perfectly happy being here with you and your family."

Again, I waited for him to reply with some kind of answer, but he didn't. Instead, he motioned toward the food. "After you."

I gathered up a plate full of food, including a huge helping of sweet potato casserole. We sat around the smaller kitchen table, enjoying our food while Colin's mother told stories of their past Christmases. It was nice to hear about the good times they had and the traditions they still upheld. Their family had deep roots that my family couldn't touch. I hadn't seen my aunts, uncles, or cousins in years. We were all scattered across the country.

After dinner was done and we were all stuffed, we moved to the foyer and sat around the Christmas tree. Colin took his place beside me on the love seat, while Theresa stood by the tree and Brianna sat on the floor so she could grab the presents and hand them out.

She picked up the present that I'd gotten for Theresa and gave it to her. Theresa held a hand over her heart. "Layla, you didn't have to get me anything."

I shrugged. "It's the least I could do. You all have pretty much taken me in the past couple of weeks."

She opened the present gently as if she didn't want to rip the paper. Brianna shook her head and smiled. Theresa pulled out the envelope and gasped when she looked inside. "Oh my goodness." She looked at me in awe. "This is too much."

Inside were two plane tickets and vouchers for an exclusive resort in the Virgin Islands. Brianna grabbed the contents and squealed. "I'm totally going with you."

Theresa took it all back. "Says who?" She winked, and Brianna hugged her.

The next present Brianna grabbed was labeled to me. She set it on my lap and bit her lip. "I honestly didn't know what to get you, but I think I made a good choice."

The box was heavy, and I could hear the sound of glass clanking together. When I opened it up, my eyes burned with unshed tears. Inside was a dozen jars of my three favorite pickled vegetables: beets, okra, and carrots. "I love it, Brianna. Did you pickle them yourself?"

Brianna nodded. "I didn't know what to get you since you have everything, so I thought this would be more appropriate. You told me your grandmother used to make them for you when she was alive."

A tear fell down my cheek. "She did. This means a lot to me. Thank you." I hugged her hard and nodded at the presents. "Yours is the big one over there."

She walked over to the largest present in the room. Her face lit up when she saw it was hers. She ripped the paper open and tore into the box. It was filled to the brim with my designs. "Holy . . ." She screamed so loud we had to cover our ears. "This is seriously the best gift ever." She ran over to me and hugged me so hard I could barely breathe. "Thank you so much."

I laughed. "You're welcome. I had them all flown in."

While Brianna was busy sorting through all of her clothes, Theresa picked up the last two presents and handed them to Colin. My heart raced as he looked at the tags. Sighing, he looked over at me. "You didn't have to do this."

I rolled my eyes. "Just open them. Do the small one first."

He opened the small one, which revealed the manual for a coffeemaker I'd bought him. It was an espresso machine as well. Shaking his head, he held it up. "Didn't like my coffeemaker?"

Sheepishly, I shrugged. "I thought you could use a new one. It works a lot faster. I already have it in your kitchen, ready to use. You can try it out tonight if you want."

His lips lifted slightly. "I might just do that."

When he got to the next present, my pulse was in overdrive. He opened the box and moved away all the tissue paper, revealing what was underneath. He stared at it for the longest time, his eyes taking in every single inch.

Theresa and Brianna rushed over, and both gasped. "It's beautiful," Theresa cried, wiping a tear away.

Brianna agreed with a nod. "It is. It's almost like they're here."

Colin held up the canvas, giving us all a good look at it. After I'd met Mrs. Denton, Glenda, from the art gallery, I had her paint a picture of the Snowflake Lane Inn. On the front porch swing were Theresa and Brianna, and standing in the front were Colin and his grandparents with his arms around them. Brianna had nailed the meaning behind it. I wanted it to be like they were still around.

Colin handed the painting to his mother and pulled me into his arms. It was the closest I'd been to him in days. "Thank you, Layla. That picture means a lot to me."

"You're welcome," I murmured. I didn't want to leave his arms, but my phone rang. Reluctantly, I stepped away from him and focused on the number. It was from New York. "I'll be right back," I said to everyone. I stepped into the library across the hall and answered it. "Hello?"

"Ms. Aberdeen?"

"Yes," I said, trying to recognize the voice. It sounded familiar.

"Hi, I'm Andrea, Mrs. Parrish's assistant. I've spoken to you before, but I didn't know if you'd remember me."

Completely caught off guard, my knees gave out, and I fell into one of the brown leather chairs. "Andrea, yes. I remember you. How are you?"

"Great, as a matter of fact. Miriam's been dying to talk to you. She's on the other line. Do you mind if I connect you?"

The breath left my lungs. "Seriously?"

Andrea burst out laughing. "Yes, seriously. I'll let her tell you the good news."

Good news? I was clueless. The line beeped, and Miriam cleared her throat. "Layla?"

"Miriam," I replied nervously, "to what do I owe this pleasure?"

"Your new designs, of course. I've looked over them all, and I'm in love."

"What? How?"

"Your assistant, Brianna, sent them over to me. Amazing job, my dear. I know you took it hard after your last line, but you've totally redeemed yourself. I'd love to meet with you after Christmas."

I was in shock and didn't know what to think. "Of course," I blurted. "After Christmas is great."

"Wonderful. Andrea will get it scheduled in. Right now, I have to finish drinking my eggnog. See you soon." She hung up, and I stood there, mouth gaping.

Brianna walked by with a sugar cookie in her hand and stopped when she saw me. "You okay?"

I held up my phone. "You tell me. I just got a call from Miriam."

She held up her hands and stepped back, a look of terror on her face. "Please don't be mad at me. When you left your sketchpad in Colin's truck, I was afraid you wouldn't do anything with them so I made copies. I knew that Miriam Parrish was the woman to speak to, so I called, pretending to be your assistant." On the verge of tears, she walked into the library. "What did she say?"

Without a smile on my face, I stared at her for a few seconds, hoping to make her sweat. She lowered her head, and I smiled, drawing her attention back when I snickered. "She loved them," I announced happily. "She wants to get together after Christmas."

"Everything okay in here?" Colin asked, standing in the doorway.

Brianna jumped up and down excitedly. "Miriam liked Layla's designs. They're going to discuss everything after Christmas."

Colin looked over at me. "Congratulations, Layla. You've worked hard for it."

"Did you know?" I asked him.

Sighing, he glanced down at Brianna. "I was told yesterday to keep it a secret."

Sheepishly, Brianna shrugged. "Sorry."

"It's okay," I said, draping my arm over Brianna's shoulder. "Looks like I have an assistant now. That is, if you're up for the job."

Her eyes widened, and she froze. "This is literally the best Christmas ever. Someone pinch me."

Theresa peeked her head around the corner and motioned for me. "You haven't seen your Christmas present yet. Come on." Colin smiled and stepped out of the way when I walked past. Theresa pointed to the front door. "Look out there."

I walked to the door, and outside, there was a couple getting out of a car. It didn't take long to realize who they were. "Oh my God."

I raced outside, and my mom flung her arms open. "Merry Christmas, sweetheart."

Excited beyond belief, I hugged both my parents. "What are you two doing here?"

My dad kissed the top of my head. "We were hoping to surprise you. We've been planning this for weeks."

I hugged them again. I couldn't believe they'd kept that from me. "Thank you. I didn't want to spend Christmas without you two."

By now, Colin, Brianna, and Theresa were all outside. I introduced them to my parents, and Colin helped grab their bags from their rental car. We walked side by side back into the inn. "You should spend tonight with your parents. We can take a rain check on the new coffeemaker."

Sadly, I nodded, but I had my parents for Christmas, which made me extremely happy. For once, in a very long time, everything was looking up for me.

Chapter Fourteen

Layla

Christmas Day

My parents stayed in Colin's cottage with me. We spent the entire night talking about anything and everything. They were extremely excited about my new line. There was a lot to think about as far as where I wanted to go after that. Did I want to move back to the big city or keep a low profile? I knew what my heart wanted.

"Layla, we're going to the main house for breakfast. Are you coming?" my mother called out.

I leaned out of my bedroom door, holding my red sweater over my chest. "I'll be there in a minute. Go ahead without me." The front door shut, so I quickly slipped on my sweater, jeans, and boots.

It was Christmas morning. Colin's entire family would be arriving soon at the inn. I was going to meet the whole Jennings side.

Once I grabbed my phone, I opened the front door, only to

come toe to toe with Colin. "Whoa," I said, sucking in a breath. "You scared me."

The wind blew his cologne my way, and I breathed it in. He chuckled and glanced down my body. "Sorry. You look beautiful, by the way."

"Thanks. You look rather dapper yourself." And he did, dressed in his jeans and gray sweater. I missed him wearing his plaid shirts. I had begun to get used to them.

Clearing his throat, he glanced down at a small wrapped box in his hands. "I wanted to find some time to get you alone. When I saw your parents leave, I figured it was now or never."

He handed me the present, and I opened it. Inside was a gorgeous, sparkling snowflake necklace. "Colin, it's beautiful." I pulled it out, and he fastened it around my neck.

"I wanted to give it to you last night but never got the chance."

I placed a hand over the snowflake. "Thank you." It was obvious there was more to say by the determined look on his face. "Why are you really here, Colin?"

With a heavy sigh, he stepped back and ran a hand through his hair. "Layla, there's so many things. After last night and hearing about New York, it made me realize how stupid I've been."

He closed the distance and grabbed my hands. "When we ran into Gabe at the tree farm and he told us both to take a chance, I didn't realize what he meant at first. But then, I got to thinking. For so long, I was afraid to take a chance on anyone, least of all you. You're famous as hell. What would you ever want with someone like me?"

I started to speak, but he held up a hand. "I have to get this out." Taking my hands again, he held them to his chest. "I've fallen for you, Layla. I tried to keep my distance because I knew there was a huge chance you were going to leave. And then I started second-guessing myself on whether I was good enough for you."

"Colin," I breathed. My heart pounded so hard I was sure he could hear it.

He moved closer, his lips only a breath away. "It turns out, it doesn't matter if I am or not. I want to be with you, Layla."

I looked right into his emerald eyes. "Do you have any idea how long I've waited to hear you say that? You've dodged me every time I've tried getting answers from you."

He sighed. "I know. All I wanted to do was tell you how I felt. I couldn't let you leave without knowing the truth."

I smiled up at him. "I'm glad you did ... because I fell for you too."

That devilish smile of his was back. "You did?"

"Yes," I said with a giggle. "And just so you know, I'm not going anywhere. I've decided to stay here no matter what. Granted, I'll have to travel every now and again, but my home is here."

He held my hands tighter against his chest. "I don't know what to say. What happens now?"

I looked up above his head where a bundle of mistletoe hung from the doorway. He followed my line of sight and chuckled. "Guess that answers it then."

We stared into each other's eyes and he leaned in close, our lips touching gently. I closed my eyes and he deepened the kiss. Our lips parted and he rested his forehead to mine. "Merry Christmas, Layla. Moving here wasn't so bad was it?"

"It was the best decision I ever made."

Runaway Christmas Bride

CINDI MADSEN

Chapter One

This was the day she'd dreamed about for so long, of having a winter wedding and being a Christmas bride. Then all her plans, her future—everything she'd been so sure about—had been ripped away the instant her groom had looked at her and said, "I'm sorry, Regina. I just can't. I can't marry you."

Naturally he'd chosen to say it while they were standing at the front of the chapel, their family and friends all witnesses as she was dumped at the altar. Her bridesmaids had tried to stop her from fleeing the scene, but she'd needed out of there so she'd hopped in her car—decorated with streamers and cans, and don't even get her started on the "Just married!!!" written in white shoe polish on the back window. The stupid, overly cheery phrase taunted her every time she glanced in the rearview mirror.

Tears had streamed down her face as she'd driven north. She wasn't even sure how long she'd been on the road or where she was—she was almost sure there'd been a sign about entering Massachusetts—but the tears had finally mostly dried up. The gas tank was about to go dry too, which meant she needed to stop soon.

I should've seen this coming. Steve had always told her she didn't know how to relax and have fun. They'd had fights about having fun—talk about the *opposite* of a good time. He thought she was too structured, and she thought he needed more organization and responsibility in his life. Silly her, she'd thought that was why they would make a good pair. Their weaknesses were each other's strengths, and wasn't there something poetic in that? She thought love would smooth out the times they grew irritated at their differences.

Perhaps, over the past few crazy months, she'd been a little too fixated on plans and the future instead of the groom. Still, he could've pulled her aside a dozen times to tell her he wanted to call off the wedding. It would've stung, sure, but there was stinging and then there was feeling naked and exposed in front of your family and friends.

We were supposed to be spending Christmas on the beach, and now I'll spend it all alone.

A figure on the side of the road caught her eye. She'd never been able to walk by someone in need without handing over any spare change she had, and while her parents had made her promise to stop picking up hitchhikers unless she at least had company, she couldn't leave the guy standing there with his thumb up. Not with the brewing snowstorm, and not when she'd experienced enough desperation today to have empathy for someone else who might be in a dire situation.

Regina slowed the car and pulled onto the side of the road. An icy gust of air whooshed inside as she unrolled the window, and she shivered, her bare shoulders breaking out in goose bumps. She'd worked so hard to get extra definition in her arms, and while she had a fluffy white wrap to go over her dress, she'd abandoned it like the rest of her wedding.

"Need a ride?" she asked, which she supposed was unnecessary considering most people didn't hail cars if they didn't need a ride.

A scruffy guy, wearing a dirty, worn beanie with holes and a coat that had seen better days, stuck his head inside. His bloodshot eyes widened as he took in her wedding dress. She could only imagine how crazy she looked, driving a car in poofy layers of white tulle, her veil batted back over pinned curls she felt coming undone, her professionally applied makeup a smeared mess by now, no doubt. "I'd love a ride," he said. "Just down the way."

"Hopefully, not too far down the way. I'm running low on gas."

"It's about fifteen miles, give or take. Friendship is a pretty small town, but you can refill your car and stop and have some dinner. Like its name suggests, there are a lot of friendly people there. It's sort of my makeshift home for now," he said with a chuckle. "House or not."

Regina assumed that meant he didn't have a house, and a pang of sympathy went through her. Here she was feeling sorry for herself because she'd wasted money on an extravagant wedding that had fallen through, and this guy didn't have a place to live. "I'll gladly take you there."

He grabbed a worn bag and eyed the backseat, probably thinking she'd rather have him there. She wasn't sure what proper etiquette in this situation was, possibly because there wasn't any.

"Feel free to sit up front," she said. "I don't bite. I might cry, though, so I hope that doesn't scare you."

"I think I can handle a few tears." He settled into the passenger seat, and she cranked up the heater as he reached out to warm his hands. He smelled like it'd been a while since his last bath. "Anything I can do to help?"

She shrugged. "I could use a new groom," she said with a mostly sarcastic laugh. Apparently it wasn't quite funny yet. "Or maybe what I need is the desire to never have one." All her life she'd pictured her future self with a loving husband and a couple of children, an idyllic little family who often laughed together.

"You'll find somebody. Somebody who deserves you and will love you for you." The confidence in his voice assured her, despite the fact that he had no way of knowing something like that.

"Thank you." She extended her hand. "I'm Regina, by the way."

He shook her hand, one firm shake that convinced her he was of good, solid character. Sometimes you could just tell. "Gabe."

After carefully checking over her shoulder for oncoming traffic, she pulled onto the freeway. Or was it a highway? Come to think of it, there hadn't been another car in forever, and the road looked too dinky to be an interstate.

Well, that's mildly disconcerting. Then again, on a scale of one to sucky, it couldn't compare to the rest of her day. But if she thought about that too much, she'd start crying again, so she made small talk with Gabe.

He wasn't a man of many words, answering most of her questions with a simple yes or no, but it helped pass the time. Then he pointed out the turnoff into Friendship, its big happy sign greeting them as they officially entered town. Flurries danced through the air, falling to the window in pretty white puffs, and she glanced at the time.

She'd been driving for almost seven hours without so much as one bathroom stop, and now that food had been mentioned, she couldn't stop thinking about it. On top of the exercising, she'd been on a low-sugar diet, one that basically meant that if a food brought you joy, it was out. She'd kept motivated on the treadmill by thoughts of her gorgeous, tiered wedding cake with the spongy chocolate goodness waiting under the fluffy white frosting. She'd told herself it'd be that much better after a month of no sweets, and since she hadn't had so much as a taste, she was planning on ordering dinner *and* dessert. Maybe even *two* desserts.

Considering the looming storm, she should probably also think about settling somewhere for the night. Not only did she hate driving in the snow, she wasn't used to it and didn't have the vehicle or the tires for it.

Regina turned down Main Street, heading toward the lights of the town, which appeared to be even tinier than she'd expected. "Does this place have a hotel?"

"The Snowflake Inn's on the other side of town and is usually pretty booked," Gabe said, "but there's a nice B and B nearby called the Cozy Cottage, and I'm sure they have an open room or two."

All she needed was a bed. "Sounds perfect." Tomorrow she'd make a different plan, a new sensation for someone who lived and died by them. "If you need a room, I could—"

"Thank you, Regina, but you've done enough for me. In fact, if you'll just drop me off up here, that'd be great."

Gabe's steady presence had been comforting, and it was odd how sad she was they had to part ways already. She could tell a good soul when she met one, and in spite of her misguided choice of groom, she still believed her gut instincts were good.

Once she'd stopped the car, Gabe gathered his stuff and flashed her a warm smile. "You should stop by Grumpy's Bar and Grill a few blocks down. The food's amazing, and trust me, you won't be sorry."

"Grumpy's in Friendship?"

"Yeah, the owner has quite the sense of humor. But don't let that scare you. Best food in town." He lowered his voice. "Don't tell Fern I said that."

"Your secret's safe with me," Regina said with a laugh. Especially since she didn't know Fern and doubted she'd come across her in her short stay here. Her stomach rumbled at the thought of food, though, making its vote known. Striding inside a restaurant in a wedding dress was a special kind of crazy, but it was like her brain couldn't even entertain the thought of stopping and changing first. Not that she had anything besides clothes meant for the tropics anyway. "Nice meeting you, and good luck with everything. And happy holidays."

Was that stupid? His holidays might not be happy, and she wanted to make them better, even if she didn't know how.

"Happy holidays," he said, and then he closed the door and she was alone again. Just her and her wedding dress and her decked-out car that looked like Cupid threw up on it.

It'd been a long day, and Emmett wanted to kick back and relax with a late dinner at Grumpy's. As sheriff of Friendship, he was never truly *off* work, but at least his job in this sleepy town mostly involved giving gentle reminders to abide by the rules and arbitrating minor disputes.

Of course, a few citizens remained sore at him when he didn't automatically pick their side. More than once he'd been told, "But you've known me for decades/most of my life/since high school!" Today was one of those days, and Fern Simpson didn't seem to care he'd known the other party for equally as long— both citizens had a decade or two on him, so he'd known them pretty much since birth.

As if having the town's B&B owner mad at him wasn't enough, Fern's daughter had jumped in to defend her mom's side of the debate, so now he had two females irritated with him. Fern had also been nice enough to remark that he was always in a sour mood these days. He couldn't exactly deny it, though he also couldn't pinpoint why.

As he entered Grumpy's, he heard a blend of voices yelling "cheers," and within seconds, he sensed the vibe was different somehow.

And that was *before* he noticed the woman in the wedding dress seated among the regulars. All he could make out from here was dark hair and a whole lot of white fabric. The bartender's gaze met Emmett's over the top of her head, and he gestured him over.

Three seconds in, and something tells me there'll be no relaxing dinner in my future.

"I think it's time to cut her off," Grumpy sternly said when one of the guys requested that he pour her another shot.

A drunken disorderly bride. That was a new one. Emmett racked his brain for who was getting married, but he didn't recall any upcoming weddings, and those types of celebrations usually involved the entire town—whether or not the bride and groom technically invited them.

The woman rocked on her stool and then gripped the bar. "Thass prob-ly a good idea. I ... Where'd my fries go? Didn't I have fries?"

All he'd wanted was a burger and a few minutes of quiet before he went home and crawled into bed. Emmett raked a hand through his hair and moved closer to the rowdy group. "You heard him. Let's give her a little breathing room and get her some water. Has she had food?"

"*Jeez.* Someone's a party pooper." She giggled and wobbled again. She remained facing forward as she focused on regaining her balance, and while he hadn't gotten a good look at her yet, he didn't recognize her. "But have no fear, I've had all the things. These guys made sure I was taken care of and had lots of drinks to choose from."

He scowled at the men lining the bar. "You guys bought her drinks? How many did you think she needed?" If he didn't know the crowd so well, he'd be angry, assuming they were trying to get her drunk, but since these were guys he'd grown up with, he leashed his anger, hoping he wouldn't have to let it out once he got the full story.

Guilt bled into their features, and Jack spoke up. "Some jerk left her at the altar, and we took it upon ourselves to welcome her to town and to help cheer her up."

"We didn't know she was a lightweight," Corbin added.

She smacked her palm on the bar. "See? I *can* be fun!"

"Well, I can't," Emmett muttered. He put his hand on her arm and slowly spun her around so he could assess just how drunk she was.

Her gaze moved to the handcuffs on his belt, and her eyes widened. "Are you gonna arrest me?" She tipped her face up to him, and he got caught up staring at her delicate features and big blue eyes, and man, she was pretty. He had the urge to cup her cheek and assure her everything would be okay, and then he wondered what had gotten into him and tried to shake off the surge of attraction—the woman had just been left at the altar. She was wearing a *wedding dress*, for goodness' sake.

Her shoulders slumped. "Perfect. Might as well end this crappy day in jail."

She attempted to stand. One of the legs of the stool pinned her skirt to the floor, so she tugged at the material. It came free, and she stumbled right into him. "*Oof!*" She braced her hands against his chest to steady herself. Then she turned her arms over, extending her wrists and accepting her fate—like he'd really cuff her. He only handcuffed belligerent offenders, and that was usually for their own good.

Emmett frowned down at her, telling himself to stifle the spark that ignited deep in his gut. "I'm not going to arrest you. I'll take your car keys though."

Her mouth dropped, and judging by the offense in her features, maybe he'd underestimated her ability to get belligerent. "I'd *never* drive like this! I can't believe you'd think I'd drive while under the influence, something I hardly ever am, by the way."

Funny enough, this was the second time he'd been accused of believing bad things about someone today, but at least he'd actually *known* the other party. "Not something I'd know, ma'am."

She scowled and flopped back onto the stool. "Well, now you do. Plus, I'm not sure where my purse is anyway, and my keys are somewhere in there, and ... " Her eyebrows drew together, and she rubbed her forehead. Evidently it didn't help, because she dropped her head on the bar and groaned. "I'm supposed to be on my way to Jamaica. Nice, warm Jamaica."

"You must've taken a wrong turn at Albuquerque," he said, because his grandparents had raised him on Bugs Bunny cartoons and it'd just sort of popped out.

Sputtered laughter shook the brunette's shoulders. "So *that's* where I went wrong."

Emmett exhaled and gestured for Corbin to move off the stool next to her so he could occupy it. "Look ... "

"Regina," she supplied, her forehead still on the bar, which couldn't be comfortable, although it didn't seem to bother her.

"Regina. I'm Sheriff Haywood."

"If it's okay with you, I'm just going to call you Sheriff Party Pooper."

He gritted his teeth. "Not really okay with me."

She twisted her head and blinked at him, her cheek on one of those cardboard coasters Grumpy handed out but nobody used. "Not really surprised."

He fought back a smile. There was something about her underneath the layers of sadness and alcohol, and there he went, having the urge to touch her again—cheek, shoulder, a comforting hand to her back. He wasn't picky.

Focus, Haywood. "As I was saying, I'm glad to hear you wouldn't drive under the influence." Most people needed reminders about the laws now and then, especially in this town where they thought the small size and the fact that they'd known him forever left certain laws open to interpretation. "I'm happy to give you a ride to wherever you're staying tonight."

"I haven't checked to see if they have a room for me, but I was told to go to the Cozy Cottage."

Since the lady who owned the Cozy Cottage was one-half of the pissed-off party, Emmett also knew that she and her daughter had left town for the night, and that meant there was no getting her checked in right now. Add in the burst pipe that had shut off access to at least one or two of the spare rooms, and they were up a creek.

Maybe water's a too-accurate analogy. The town plumber wouldn't drop everything to fix the pipe since he had other jobs scheduled, and that was when Emmett had been called in. A few of the local boys had at least slowed the leak, but pipes needed to be purchased from the next city over, and Fern was hopping mad the plumber wouldn't bump her to the top of his list.

Fern had insisted that, with the Snowflake Inn booked, it

was important she have spare rooms, and Emmett had inwardly rolled his eyes that she thought anyone would unexpectedly enter their tiny town and suddenly need a room. At one point it'd even been suggested that *he* drive to get the pipes, like he could simply abandon his post. Now he got to be the one to tell the woman across from him that there was no room at the inn. A little too ironic considering the time of year.

"The Cozy Cottage had to close for the night, but I'm sure we can find you a place to stay."

"How far's the next town? I can't drive, but maybe if I get a taxi?"

"It's a good hour's drive from here. Not to mention it's snowing pretty hard now." He glanced at the guys who'd been so helpful at plying her with alcohol. "Jack? Don't you guys have a spare room?"

His eyes flew wide. "My wife would kill me if I brought home a pretty girl I met at the bar, no matter what the explanation. I just got my bar privileges back, at that." He glanced at her. "Sorry, Regina."

She swiped a hand through the air, the *don't-worry-about-it* in the gesture clear.

Emmett turned to Corbin.

"Don't look at me," he said. "I got more kids than beds, and the dogs occupy the couch."

The other guy down the bar was married to Fern's daughter, so Emmett couldn't exactly ask them to do him a favor.

More head shakes all around, and he noticed that Grumpy had backed away before he could even ask. Great. He'd just promised not to arrest her, and not that he would, but he could hardly cart her to the jail to sleep on an uncomfortable bed in her wedding dress. Obviously, she'd had a hard enough day.

Taking her to his house? The words *bad idea* flashed through his head. Not only because he couldn't stop thinking about how beautiful she was and forgetting that he needed to remain professional, but also because she shouldn't go home with a perfect stranger who lived alone. *He* knew she'd be safe, but she was drunk, her judgment impaired, and he wouldn't put her in that situation. In fact, if she accepted an offer like that, he'd have to lecture her about reckless decisions.

There was only one option, as he saw it. He only hoped it didn't mean more of Friendship's female citizens being upset with him.

"I have an idea. I've just gotta make a call . . ."

Chapter Two

Regina's first thought upon entering the bar and grill earlier, only to have everyone stare at her, had been to run for the second time that day.

But then someone had shouted, "Hon, you look like you could use a drink!" And every time her smile had faltered, both during and after the retelling of her failed nuptials, the guys called for another shot, and she might've gotten carried away.

Mr. Hottie Police Officer placed his hand on her lower back as he guided her out of Grumpy's but then quickly jerked it away. Apparently, she was the only one feeling the attraction vibes. Or maybe that was the alcohol. Given the dirty blond hair, kept short, the shaven face, the deep brown eyes, and the way he carried himself—almost as if he owned this town—she'd be attracted sober or drunk or any stage in between. But hello, she'd just gotten out of a relationship—*understatement*—and he was so dang serious. Which was something she'd been accused of being more times than she could count.

Can't you just relax and have a little fun? Steve had asked after dinner a couple of weeks ago.

I'll relax after the wedding, she'd said, the way she often put off her relaxation until the next thing was done, and then the next thing, until she couldn't remember the last time she'd relaxed. About thirty or so minutes ago was rather blissful, but reality was knocking at the door now, and as hard as she pushed against the other side, it'd come busting in soon enough.

Regina stepped up to the back of the police car, but Sheriff Haywood opened the passenger door instead and guided her toward it. "You're up front with me. And here." He shed his police coat and thrust it at her.

"I don't really feel cold." Weird, because a layer of snow covered the ground and more of the white stuff drifted down around them, like they were in one of those pretty globes. An officer and a bride—not the usual snow globe characters, but it made her smile anyway.

"You've got goose bumps, so you're cold. Just put it on."

"A 'please' wouldn't hurt," Regina muttered, but did as he asked, and with the material still warm from his body, a different type of warmth rose up. The coat smelled nice, too, musky and woodsy, and if he wasn't staring at her with a confused, frustrated expression on his face, she might've even lifted the fabric and taken a sniff.

He opened his mouth as if to speak, but someone walked by, and the sheriff's gaze moved to them. He nodded at the guy. "Hey, it's getting bad out, and the storm's supposed to dump more snow. You need a place to stay for the night?"

"Thank you, Sheriff, but I've got somewhere to stay."

The voice sounded familiar, and as the guy stepped into the puddle of lamplight, Regina recognized the hitchhiker.

"Hey, Gabe! You were totally right. That restaurant was the best, and the people here are the nicest." She lifted a hand to the side of her face and stage-whispered, "Even if the sheriff is a bit grumpy." She snorted a laugh. "Maybe *he* should own Grumpy's."

The sheriff glanced at her, and remorse crept in. He was helping her out and had offered Gabe a place to stay too. And right when she'd decided he was the gruffest person she'd ever met, he'd made that Bugs Bunny joke. So now she struggled to land on the exact right description for him.

"Um, thanks again for not arresting me," she said.

One corner of the sheriff's mouth turned up a fraction of an inch, and her nerve endings pricked up as she anticipated getting a whole smile. But then his mouth flattened into a firm line, the good humor leaving as quickly as it'd come. He turned back, assumedly to address Gabe, but he was nowhere to be seen.

Hmm. I'm even more buzzed than I thought. She was returning to her one glass of wine limit from here on out.

Now I'm making plans for all my future drinking. Yeah, Regina, you really are a barrel of monkeys. No wonder Steve got out while he could.

"What's with the face?" the sheriff asked.

"What's with *your* face?" she countered so she wouldn't have to explain—and honestly, her outfit should say enough. Spoiler alert: any woman wearing a bridal gown not in a shop, the privacy of her own home, or while standing next to a groom, has had a bad day.

"How do you know Gabe?" Sheriff Haywood asked.

"He was out on the highway hitchhiking, so I gave him a ride into town."

A scowl creased the sheriff's face. "You make it a habit of picking up strangers?"

She swung out her arm, toward the spot Gabe previously occupied. "You just offered him a place to stay."

"Yeah, because he's not a complete stranger to me, and I'm a big guy who could handle myself if someone attacked me."

"I have good gut instincts."

He gave her dress a pointed look, and her jaw dropped for the second time that night. Before she could say anything, he said, "Just . . . maybe don't pick up too many hitchhikers. It makes it hard to keep people safe, even if I admire that you'd do something so nice for a stranger."

"Lucky for you, I'm not your concern most of the time." She yawned, exhaustion suddenly hitting her hard. Cold was setting in, too, and she wrapped her arms around herself, glad for the jacket.

"Well, here and now you are, and I plan to make sure you have a safe, comfortable place to sleep tonight, so why don't you get in the car?" The sheriff nudged her inside, shoving the extra layers of her now snow-covered skirt into the car before shutting the door.

Regina put on the seat belt, and as he drove down the road, she leaned back farther in the seat. Her brain told her to pay attention to her surroundings and what was happening, but her eyelids kept drifting closed, and all she vaguely recalled was being carried inside a warm house and laid on a couch. Voices, male and female, and then someone took off her heels and dragged a blanket over the top of her.

She sighed at the comfort, and right before drifting off into that deep, blissful sleep, she swore that a callused hand cupped her cheek, there only for a moment before it was gone.

Chapter Three

The sound of clanging pots and pans jerked Regina awake, forcefully enough that she tumbled to the floor, something binding her legs and keeping her from catching herself. White tulle obscured her vision, along with a few dark curls, and as the scent of coffee invaded her senses, yesterday came screeching back to her. Standing at the front of the church, Steve telling her he couldn't marry her, driving for hours, a bar and grill with friendly people, drinking way too much, and a very sexy cop.

"You okay?"

The deep voice washed over her, waking up every single cell in her body. She glanced up, wishing she were less of a hot mess and then deciding that ship had sailed last night when she asked if he was going to arrest her.

She attempted to stand but found her legs still inexorably bound, so she flipped the veil off her face—she couldn't believe she still had it on—and then tugged at the multiple layers of her gown, trying to free herself. "Things are a tad fuzzy. Are we at … your place?" A sober Regina would've never agreed to go home with a man she didn't know, no matter what the circumstances.

"My place." A blond woman stepped into view and gave a little wave with the spatula in her hand, and Regina experienced an insane moment of jealousy. Of course, he had a gorgeous girlfriend. "I'm Callie—his sister."

"Oh. *Oh.*" Crap, had she accidentally revealed her relief? It didn't mean he didn't have a girlfriend, and since she was merely driving through town, that didn't matter anyway. "But you don't live together?" A weird question, but her brain wasn't at the top of its game.

"I have a place of my own not far from here," the sheriff said, his eyebrows knitted together, acknowledging the weirdness of the question.

"So you stayed to watch over me?" A swirl of warmth went through her. For such a gruff guy, that was surprisingly considerate. She had on a dark brown coat with a badge emblem too—his coat. "Because you were worried about me?"

His expression made it clear that not only was she miles from the truth, he definitely thought she was a crazy person. Considering her current situation, she wasn't sure she could contest that assessment.

Her stomach dropped as dawning hit. "Because you were worried I might be a psycho, and you didn't want to leave me alone with your sister." She finally managed to get her skirt untwisted enough to push to her feet.

"You were drinking in a bar while wearing a wedding dress," he said, and his sister smacked his arm and whispered for him to "Be nice, Emmett."

Emmett. That name fit him, although since he'd introduced himself as Sheriff Haywood, clearly Regina didn't get to use it.

"It's okay. He did a nice thing bringing me here instead of making me sleep it off in jail. Can't ask for much more than that.

And my name's Regina, by the way." She reached up, removed her veil, and tossed it on top of her purse, which had been placed on the coffee table, and not by her. At least, she didn't remember doing it. "Obviously, yesterday was a rough day. I'm sorry if I caused any inconvenience. I'll, um, find my car and then make a plan to get out of your hair."

"We'll get to that after breakfast," the sheriff said. "How do you like your coffee?"

"Caffeinated."

He cracked a smile—an actual, full smile with a hint of teeth. And as she walked toward the steaming mug he offered, it felt like maybe one day she could look back at this whole ordeal and there'd be more than just bad memories in the mix.

Emmett glanced across the cruiser at Regina, who was now wearing a pair of his sister's too-short jeans along with a fuzzy sweater that made him want to pet it and see how soft it was. The thought of her leaving bothered him for some reason, even though the woman had only brought about a lot of complications.

Regina made a wistful noise as she peered out the window. "Look how cute this place is with all the garland, ribbon, and 'Season's Greetings' flags. You've got the whole town decorated, and I bet there was a tree lighting ceremony and everything."

"It's tonight, actually. It always causes a big ol' fuss too. Every year I nearly have to break apart fights over who gets to flip the switch to light the tree."

She laughed. "Okay, Grinch, I hear you loud and clear. You think the town celebrations are silly."

He sighed. "Not all of them. People here just take every little event so seriously, and someone always gets offended, and guess who they come running to?"

"The obvious answer says you, although I'm not sure why. If I wanted to rant, I'd choose a more sympathetic ear."

"And how do you know I'm not sympathetic?" he asked, trying not to be offended and experiencing a pinch of it anyway.

"I never said you weren't. In fact, between the help you gave me and offered to Gabe last night, I know you are. But sympathetic acts and a sympathetic ear are two different things, and I bet you cut rants short by telling people things like 'suck it up.' Possibly even suggest they're complaining about First World problems."

"I would never use that phrasing, even if it fits."

She grinned like she'd caught him red-handed, and her smile hit him right in the chest. He'd already figured out plenty about her too. For example, she seemed like the type to expect a lot, which led to constant disappointments. Emmett had dated a woman with the same personality, and he and his small town had fallen short. Still, he felt bad Regina had been left at the altar, and clearly that guy should've had the guts to tell her before she'd gotten all dressed up in that beautiful gown. On account of that, he'd help her to her car and then wish her good-bye and get to work—he was already an hour behind schedule thanks to last night's shenanigans.

"That's my car," she said, her entire body tensing, and he frowned as he looked it over. The snow had dusted it, but with the sun moving higher in the sky, most of it had melted, revealing decorations that declared her "Just married!!!" Someone had really gone overboard on those exclamation points.

"Why don't I drop you off at the Cozy Cottage—I've got some business to settle there anyway—and then you can get your car later. It's only a couple of blocks to walk it, or you can ask most anyone to give you a ride."

She arched an eyebrow at him. "So I can't give away rides to strangers, but I can accept them?"

"I can vouch for the people at the Cozy Cottage, along with the folks who run the convenience store and the diner, as well as Grumpy, who you met last night even if you don't remember." He leaned in conspiratorially. "It's the gray-haired quilting ladies you have to be careful of. One minute you're walking by, the next they're trying to teach you to sew."

Her laugh filled the air, lifting the mood in the cruiser and causing a sensation in his gut that he hadn't felt in a long time.

"What do you say? Will you let me take you to the B and B?"

"Sure," she said. "Let me just grab my suitcase."

He pulled next to her car, and when she ducked inside, he sent a group text to the guys who'd been so sympathetic to her plight last night. He told them to make sure that, by this afternoon, her car no longer showed any sign of her failed nuptials. He figured with the help of Fern—mad at him or not—he could at least convince Regina to stay for long enough that she didn't have to drive around with the reminder of her failed wedding trailing after her.

The conversation died when Regina and Emmett stepped into the Cozy Cottage, all eyes moving to them. Emmett had insisted on carrying her suitcase inside, and he moved it in front of him, almost like a shield, setting Regina's nerves on high alert. What kind of place was she walking into?

"Are you our bride?" a woman with a knotted gray bun on the top of her head asked, and Regina glanced down to make sure she had, in fact, changed out of her wedding dress.

"This is her?" another woman inquired, taking a step toward Regina, and then several others were closing in.

Regina clamped her hand on to the sheriff's rather firm arm without thinking, and when she peered up into his brown eyes, her heart skipped a beat, making it that much harder to convince herself to let go. "These are the people you vouch for, right?"

The corner of his mouth twisted up a fraction, but it was like he refused to let himself *actually* smile because that was as far as he let it go. "You'll be perfectly safe. Now, whether or not you'll ever get a moment's peace again ...? That's another story." He gave her an encouraging nod and turned to the woman with the bun, calling her Fern and asking if she had an open room for Regina.

"Of course! I mean, it'd be easier if *someone* made the plumber fix our burst pipe yesterday, but since I went and got the parts myself—in a snowstorm, no less—I should have that issue fixed soon." Fern tapped away at the keyboard of her computer. "In the meantime, I do have one last open room, although it's one of the smaller ones."

"That's fine," Regina said.

The woman peeked over the top of her computer screen. "And how long are you planning on staying?"

"Um, for the first time in my life, I don't really have a set plan."

"That's okay, dear. How long were you going to be on your honeymoon?"

Regina automatically flinched, and one of the other women scolded Fern and then took Regina's hand and patted it like they were old friends.

Which made her even more hesitant to let go of the sheriff's arm. He glanced down at her hand, and his throat worked a swallow, and she probably shouldn't be noticing that.

She dropped her hand, wrapping her arm around her middle

instead. Because she loved her finance-director job and felt the company could hardly run without her, taking time off was difficult and her workaholic sensibilities kicked in. "Um, two weeks, which seemed like an extravagant amount of time to me, but I never take time off." *Just another reason my fiancé decided to get out while he could.*

Ex-fiancé.

The woman holding her hand squeezed it. "Everyone needs time off, and I say you take that time to relax and just work on you, honey." A lightbulb went off, lighting her eyes. "You should spend it here with us."

"Oh yes," and a few other enthusiastic responses went through the group. "There's nothing like Christmas in Friendship."

"We've got enough things going on to keep your mind nice and occupied," Fern said.

"I know that *I'll* be nice and occupied with the events," Sheriff Haywood added. "The town makes sure of it."

Fern clucked her tongue. "Ignore him. He's a stick in the mud about Christmas."

"Funny," Regina said, getting swept up in the teasing. "I just accused him of being the Grinch, and would you believe he tried to deny it?"

The ladies laughed, and she glanced at him, hoping it was okay she'd said that. He shook his head but there was that almost-smile; if she'd known she'd only get the with-teeth smile at his sister's house, she would've taken an extra second or two to appreciate it.

"And you *have* to stay for the big Christmas party. There's a dance and everything," the woman still holding her hand said. Evidently, she wasn't planning on letting go, which meant Regina might no longer have a choice in the matter. The woman's gaze lifted over the top of Regina's head. "Shouldn't she stay for the dance, Sheriff?"

Regina glanced at him again. She couldn't seem to help herself, and now that she'd gotten used to so many people she didn't know crowding her space and asking about her personal affairs, she found herself swept up in the sense of camaraderie.

The sheriff's eyes locked on to hers, mischief dancing in their depths. "Pretty sure it's illegal not to go to the Christmas party 'round these parts, and I already gave you one free pass on being arrested, so ..."

She tilted her head, giving him her best haughty expression. "So you're saying, if I don't stay for the festivities and go to the dance, I'll be spending my vacation in jail?"

"Afraid so. I don't make the laws, I just enforce them."

"When he feels like it," Fern said, and his scowl returned.

"No, you just want to be an exception to the rule," he shot back.

The B&B owner made an offended noise before turning back to Regina, who'd always thought these kinds of towns only existed in fiction. She liked how involved they already were in what happened to her, even if she also worried it was a bad idea. She was in a fragile state as it was, and getting attached to people only to leave? Well, after the one person she'd planned to spend her life with walked away without a second thought, attachment issues were sure to follow. She'd do some research so she could find out what to expect and how long it might take to get over.

Still, two weeks in a cute little town that celebrated Christmas on such a grand scale sounded like just the vacation she needed. "Okay, book the two weeks. But if I need to leave early ... ?"

"We can work with whatever you need, dear," Fern said.

"Thank you. I appreciate that." As Regina dug out her credit card to finish booking the room, a lightness filled her. Her parents always vacationed in exotic locations for the holidays—this year it was Italy—and while she had friends and distant relatives, she didn't have anyone she felt she could burden for Christmas now that she was a gloomy party of one. And she certainly didn't want to go back to her place. That would only accentuate her loneliness.

"I can call in Aaron to take your bag if you—"

"I'll take it," the sheriff said, and the women exchanged curious glances. It would seem he didn't offer to tote suitcases around very often.

Admittedly, it made her feel sorta special, even though her heart was far too beat up to go getting any ideas about the surprisingly cute law enforcer and resident grinch.

He walked her down the hall, and when she unlocked the door, he rolled the suitcase across the threshold but remained on the other side. "Just wanted to make sure that you felt safe here, and that you didn't feel too pressured into agreeing to stay, even though you wanted to escape."

"Are you saying you'd break me out if needed?"

He leaned a hip against the doorjamb, and the way he filled the doorway made it clear he was every inch a man who could handle himself, just as he'd claimed to be. "Guess I'm not as hardcore at enforcing the town's Christmas Party Decree as I pretended while we had an audience."

She smiled at him. "I feel safe and happy, and I think staying here for a couple of weeks is just what the doctor ordered." She leaned on the interior side of the doorjamb, her hip a few inches from his. It struck her how tall he was, something she noticed as a tall woman who often looked eye-level with men.

"Thank you for all your help, Sheriff Haywood. This morning and last night."

"It's Emmett," he said, dipping his head a few inches, and they were close enough that she could feel the heat of his body coming off him. Then she was recalling how firm his biceps had felt underneath her palm.

Her heart went to fluttering in her chest since it was worse at listening to reason than her brain was. "Thank you, Emmett."

Chapter Four

Thanks to the group of women who frequented the main room of the Cozy Cottage to drink coffee and tea and gossip, Regina had ended up with a coat, gloves, and a scarf that was long enough to mummify her entire body. She wound another loop around her neck so she wouldn't step on the end and trip and fall—no need to embarrass herself every day she was in town.

People milled about the park, chatting and enjoying hot chocolate and apple cider as they waited for the tree lighting ceremony. Regina accepted a cup of cocoa, holding it in her hands and sighing at the added warmth. It was significantly colder here than it was in Maryland. Her gaze skimmed the area, and while she told herself she was merely observing the cheerful gathering, her heart skipped extra quickly, hoping to find and observe the sheriff.

Emmett. He said to call him Emmett.

And I need to find him and say thank you, so it's okay to be looking for him.

After lunch at the Wallflower Diner, she'd fortified her nerves the best she could to face her decorated car. But it was cleared of the streamers, cans, and that mocking "Just Married!!!" scrawl. She suspected he'd noticed how much it'd bothered her.

As Regina moved closer to the action, several people introduced themselves. Word had obviously gotten around about who she was and why she was there, but everyone was so kind, and even better, nice enough not to mention how much of a mess she'd been last night.

The crowd gathered closer to the stage as the mayor welcomed everyone to their annual tree lighting ceremony. Regina tipped onto her toes, still searching for a dirty blond head of hair.

"You're not making a play to be the one to flip the switch, are you?" a deep voice said near her ear, and butterflies erupted in her stomach. She turned to the very guy she'd been looking for.

"I feel it's only fair, what with me having been part of the town for almost a whole day. Plus, don't tell the cops, but my goal is to get arrested by Christmas." She pretended she'd only now noticed his clothing and the big shiny badge on the coat she'd had wrapped around her last night. "Oh, this is awkward."

His lips quivered but not enough to count as a smile. He lifted one of her colorful scarf coils. "Let me guess. Marge got a hold of you?"

"She let me borrow it. In fact, I don't have a stitch of clothing on that's mine. Save the underwear." Her cheeks blazed, embarrassment doing a far better job than the layers at keeping her toasty. "I mean . . . You know what I mean."

It was as if someone had pressed the pause button on him. He didn't move, didn't seem to blink or even breathe.

"So, um, this hot chocolate is really good." She licked it off her upper lip, and his eyes tracked the movement. "Emmett?"

He cleared his throat. "I wouldn't know."

"Can't drink any because you're on duty?" She lifted the cup and eyed it suspiciously. "What exactly do they put in it? If I get sloppy drunk one more time, I'm pretty sure the sheriff will haul me to jail."

"Ha-ha. I just haven't had time to try a cup, because anytime I go near the table, someone needs something. Plus, there are doughnuts over there, and I'd hate to become a walking cliché."

Regina opened her mouth to tell him she'd cover for him if he wanted to grab a cup now—no promises about refraining from cop/doughnut jokes—but before she could, an older lady burst right into their cozy bubble.

"Oh good, I found you." Her words were spoken on a huff, her movements urgent. "Jack parked in the spot where Santa Claus arrives in his sleigh. You need to make him move his truck."

"I think there's an opening on the other side of the stage," Emmett said. "Just have Joe circle—"

"*Shhh.*" The woman wildly looked around. "*Santa* always comes in the same way. It's what everyone expects, and you can't change the rules because Jack is your buddy. I warned him I'd get the law involved if he didn't listen, and typical, he has to do things the hard way."

Unlike the woman, who was clearly so easy-going. She charged through the crowd, obviously sure the sheriff would follow. Emmett sighed and raked a hand through his hair, causing some of the strands to stick up at different angles. "Guess I better go deal with that."

"Okay, but just so you know, this is all part of my evil plan," Regina said. "Distract the sheriff with Santa problems so I can elbow my way to the switch that'll light the tree. Where is it again?"

"Sheriff!" the woman demanded, and he began walking backward.

He pointed a finger at Regina. "Behave till I get back."

"No promises," she said, while her inner voice squealed over the phrase *till I get back.*

He shook his head, a slight curve to his lips. "Out of towners, man."

Over the next several minutes, a Christmas carol was sung by the crowd, the middle school band struggled through a trumpet-heavy rendition of "Silent Night" that was anything but silent, and then everyone leaned forward as one as they waited for the tree to light up. The effect was breathtaking. Twinkling lights lit up the ornaments and tinsel, and as if the universe was punctuating the night, fat flakes of snow began floating down.

Santa Claus rode in on a sleigh—from the area the woman had indicated he *always* came in from, so evidently Emmett had cleared up the parking disaster. The children surged toward the jolly old elf, and in spite of the chaotic state of her life, their excitement washed over her, giving her that tingly, Christmas sensation she hadn't experienced since she was a kid.

"Looking for Regina?" Callie asked Emmett as he glanced around the area.

"I'm doing my job," he said. "Making sure that everyone peaceably disassembles."

"Sure."

You didn't get to his position without being able to observe a lot at once, and sure, Regina was on the list of things he wouldn't mind seeing right now. Most likely she'd gone back to the B&B already, the cold too much, even with that boa constrictor scarf.

For the first time in a long time, he'd been enjoying one of the festivities, right before getting a reminder of why he disliked them. Talk about drama. Over parking, even though most of the lots didn't have lines, and the ones that did, people took as a loose suggestion. Technically, everyone who'd been parked in the grassy area where Jack left his truck had been parked illegally, but no one seemed to care about actual laws, only tradition.

Just another night in Friendship.

Only then he spotted Regina, and it wasn't another regular night. Of their own accord, his legs took him closer to her. "Hey," he said when he reached her.

"Hey. Not sure how warm it is now, but I grabbed an extra, just in case you hadn't had a chance yet." She extended a cardboard cup, along with a doughnut wrapped in a napkin. "And cliché or not, it's a shame to pass up doughnuts—if I were a cop, that's what *I'd* arrest people for."

Was it sad that it was probably the nicest thing anyone had done for him in a while? Sure there was the general friendliness that abounded here, but this was a deeper level, one that said she'd noticed.

"Thank you." He juggled the doughnut in his left hand and sipped the hot chocolate. Lukewarm but still good. "How'd you like the ceremony?"

"It was beautiful, and for the first time this year, it actually feels like Christmas. Admittedly, I was a tad disappointed in the lack of fisticuffs over pulling the switch."

"Yeah, it doesn't feel like Christmas until someone gets punched in the face," he said, and she laughed. "It means I was doing my job."

"Oh, so now you're taking credit for the whole thing?"

"Basically." Had he stepped closer? Or had she? The lights from the tree lit up her face with a soft glow. He wanted to tug her scarf down a couple of inches so he could see the smile lifting her cheeks instead of simply knowing it was there.

"Before I forget, I assume you're responsible for the fact that my car no longer looks like Cupid threw up on it?"

"Can't take all the credit. Your drinking buddies helped."

Another laugh. "Drinking buddies. Never had those before. Honestly, I was a bit antsy all day, trying to figure out what to do with myself. Usually my days are cram-packed with meetings and spreadsheets and reports, and without a long to-do list ... well, I'm trying to live in the now a bit more, but it still feels weird."

"I find the people who live in the now are the ones who end up in jail."

She tilted her head. "Is that supposed to be encouraging? Because if so, I've gotta say, it needs work."

"The truth's the truth, no matter how you dress it up. Not that I'm saying you should schedule every second of every day."

"How much of your life is planned out?" She was definitely the one who moved closer this time, and the scrutinizing scrunch of her forehead made him way too self-conscious, another emotion he hadn't experienced in a long time. "You don't seem like a go-with-the-flow guy, but you don't seem like much of a planner either."

"Hard to plan when you don't know what people are gonna get themselves into. Mostly I just plan to go to work and deal with issues and perceived disasters as they inevitably arise."

"There's the Grinch making an appearance again."

"If the green shoe fits, I'll go ahead and wear it."

She glanced down at his boots.

"It was a metaphor," he said.

"Careful what you say, because now if I see green shoes, I'm going to buy them for you."

"You'd be hard pressed to find any in this town, so I'll take my chances."

She grinned, and he thought again about how nicely the tree lights played across her features. A quick check made it clear most people had gone home, leaving only a few stragglers out and about, along with a few couples. The couples were caught up in each other, but several of the stragglers were looking their way, as if he and Regina were a television show. *The rumors will be flying tomorrow.*

He gulped down what was left of the hot cocoa and then crumpled his cup and tossed it in the nearby recycling can, his plan to tell her good night.

"Wow. Nothing but net—or plastic, as it were," Regina said, and the fact that she sounded so impressed made him feel like a superstar over such a menial thing. "I'd definitely miss."

"Just takes some practice." Emmett debated following through with his plan to tell her good night but found he didn't want the night to end quite yet, onlookers or not. The townspeople were going to talk anyway, so he might as well have the benefit of spending time with her. "Try it."

As she bent to grab a discarded cup, her scarf came undone enough to loop around her knee. She battled it for a moment before he stepped in to help.

"Not sure you can throw with so many layers on," he said.

"Honestly, my fingers turned numb long ago anyway. So now I have two excuses to blame if I miss." She cocked her arm, and he stepped in front of her, blocking her throw.

"Wait. You've got to crumple it so the air doesn't catch it." He squished the cup into a tight ball and returned it to her.

"Were you a sports guy in high school?"

"In this town, everyone has to play every sport or you don't have a team. What about you?"

"I was the girl who studied and lost sleep over SATs. Even after I graduated, there was college, where I'd have another test or project to worry about. Then I went right to work, where there were reports and performance reviews and slaving away to climb the ladder as fast as possible. Save last night, I don't remember the last time I relaxed, and that wasn't so much relaxed as . . ."

"Wasted."

She gave his shoulder a light shove. "Gee, thanks. I was going to say slightly tipsy—sounds much better."

"Stop stalling and shoot the cup," he teased, gripping her hips and turning her to face the trash can.

She cocked her arm and then let it fly. Her throw went wide and short, landing feet away from the can. "Oh great. I've gotten worse."

Emmett retrieved another cup and crumpled it. He wasn't sure why this suddenly seemed important, but while she'd been joking before, her expression spoke to a sense of failure that had to do with more than her toss. "Not to do the cheesy-guy-showing-a-girl-how-to-shoot thing, but . . ." He stepped up behind her. "I'm going to teach you how to aim and follow through."

"Usually follow through is my thing," she said, her lips slightly pursed.

"Good. Then you'll be a natural." He gave her the cup and slid his hand down her arm. Even with all the layers, his pulse quickened. He guided her arm up and put it through the motions a few times. "We're gonna let go this time. Ready?"

She glanced over her shoulder at him. For a moment, time froze. Determination set in to her jaw, and then she nodded. "Ready."

"I did it!" It took a couple of times with Emmett's help—and okay, they'd scooted a yard or so closer—but she'd finally managed to land a cup in the recycling bin. She spun in Emmett's arms and peered up at him. His teeth weren't showing, but that was definitely a smile.

Her heart skipped a few beats, and without notice, her body went haywire on her.

What was she doing this close to a guy? One she barely knew, the day after she was supposed to get married. She took a large step back. "I, uh, guess I'd better get back to the B&B."

"I'll walk you."

"Can't vouch for everyone out and about tonight?" she asked, attempting to infuse a teasing tone into her voice. She needed to steer things back to lighter territory. *Safer* territory.

Emmett's eyes remained steady on hers. "I can. I'd still feel better if I walked you there myself."

A torn sensation went through her, half celebration, half fear. But it was only a couple of blocks. Not like she could fall for a guy in that short a distance. She was relatively sure anyway, although these days everything she thought she knew kept coming unraveled.

They picked up a few more stray cups on their way out of the park, opting for dropping them into the bin instead of shooting them inside.

Without Emmett's heat at her back, the icy air cut through all her layers, and she tugged her borrowed coat tighter around her. She went ahead and added another scarf coil around the lower part of her face because maybe that'd keep her from thinking about silly things like what it'd feel like to press her lips to the sheriff's.

They walked mostly in silence, the majority of the talking done by people they bumped into on the sidewalk. After parting ways with another pair who'd stopped to inquire about their evening and wish them a good night, Regina said, "Um, you might want to vouch for me, because everyone we pass is studying me super closely."

"Correction, they're studying *us* closely. And I'm not sure I know you well enough to vouch for you."

As tended to happen around him, her jaw dropped. She made an offended noise and smacked his arm.

"For one, you go around hitting the sheriff," he said with a chuckle. Both of them slowed their pace as the Cozy Cottage came into view. Mere minutes ago, she wanted to hurry and get there so she could lock herself in her room. Perhaps take a hot bath and see if she could get feeling back in her extremities. But now she wanted to slow down again. Her emotions really needed to make up their mind.

Logic said this guy was dangerous—when it came to her already beaten-up heart anyway. And she was only here temporarily. And a hundred other "ands."

Emmett walked her all the way to the front porch and then braced his hand on the beam next to her.

"One more citizen delivered safe and sound," she said, her voice slightly breathy, and not from the walk or the cold. "You deserve a gold star. Oh, wait. You've already got one."

He bit back his smile.

"Why do you do that?"

"Do what?" he asked.

"Refuse to smile. The only full smile I've seen was at your sister's. And don't act like you're not holding it back, because I'm hilarious."

"You do look kinda funny in that scarf."

She shoved his solid chest, and he chuckled, his laugh and corresponding smile subdued but there. Then his brown eyes landed on hers. "Maybe I forgot how." When she aimed a skeptical expression his way, he added, "It's not easy walking the right line between friendly and stern. Going overboard on the stern is better than everyone thinking they can take advantage of the friendly."

"But Fern said you've been grouchier lately." Perhaps she shouldn't have started this line of questioning, but she couldn't help herself. Even as she told herself to tread carefully, she wanted to know more. "Is there a reason for that?"

"Besides the fact that there's an event every night, and at each one of those, someone will park in the wrong space, or think they should have special privileges, or a hundred other ... what did you call them? First World problems?"

"Yes, besides that."

"Not sure. Just haven't felt like myself." His gaze dipped to her mouth for the briefest second. "But tonight's been the best night I've had in a long time."

She leaned closer and toyed with the edges of his jacket. He should zip it up. She couldn't believe he wasn't too cold, but she liked that she could peek at the form-fitted shirt under the layers. Before tonight, she might've claimed a man in uniform didn't affect her. "Does that mean I get a full smile?"

"Not yet," he said, a slight curve to his lips. "But maybe if you stick around long enough, you'll see one eventually."

"Oh, I'll get one out of you yet."

"Good night, Regina." Even though he'd wished her good-bye, he didn't move, his palm still braced by her head. Now she was the one staring at lips—his, obviously.

Nope, the scarf didn't stop thoughts of kissing him. It did help her from following through though. "Good night, Emmett."

He closed his eyes, so fleetingly she almost thought she imagined it, and his fingers lightly brushed her cheekbone as he pushed back, turned, and walked back the way they'd come.

Chapter Five

"So, we couldn't help noticing you spent most of the time at the tree lighting ceremony with the sheriff," Fern said Monday morning, pulling a chair away from the table in the living room of the B&B and plopping herself into it.

"And that he walked you home," Marge, the woman who'd given her the giant scarf, added.

While Regina kept her attention on the breakfast plate in front of her, she was no longer worried about her lack of personal space. She was quickly learning that didn't exist here in Friendship. She sipped her orange juice, taking her sweet time as she calculated how to respond. "He was just being a gentleman."

Two unconvinced faces stared at her, clearly waiting for more.

Fern sighed. "Come on. We need more than that. He's a right grouch lately, and we were hoping you could help him get over that."

"Careful. It sounds like you're pimping out your guests."

"Hey, I'm not entirely opposed to it," Fern said, and Marge hooted like she'd told a grand joke. Most of the time when the words *bad influences* got tossed around, people automatically pictured rebellious teenagers, but these two were definitely up to no good.

Emmett warned me to look out for the gray-haired ladies. Next thing you know, they're going to insist on teaching me to sew. Or knit. Stifling a laugh, Regina picked up her biscuit and split it so she could add butter and jam. "You remember how I was supposed to walk down the aisle a few days ago?"

The chair legs scraped across the wooden floor as Marge scooted her chair closer. "We remember that you didn't. That's the important part."

"Doesn't mean my heart didn't get plenty beat up."

Both women appeared slightly reprimanded, but Regina doubted it'd last so she figured she should change the subject. "If I'm going to stay two weeks—"

"You are," Fern said in a no-room-for-argument tone.

"Then I'm going to need more than the outfit I borrowed from Callie and the suitcase full of summer clothes I packed for the beach." This morning, she'd put on Callie's jeans along with a ruffled short-sleeved blouse that'd have her freezing to death in five minutes flat if she dared to step outside without her also-borrowed coat and scarf. "Where does one shop for clothes around these parts?"

Fern's eyes widened in a way that sent a prickling sense of foreboding across Regina's skin. "You could ask the sheriff to drive you into the city. Takes just over an hour to get there, so that'd give you lots of time together."

"Or I could take my very own car." The thought made her blood pressure rise. Snow didn't exactly melt here, and she worried she'd end up sliding into a ditch somewhere, and then she'd be another problem for Emmett to solve. Or worse, she'd discover she didn't have cell reception and end up alone for hours. More than that, now that she'd settled in, she didn't want to spend any more of her vacation time traveling. Although, if it meant being with Emmett . . . "I'm sure the sheriff's busy."

"I'm sure he wouldn't be if he knew spending time with you was an option. You'd be doing us a favor, really. Like I said, we could all use a break from his grumpy-Gus attitude."

"At least you aren't overdramatic about it," Regina said.

They nodded, and she wasn't sure if they were faking not understanding her sarcasm or if they truly didn't get it. He wasn't as bad as they made out either. Sure, he refused to smile, something she was going to work on, but he was fair and kind, and only a pinch grumpy, on top of being overworked.

"I'll call him right now." Fern whipped out her phone and tapped the screen.

"No, don't!" Regina dove across the table, sending everything on it rattling and overturning the last half of her water, and the two older ladies looked at her like *she* was the crazy one.

"Hey, Sheriff," Fern said, and a mix of apprehension and anticipation churned through Regina's gut. "I'm here with our lovely guest, and she was hoping you could take her clothes shopping in Somerhaven. Like, say, if someone asked her on a date and she needed a fancier outfit."

Regina dropped her head in her hands as heat crept up her neck. She should get the water cleaned up, but it was quickly soaking into the tablecloth and no one else seemed concerned about it.

"Well, no one's asked her out just yet, but I'm sure it's only a matter of time. Maybe you'd like to be the first to—" Fern frowned. "It *is* an emergency. Do you want her to freeze to death in this tiny outfit she's wearing? She's going to catch pneumonia *inside*, much less what'll happen if she ventures outside."

And it keeps getting worse and worse. She should've asked for Emmett's number last night. That way she could at least text him and explain that she hadn't asked Fern to call, and she certainly didn't expect him to come.

"Oh, the town can take care of itself for an afternoon. Tell your deputy to do something for once." Pause. "I don't know about you, but I worry she'll get into the city and forget how charming we all are—especially if no one will be nice enough to take her shopping, and then we'll lose her for goo—"

Fern nodded and glanced at Regina. Her glasses made her eyes cartoonishly wide and amped up her scrutiny. "Fine. I'll let her know." She hung up and sighed. "I tried, but he says he has to work."

How stupid was it that disappointment seeped in, in spite of not expecting him to take a day off to go shopping with her? What was he going to do? Sit outside the dressing room and give a thumbs-up or down as she modeled clothes for him like they were in some kind of cheesy movie montage?

Regina kept her expression neutral, faking it in hopes she'd eventually make it. "I'm perfectly capable of shopping for myself, and I'm afraid you ladies are getting the wrong idea about me and Sheriff Haywood." Honestly, she was afraid her heart was getting the wrong idea too. Hadn't it learned its lesson?

"I don't think so," Fern said. "While he might be too much of a stickler to take time off, you should've heard the bark in his voice when he asked who you were going on a date with. More than that, he's sending his sister to help, so you'll find enough clothes to keep you warm without falling victim to the allure of the city. All good signs, trust me."

Fern's logic was nowhere near the realm of actual logic, and spending time with his sister would just be weird. Part of her thought she should grab her bags and flee this small town before she found herself living in a *Twilight Zone* episode where everyone was setting her up on forced dates.

It all seemed sudden and unplanned, and . . . It hit her that she was supposed to be letting go of plans and expectations. And if she was going to sincerely try out the whole throwing-caution-to-the-wind thing, she figured this town with its ridiculously friendly people was as good a place as any.

Emmett hung up the phone and pinched the bridge of his nose. Last night he'd been too careless. What was he thinking flirting with Regina? Especially with the whole town watching on.

Now Fern was calling and requesting he take Regina shopping? He was sure that the B&B owner was behind it because he doubted Regina, who talked about how regimented her life was, thought he'd take time off work to shop for women's clothes. Especially when he had no idea about women's clothes, besides that Regina seemed to make everything look good.

There he went again, thinking things he shouldn't. *She was just dumped.* A person didn't simply bounce back from that in a matter of days, even if the guy was obviously an idiot to let Regina go.

When Fern had mentioned a date, jealousy had bubbled up, and he'd mentally begun compiling a list of every bachelor in town who might've asked her out, along with what dirt he had on them. Not that he'd use it.

Most likely.

Unless he needed to.

He grumbled and leaned back in his chair. As if he hadn't already been having enough irrational thoughts, Fern had added the remark about how Regina might not come back, and that'd fed a worry he didn't realize he had. "This is ridiculous."

The receptionist glanced up from her desk. "What is, boss?"

This town. His strong feelings for a woman he hardly knew. The fact that he suddenly wanted to blockade the roads out of here. He was losing his mind. "Nothing."

"This wouldn't happen to have anything to do with the pretty woman you were teaching to shoot baskets last night, would it?"

"You too?" he asked. Usually Sarah remained neutral when it came to gossip. While he was sure she knew it all, she kept it away from work.

"All's I'm saying is that you seemed happier this morning than you have in a long time. And if a certain brunette is responsible, maybe you should let yourself enjoy it."

"And maybe the mistletoe hung all around town is going to everyone's head. Did you know the plant's a parasite that feeds on other plants? Doesn't seem so romantic now, does it?"

Sarah simply smiled and began to hum a Christmas tune under her breath. With a sigh, Emmett dialed his sister and attempted to prepare himself for yet another woman in his life who'd inevitably tell him he should ask out Regina before he went and lost his chance.

Chapter Six

Regina couldn't remember the last time she'd read a book in just two days. Most of the time she had far too much to do, but after spending most of her Monday with Callie, she now had a handful of outfits and a couple of paperbacks she'd picked up at the cute bookstore on Main. The nice thing about bookstores was how universal they were. You could almost always find a great mix of books.

Clothing stores were a bit trickier. Being on the tall side meant her legs and arms were longer than most. Callie's clothes had barely fit, while still being on the too-short side, and apparently the clothing stores in town didn't even have pants or sleeves long enough for Callie. Because the outfits also needed to fight off the cold, Callie had concluded the best—and only option, really—would be the sporting goods shop.

Regina was now the reluctantly proud owner of flannel and fishing logo shirts that she normally wouldn't be caught dead in. At least they were comfy, if not terribly stylish. Perfect for lounging around and reading—she'd even started the last two mornings with a relaxing bath. While a hint of anxious energy still hung in the background, for the most part, it'd been extremely rejuvenating.

The rotary phone on the side table rang, and she eyed it suspiciously. Yesterday her cell phone had started buzzing with a stream of never-ending texts and messages. Everyone from friends and family to her coworkers who were just hearing the news wanted to know why and how and what'd happened after Steve said I don't. In the mix was a text from Steve, saying he was sorry, and that when she was ready, they needed to talk. *A big no thanks to that.* She'd sent a text to her parents telling them she was safe and enjoying a getaway of her own, just in case they bothered worrying about her between yachting and dining on Italian cuisine, and then turned off her phone.

The ringing continued, past when voice mail would usually pick up, and Regina considered not answering. *It's probably just Fern being nosy about why I haven't come out of my room except to grab breakfast to go.*

Finally, she lifted the receiver off its cradle, idly thinking she hadn't handled a phone this old or bulky in years. "Hello?"

"Regina, hey." Emmett's voice danced along her nerve endings, sending them into a tizzy, and now she was mad she hadn't picked up sooner. She'd gone far too long without hearing his voice.

Whoa. It's only been two days. Plus a half.

"Regina?"

Oops. She supposed she needed to make her mouth work, which was trickier than expected after two days spent in near silence. "I'm here. Not doing anything illegal, either, in case you were wondering."

"I'm always wondering," he said with a soft laugh, and butterflies stirred to life. While she told herself it was too soon to experience the floaty sensation overtaking her, it didn't stop it from happening, and she wondered if she should simply enjoy knowing that she could actually feel that away again. That her failed nuptials hadn't killed her ability to experience flutters.

Come to think of it, she couldn't remember the last time Steve left her with happy tingles. Since thinking about him would be a downer, she focused on the guy on the other end of the line. "Well, I haven't left my room in hours so, even if I *had* been getting into trouble, it's not in your jurisdiction."

"Wrong. Your room is in my jurisdiction."

A tendril of heat unfurled in her chest, and he cleared his throat. "Anyway, I was just calling to check in. Callie said you two had fun the other day."

"We did. We both got the giggles at my limited clothing options, and I'm putting it out there right now that I'm going to look mostly ridiculous for the duration of my stay, although I guess getting frostbite would be more ridiculous, if only slightly so."

Regina *might've* tried prying out a little more information about Emmett, but Callie wasn't spilling and instead turned the questions on her, which made her clam up. With overly personal questions off the table, they focused on shopping, and it'd been her most fun shopping trip ever. If Regina were going to be here longer than a couple of weeks, she could see herself becoming good friends with Callie.

"Figured she'd be helpful. That's why it was better for me to send her."

"For the record, Fern was the one who asked you to accompany me. I understand that you have a job to do, and you don't strike me as a guy who really loves clothing shopping."

"I also figured that. And you're right about the shopping, although now I'm wondering if that's a slam on my wardrobe choices."

Regina laughed and shifted on the bed, tucking a pillow under her stomach and kicking her feet like a twitterpated teenager. "Since I've only see you in your uniform, I don't think I'm qualified to slam your clothes."

"So, what you're saying is that you'd like to meet me for dinner, and that I'd better be wearing street clothes so you can properly judge."

More kicking. "I think that's rather presumptuous on your part."

"Pick you up in thirty? I don't have long to eat before I'm required to be at the community center so I can judge the gingerbread house contest."

"Oh shoot, I forgot about that. I was told I have to be one of the judges because I'll be neutral, thanks to the fact I don't know anyone."

"And I was told I'm a neutral judge because I already judge everyone," Emmett said, and Regina laughed again. "Regina . . . ?"

"Yeah?"

"You never answered the question about dinner."

"That's because you never posed a question." Regina bit her lip. "But if you had, I might wonder if it's a bad idea, considering I just got out of a serious relationship and I'm only here temporarily and a dozen other complications."

"Let me tell you some things that aren't complicated. We both have to eat to survive, and there are only two places to do that in town, so we might as well have dinner together. Nothing big or serious. Just a meal between two people who are getting to know each other."

"Well, when you put it that way . . . "

"I'll see you in twenty-eight minutes."

Her smile spread across her face, and while she'd definitely need that time to get ready, she couldn't help thinking that twenty-eight minutes wasn't nearly soon enough.

*

"Wow, Sheriff," Fern said with a knowing grin. "I don't think I've seen you dressed up in months."

"I'm not dressed up. Technically, I'm dressed down." Put on a pair of non-holey jeans with a gray Henley instead of your usual uniform, and suddenly everyone thinks you made a huge effort. Not that he hadn't spent a few extra minutes on gelling his hair and finding his good cologne, and yep, he was getting way too wound up over a woman who'd be leaving town soon.

Then Regina came down the hall, her dark hair in loose curls around her shoulders, the blue shirt she had on accenting her eyes, and he thought it was worth being tangled up in knots if it meant spending more time with her. Maybe even worth the whole town gossiping about it.

"Sheriff," she said with a nod. Then she tapped a finger to her lips and looked him up and down. "Now that I'm qualified, I have to say that, maybe next time, I should demand you go shopping with me. Clearly you've got good taste."

"Stop, or you'll make me blush." He walked a few steps closer. "You hardly look ridiculous, so I'm calling that bluff right now."

"Are you serious? While these snowmobile pants are fleece-lined and warm, they make a swooshing sound when I walk." She demonstrated. "As for the shirt, the front's pretty normal, but then ... " She spun around and lifted her hair off her neck, displaying a colorful fish. "At least it's a pretty fish, but yeah. A fish." She turned to face him, a mesmerizing curve to her extra-pink lips.

He almost told her she made sporting-goods-chic hot, but that was too bold for two people having a simple dinner, so he stuck with a simple question. "Ready to go?"

She nodded. "I'm starving too."

Emmett put his hand on her lower back and guided her

toward the door. He liked how tall she was—how she lined up so well with him.

"Don't forget we need you both at the community center for the gingerbread contest," Fern called after them, and they shared a smile before pushing out the door. The odds of anyone letting them forget about their judicial duties were slim to none.

A quick drive later and they were at Grumpy's.

When they walked in, several people called out greetings, and Emmett wanted to pull Regina to him and make sure they knew she was here with him, but again, that wasn't keeping things light. Just two people getting to know one another.

So that the other one could leave.

Maybe she'd been right when she said this was a bad idea. But then she flashed him a killer smile, and just like that, he was back on the hook.

They sat at a cozy table in the corner and ordered the special.

"I don't want to bring up a bad subject, but in the interest of getting to know each other better . . . " Regina ran her fingers along the rim of her water glass. "Neither you nor Callie have mentioned your parents. Are they . . . ?"

"In Florida enjoying the warm weather? Yes, yes they are."

Relief flickered across her features. "I was worried it was some tragic holiday story, and I didn't want to say the wrong thing . . . "

"Just the typical story. They like the warmth, and my mom's parents live down there, so they're visiting them now. They'll be back next week so they won't miss the big holiday party and so they can spend Christmas here. I'm sure you'll meet them."

She nodded, the thought of meeting his parents clearly overwhelming even though she was the one who'd brought them up.

"Not officially meet them. Just . . . small town."

"Right." She tore the wrapper that held her napkin around

her silverware and smoothed it with the side of her palm. "My parents prefer to travel over the holidays. They almost canceled Italy this year since my wedding was so close, but I told them they might as well go since I'd be on my way to Jamaica." She shrugged, the gesture too forced to come off as casual, and her fingers trembled a bit. "I'm glad they didn't or there would've been a fancy soiree at their house that I'd be expected to attend, and I'd have to deal with all those pity-filled looks."

The mention of her failed nuptials hung over them for a couple of beats. It was always there in the background, and again he wondered what he was doing. But the thought of her returning home to no one rubbed him the wrong way too. He'd rather she be here, where people would smother her with affection whether she wanted it or not.

"Thanks for not pitying me," she said. "Or doing a good job of hiding it anyway."

"I don't pity you. I pity him. That idiot walked away from what I'd bet is the best thing that ever happened to him." A bold statement, but he meant it. Maybe his simple life here wouldn't satisfy her for long, but she was kind and funny and sharp-witted, on top of being beautiful, and you didn't run across those traits every day.

She covered his hand with hers. "Thank you for saying that. I'm sure I did a lot of things wrong, and I tend to get lost in the details, but I never thought I'd get so lost in them that I failed to see things had fallen apart. Maybe my perfectionist side just refused to let that happen. And admittedly, I'm not always this fun." She leaned closer. "Another confession? While I thoroughly enjoyed my relaxing days of reading, my antsy side was kicking in, and I was relieved when Fern demanded I be a judge because it gave me a purpose."

"Relief definitely isn't what I felt when they asked, but I think it's good to have a purpose. And you are fun."

"Don't take this the wrong way, but you're not exactly a barrel of monkeys. I mean, the other night with you after the tree lighting was super fun, but I'm guessing that's not your usual either."

"I'm not sure how to take that. What's the wrong way and what's the right way?"

She shrugged. "I guess I want to be a perfectionist, even when it's deciding to have fun."

"Yeah, that sounds like fun."

"*Exactly.* I can't even have fun having fun. It's too stressful."

The waitress came and delivered their food.

Since Regina still looked perplexed over her inability to have fun—which was silly—Emmett turned his hand over, locking their palms together. "Are you having a good time now?"

Her eyes met his, and she swallowed and then nodded.

"Good. Then let's not worry about later fun." Maybe he *had* been on the grumpy side recently, but he was slowly coming out of it, and the woman across from him was at least partially responsible. "Let's focus on the now."

"Just live in the snow globe world until time's up?"

A pang went through his chest at the phrase *time's up*, but that was silly. It was way too soon for that. "Why not?"

"Well, I like that it's a perfectly defined plan."

He shook his head but couldn't help smiling.

"Still no teeth," she said, propping her chin on her fist. "I'll get that full smile out of you yet, Sheriff Haywood."

An electric current traveled across his skin. He probably shouldn't like her calling him that so much, but it didn't change the fact that he really did.

Chapter Seven

Regina studied Emmett as he bent over the sheets of gingerbread, bag of icing in hand, tongue out in concentration. Evidently, judging the competition wasn't enough. They had extra supplies they'd 'brought for the kiddos,' and Fern, who was running the event, told them they might as well make a house instead of 'standing around like bums'.

So they were making a house.

Icing dripped out the back of the bag, and Regina couldn't help it. She stepped forward and placed her hand over his. "You've got to squeeze from the end. I know it's not fun and carefree, but icing is spilling all over the floor."

Emmett glanced from her to the bag and then to her again. He swiped a glob of icing onto his finger and popped it in his mouth. "Mmm. See, I do it this way because then I have no choice but to clean up the mess with my tongue."

"That would be nice, except now I'm not going to have any icing left for the decorations I've carefully divvied out, and how can we be judges if we can't even complete a house of our own?"

Emmett raised an eyebrow and swiped another finger through

the icing. But instead of licking it off himself, he extended it toward her. "Go on. You know you want a taste."

Her pulse spiked. They were going to get in trouble, first for eating all their icing and second for causing a scene in the middle of the community center. Still, she stepped closer to him and took a taste.

His pupils dilated, and the temperature in the room shot up about a billion degrees—those houses would be melted here pretty quick.

"Only fifty minutes left," Fern said, and they jumped apart. She glanced between them, far too smug.

Regina cleared her throat. "Oh, I'm a really good multitasker," she said without thinking how exactly that sounded.

Emmett snort-laughed behind her, and she elbowed him in the gut, satisfaction going through her at the sound of his grunt. Fern strode off, and Regina longingly studied their candy. "I hope that I can eat one of those Twizzlers after our house has been on display for a while."

"Or you could just eat one now, like I'm going to do with my favorite Christmas candy." Emmett grabbed a gumdrop and tossed it in his mouth.

"Yuck! Gumdrops are the worst, and you ate a green one at that."

He reached out, snagged another, and placed it on his tongue.

She bumped him away from the candy so they'd have some left to decorate with. Much more of his snacking, and they wouldn't be able to make the trees in the front, unless they decided to make pink or red ones, but those colors were needed for the windows. "You make icing glue spots; I'll place."

Emmett saluted.

"Smart aleck. I'm taking that as your total obsequiousness."

They circled the gingerbread house, and while Emmett had made a mess of the icing bag and floor, his foundation and seam work was solid. They made a good, efficient team, which was fun for her. *Take that, Steve.*

Emmett reached for another gumdrop, and she playfully smacked his hand.

"Just wait and see if we have any left." They wouldn't with the schematics she'd mentally drawn up, but she'd wait to drop that gummy bomb.

Emmett circled an arm around her waist, anchoring her to his chest and then reached around her, grabbed a pink gumdrop, and ate it.

"Now the top floor won't have all its windows!"

"Better even it out then," he said, stealing another as she attempted to wiggle free and block him from putting that one in his mouth.

She failed.

"My mom puts gumdrops in her fruitcake," he said. "This is making me crave a piece."

"I repeat my earlier 'yuck.' I've never seen anyone actually eat fruitcake. I have this theory that only a hundred or so have ever been made, and every Christmas, people just re-gift the loaves they received the year before."

"Not true. I've eaten a lot in my day." He took a handful of M&M's out of the bowl, and she kicked up her efforts to break free.

"Emmett Haywood, don't you dare eat my roof tiles."

"I'm not going to. You are." He brought them in front of her face. "I've decided that I'm in charge of you having fun tonight. Open your mouth."

On principle, she thought about fighting him, but they

smelled amazing, and she loved M&M's. For the first time pretty much ever, she complied. So much for him being her subordinate.

Regina couldn't help the moan that slipped out. No sugar for two months could do that to you. "They're even better than I remembered." She snagged another, and then she realized she'd relaxed into Emmett's embrace. She glanced around, but everyone seemed to be super focused on putting the finishing touches on their houses.

She studied theirs. It wasn't the prettiest or the most impressive, and she should really stop eating the candy tiles so they'd have enough for the finishing touches, but at the same time, she couldn't bring herself to care. What made it perfect wasn't how it looked, but how much fun she'd had, and that she was now cuddling with a not-so-grumpy-anymore sheriff.

The loud *bing* of the timer made her jump, and then Fern used her over-the-top megaphone to demand that everyone put down their supplies and step away from their tables.

Regina quickly snagged a couple of Twizzlers.

"You rebel," Emmett whispered in her ear.

"I grabbed one for you too."

"What I meant to say was, you beautiful evil genius."

She laughed as she spun in his arms, and her breath caught at the way he looked down at her. Time froze while her heart rate sped up. His throat worked a swallow as his hand splayed across her lower back and drew her even closer.

" . . . to the tables."

Vaguely, she realized someone had not only neared but was talking to them.

"Judges," Fern said, louder this time, *"if you'll follow me to the tables."*

"Is it just the two of us?" Regina asked when Fern extended two clipboards.

"Along with me. Judges are best in threes to help with tie-breakers, plus I have the most experience with baking."

They rounded the zoned-off competition tables that held the numbered houses. There were three categories, each item earning a rating on a scale of one to ten: overall look, originality, and difficulty.

Regina leaned closer to Emmett. "Well, they all look way better than ours, so I'm going to say everyone gets a ten on the difficulty level."

Fern glared at them. "No discussing scores!"

"Uh-oh." Regina grimaced. "Next, she's going to ask you to arrest me."

Emmett brushed by her, pausing to whisper, "It'd help you achieve your goal of getting arrested by Christmas. Really, I'd be helping you both out."

She stifled a giggle as they continued down the row. When they reached the last house, she gasped—then she felt like a nerd for gasping, but still. Spree candy tiles made up the icicle-draped roof, and Santa and his chocolate reindeer had parked on the lawn. "Wow, I didn't realize Peeta lived in your town."

Emmett glanced at her, eyebrows all scrunched up. "Peter Whibley? I assure you he didn't decorate this, and how do you know him?"

"No. *Peeta.*" Since no lightbulb went off, she added, "From *The Hunger Games?*" She swiped a hand through the air. "Never mind. This house gets my vote."

"Mark the sheet, dear," Fern said, a little extra threat in the *dear*. Yeesh. Funny how the people in the town were the least judg-mental she'd ever met, except when it came to Christmas contests.

A few minutes later, her favorite house was declared the winner, and to her surprise, it belonged to a thirteen-year-old girl. She collected her impressive cash prize, and the town of Friendship called it a night.

And even though Regina was far from ready to part ways with the sexy sheriff, she knew that another night like this and her plan to go slow and proceed with caution would be forgotten. Then she'd end up hurt all over again. So she asked Fern for a ride back to the Cozy Cottage, and along the way, decided that she was going to have to put some distance between herself and Emmett Haywood.

Chapter Eight

Over the next week, every time Emmett saw Regina, it was always too brief, and she was always surrounded by people or in a big hurry. She didn't call him, and although he hadn't given her his number, she could've called the sheriff's office easily enough. He wanted to call her several times, but she'd pulled away a couple of times now, and he was trying to do the right mix of taking advantage of what limited time they had and not scaring her off.

Still, earlier today he'd dialed her room at the Cozy Cottage. She hadn't answered.

The phone on his desk rang, and his pulse jumped, hoping to hear a certain voice on the other end, regardless of how unlikely. Undoubtedly, it was a resident wanting him to go tell someone else how they should/shouldn't do something they were doing, about to do, or considering doing.

"We're home!" Mom's singsong voice carried over the line. "Dinner at our place tonight, no excuses. Callie's on board, and while I was in the diner, I ran into that pretty woman who's visiting for the holidays and convinced her to come too."

Emmett sat forward in his chair, the legs hitting the floor

with a *thunk*. "Do you mean Regina?" Not like there was another woman in town who was visiting for the holidays, but he craved confirmation.

"Everyone's said such nice things about her, and I heard all about how her wedding went kaput, poor thing. I also heard that you two have been cozying up, so I figured I better get to know her."

Emmett scrubbed a hand over his face. "Mom, I'm not sure that's a good idea." Not only would it possibly tiptoe into scaring-Regina-off territory, but Mom fell for people in two seconds flat. She'd also been trying to marry him off forever. Callie too.

"You want me to call and uninvite her? That would be rude, Emmett."

"I'm sure she only accepted because she felt obligated."

"I'll have you know we had a lovely conversation. I offered up all sorts of facts about you—don't worry, I made you sound good, which isn't hard . . . "

This just kept getting worse and worse. Mom continued prattling on about Florida and dinner, and Emmett regretted not taking the opportunity to take Regina out at least once more before his parents arrived back in town.

There'd be no peace after this.

In fact, he predicted that come tomorrow morning, Regina would be fleeing back the way she came, never to return again.

Regina's nerves did jumping jacks in her gut as she approached the front door of the Haywoods'. She'd tried politely saying no to dinner, but Emmett's mom wasn't deterred, and when pushed, she couldn't come up with a fast enough excuse.

After all, rehashing the weird voice mail message left by your ex-fiancé wasn't exactly a normal way to spend a night, and more than that, it wasn't how she *wanted* to spend one of the few precious nights she had left in town.

Emmett was either busy or giving her space. Or taking space? She wasn't sure, but she'd wanted to call a dozen times. Wanted to forget about complications and do what he'd said—focus on the now.

Although meeting his parents . . . ? *Oh, jeez.*

The noise of an engine caught her attention, and Emmett's truck pulled up to the curb. He climbed out and she watched, mesmerized by the way his long legs ate up the space between them.

"Your mom invited me," Regina said, juggling the bottle of wine she'd brought to her other hand.

"She told me. If you want to run, here's your chance. I'll even cover you."

"Do you want me to go?" she asked, insecurity rising.

He stepped closer and cupped her cheek. "No. I'm glad to see you. Is it weird that it seems like it's been forever?"

"I'm experiencing the same feeling, so maybe, but at least I'm not alone."

"I think I'd better get your number before you meet my parents. That way, I'll have it even if they scare you off."

"Not exactly helping the nerves here," she said with a laugh, but when he gestured for her phone, she handed it over.

He sent a text to himself. "Now you have my number, and you should definitely use it."

She opened her mouth, hoping something clever would come out despite the way her brain went blank in his presence. Luckily—or unluckily?—the door swung open.

"What are you two doing out here in the cold?" Mrs. Haywood ushered them inside. "Come on in. Dinner's almost ready."

Over the next few minutes, Regina received a tour and a glass of wine. Then she crowded around the computer with everyone else to watch a slideshow of pictures from Florida. She also received a couple of smiles from Emmett—still closed-lip, but the impact sent her emotions reeling all the same.

"Now where are you from again?" Mrs. Haywood asked as they settled around the dining table.

"Cambridge, Maryland. It's definitely warmer than here, with a lot less snow, but luckily the people in Friendship have supplied me with a coat, gloves, and a scarf."

"Oh, you got a Marge scarf?" Mr. Haywood asked, and Regina nodded—Marge had told her it was no longer a borrowed accessory but a gift, and wouldn't hear of Regina paying for it either. "I think everyone in town has one. We all claim we don't wear them much because we don't want to ruin them, but really it's because we need to see and walk. Not sure why she only makes them ten feet long."

Regina laughed. "Well, during the tree lighting ceremony, I decided being warm was better than either of those things."

Emmett's chair was next to hers, his steady presence at her side an indulgence she'd missed. Conversation moved to Callie, and she caught them up on her life. "That's pretty much it, until Emmett brought home a woman in a bridal gown."

Heat climbed up Regina's neck and settled into her cheeks. Callie was clearly teasing her, but she was afraid the Haywoods would get the wrong impression of her.

Underneath the table, Emmett's hand found hers, and Regina squeezed, silently warning him that she might not let go for the rest of the night.

Emmett stepped onto the back patio with Regina, who'd slipped outside to answer a call. She hadn't immediately fled after dinner, which he took as a good sign. But there was a tenseness in her posture that hadn't been there before.

"Everything all right?"

Her breath came out in a white puff. "Yeah."

He crossed his arms and narrowed his eyes.

"Don't give me the interrogator bad-cop glare."

"Hard not to when I know that something's up."

"Not in the now, which is what I'm going to focus on. Right *now*." She smiled and tilted her head toward the trampoline. "I haven't been on one in years. I used to be really good at them."

"Let me guess. You had goals and a plan."

"I did. Achieved them too." She started across the lawn. "Come on. Let's see if I've still got it."

"I'm not sure that's a good idea," he said.

She lifted her chin, a haughty expression on her face. "I'm not sure doubting my skills is a good idea."

They reached the edge of the trampoline. "Fine, but if you get hurt ..."

She boosted herself onto the padded edge. "You'll leave me to bleed out?"

"Graphic, but no."

"You'll arrest me for trespassing?"

"Most likely not, but that's because my mom would have to agree to press charges, and she already likes you too much."

Sadness edged her smile. "I like her too." Then she arched an eyebrow. "So glad to know you have my back."

He stepped closer so that her knees were against his stomach, and placed his hand on her thigh, dragging his thumb over the top of the snowflake leggings she had on underneath a "Live, Love, Ride" snowmobile sweater. "You know I do."

Her lips parted, and he wanted to close the distance and taste them. But he forced himself to remain in place.

She cleared her throat and pushed to her feet. "So ... " She bounced lightly, as if testing the elasticity and recoil of the trampoline. "What'll you do if I fall during my big stunt?"

"Probably just say 'I told you so.'"

She bounced higher. "How about we make a wager ... ?"

"Now gambling *is* something I'll arrest you for."

Her laugh split the chilly air and left a white puff around her head like a halo. "How about, if I do a flip, you owe me a dance at the party this weekend? And if I don't, I owe you one."

He grinned, and she clapped her hands together.

"I got a full smile with teeth! I rule!" She bounced up again and again. Then she flipped. The landing was wobbly, but her excitement over it was solid.

"Okay, I can't just let you show me up. Watch out." He climbed on and then realized this was a bad idea. For as much as she claimed she wasn't fun, every minute he spent with her proved otherwise.

He bounced like he used to when he was a kid—he hadn't been on one of these things in forever. After taking a moment to recalibrate based on his extra height, he flipped, and Regina cheered. As he slowed his bounces, his weight made her slide toward him, until they were standing together in the middle of the trampoline.

He placed his hands on her hips, and desire flooded his system. More than anything, he wanted to kiss her. He dipped his head, and her fingers wrapped around his biceps as she tipped onto her toes.

Her lips were a mere breath away.

The back door slid open. "Time for dessert!" his mom called, and it broke the spell. Regina dropped her arms and scrambled off the edge of the trampoline.

"I have to go," she said.

"Regina." He wanted to ask what happened to living in the now, but by the time he made it in the house, his whole family was staring at him, Regina nowhere in sight.

"What happened?" Callie asked, and all he could do was shrug.

"No idea." But he suspected the phone call she'd gotten earlier was partially to blame, and he intended to find out who or what was interfering before they even had a chance to try.

Chapter Nine

"You can't just run away, Regina," Steve said, and Regina dropped her fork, causing it to clatter against her plate. Over-the-phone discussions weren't working so well, so he'd insisted they meet.

She'd told him, "Fine. Come to Friendship, Massachusetts, and we'll talk."

Honestly, she didn't think he'd come. She didn't want him in her room, so they were meeting for breakfast in the living room of the Cozy Cottage, and they undoubtedly had an audience. After what he'd just said, she no longer cared about keeping it quiet. "Since you did the equivalent of running from me in front of all our family and friends on our wedding day, you don't get to scold me for my reaction."

"As I said over the phone, I'm sorry for that. We have a lot of stuff to deal with though, and I can't do it by myself."

"Probably because while you were busy being the fun one, I had to be the serious one who took care of everything."

Steve sighed. "What are we going to do about the house? I can't afford to live there myself."

"And neither can I," she said. He was the one who'd wanted

the bigger house in the nicer neighborhood. It fit with her ideal image of the perfect family, so she'd gone with it. Now, the thought of that giant, empty house ... She didn't want to go back, not to there, and not to the condo where she'd lived before—although she'd sold that, so it wasn't an actual option.

Steve ran a hand through his hair. "This isn't you. Small town, not taking care of your responsibilities ..." He gave her false-advertising "I can bait my own hook!" shirt a disdainful once-over. "Whatever you're wearing. I still don't understand how you ended up here."

"I don't understand how that's relevant to our conversation."

Steve sighed again. It was quickly becoming his signature move. "Look, I should've told you when I started having doubts. I thought it was just cold feet. And my family adores you ..."

A sharp twinge lanced her chest. She'd adored his parents too. They were kind and more down to earth than her parents. Funny enough, Steve would've fit in better with hers.

A memory from two nights ago drifted up, of sitting around the table with Emmett's family, talking and laughing. Despite her best attempt to stop it, she was getting too close. In the end, she'd only have more people to miss.

"Will you at least figure out what to do about the house? Oh, and take care of shutting off the utilities, water, and everything else. We also need to return gifts, you know."

Well, it was inevitable. A week and a half of relaxation and fun was a good run. Sooner or later, reality had to come creeping back in. "My guess is we're going to have to list it, unless we want to rent it out, and I'm not doing everything on my own. You don't get to back out and leave me with all the responsibilities."

He threw up his hands. "Fine." They finished their breakfast in tense silence, and then he pushed away from the table. "When are you coming back?"

"Not sure, but I'll give you a call."

Big surprise, another sigh. "Guess I'll try to make the best of the trip and buy some presents. Any recommendations?"

"There's a gift shop on Main. They have these amazing sculptures your mom would love. And the candy shop next door has those specialty chocolates your dad loves."

"Come with me? Show me around and help me pick the right things?"

Once again, he wanted her to do everything for him. Maybe she wasn't the most fun, but he was an overgrown baby, and in this moment, she was glad he'd backed out. She could've spent the rest of her life overcompensating, and she wanted someone who'd be on her team. Someone who liked who she was, yet also made her better and happier. *Someone like Emmett*, her brain provided before she could stifle it.

"I already have plans," she said. Steve didn't need to know they involved another novel and the cushy bed in her room. If she had to return to the real world sooner than expected, she should enjoy one last day of fun.

While she immediately thought of Emmett yet again—if there was anyone who could make doing nothing fun, it was him—and she wanted him to be part of her last day. But that would make a clean break that much harder.

And the thought of saying good-bye was already enough to cause a hollow sensation she feared might never fully go away.

People accused Emmett of being overly suspicious, but he liked to think of it as more cautious and good at his job. Whenever a stranger arrived in town, he wanted to know who they were and why they were there. Which is why he stepped into the path of the dark-haired guy in a polo.

"Mornin'."

The out-of-towner vacantly nodded and looked for a way around Emmett, but this reconnaissance mission wasn't over yet.

"I'm Sheriff Haywood. I don't believe we've met."

The guy glanced at Emmett's extended hand and hesitantly took it, giving it a weak shake. "Steve Mills. I just got into town this morning, but I'm not planning on staying long. I needed to talk to my fianc—my . . . Regina."

Every muscle in Emmett's body tensed. This was the ex? And why did he almost call Regina his fiancé? Not that calling her his was much better.

Because she's mine.

Emmett instinctively knew Steve was responsible for why she'd been upset the other night. Why was he here, and was he trying to win her back, and was she considering it? The caveman in him said he could totally take Steve. As if that'd impress Regina.

". . . told me to visit the gift shop. So, if you'll excuse me, I have some presents to buy."

Emmett let him pass. His gaze drifted toward the Cozy Cottage. He couldn't see the building, but the urge to check on Regina crept over him. It'd hurt if she'd decided to work things out with Steve, but if she needed a shoulder to cry on, Emmett would happily provide one.

Only the radio on his shoulder buzzed. "Boss, we got a situation."

"Can it wait? I'm in the middle of something." About to be anyway.

"Corbin wrecked his motorcycle. The ambulance is on the way, but—"

"I'll be right there," Emmett said as he spun on his heel and rushed to the cruiser.

It'd been a long day. Corbin broke his femur and had to be taken to the hospital in Somerhaven. The town pulled together to care for his kids so his wife could stay with him, and if things went well, Corbin should be back home in time for Christmas, although he'd be on crutches for a while.

It was all Emmett could do to shower and get to the Christmas party on time. As soon as he arrived, he searched for Regina's dark hair in the crowd.

"Did you hear?" Fern asked, lips pursed.

"Don't worry. Corbin's gonna be fine."

"Oh yes, I was sorry to hear about his accident, but that's not the news I meant." Fern wrung her hands together. "Regina's leaving early—as in tonight after the party. I wasn't sure if you'd talked to her yet."

His heart sank. She'd decided to go back with that prick? Steve Mills wouldn't appreciate her the way she deserved. *Of course she's leaving. You always knew she wouldn't stay.*

Hope had crept in though, and he'd let it. For all his talk about not letting the season get to him, it'd added to it. The idea of having someone to celebrate with, and he wanted that someone to be Regina.

"Excuse me," he said, his voice tight, and Fern didn't bother stopping him or arguing, so he could only imagine that he looked as stormy as he felt.

He circulated. Tried the punch. Watched the door.

An eternity later, Regina finally arrived. She exchanged

smiles and greetings with the people near the entrance. One of the women took her coat, and Emmett's lungs forgot how to take in oxygen. She had on a strappy floral dress with a flowy skirt.

Her gaze met his across the room, and everything inside of him reached for her. *Shut it down. She's leaving.*

He arranged his features in a careful mask as she approached.

"Do I look silly?" She smoothed her hands down her skirt. "It was the only dress I had, and obviously I packed it for the Caribbean."

"You don't look silly." He didn't trust himself to say any more. "So, I hear you're leaving."

She sucked in a deep breath. "I have to go take care of things back home."

"Have to?"

"I should." Her brow crinkled for a second before smoothing. "I mean, yes. I have to."

"Would one of those things be your ex? I ran into him earlier today."

"It's . . ."

"Let me guess. Complicated." He crossed his arms. "Don't worry. I pegged you as a complicated woman the moment we met."

Hurt flickered across her face. He didn't want to hurt her, but everything inside of him ached, and he was doing a bad job of keeping the lid on his emotions.

"It's not about him," she said. "We've intertwined our lives to the point that I have to go untangle everything so we can both move on."

But she'd be moving on somewhere else, eventually with someone else, and that left a bitter taste in his mouth. He knew it wasn't realistic for her to leave behind her job and her life and stay, but he wanted her to anyway. *Stupid hope. Stupid me.*

Fern stepped up to them and nudged them toward the floor. "Get out there. Everyone's standing around, and I need a couple to start dancing."

Emmett opened his mouth to say that they weren't a couple, but then Regina placed her hands on his shoulders, and he wanted to hold her one last time.

They moved to the center of the floor and swayed to the music. He soaked in her perfume, the tickle of her hair against his chin, and how she felt in his arms. Then she dropped her head on his chest, and he was sure she could hear his heart thundering away against her ear, saying all the things he wanted to but couldn't.

At the end of the song, Regina reluctantly pulled away, and Emmett dropped his hands. He looked so big and tall and handsome, and a tight band formed around her chest. How had he come to mean so much to her at such a messy time in her life? And after such a short period too?

Somehow, he had. But things would only get messier the longer she stayed, and she had to return home and be the boring, uptight woman who got things done. And if she didn't go now, she wasn't sure she'd summon enough strength again, not if she spent Christmas here in this place she'd grown to love.

A giant lump formed in her throat, and she had to force her words past it. "Living in the moment was fun, but I can't stay in the now. I worry about the future. It's my nature, and while it bit me in the butt a couple of weeks ago, it's served me well in a lot of areas."

Emmett nodded. "Okay."

"I better go tell everyone good-bye."

He nodded again.

She wanted to say good-bye, but the real problem was that she didn't *want* to. She simply *needed* to.

Since she was a wimp, she decided to save her good-bye to Emmett for last. She circled the room, thanking everyone for taking her in and trying to return items of winter wear they refused to take back.

Tears clogged her throat as she hugged one person after another. She hugged Fern extra tightly. "I hope I'm not leaving you in the lurch. I'll pay for an extra night or two if you need me to."

"You hush," she said in a stern yet soothing way. Instead of releasing her, Fern leaned back to look her in the eye. "You're welcome here anytime. The sheriff's not the best at expressing his feelings, but he's sad to see you go."

He'd seemed . . . distant. Even with her head on his chest, he was far away. He hadn't said much, just nodded, and she started wondering if she cared more about him than he did about her, and wasn't that just her luck? Maybe she was cursed.

She should probably wish on a Christmas-tree star. Or an angel since it topped the tree in the community center.

Through the open doorway, she spotted Gabe, the man who'd—in a roundabout way—led her here. She turned to gather some Christmas goodies to take to him, but then she spotted Emmett, already approaching him with a plate. He gestured toward the building, inviting him inside, but Gabe shook his head. But his "thank you for this", was loud enough to hear.

He glanced over at her, and she gave a little wave. Cold air nipped at her skin, yet she remained in place, watching as Emmett walked back toward her. He hesitated in the doorway next to her.

"Kiss, kiss!" came from the crowd, and Regina glanced

at them, thinking they were being far too bold, even if they were shouting the overpowering thought that was already on her mind. But then several fingers pointed at a sprig of mistletoe hung in the doorway that she swore wasn't there a moment ago.

Emmett peered up at it as well, but his posture, as well as his face, remained closed off, making it impossible to read him.

Regina worried kissing him would make the longing wrapping itself around her heart worse.

But didn't they deserve a kiss good-bye?

More people joined the "kiss, kiss," chant.

"You don't have to kiss me," she whispered. "I don't want you to kiss me because you feel obligated."

His eyebrows arched, emotion finally bleeding through, passion and affection and a hint of surprise. "I've wanted to kiss you since you asked if I was going to arrest you, so it'd hardly be an obligation."

The ground whooshed out from under her feet as he slipped his hand behind her neck. He drew her to him as his mouth crashed down on hers, and the combination of soft lips and scruff sent a shock wave through her body. She moved her lips against his, wrapping her arms around his waist so she wouldn't melt right onto the floor.

Happiness like she'd never felt before washed over her, leaving her breathless and dizzy. And did she mention the happiness?

Then he slowly pulled back, his brown eyes boring into hers. "Good-bye, Regina," he said, and reality came screeching back to her. It'd been an amazing kiss, but it was edged in finality.

She glanced toward the onlookers, croaked out a good-bye,

and rushed out of the building. She just needed to make it inside her car before she burst into tears.

As she drove past the now familiar shops on Main Street, the scenery blurred, and she had to blink to clear her vision.

She'd left home crying, and now she was crying on her way back.

There was something tragically poetic about it all, but she was too busy feeling sad to sort it out now.

Chapter Ten

Emmett stood numbly in the doorway as Regina's car drove away, her taillights two flashes of red in the dark. Most everyone else in town was here at the dance.

Staring at him.

"Show's over," he barked, wanting everyone to stop looking at him with a mixture of frustration and pity.

Callie stepped forward, and he focused on her, needing a friendly face right now. "You're just going to let her go?" she asked, which wasn't the comforting he'd expected, or wanted.

"She made up her mind."

"But you didn't fight for her. You're as bad as her groom!" Fern voiced it, but there was a lot of nodding in agreement.

Below the belt, but Emmett *had* thought the guy was a fool to let her go.

Mom stepped forward—he hadn't even realized she and Dad were here. "Well, don't just stand there. Hurry up and go get her!"

Regina had only been on the highway for a handful of minutes when she caught sight of red and blue lights in her rear-view mirror.

Emmett was at the dance, so it was probably a deputy—or worse, state police—and she'd probably been speeding in an attempt to outrace the heartbreak before it hit.

As she maneuvered onto the side of the road, the ache that'd overtaken her chest deepened. It felt like she'd left her heart in Friendship with a certain sheriff.

Here she was, getting in trouble with another cop, in another inappropriate dress. At least this one was slightly less mortifying than her bridal gown.

The dark figure approached her car, and she reached over to get her registration and proof of insurance out of the glove box.

The cop pulled on her door handle, and she jumped. Her mind must be playing tricks on her, because she swore it was Emmett's face in the window. She leaned closer to the fogged-over glass, and her heart rate kicked into high gear.

The second she hit the unlock button, Emmett threw open the door, reached over her and unbuckled her seat belt, and then hauled her out of the car and into his arms. "I forgot to tell you something. A whole lot of things, actually."

"Yeah? And this was the best way you came up with to do it?"

He grinned, full-out, teeth and all, and her stomach raised up, up, up to kiss her rib cage. "I was desperate. And I just so happened to have a cop car at my disposal."

"How convenient," she said, and his grin widened even more.

"Regina, I didn't know quite what to make of you when you stormed into my life, and I still don't, but I know you're far from boring, you make me smile, and I'd be an idiot if I let you go without a fight." He brushed his lips across hers. "I want you to stay. I know it's fast and there are a lot of things we need to figure out, but I've never felt a connection so strong in my life. Stay till Christmas at least, so I convince you to stay even longer."

Before she could answer, he kissed her again, backing her up against the car and kissing her until her bones turned into liquid fire. "Okay, I'll stay," she said, her voice breathy. "I'll still have to go home in the near future and take care of some things, but I'm not ready to let you go either."

Emmett dropped his forehead against hers. "Thank goodness. I'm pretty sure that they'll throw me out of office if I return to town without you."

"Oh, so this is for the town?"

He took off his coat and draped it around her. "It's definitely for me. But we'll let them *think* it's for them too. Then maybe they'll give us a moment's peace as we figure everything out."

At the same time, they both said, "Probably not," and laughed.

Then kissed some more.

Fat flakes of snow drifted down around them, making her cuddle tighter into his embrace. Regina basked in the feel of his warm lips against hers as the snow dusted their heads and the ground around them.

Two weeks ago, she didn't think there was such a thing as Christmas miracles, but as she made her way back to town with a guy she was crazy about, she thought maybe it was like one of those snow globes she loved. You had to shake your life up a bit before you got to be one of the blissfully happy people in the perfect scene with all that magical snow swirling around you.

Epilogue

One year later ...

"I'm so nervous," Regina said to Callie, who was walking around the train of Regina's wedding dress, fluffing and arranging. "What if he doesn't show? Or what if I get up there and he says he can't marry me?"

Getting married one year to the day they'd met seemed romantic when Emmett proposed it—after he'd proposed to her. These days she did her financial directing from home, which was now in Friendship, occasionally having to travel to consult when businesses wanted more than virtual support.

In a lot of ways, it felt like she and Emmett had fast-forwarded through the beginning parts of a relationship during her first two weeks in town, so they'd gone back and taken their time dating and getting to know each other. She was now part of the town, and they were always in her business and either thanking her for the sheriff being in a good mood—or asking her if she could do something when he was in a bad one—and she loved it.

Loved the town, loved her life, loved Emmett Haywood. She used to think she knew what she wanted and what the ideal family and life looked like, but now she *did know*, and she couldn't wait to take that next big step.

"I've never seen any dude as excited to get married as my brother," Callie said. "Trust me, he's going to say 'I do' as fast as humanly possible."

Regina blew out a shaky breath. She believed her almost sister-in-law, she did, but she'd been in this position before. With the wrong guy, she realized that now, but it didn't stop her nerves from going haywire on her.

But before she could overthink it too much, they were lining up and then marching down the aisle of the church.

Regina's parents hadn't fallen in love with Friendship quite the way she had, but they were supportive and planning to stay through the holidays to experience all the traditions, from the tree lighting ceremony to the gingerbread contest, to the party with the dance.

As her father neared the end of the aisle, he lifted her veil off her face.

Regina slowly turned toward Emmett, and in that moment, she was sure of everything. His expression spoke of unconditional love. Of shared laughter, the many conversations they'd had, and the countless kisses they'd exchanged over this past year.

He was also giving her the full smile, with teeth.

She returned it, excitement zipping through her on a high-speed, high-voltage circuit.

Then Emmett extended his hand, and she happily placed her palm in his. They walked the last few steps to the pulpit together.

Reverend Jones read some lovely words, and as he repeated the vows to Emmett, Regina held her breath.

"I do," Emmett said, loud and clear, without any hesitation.

And of course she did too.

Pronounced husband and wife, the only thing left to do was seal it with a kiss.

Naturally, Emmett went for broke, adding a dip to the kiss as their family, friends, and the entire town cheered for the start of their forever future.

Christmas Lights

AMY BRIGGS

For everyone willing to believe in Christmas and all its magic, even when life makes it hard.

Chapter One

Samantha

It was that time of year again. The annual pep talk with my sister, Robin, about the holidays. "We go through this every year, Sam," she said in a motherly tone.

"What?" I asked, only half listening and still looking through my closet. I was thinking about how my wardrobe needed an update, not just for the winter weather ahead of me.

"You are always freezing when you get here," she teased.

"I could have thirty-two layers on, and I'd still be cold in Massachusetts in the winter, Robin. I live in Florida. Come on. You were born a Floridian. I don't know how you manage to function at all in that weather after growing up here."

We were both born and raised in Florida, went to college in Florida, and we were Southern through and through. So the fact that she was lecturing me was even more annoying than the thought of freezing to death over Christmas.

"It wasn't easy at first." She chuckled. We have had this banter every single year during the holidays since she moved away, and it was tradition at this point. "Anyway, just remember it'll be cold." Changing the subject, she brought up one of the only topics about my annual trip to the tundra that brought a huge smile to my face. "The kids are excited to see you."

Robin always tried to lift me up during the holidays; she made it her job. She wanted me to enjoy the season even if it wasn't really my thing anymore. My nieces were eight-year-old twins, and they were absolutely hysterical. I did love playing in the snow with them every Christmas. It was usually the highlight of my trip, even if I was a human icicle. Each year, they were turning from babes into little women, and I definitely didn't want to miss that. Playing with them and establishing myself as the cool aunt was worth the trip all on its own.

"Tell those little pretties that I can't wait to see them. They're going to be performing this year, right?"

"Yes, they are, and they're so excited to show you their costumes. But I've been sworn to secrecy. They asked me not to give you any details so that they could share everything they're up to themselves. They were very specific with me about this. They're basically turning into eight-year-old teenagers."

I laughed. "I can't wait to see them."

"Well, I can't wait to see you. When do you get here? Are you sure you don't want me to pick you up?"

"My flight gets in at around noon on Thursday, and I should be at your house by early afternoon if all goes well. Don't use up time off for that. I'd rather we got to spend time together when you're on vacation."

"Sounds good." She paused. "I'm really glad that you are staying longer this year. I miss you, Sam," she said softly. "I promise that we're going to have a great time, and make some new memories, okay?"

"I miss you, too, Robin. I'm looking forward to some quality time with my sister. It's been far too long. This year, we'll have lots of time to catch up over hot toddies and cookies when I get there, I promise."

"Okay, I'll see you soon. Love you!" she shouted, emphasizing the *you* dramatically, making me giggle.

"I love you, too, dork." I hung up the phone grinning, dreading the season a smidge less.

As much as I didn't love flying all the way to Friendship, Massachusetts, every December, it kept me celebrating Christmas, even if I was phoning it in emotionally a good chunk of the time. If it weren't for my sister pulling me back in, I'd probably just order Chinese food and read books instead of acknowledging there was even a holiday happening around me. In fact, just hearing people say "Merry Christmas" made me sad, and I usually replied with a simple "Thanks, you too" instead of saying it back. Saying it was disingenuous; I didn't say it because I didn't feel it.

It had been my mom's favorite time of year, and she and my dad had made a big deal out of the holidays. Even though we lived in Florida and many people felt the warm weather wasn't festive, she'd wrap the palm trees in Christmas lights and put out every decoration she could find. Her stash had grown to epic proportions over the years. We had one of those National Lampoon decorated houses, the kind that blinded the neighborhood with twinkle lights, and a yard full of decorations from blow-up Santas to flamingos with Santa hats.

Planning the trip brought me back to my favorite memory of Christmas with my parents. It was when I was around twenty-two, my senior year of college. I came home for the holiday break, and they'd filled the entire yard with snow they'd had brought in for my arrival. I only went to college in northern Florida—it wasn't like I'd been gone across country or anything—but they wanted to surprise me nonetheless. I didn't even know that was something that could be done. They had it timed perfectly, and when I pulled into the driveway, my sister and my parents were beside themselves with laughter. I remember thinking that I had the coolest family in the universe. I mean who would go through the trouble of filling their front yard with shaved snow, knowing that it would almost certainly melt by the next day? My parents did. They were over the top in the best of ways, and making my sister and me laugh and smile was always the end game.

The more I reminisced, the less I wanted to celebrate. I stared at the hanging clothes while standing in front of my closet, knowing full well I had no decent winter clothes to speak of, and the sadness and anger took hold again, like always.

Christmas was devalued to becoming nothing more than a reminder of my parents' absence. It had been five years, which wasn't long to me, and I hated the thought of pretending to be full of joy. Part of me knew that was ridiculous, but my solitary life had become my security blanket. In that moment, all I wanted to do was call my mom, of course. Instead, I made a note to try braving the crowds at the mall for a new coat before I left.

Chapter Two

Jason

I was working on my single-engine plane, tinkering as usual, listening to Emily sing Christmas carols while running around the hangar. It was getting to be about dinnertime, and I needed to wrap things up, but I kept stopping to enjoy her songs. Her tiny voice belted out "Jingle Bells" as loudly as she could and reverberated around the hangar and brought a smile to my face. I loved hearing her sing. As I put down my wrench to rub my hands together, I noticed that the cold weather had started to become biting. It was going to be one of our coldest winters.

"Em?" I called out, not entirely sure where she was although I could certainly hear her caroling.

"Present!" she yelled back. We'd established that as our code for calling out to each other from the time she could talk. I couldn't even remember how it started, but she'd always announce herself as present if her name came up or was called out.

"You cold?" I yelled out. I had bundled her up in her favorite pink scarf with matching gloves and hat and a very loud hot pink puffy coat she insisted on having. I never imagined that my life would ever contain so much pink. She was probably sweating under everything I'd layered on her tiny body, but you could never be too careful.

"Nope!" she yelled back again. She clearly didn't want to be bothered with her boring dad's questions.

"You want to get our Christmas tree tomorrow?" I called out, grinning. I knew that would cause her to come running.

Suddenly skidding to a halt in front of me in all her pink, puffy glory, blond curls peeking out from under her hat, Emily placed her hand dramatically on her little hip. "Well it's about time, Daddy. I thought you'd never ask. I mean Christmas is in, like, *one week*. Sheesh." Her pink lips turned into a smile.

"It's more than a week away. Come on now," I replied.

"Listen, Dad, I'm just saying, the good ones could be gone by now, and it's not our first rodeo." She started to giggle. She was always cracking herself up, which in turn made me laugh all the time.

Putting my tools away in their box, I turned back to her, opening my arms for a hug. As she jumped into them, I squeezed her a little too tightly, causing her to let out a little squeal.

"Dad! You're squishing me! Put me down!" she cried out.

"Okay, okay." I gently set her down and kneeled down to her level. "You know I can't help it. You're getting so big, I just want to enjoy every minute of hugging you. When did I stop being Daddy and become just Dad?" She was growing up so fast that I could hardly stand it. It seemed like just yesterday she was learning to walk, and now she was running circles around me.

"Oh, Dad, you're so dramatic. You'll always be my daddy, but I'm a big girl now," she said with a little eye roll and a huff.

Talk about dramatic; she didn't get that sass from me, that was for sure.

"All right, well, let's get home and get some dinner. We can talk about what kind of tree to get this year after you do your homework," I replied.

"Can we have mac and cheese for dinner?" she asked as she grabbed my hand and started pulling me toward our truck.

"Mac and cheese again? How about we try having some vegetables in our life, kid." I knew this was a losing battle, but I had to try.

"How about we just have mac and cheese?" She grinned at me, knowing she would likely win this game tonight. I wanted to be a good dad. I had no idea what I was doing half the time, but she was an easy kid. Always well behaved, sweet, and kind to others, what more could I ask for really?

After we got buckled in, I peered in the rearview mirror at her in the backseat. "You want to go out for dinner instead?" I didn't really feel like cooking, and this way we could have the best of both worlds.

Her tiny lips curled into a smile again. "Can we go to the Wallflower?" She raised her eyebrows at me expectantly.

Knowing that diner was where she'd want to go, and where I also wanted to go, I nodded my approval. "Anything for you, kid."

Our little town of Friendship was small, and it didn't take long to get there. I noticed a homeless man sitting outside on the bench between the diner and the teashop next door. It was too cold to be fending for yourself out there, especially at night. As I opened the door to let my little lady in, I made a note to order him some food on our way out.

I waved to a few of the locals I knew, and Emily skipped

around the diner hugging folks and saying hello while I grabbed us a booth.

"How's it going, Jason?" she asked me, pen in hand. Her bright red hair was piled on top of her head in an old-fashioned bun, pulling tightly at the wrinkles that time had offered.

"It's good, Diana. Hey, question for you," I began.

"Sure, what is it?"

"That man outside, I've never seen him before, have you?" As I leaned back, I could see him on the bench, sitting quietly. He wasn't begging or anything, but he did look cold, and his matted hair and beard appeared as if he'd been on the streets a while. Friendship wasn't a place that had many people in his situation, and I'd never seen anyone homeless in our little town before.

Diana leaned forward to peek out the large glass front window. Shaking her head, she replied, "Nope. I've never seen him before. I'll have to call the cops to have him removed. We can't have bums sitting outside the diner scaring customers off. I hope this isn't going to be an issue in this town like it is in the city." She huffed.

"No, wait. It's almost Christmas. And maybe he's just passing through. Can you put a holiday plate together for him and put it on my tab? You can make it to go." I wasn't going to give the guy money so he could go blow it on booze and such, but I wanted to do something to help him out.

Diana nodded without reply and gave me a small smile. She was born and raised in Friendship, and while her disdain for the man outside was evident, I knew she was a good person and would take care of the meal as I asked without question.

Emily finally came to take her seat and began sipping the chocolate milk I'd ordered for her. "What were you talking to Diana about?" she asked me.

She was so young and innocent that I was tempted to lie, not wanting to draw attention to the man outside. But I never lied to her, and as sad as it was that the man clearly didn't have a home of his own, I was honest. "I was talking to Diana about getting the homeless man outside some dinner." I paused, waiting for the barrage of questions I expected. Sometimes her curiosity could be overwhelming. Emily surprised me, though, and asked me a question that made me realize I hadn't done such a bad job raising her alone after all.

"May I please give him my dinner too? And I think he probably needs some pie, because it's the best pie. And also, in case he needs something for later, because everyone needs a snack at bedtime." Her steely blue eyes met mine, and I had to fight back the tears I felt forming.

"You know what, Emily? We'll order him what you're having too. You need to eat some dinner, but I promise, on our way out, we'll make sure he's got a hot meal and a sweet treat to have before bed, too, okay?"

"Thanks, Daddy." She sent her sweet smile across the booth to me, and as my thoughts shifted to how this man ended up in our little town, I decided I was going to make sure he had what he needed to get by through the holidays. It was the least that Emily and I could do, as fortunate as we were. After all, it was the season of giving.

Chapter Three

Samantha

I'm fairly certain that the chill hit me before the plane even landed, while we were just descending into the great Northeast. It was an uneventful flight thankfully, and we touched down in Massachusetts right on time.

I was spending two weeks in Friendship, which was quite a bit longer than usual, but I missed my sister, and it had been an entire year already since we'd seen each other. She was taking most of the time off as well, leaving plenty of time to relax, chat, and participate in the numerous holiday activities. Since it was the middle of the day and the family was still working, I got my own ride to Robin's house. Even though I live over a thousand miles away, I still had my own key. I'd planned to drop my bag off and then head right back out to Main Street and pick up a few winter items.

I'd attempted to find a few warm items at the mall in Florida, but it was a wasted trip. I always found it strange that you could buy sweaters and coats in Florida. The stores changed out their inventory as if it were going to get cold, even though it never did. What they didn't carry, though, were clothes warm enough to keep you toasty in New England. Sure, I could have ordered some things online, but I liked Robin's downtown strip, and I loved supporting local businesses instead of the big-name manufacturing companies. And after the long flight, I knew it would be nice to walk around as well.

Friendship was exactly what you would envision if someone said to you, "New England at Christmas." It reminded me of a holiday card with its small shops and local businesses that had been passed down from generations in many cases. There was a small pond near the center of the town that you could actually skate on when it froze over, and they held a Christmas tree lighting each year in the square. The entire two weeks leading up to Christmas in Friendship was filled with choir concerts, the annual Christmas play, as well as a little winter wonderland downtown chock full of things for the families to do together. My nieces would be performing in the concert, and their enthusiasm was always contagious even for a scrooge like myself. Thank goodness for the joy of children at Christmas.

A short ride from the airport later, I let myself into my sister's house and looked around. Everything already looked and smelled like the holidays. I could tell she'd been baking, the aroma of vanilla and sugar wafted through the house. On a small table just inside the door was an envelope that had my name on it and a little wooden block that had been carved to look like a Christmas tree. I grinned and shoved my suitcase out of the way, grabbing the envelope greedily.

When I opened it, I read the little note from Robin.

Sister,

    *I know it's not your favorite time of year, but I promise
you that this year we will make new memories and eat all
the cookies our pants will allow us to. There's a batch on the
counter for you to get started with now! I love you so much,
and I'm so happy you're here with us. We're getting a tree
tonight, and we have lots of fun surprises planned for the time
you are here.*

    *Now go shop for some warm clothes because I know you
didn't bring enough.*

    See you soon!

    Love you,

    Robin

I grasped the letter close to my heart, holding back tears. She
was trying so hard to make the holidays something different
and wonderful for all of us as a family. As I let out a big sigh, I
resolved to put in a little more effort to enjoy the season with my
family and to appreciate what they were trying to do for me. It
wasn't fair to everyone else if I had a bad attitude, and even if I
had to pretend, it was worth it.

After I read the note a few more times while shoving some of
the peanut butter blossoms, my favorite cookie, in my mouth,
I grabbed my jacket and took off to do a little shopping. I was
craving a good cup of coffee, too, and the coffee shop downtown
was exactly what I needed. It was no big chain, just an awesome
older woman running a coffee- and bakeshop with her daughter,
and it was the best coffee in the world. I had bought some the
year before to take home, but it wasn't the same. I mused to
myself that they must make it with melted snow or something,
giving it the perfect flavor.

As I approached the coffee shop, a homeless man stole my attention with a warm smile. Normally, I would have gone about my business, but I was drawn to stop and talk to him.

"Bah humbug," he said.

"What?" I asked, surprised.

"Bah humbug, right? The holidays are dreadful."

"Um, I guess," I replied. I agreed with him, of course, but was taken aback by his blatant disregard for the holiday. Most people this time of year were filled with cheesy smiles and brimming with cheer. "Can I buy you a cup of coffee, sir?" I asked quickly. It seemed like the Christmassy thing to do. I was holding on to myself as the wind whipped, causing me to shiver.

"What a kind and generous offer, miss. I would love to take you up on it." He smiled kindly at me as if he'd never said "bah humbug" in the first place.

"Okay, just hang on, and I'll get us both some coffee to warm ourselves up with," I replied.

"Thank you so much." He rubbed his hands together and huffed his breath into his palms.

"I'll be right back."

I ran in and ordered two large coffees, taking in the warmth of the shop. That New England air had a chill to it that needed to be eradicated from the inside out with that piping hot coffee. As I turned quickly to leave with my two cups, I smashed into the rock-hard chest of an innocent bystander as if he were a brick wall.

"Shit!" I blurted out, hot coffee covering my gloves and seeping through to my skin. "Oh my God," I exclaimed, as I looked up at the man before me.

As his strong arms righted me and took the smooshed cups from my hands, he asked me, "Are you okay? Those were hot coffees. Let me get you new ones." I met his eyes, and as I locked with the crystal blue in them, I forgot how to speak for a minute. He was beautiful.

"I ... uh ... No. I'm fine." I had been traveling all day and looked my worst. I was annoyed even more after catching a glimpse of his New England lumberjack hotness. *You have got to be kidding me.*

Laughing, he said, "No, I won't take no for an answer. Come here. Let me help you get cleaned up, and let's get you some new coffees. It's the least I can do for barreling into you to get my fix." He pulled me to the side of the shop, handing me a stack of napkins.

Regaining my composure but not losing my attitude, I forced a smile. "It's not a big deal. I'm totally fine," I replied as I dabbed at my gloves with the napkins. I watched as he motioned to the young girl working the counter that he needed two more coffees.

"You're sure you're not burned or anything?" My hands were now out of their coffee-soaked gloves. He gently took my hands in his and examined them, turning them over, presumably to see if they were burned. It was extremely awkward, and I wasn't feeling particularly cold anymore. In fact, I was equally hot, flushed, embarrassed, and annoyed, I'd say.

I replied, "Really, I'm fine. I just need to get my friend a coffee." As he looked around for the friend in question, I looked around to see where the damn coffees were.

"They should be right here." He smiled at me, as if he were advertising for a toothpaste commercial. My fight-or-flight response had reached overdrive, and I scanned the room hoping for an escape plan to present itself.

Thankfully, our new coffees arrived in a moment's time, and I took my hands back. "Thank you for replacing my coffees, not at all necessary," I said. "It was very nice to meet you ..." I continued as I skirted toward the door.

"I didn't get your name," he said, watching me carefully.

I ignored his question. Not because I'm awful but because I'm awkward. I had absolutely no idea how to behave between the shock of the spilled coffee, the insanely hot guy, and the desire to get the man outside a cup of coffee. My brain was in conflict, and I couldn't wait to get back outside into the cold for some relief. "Thank you again," I said quickly as I made my way back out of the shop.

"Hope to see you again soon ..." he said quickly as I hustled out. I couldn't possibly say another word for fear of saying something incredibly stupid, simply nodding as I rushed out, my hands full of coffee. I'd become a bumbling fool out of nowhere.

So annoyed with myself and the whole encounter, I tried to shake it off and then realized I'd left my damn gloves inside. Completely irritated, it seems I'd forfeited them. There was no way I was going back in for them. They'd been sacrificed for humility, and I'd have to just get a new pair in my shopping adventures.

As the cold air stung my face, I came to my senses. Inhaling dramatically, I regained my composure and found the homeless man I was trying to do a holiday good deed for. No good deed goes unpunished.

Chapter Four

Jason

I always stopped for coffee after dropping Emily off at school and sometimes again in the afternoons. We lived just far enough outside of town that the school bus didn't come to our house. Even if it did, I'd still take her. It was one of my favorite things to do each morning and had become part of our normal routine.

On that particular day, I needed an afternoon pick me up, and I swung by the coffee shop. Running into the mystery woman was certainly outside of the routine.

She was stunning, and something about her made me laugh. How I didn't insist on getting her name was beyond me, but she'd run out of the coffee shop before we had a chance for a real conversation. I knew just about everyone in town, and she was definitely not local. Maybe visiting her family—it was the holidays after all. There were always a lot of visitors and even quite a few tourists this time of year.

Through the window of the coffee shop, I watched her leave

and then discovered that, not only was she beautiful, but she was kind as well. Her friend, the one she was getting coffee for, was the homeless man I'd encountered the night before. She handed it to him, chatted for a moment, and then walked away. I needed to find out who she was.

Outside the shop, the homeless man was warming his hands with the coffee and saying hello to those who would acknowledge him. I continued to wonder who he was, but at the forefront of my mind was finding out who *she* was.

"Hello there," I said as I approached him.

"Ah, good afternoon, Jason."

"How did you know my name?" I never spoke with him at the diner.

He laughed joyfully. "Why, the waitress, Diana, from the diner, gave me your name. Thank you for the hot meal on a cold evening. You helped keep an old man fat. Much appreciated. I'm Gabe." He rubbed his belly and then returned his hand to his coffee cup.

I found it strange that Diana would tell him my name. She had offered to take the food out to him while Emily and I ate the other night, and when we left, he was gone.

"Gabe, nice to meet you. And you're welcome."

"That pie really hit the spot." He smiled.

"The pie was my daughter's idea. Everyone needs pie apparently." I grinned, thinking about what a kind little girl she was.

He chuckled. "Yes, everyone does need pie. She's an adorable young lady." He looked around and then took a step closer to me. "Is there something I can help you with, Jason?"

Standing there, I wasn't sure why I was so compelled to talk to this guy, but I was. He seemed like a genuinely nice person, who was probably just down on his luck, but I had no idea. "I was wondering, do you know that woman? The one that brought you coffee?"

"Oh, she's quite lovely, isn't she?" He smiled, as if he were musing at something. For being homeless, and likely quite cold, he seemed happy.

"Uh, yes. Yes she is." It was windy, and I pulled my coat a bit tighter around me.

"So, you like her?" he asked me.

I didn't quite know what to say. "I . . . uh . . . " I stuttered. He was rather blunt, and I was taken aback by his comment, which wasn't altogether untrue.

"I can see these things," he said.

"Oh, you can, can you?" I was beginning to think this guy was crazy after all, and I was about ready to get out of there.

"That kind and generous young lady is Samantha. She's visiting her family for the holidays." He looked as if he was waiting for my reply, eyebrows raised. Suddenly, I felt like a teenager with a crush, and I didn't know what to say.

"Oh, that's cool." *That's cool.* That's what I said. I didn't know what else to say.

The old man laughed, hard. "Today won't be the last you see of her." He turned to walk away.

"How do you know?" I called after him, almost desperately. His crazy talk was just enough of what I wanted to hear.

Turning back to me, he replied, "I know all kinds of things, Jason. You'll see her again. And you'll make her smile again. Not to worry."

He winked and walked away, leaving me standing there a bit taken aback. The familiarity I felt toward him was so unusual. It was as if we'd been old friends. I switched my gaze to the square around us, thinking of what to say, what to ask, but when I looked back, he was gone. He'd disappeared into thin air.

The old man was on my mind all day, as was Samantha. I spent the day as I usually did, working in my shop. I worked as a mechanic as well as a pilot. One of our residents, old Mr. Macintosh, had a 1967 Plymouth Barracuda that he wanted restored. It was a hell of a job—he'd seriously let it go over the years, but when his wife passed away last spring, he pulled it out of hiding and asked me to take on the project. We agreed that the restoration should be all original parts, and so it wasn't an overnight job. I worked on it in between regular jobs, a little bit each week. I'd been working on cars since I was a kid and took over my dad's shop when he retired. Some days, my dad would come and work on the Barracuda with me and talk about the old days. This day, though, I was alone with my thoughts, the confusion swirling.

I couldn't get the homeless man off my mind, and as I racked my brain trying to figure out why he seemed so familiar, I completely lost track of time and almost forgot to go pick up Emily. She got out of school in the late afternoons, and typically I left work to get her and brought her back to the shop to finish up my day while she did her homework. After the strange day and the distracted thoughts, I decided that I'd close up shop, pick Emily up, and take her for a plane ride. It was always so much fun for both of us, and we didn't do it as often as I'd like.

When I picked her up from school and told her the plan, she was beside herself.

"Daddy! Seriously? It's been forever. I'm so excited!"

"Yeah, why not, kiddo? I gotta take her up to keep the motor going, and seeing the Christmas lights from above should be a sight, don't you think?"

"Oh yes! Will you take us over the old barn?"

"Of course I will, sweetie."

The McIntyre Farm was known for their holiday lights. They covered their barn with so many lights that you could practically see the glow from across town. It was amazing to see it all lit up below you, and I'd become known for giving a few rides in my little plane here and there to spread the joy. It was one of my many favorite things about the holidays.

Chapter Five

Samantha

The coffee-toting, rugged, and handsome man I'd run into that morning was all I could think about. Well, that and the fact that I was a blundering idiot and freezing. His short beard had just a few gray strands, and his eyes, they were welcoming in a way that was paralyzing. I felt a sly smile spread across my face as I mused about him. All that time alone must've been getting to me because I felt a bit of my cold heart defrost and flutter.

As my sister suggested, I went shopping for some warm attire and re-acquainted myself with Friendship. After a lovely afternoon daydreaming of the handsome stranger and getting some warm sweaters, I made my way back to my sister's house where she was waiting for me with open arms.

"Sam!" She ran toward me as I entered, her blond curls flying behind her.

As she nearly tackled me, I squealed. "Robin!" Transported right back to our childhood when we were the best of friends, I hugged her back, holding on for dear life. Family time always caused a flood of emotions for me, and I was laughing and crying all at once.

"Oh, Sam." She pulled away. "Don't cry." She wiped a tear from my cheek with her thumb and then swept a stray hair from my face.

"I'm not sad, I promise. I'm so, so happy to be here. I don't know what's come over me." I started to laugh more.

"Put those bags down and come into the kitchen. I've been baking. Someone got into the peanut butter blossoms today, so I made more." She winked at me and reached down, tugging at my hand to follow her. "The kids will be home from their show practice soon, so let's catch up before they get here. I want to tell you about all the fun stuff we've got planned!"

I'd not forgotten about all the activities this town holds for Christmas. You'd think it was one of those movies they show during the holidays. Almost every day there's an open house or a decorating competition of one kind or another. However, the town's children performing the Nativity is one of my favorite events. The rest could be rather overwhelming.

"Do tell. I'm assuming that it's the same as usual?" I tried to quell my sarcasm as I joined her in the massive kitchen.

"Well, not *every* night," she replied.

I raised my eyebrow. "Oh yeah?"

"Okay, almost every night. But it's Christmas. It's about being together. Don't be a grinch." Disappointment spread across her face.

"I'm not being a grinch! I want to spend time with my family. I'm here for almost two weeks. We will have some time together, just relaxing as a family, right?"

She reached her hand across the island in the kitchen to take mine. "I promise we'll have lots of time together as a family.

And I want to make sure you and I are able to have some sister time too. The moms club is having a cookie exchange, aka wine night with cookies, and you and I are going to attend without the kids or the husband. Just us girls. I have lots of awesome things planned to make this year special."

"I'm excited, Robin, I promise." I felt the need to reassure her. The elephant in the room, my well-known lack of holiday cheer, had yet to be brought up, which was refreshing and yet ominous. I was waiting for the topic to arise, prepared to defend myself. And then there it was.

"I know you're not completely thrilled with all of the festivities, but I appreciate you making an effort. Particularly for my children." Her tone shifted to slightly stern with me.

My face got hot. "I'm not going to ruin your Christmas wonderland, Robin," I replied defensively. I resented the implication that I was going to make the holidays something other than enjoyable. We'd already been through this before, and I was tired of hearing it. I never spread my ill feelings toward the holidays to her, and certainly not to the girls.

"I didn't mean it like that, Sam."

"Well, how did you mean it, Robin? If you didn't want me around, then what am I doing here?" Part of me was almost looking for a reason to leave in that moment, even though deep down I wanted to be there, celebrating with my family.

"I never said I didn't want you here. Stop putting words in my mouth!" We were both growing upset, and her voice became higher pitched. "I lost them, too, you know. I loved them too. It's not just your grief. It was Mom's favorite time of year, and it used to be yours. Don't lose that." She paused and softened her tone. "I didn't mean to make you feel like I don't want you here. I'm sorry if it came out that way." A tear rolled down her cheek.

I got up to hug her, pulling her into my arms, and tried to control my own tears. I avoided family so that I didn't have to feel this way. It was going to be a hard two weeks. "Robin, I'm sorry. I know you lost them, too, and I didn't mean to make you feel like it's all about me. I'm actually very excited about wine and cookies with the girls and the show and whatever other amazing winter adventures you have planned."

I began to laugh a bit, lightening the mood. I wasn't excited about all of those things, but I could pretend. Robin was all I had left, and I wasn't going to ruin Christmas for her and her family just because I couldn't move on.

"What do you say we practice wine and cookie night right now?" She wiped her tears away and let out a small laugh.

"I think that's a grand idea." I hugged her again and then took it upon myself to peruse the wine rack. The wine rack was a bit of an understatement. It was actually a rather large section of wall that had a built-in wine storage unit. The selection wasn't lacking either. My sister had a good job. She worked as a project manager in technology, and her husband, Michael, was a financial analyst or something like that. I wasn't totally sure except he talked about investing a lot, and they made a ton of money between them. Their house was huge and beautiful.

The holiday decorations were like what you'd find in a magazine. From the garland along the bannister, to the multiple trees of varying sizes around the house, the decor was amazing. If the holidays made you feel good, this house would be the Vatican for your joy. Robin had the majority of my parents' decorations, and I had noted them throughout the house earlier that day. Intertwined with her and Michael's things, they seemed right at home. I'd be lying if I said that it wasn't striking and magnificent really, but it was still a reminder to me of what was lost more than anything else.

The rest of the evening, I caught up with my sister, talked about the million and one activities we were participating in, and played with my nieces. Their excitement over seeing me gave me a reprieve from my pretending, and I ended the night tucking them in with a story. They wanted me to read the Nutcracker to them, which was my favorite holiday story growing up as well. As I settled into my bed that night, the handsome stranger from the coffee shop crossed my mind again. I wondered what he was doing, and for some reason, I wondered how he felt about Christmas.

Chapter Six

Jason

There's no such thing as a vacation when you're self-employed, but I was determined to take a few days off to enjoy the holidays and all the fun things going on in town with my girl while she was still young and full of Christmas spirit. I didn't want her to spend her entire week off hanging out with me at the shop or the hangar, so I rallied to get all my loose ends tied up. She wasn't always going to be a kid and that innocent and excited about everything, so every moment counted. She had choir practice after school, and one of the moms was going to bring her home afterward, so I had a little bit of extra time to myself. I hadn't finished giving my plane a tune-up, and that was the first order of business.

Several folks had already called me asking if they could rent time with me up in the air to view the lights and spend a roman-tic flight with their loved one. It was so awkward that people could have a romantic experience with me three feet away, but it was good money, especially around the holidays, and it wasn't always a couple. In fact, I'd booked a flight for Robin Jameson, who wanted me to show her sister the lights. Robin's sister was in town visiting for the holidays, and Robin's twin daughters were in Emily's class, so I happily agreed to fly them around later that week.

I couldn't help but be on the lookout for Samantha while I was out and about. Hoping to see her again, I milled around the coffee shop longer than I needed to when I ran into Gabe again. He seemed to pop up at the oddest times, and I was still confused by our previous conversation but also equally intrigued. I decided to grab him a coffee and join him on the bench outside, weather be damned. We had plenty of snow already, but all the sidewalks were clear, as were the benches around the square. Families had already begun their vacations, and it was lovely to see so many people enjoying time together.

I picked up the coffee for Gabe and headed over to his bench. He didn't seem to be cold or even in need of anything really. He was just watching people and smiling when I approached.

"Afternoon, Gabe. I thought you might like a coffee to keep warm." I handed over the paper cup.

"That was very kind of you to think of me," he replied.

"You're welcome," I said.

We sat silently for a moment before he finally broke the ice on our conversation.

"So, are you all ready for Christmas, Jason?" he asked me.

"I think so. I had a few errands to run today, some last-minute gifts and such."

"Will your parents be joining you and Emily for Christmas?" he asked me. His question surprised me, but he seemed to know things, so I answered.

"No, they're in Maine now. They retired there, and we all

agreed that with the impending weather, it was better that they stayed off the roads." I paused. "How did you know my parents don't live here?"

"I told you, Jason, I know all kinds of things."

"Who are you?" I asked pointedly. I didn't want to befriend some weirdo stalker guy who knows about me and my kid, and if he thought he was going to get something out of us, he was mistaken.

"Oh, I'm just a harmless old man, Jason. You needn't worry."

"How do you know so much about everyone in this town? Are you from here?" I asked.

"Oh no, I'm not from here. I'm just a very good listener. You'd be surprised how much people say around someone who they perceive as invisible," he replied.

"How did you find yourself in Friendship?" I asked. Feeling bad that he felt invisible, I wanted to know more about him. No one should feel that way, and maybe he was just a kind old man.

"I tend to go where the magic is. Friendship is full of Christmas magic, you know," he said. His gaze drifted back to the people shuffling around the square, and he smiled. "Just look around you. I know you can see it too."

He was right. I always felt that way about Friendship. But how he knew that was still lost on me. And it was a weird conversation to be having. Yet I didn't cut and run either. "This town definitely takes its Christmas celebrations seriously. There's no doubt about that. Have you been here before?" While he seemed familiar, I was quite sure I'd never met him before, and no one else seemed to know who he was or where he came from.

"No, this is my first time here." He smiled joyfully.

"How long have you been here?" I asked.

"I just arrived recently. And I told you before, I listen." He turned to me. "Have you seen Samantha yet?" he asked.

"Samantha?" I repeated, buying myself time to come up with an answer. "I don't even know her."

"That isn't what I asked, now is it, Jason?" He grinned. Even through my embarrassment, I couldn't help but smile back.

"No, I suppose it isn't, Gabe." I chuckled at the situation and at how I was feeling. Even though there was nothing to be embarrassed about, I couldn't help but feel a little uncomfortable talking to him about her. I had only had a single encounter with her, which was awkward at best. Yet she'd been on my mind constantly, and somehow he knew. "I have not seen her," I admitted.

"You will," he replied.

"Gabe, what's all this about Samantha? Seriously?" It was one thing to have a new woman in town on my mind, but it was entirely another to have this homeless man weighing in on the situation.

He took in a deep breath. "Jason, some things you'll need to figure out for yourself. But here's what I can say." He paused as I leaned in, on the edge of my seat. "Samantha is someone that should be in your life."

"How could you possibly know something like that?" He was back to sounding crazy again.

"May I ask you a question?" he asked, ignoring mine.

"Sure, go ahead," I replied.

"Okay. Are you happy?"

"I'm as happy as anyone else, I suppose." I wasn't sure where this was going, but I did give it some real thought. "Why do you ask?"

"Happy means different things to different people, right?" he asked.

"Of course it does."

"But there are some things that everyone needs in their life to be truly happy."

"What are those?" I asked.

"There's many. Love, growth, certainty, uncertainty, significance. These are all important components of true happiness."

"I see." I thought over what he said for a moment, but wasn't sure I understood where he was going with it or what it had to do with Samantha.

"You will," he replied.

Gabe stood up and looked down at me. His shaggy hair was unkempt, and his tattered jacket had seen better days. He smoothed out the front of his coat with one hand before returning it to the coffee cup, which was surely keeping his hands warm.

"Is there anything that I can get you, Gabe? Do you have a place to stay? It gets very cold here at night." He had to be sleeping somewhere, and with the storm approaching, I was concerned whether or not he'd be able to survive out on the streets. He may have been strange in many ways, but no one should be sleeping out in the snow.

"Oh, I'll be just fine." He picked up his small bag and readied himself to leave. "Don't you worry about me, Jason. I'll be just fine." He began to walk away but then stopped and turned back around to me. "You deserve to have all of those things in your life, Jason, most of all love."

"I have plenty of love in my life, but thanks, Gabe," I replied. I had my daughter. I had my parents. I didn't need more. I was content.

"There's still a little piece of your heart that needs filling, my friend. Don't turn away from it, even if it doesn't make any sense to you. It will."

I didn't know how to respond to what he said. I felt like my heart was plenty full. Clearly our conversation was over, though, and when he was about twenty feet away, I called out.

"Take care of yourself, Gabe."

"I always do," he replied without turning back around. As he walked away, I noticed a limp I hadn't seen before.

I sat on the bench for a few minutes, watching Gabe hobble away and mulling over our conversation. He was a strange guy, but he also seemed rather insightful in many ways. His constant reminders of Samantha were off-putting at first, but somehow it just made me want to get to know her, and a twinge of disappointment I hadn't run into her yet crept into my mind. If she was here visiting, I was bound to see her at one of the many events over the next week, but what would I say? *Hey, the homeless dude you bought coffee for the other day said that you need to be in my life, and I'm inclined to find out why. What do you think?* Unlikely to happen.

Gabe had disappeared. I had lost sight of him, distracted in my own thoughts. I knew I needed to get off the bench and get going. The afternoon I had to myself would be over soon, so I decided to head over to the toy store. I needed to pick up the bike I had ordered for Emily and get it home before she got back to the house.

Chapter Seven

Samantha

I still had a bit of shopping to get done, but I didn't want it to interfere with any of the family time we had planned, so I headed downtown while the girls were still at school, and Robin and Michael were still at work. Of course I wanted to get some coffee first, so I made the coffee shop my first stop. I had borrowed some new gloves from my sister, who thought my exchange with the mystery man was hysterical. She grilled me incessantly to try to figure out if she knew who he was. She probably did, and when I blushed telling my story, it sent her into full detective mode.

I grabbed my coffee quickly but cautiously this time, looking around for any hot guys I might accidentally run into. Alas, there were none, just the usual folks grabbing their afternoon fix like me while out running holiday errands.

The next stop was the toy store. I'd already gotten the twins a couple of cute outfits that I'd found in Florida, but being the cool aunt that I am, they needed fun gifts from me too. They no longer dressed alike, and while they were still very close at eight years old, they had developed different personalities. Daisy was much like her name, full of energy and a bit of a dreamer with an active imagination. She loved reading. Delilah was her scientific counterpart. She had explained to me how the cells in the body do a variety of things, and from what her mother told me, she enjoyed taking things apart to see how they worked.

The toy store in Friendship was small and unique, full of unusual gifts for children. Everything from children's books to stuffed animals to mini laboratories was available there, so I knew I'd be able to find something fun. I could've taken the trek out to the mall, but it was over an hour away and would've been crowded with miserable people. Not to mention the fact that the gifts wouldn't have been as cool and different. While meandering through the aisles, I found exactly what I wanted. An artist kit for Daisy and a miniature forensics laboratory for Delilah complete with fingerprinting and investigation tools. They'd love them.

As I walked toward the register to complete my purchase, I heard a familiar voice. It was him. The mystery man. He was in the toy store. My heart rate picked up, and my stomach dropped. I wasn't sure if I was excited or scared, but before I could hide behind the giant teddy bear in aisle four, I was spotted.

"Samantha?" he asked. *He knew my name. How did he know my name?*

"Oh . . . uh . . . hi there," I replied, attempting not to look like I was about to hide behind a colossal stuffed bear.

"How are you?" he asked, grinning broadly. He was just as handsome as I'd remembered with his closely shaven beard and striking blue-gray eyes that shone from the light in the store-front's window.

"I'm good. I'm good." It was like I'd forgotten how to form complete sentences. For an editor, I was lacking in any use of the English language.

"That's good to hear," he said. I wanted the moment to end, but I also wanted to think of something adorable or clever to say. If I could smack myself in the forehead without him seeing I would have.

"What are you shopping for?" It was the best I could come up with. Dorky small talk was what I'd been reduced to. I edit best-selling novels for a living, and I couldn't come up with anything better than *What are you shopping for* in a toy store at Christmas.

"Oh, my daughter's bike. It's about that time for an upgrade, so of course Santa needs to get one."

I knew it. He was married with kids. Of course he was. Who would let a stunner like this guy go? I bet his wife was a knock-out too. "That's awesome. I'm sure she'll love it. How old is she?"

"She's eight. She's at choir practice for the show right now, so I'm taking advantage of a few minutes to myself to get this taken care of. Who are you shopping for?" He looked at the items I was holding and then met my gaze again. "Looks like you've got an artist and a scientist on your hands?"

"Oh yes. These are for my nieces. They're also eight. I like to get them one fun present to go with all the stuff their mom insisted they need. How boring to get what you need for Christmas." I let a little giggle escape.

Letting out a laugh himself, he nodded. "Yeah, I agree. You get what you need when you need it. There's no fun in opening up a wrapped pair of socks. Even as an adult that's super lame." He tilted his head, thinking. "Your nieces are both eight? Are they the Jameson twins?"

My eyes widened. He knew them. Oh, this was getting

so much more awkward. "Uh, yeah. They are. How did you know that?"

He laughed again. "My daughter is in the same class as Daisy and Delilah. They hang out together ... or play rather. I guess eight-year-olds don't really hang out." That made both of us grin, and I loosened up my death grip on the box of forensic tools for children.

"Small town, I guess." I didn't know what else to say, and my general awkwardness was about to return at any moment. Then I remembered that he knew my name, and I wanted to know how. "You knew my name, how is that?" I squinted at him suspiciously.

"Oh, Gabe told me your name." He shrugged.

"Gabe, the homeless guy?" Why would he be talking to Gabe about me?

"Yeah, I bought him coffee the other day, and my daughter and I got him some dinner a couple nights ago. I keep running into him." He paused. "He mentioned that Samantha brought him coffee the other day, which obviously I saw you do. So I put two and two together," he said hurriedly as if he were trying to change the subject.

"I see," I replied.

"Well, uh ... in the interest of full disclosure, allow me to introduce myself. I'm Jason Hayes." He stuck his hand out, so I awkwardly put my purchases down on the nearby counter to shake his hand. His handshake was firm and soft at the same time, and I definitely didn't mean to keep my hand in his for as long as I did.

"Nice to meet you, Jason. I'm guessing you've figured out that Robin is my sister, and I'm here for the holidays?" I asked.

"Yes, I didn't even need a detective kit either."

I didn't get the joke, then he nodded toward the kit I was getting for Delilah. I let out a little giggle, but I was still feeling like I needed to get the hell out of there for fear of inserting my foot in my mouth again at any moment. But the world had other plans for me.

"So listen, can I buy you a drink or something? A coffee? I drink a lot of coffee, and obviously you drink coffee too?"

What was happening here? Was he asking me out? I was so confused. So of course I said something dumb. "Don't you have to get home to your family?" So that came out far ruder than I meant for it to, and it was my way of shutting down coffee with a married man because he was way too good looking for me to go have a beverage of any kind with.

"Actually no, I don't. It's just Emily and me. Is that what you're really asking me?" His grin spread across his face. He called me out on my trickery. I pretty much just asked him if he had a family to get back to, but damn, he caught me fishing.

My face was hot with embarrassment again, but I folded. "Yeah." I had to laugh at myself. Not smooth. Cool and collected was something I very much was not, unless it was related to my work.

"I am very much available for a cup of coffee and would love for you to join me before you wrap up your afternoon of shopping. I know you can't stay late. Robin has Christmas on a tight schedule. She's known for it, so I know you have some Yuletide celebration of one kind or another just about every night. But, if you could spare a little of your afternoon, I'd love to continue chatting."

What the hell. I didn't have anything to lose. And my coffee addiction was never truly quenched. I could drink it day and night and never have enough. Plus he was right. There was some kind of activity I couldn't quite remember that the caffeine would surely make better.

"Sure, why not?"

"Okay great. You get those presents taken care of, and we'll take this bicycle out to my truck and head over to Wallflowers. We can sit, and I promise not to spill coffee all over you again."

His smile was warm. In fact, I wanted to rip my coat off I was so hot. Between his smile and the fact that I was perpetually blushing and the temperature inside the store, I was dying.

But I was going to have afternoon coffee with a handsome stranger while on vacation. Life could be worse. For a few minutes, I'd forgotten how little I cared for the season, and I was enjoying myself.

Chapter Eight

Jason

The warm air from the diner hit me in the face as soon as I opened the door. Samantha walked in, and I couldn't help but to ogle her. She had on a huge, puffy coat that practically engulfed her, and boots that went up to her knees. Her long blond hair was tucked under a wool hat, and her pale cheeks were flushed from the cold.

I grabbed us a booth and motioned to Diana for two coffees. Samantha sat down across from me and removed her hat before unzipping her coat.

"Cold?" I asked.

"I don't know how y'all handle this all season," she replied. "It's like seventy-five degrees at my house right now." She ran her hands through her hair, and the sun from the front window reflected off the blond. Her sister had the same color hair, and so did the twins. It was clear they were related.

"It's not so bad. You get used to it. The seasons are nice here. We get a little bit of everything throughout the year. You should come back in the spring when everything is green and flowering. You'd like it."

"I've been to visit in the spring. You're right; it is nice. But you can go to the beach almost all year-round in Florida, you know." She smiled at me, a teasing grin.

"I'll give you that. It does sound nice to go to the beach, especially since we have a couple more months of cold. But this weather makes it feel like Christmas, don't you think?" I asked.

She hesitated. "I suppose that it does." Then she changed the subject. "So, you said it's just you and Emily?"

I didn't talk much about Emily's mom, but I wanted to be transparent with Samantha. Something about her made me feel comfortable, like I could just say anything I wanted. "Yeah, it's always been just the two of us."

"I'm sorry, you don't have to explain anything to me," she said.

I reached across the table and touched her hand gently. "No, no. It's okay. Most people in this town know me and know my story, so I just haven't told it in a long time. Emily's mom left shortly after Emily was born. She didn't want to be a mom. It wasn't a planned event. She didn't want to keep the baby, but I begged her to, and once Emily was born, she gave me full custody and left Friendship."

"Oh my God, I'm so sorry."

"Oh no, don't be sorry. Besides, it was a long time ago. We were young, and I knew that she wouldn't stick around. She never wanted to settle down in Friendship. We were high school sweethearts, but it was never meant to be. Emily is a gift, though, and my life wouldn't be the same without her. I thank God for her every day. She keeps me on my toes." I laughed thinking of the conversations we've had. Emily made me laugh constantly. She kept me young.

"So you don't talk to her or anything?" Samantha seemed surprised.

"Nope. She'll write once in a while. She travels a lot. That's what she always wanted to do. But it's not a thing, if that's what you're asking." I answered honestly. I liked Samantha, and even though she wasn't staying in Friendship—she was just visiting—being the real me was important.

"Well, that's really amazing of you. There aren't a lot of stories like that, where the dad is the full-time caregiver. Having an eight-year-old girl must be funny."

"She's a riot. She cracks me up every single day." I wanted to talk about Samantha, not Emily, so I changed the subject. "So, what about you? What's your story, Samantha from Florida?"

"My story? Gosh, I don't know. I'm not into winter. We established that already. I love coffee, long walks on the beach?" she joked.

"What do you do for a living?"

"I'm an editor. I read novels for a living. It's a quiet life really, but filled with amazing stories. I love it. What about you?"

She was smart and beautiful. Of course. "I'm a mechanic, and I also have a small plane that I use for recreation and occasionally take passengers out and about. In fact, your sister booked a flight for this week, did she tell you?"

"She did not! That sounds wonderful."

"Well, don't tell her I ruined the surprise. I won't tell you anything else about it, so you can pretend to be totally shocked." I laughed.

"The secret is safe." She smiled. She took a sip of her hot coffee, wrapping both hands around the mug. She was beautiful and charming, and as we continued chatting, I felt at ease with her, more so than with anyone in a long time. In fact, I had to remind myself several times it wasn't a real date. She was just on vacation, and it was just coffee.

I hadn't dated much after Emily's mom left. Not that I was heartbroken or anything like that, but I was busy with a baby. We had broken up before the baby even came and just agreed to terms that worked for both of us, but the thought of dating was the furthest thing from my mind.

As time went on, I'd gone out with a couple of lovely women here and there, but I wasn't looking to jump into a marriage, and the girls I'd gone to school with around here wanted to get married and have kids, and I already had one.

My parents helped with Emily until she was about five, when they retired north. They came down a lot, but before they left, we were a team of three raising my daughter. Anyway, the dating scene turned pretty dry over the years, and seeing someone seemed out of the realm of possibility without moving, which I just wasn't going to do.

Samantha and I talked a bit more. She told me some of her favorite things that her family does for Christmas, and we realized we would be at many of the same events.

"It's very nice to meet a new friend here. Family is great, but this is pleasant," she said.

"Well, it seems that we'll be seeing a lot of each other this week. So tell me, in the spirit of the season, what's was your favorite thing about Christmas growing up?" I asked.

She checked her watch. "I really should be going, Jason. We've got the open house and holiday lights party tonight, and I need to help my sister get ready." She stood up and began zipping her coat.

"Okay, well would you like me to drop you off? It's on my way." I didn't want our afternoon to end, but I could also tell that something was wrong, and I wanted to fix it.

"Oh no, that's not necessary. I have one more quick stop to make before heading home. And I have my sister's car. I'm sorry to rush off, but I gotta go. Thank you for the coffee, Jason. It was lovely chatting with you, really."

"You're welcome. I'll see you later then," I called after her as she rushed off. I definitely said something that upset her in some way, and it was gnawing at me.

I paid for the coffees and was headed back to my truck across the square, when I ran into Gabe yet again. I wasn't in the mood for one of his weird talks about love, and I definitely didn't want to talk about Samantha with him. I felt like he pushed me in the wrong direction there. It was a total waste of time to get hung up on a woman who didn't even live here.

"Jason! How was coffee?" he called out to me as I walked by.

I'd intended to ignore him and keep on walking, but I couldn't. I stopped, turned around, and addressed him. "Hi there, Gabe." I waited a moment, trying to choose my words. "What's your deal?" I asked.

"What do you mean?" he asked, innocence in his tone.

"I mean, why are you trying to get me to spend time with Samantha? Who is she to you? She doesn't live here and isn't planning to. In fact, she pretty much hates winter, so what is going on here?"

"Things aren't always what they seem, Jason."

"You're just going to talk in riddles?" I was exasperated.

"Samantha is special. What she feels deep inside and what she tells you aren't the same yet. But they will be," he said.

"What in the hell are you talking about? She is going to be here for a few days, and then she'll be gone." Saying it out loud was even more frustrating than the conversation itself. We had a great time chatting and everything was fine until I asked her about Christmas. Then it hit me, something about Christmas upset her. Why didn't I think of it before? My expression must have changed when I realized her problem was Christmas, not me, because Gabe began to grin.

"You figured it out?"

"Something happened to her that made her not like Christmas, didn't it?" I asked.

"Now you're paying attention." He nodded.

"But she was fine talking about all the things she was doing for the holidays here. So, what was it?" I asked.

"That is for her to tell you. And she will. In time. Be patient. Be persistent. It's not for nothing."

"How do you know that, Gabe?" Then before he could answer, I replied. "Let me guess. You know some things?"

He grinned and bundled his coat against his belly. "You're listening. Keep doing that." With not another word, he walked off, leaving me once again standing there with my thoughts.

Well, if she needed Christmas to be awesome, I was the guy for the job. Christmas was my thing, and I'd make this the best Christmas since whatever had happened to her.

Chapter Nine

Samantha

I hustled out of the diner like my hair was on fire, probably making a spectacle of myself. While I knew that Jason had no idea that I didn't want to reminisce about the holidays growing up, I didn't want to explain it either. Up until that moment, it had been amazing. We chatted about all kinds of things. He asked about the books I had read. He'd even heard of some of the authors that I edit. I love a man that reads.

There were no awkward moments, and I didn't even stumble over my words like I usually do. Although I didn't typically find myself having coffee with terrific-looking men all that often. I was actually done with my errands that day, contrary to what I told him, and when I left, I power-walked to the car where I banged my head on the steering wheel repeatedly.

It wouldn't ever go anywhere. It couldn't. We live a thousand miles away in what may as well be a different planet. But that didn't mean that I shouldn't be nice or even enjoy the flirtation. He was such a nice guy. I felt like a total fool.

I headed home to my sister's house, where she was waiting for my return. When I sighed audibly, she put down her glass of wine. "What happened?"

"So, I ran into the handsome stranger again," I said.

"And?" she asked excitedly.

"And his name is Jason Hayes. Apparently his daughter is friends with the girls?"

"Oh yes! How did I not figure that out?" She exclaimed. "He's so handsome, Sam. And such a good dad. All the moms have a crush on him." She laughed. "So, tell me what happened!"

I rolled my eyes dramatically before telling her about the afternoon. "So, yeah. I bolted."

"Oh, Sam, come on. Why would you do that?"

"I don't know!" I replied, flustered. "He asked me what my favorite Christmas memories were, and I froze. Look, you know how I feel about this topic."

"Sam, I'm so disappointed," she said. It felt like a knife in my stomach.

"You're disappointed? What is that supposed to mean?" She's my sister, and not having my back was devastating.

She placed both of her hands down on the counter as if she were trying to calm down. "Sam, I love you. You know that I do. But give me a break. This whole 'I hate Christmas because my parents are dead' routine is getting old."

"Are you kidding me?"

"No, Sam, I'm not kidding. I'm not saying that you can't wish they were here—hell, I wish they were here—but they're not. And you being some kind of Christmas phobic to everyone is just . . ."

"It's just what?" I interjected.

"It's childish, Samantha. You don't have to forget about them, but you do have to move on for crying out loud. Make some new memories. The holidays are supposed to be about sharing and giving and loving. All you're doing is making yourself miserable, and frankly, making the people who love you miserable."

She ran her hands through her hair and continued. "You need to get it together, Sam. I love you. I love you so much. But honestly, you have to move on. At this point, it's become a choice. You're not a little girl anymore. You have the ability to cherish their memories and move forward, it's up to you."

"I cannot believe you're calling me childish because I didn't want to tell a complete stranger my favorite things about Christmas. You cannot be serious right now."

"I'm completely serious, Sam. It's Christmas. That's what people do. They exchange stories about their family traditions. They bake cookies for each other. What the hell is wrong with you?"

She was right. I knew that every single thing she was saying was true, but I didn't want to hear it. I wanted to retreat, not face my feelings. My immediate reaction was to pack my things and get on the first plane back to Florida to be by myself, to wallow in my misery. But I knew better.

Robin paced around the kitchen, nothing left to say, so I had to speak up. "Look, Robin, I'm sorry. He's just a guy I met. It's not that big of a deal. I will try harder."

"Sam, he's not just some guy. He's our friend. And his daughter is friends with our kids. Do you not see how your behavior impacts others?"

"I'm sorry," I replied.

"Look, the girls are going to be home any minute, and we're going to get ready for the open house tour. I'm planning to make this Christmas, like every Christmas ever, special. If you want to come, then go get ready. But you need to put on a good face for my kids, okay?"

"Do you not want me to go?" I asked. I was hurt that she seemed to not want me there. Her tone was frustrated, and I understood it, but she always tried to make me feel better in the past. This time was different.

"Honestly, Sam, it's up to you. I wouldn't have asked you to come here for the holidays if I didn't want you. But seriously, figure out how to fake it, or better yet, move forward like the rest of us have."

She walked off, and I let her go. It was clear that we both needed some space, and I wanted some time with my thoughts. I went to my room and flopped down on the bed, trying to decide if I should stay away for a bit or if I should put on my big girl pants and just make more of an effort to keep my feelings to myself. Originally, I thought that I could just be myself and be sad when I wanted, but that clearly wasn't the case. I didn't know how to get out of my funk, though, and pretending was going to take some real effort at that point.

The girls came home, and I could hear them running around and getting ready. The Christmas open house tour was basically going from historical house to house to view their decorations, have a drink and a snack, and then move on to the next. Friendship had a decorating contest for the participants, and they received a trophy or something, and of course bragging rights. It was a fun way to stop by your neighbors' houses and catch up while checking out their decorations and spreading some holiday cheer.

Inhaling a deep breath, I heaved myself up off the bed. It was time to get it together and be with my family. I changed into a fresh pair of jeans and boots, and one of the new sweaters

I picked up while I was here, and headed back to the kitchen where the family was all gathered and getting ready.

"Aunt Sam!" Daisy shouted.

"Are you ready to go? It's going to be so fun, and there's so many good snacks," Delilah added.

"Well, who can say no to good snacks? Certainly not me," I replied.

Robin looked over at me and raised her eyebrows questioningly, so I smiled and shrugged slightly. What else could I do, but buck up? I wanted to be with my family, and I didn't want them to have a terrible time because of me. Besides, the girls were right. Snacks are great, so I could pull it together for snacks and family.

As we walked up to the first house, Robin put her arm around me. "I'm sorry that I was so harsh with you, Sam. I don't want you to ever feel like I don't want you here with us."

"I know, Robin. I'm sorry that I let my emotions get the better of me, and I promise to try harder," I replied.

I gave her a squeeze back, and we didn't mention it again. I thought the whole incident was behind us when we walked into the first house, and there he was. Jason Hayes, with his adorable smile, and with him was the cutest little girl who was racing toward my nieces at full speed.

Chapter Ten

Jason

It could not have been more perfect timing. I had been trying to figure out for a good chunk of the late afternoon how I could run into her again, and there she was. Emily ran like the wind toward her friends, and I greeted the Jameson family. Lastly, of course, was Samantha.

"I believe you've already met my sister, Samantha?" Robin grinned at me.

"Yes, yes I have." I winked at Robin, and she walked away to talk to some of the other people milling around, and the kids took off together in another direction. Likely, they made a bee-line toward the Christmas cookies.

Samantha was left standing in front of me all by herself. Absolutely stunning, she was smiling bashfully at me. "So, about today . . ." she started, but I interrupted her.

"Today was fantastic, Samantha." She was trying to explain, but I didn't want her to feel self-conscious, and my theory was that, if she were comfortable enough with me, she'd tell me what she wanted me to know when she was ready.

"Thank you." She smiled. "I enjoyed chatting with you today." Her eyes shifted around the room anxiously.

"Let's grab a drink, what do you say? Something a little more festive than coffee," I offered.

"That would be great." She smiled at me, relaxing her shoulders.

There was some kind of holiday punch in a bowl, which seemed like the most festive choice, so I scooped out two cups for us and handed her one. "This looks like Christmas, so let's give it a try," I said.

"Thank you."

We walked over to a quieter corner of the foyer area, near one of the many Christmas trees in the home, and I leaned up against the wall. "So, Christmas isn't really your thing, is it?" Her eyes widened while she took a sip of the punch. Clearly, I'd hit the nail on the head. "It's okay you know. You can feel however you want about the holidays."

"It's not that I don't like Christmas. It's just . . ." She paused.

"But it brings up bad memories?" I offered.

"Well, yeah."

"Happens to a lot of people. We associate things with each other. It's human nature. It's like how some people don't like the smell of a certain alcohol because they almost died in a field drinking underage. That shit can stick with you forever." I smiled, hoping my analogy made sense.

She laughed. "That's exactly what it's like."

"Sometimes, you just need new memories to create a new association."

"I never really looked at it that way," she replied.

"You want to take off?" I asked.

"You mean leave?" she asked.

"Yeah, let's get out of here. We can go walk around. It's not insanely cold tonight, and you appear to have the proper attire for a walk." He grinned.

"What about your daughter?" I asked.

"Hang on for just a second." I took off, leaving her there briefly. I found Robin and asked her if she'd take Emily with them to the next few houses. For the kids, it was basically a cookie tour of the neighborhood, and Emily wasn't going to miss me now that she'd found her friends. Robin grinned at me knowingly, and I just gave her a little shrug and she agreed. I told Emily I was going to go for a walk with my new friend and that she could stick with the girls. She was more than happy to see me later.

I went back over to Samantha, who was right where I had left her. She was watching the families mingle, and saying hello to the folks who were walking past her on their way in. "Oh, there you are. I've turned into the holiday-greeting committee," she said with a smile when I approached her with my coat in hand.

"Told you I'd be right back. Let's get out of here." I took the cup from her hand and set it on a nearby tray and then led her outside. There was still quite a chill in the air, but the wind had died down, so it was calm and fresh. Not biting like it could be this time of year. "Are you warm enough?" I asked her as we made our way down the driveway.

"I am. I guess I'm getting used to it after a few days," she replied.

"All the socializing and group activities can be a lot. Especially if you're not used to all these people," I said.

"Yeah, that is true. I work by myself, so I tend to have a fairly quiet life. Sometimes all of the hullabaloo of the holidays can be a bit much."

"I get it," I replied.

We walked through the neighborhood, most of the houses covered in lights. Their doors opening and closing with visitors coming and going. Samantha was quiet but seemed to be enjoying the peaceful walk. I led us toward the square, which wasn't particularly far away.

"I don't hate Christmas."

"I never said you did." I smiled and nudged her.

"Okay, no, you didn't. But you think I do. I'm not a scrooge or anything."

"You are far too pretty to be a scrooge," I replied. She let out a little giggle. I'd hoped that she could see that I had no intention of pressuring her into telling me anything she didn't want to and that she realized that it was just a walk, away from the crowd. Nothing more.

"Christmas was a huge deal in our house growing up," she offered.

"Oh yeah?"

"Yeah. My parents went all out. It was a lot of fun. I always looked forward to it. It used to be my favorite time of year."

"So what changed?" I asked, hoping she was ready to give me a hint.

"Christmas was always the big thing. It was the celebration of the year for our family. My parents did all kinds of crazy things to celebrate. When they died, I just didn't want to celebrate it anymore. That probably seems a bit much, right?"

"No, it doesn't."

"No?" she asked.

"Not to me. Your feelings are just that. They're *your* feelings.

Who's to say how you should or shouldn't feel? Loss affects everyone differently. Do I think you should make some new Christmas memories? Sure I do. But whether or not you do that is totally up to you."

I led us toward the gazebo in the middle of the square. It was empty and completely lit up. When you stood inside of it with all the lights shining, it felt like being inside of a Christmas ornament to me. A glow surrounded you, and from a three-hundred-and-sixty-degree angle, you could look all around the town as if you were inside of a viewing window made just for you. "Come on."

I took her arm in mine to lead her inside the gazebo and positioned her square in the middle. I wouldn't have discovered this little trick, had my daughter not pointed it out to me. "Now spin around slowly and tell me what you see."

She looked at me with skepticism, pursing her lips slightly. "What am I looking for?"

I laughed. "You're not looking for anything, Sam. Just look."

She humored me and started to spin slowly. The shimmering lights bounced off her blond hair, and as she twirled around, she looked like an angel.

"So what do you see?" I asked.

Still twirling slowly, she replied. "I see a toy store. I see the bank. I see an ice cream shop and bakery." She stopped twirling. "This is silly. What am I supposed to see?"

I stepped up behind her and pulled her gently into me and started to spin us both slowly. "Here's what I see," I whispered. "I see Mrs. Manor's flowerbed filled with little wooden snowmen, where there's always flowers in the spring. I see a rocking horse in the toyshop window, which reminds me of a simpler time when toys weren't so complicated. I see snow art drawn on the window of the bank with that weird spray snow. It reminds me of powdered sugar on cookies." She softened into me, and I stopped spinning and turned her around to face me.

A soft smile appeared on her face. "I guess maybe I needed someone to show me a little."

"Well, there's one other thing I have to show you right now." I grinned and pointed above us. Honestly, I hadn't even planned it, but there was mistletoe hanging from the center of the gazebo. I was still holding on to her, and she hadn't let go, either, as her eyes averted overhead as well.

She lowered her head back down and then smirked. "What the hell," she said as she raised herself up on her toes, pressing her lips softly to mine.

Chapter Eleven

Samantha

So I kissed a stranger. I guess he wasn't really a stranger by then. But pretty damn close. After all was said and done, he opened my heart up, and I genuinely started to feel like the holidays could be different. I was already making some new memories.

We sat outside, just enjoying the crisp, cool air for hours. He asked me all about myself. What I loved about my job, what I loved about my life. I told him my favorite Christmas memories with my parents. The flamingos—I told him all about those silly flamingos—and for the first time in five years, I reminisced without anguish. I relished in sharing my stories, instead of dreading the return of their memory.

We walked back toward the houses, and I had a spring in my step. I felt lighter. Many of the families had gone back home, including my own. They'd taken Emily back with them, and it seems that my sister and Jason had arranged via text that he'd bring me back home where he could then pick up his little girl.

On the walk back, he'd casually reached for my hand, which

I willingly nestled into his. I hadn't felt so connected and at peace with someone in as long as I could remember. Just the two of us, without all of the chaos, all the noise of the holidays, was calming.

When we arrived back at my sister's house, the little girls were all dead asleep in the living room. With three tiny, little bodies amassed by innumerable pillows, it looked like they'd passed out in the middle of playing.

"Hey guys," my sister whispered when we walked in. "They finally crashed from all the sugar," she joked.

"They look so peaceful," I said.

"It's a trick. When they wake up, the chaos begins again," Jason said.

"Jason, if you want, Emily can sleep here tonight. I'm going to let the girls camp out in the living room. It's vacation, after all. I can bring her by tomorrow after breakfast?" Robin suggested.

"Are you sure? I don't want her to be an inconvenience, Robin," he replied.

"Once you have two eight-year-olds, you may as well have ten. It's no trouble at all. Besides, they're all sacked out anyway."

"Okay, that would be great. Thanks, Robin."

"You're welcome." Her eyes shifted to me and back to him again. "I'm going to head off to bed myself. You two have a good night now." She grinned knowingly, which was completely embarrassing. I suddenly felt like a teenager who was doing something she shouldn't be.

"I should head home myself," Jason said. Robin walked off to her room, and I could hear the door shutting softly. He turned to me, taking my hands in his. "I had a really good time tonight. I'd like to see you again. You'll be at the concert tomorrow night?"

"I will," I replied. Nervousness washed over me, and I could feel my face getting warm.

"So, until tomorrow," he said just before leaning down to kiss me. It was a deep kiss, the kind that tangled up your insides and made your knees weak. I steadied myself, placing my hands against his chest.

As he pulled away to leave, I opened my eyes, taking him in. His dark hair contrasted with his light eyes, and he seemed to be thinking something he didn't want to say. "What is it?" I asked.

"I don't want to go," he replied, a broad smile forming.

I grinned back shamelessly. He was so handsome, and his charm was downright captivating.

"I'll see you tomorrow," I said.

"Okay, okay." He pulled away and then leaned in for one more quick kiss.

"Get out of here!" I pretended to shove him out.

"Good night, Sam," he said as he walked away.

I shut the door gently, and then leaned up against it and put my face in my hands. I wanted to squeal. My heart was racing, and I practically danced my way back to my room.

The next morning when I walked into the kitchen, Robin was already up and sitting at the counter drinking her coffee and reading something on her phone. The girls were awake, and having pancakes at the table, giggling and laughing about something.

"Well, hey there, sister," she said mischievously.

"Good morning," I replied with a sly smile.

"I trust you had a good evening?" she asked.

"I did indeed." I walked over to the coffeepot to pour myself a cup.

"So, give me the scoop. Come on!" She was done playing games with me, and it was hysterical.

"The scoop? On what?" I teased.

She slapped my arm gently. "Come on!"

"What do you want to know?" I asked. I wasn't sure what to say really. I had an absolutely wonderful night, with a wonderful man, who lives a thousand miles away from my house. That was the truth of the matter.

"You two seemed cozy last night," she said.

"We went for a walk, and then we talked out by the gazebo for a while. We had a really nice evening."

"And?" she pleaded.

"And what?"

"Did you kiss him? You kissed him, didn't you? Give me all the details!" she demanded.

"A lady never kisses and tells," I replied coyly.

"She tells her sister dammit!"

I couldn't help but to laugh. Robin was on the edge of her seat, she was dying for information, and I couldn't deny her any longer.

"We kissed. Under the mistletoe in the gazebo. It was like a movie, Robin. It couldn't have been a more perfect moment in time. But it doesn't mean anything—I mean, come on."

"What do you mean it doesn't mean anything? Of course it means something. That's Jason frigging Hayes, Samantha! He's only the most eligible bachelor in Friendship. And you had a little Christmas kiss with him under the mistletoe. That's something," she insisted.

"Robin, I live a thousand miles away. It was just a kiss." I was lying to myself. It wasn't just a kiss. It was a brand-new Christmas memory. For the first time in a long time, the idea of a Christmas memory made me smile.

"It's never just a kiss," she said.

"Well, this time it was. It can't go anywhere. I'm going home right after Christmas. To Florida, where I live. You remember? Palm trees, sunshine, a distinct lack of snow?"

"Uh-huh. Whatever, Sam. You can tell yourself that all you want, but I know you."

"What does that even mean?" I asked, intrigued.

"It means that you don't go around kissing people at random. And especially not at Christmas. It's a goddamn Christmas miracle!" she exclaimed.

"Oh my God, Robin, shut up."

"It's a blessing. Like the baby Jesus," she teased.

"I cannot even believe we're related," I said, rolling my eyes dramatically. She was cracking me up to be honest, but I wasn't going to give in.

"Oh, we are related. And I know you. Better than anyone else. You like him," she said, quite matter of factly.

"I can't deal with you right now." I started to laugh.

"Oh, but you can. And you will. Because I'm your sister, and you're stuck with me," she said in singsong fashion.

"Good lord." I let out a small giggle. "I'm going to shower. What's on the agenda for today?"

"Today, we are lounging. I'm done with work through the holidays, and the girls have their concert tonight. So, tonight will be about those shenanigans. But until then, we have no obligations whatsoever, which pleases me to no end. That work for you?"

"That sounds amazing actually. Wanna bake more cookies?" I asked.

"Well, of course I do. It's the holidays. We're gonna go ahead and get fat and nap after we get high on sugar, before we do it all over again."

"Sounds like the best day ever."

I sat down with my coffee and listened to the girls talking and laughing. The house felt warm and inviting. I was relaxed and genuinely happy, which I can't say I'd felt in years. Part of me knew it would have to come to an end, but I decided that very moment, that while I was in Friendship, I would enjoy all it had to offer. Including one very rugged and handsome pilot-slash-mechanic.

Chapter Twelve

Jason

That night couldn't have turned out better if I'd planned every bit of it myself. I didn't, though, and considered myself lucky as hell. Deep down, I wasn't really sure where it was going with Samantha, but it felt right. I had felt some kind of pull to her and then a push from Gabe, and that propelled me toward her at almost top speed. How Gabe knew was still lost on me. There was no way that he figured this out on his own simply by being a good listener. I didn't really care what it was. I felt good, and I was going to enjoy it.

The next day when Robin came to drop Emily off, she teased me a little bit but then helped me plan a surprise for Samantha. It was outrageous and required a ton of legwork, but the wheels were already in motion. Robin couldn't believe what I was planning.

"Wait, you've already found a place to get plastic flamingos in December, a week before Christmas? How is that even possible?" she asked me.

"I have a buddy who's in the business of getting people what they need," I joked with her as if I had to call the mob or something. In reality, if you're willing to pay, you can get almost anything you need. Besides the fact that it's the season of giving, and people wanted to help me make Christmas wonderful for someone special.

"What about the hats?" she asked.

"That's where I need your help," I replied.

"Okay, what can I do?"

"I need you to get me two hundred Santa hats."

"Two hundred?" she repeated. "That's a lot of Santa hats, Jason. Where am I going to get that many?"

"Call the moms club and initiate the emergency phone tree," I replied, completely serious.

"You want me to initiate the phone tree for Santa hats?"

"I do. Someone in Friendship needs their Christmas spirit brought back. I consider that an emergency. There are at least twenty moms on that list, and me of course. Hell, we can make them if we have to. Whatever it takes. The flamingos need hats."

"This is crazy." She laughed.

"Crazy and amazing, though, right? I mean, you think she'll like it, right?" I asked. It was totally over the top, but this was a holiday emergency ... sort of. I probably should have asked Robin what she thought of the idea before I started procuring yard flamingos from all over the place, but I had an idea and needed to run with it.

"I think it's going to blow her mind, Jason." Robin had a thoughtful look.

"You don't think it will upset her, do you?" That was the last thing I would want.

"Honestly? I think it might bring a tear to her eye." I must have looked worried because Robin continued right away. "But I don't think that is a bad thing! Don't worry. I think it's time for her to see that she can enjoy the traditions of the old days with our parents and make new memories at the same time."

"That's what I'm hoping for here, Robin. I want to make her happy," I replied honestly. She grew silent and observed me with a bit of a smirk, which gave me pause. "What?" I asked.

"What do you hope to achieve from this grand gesture?" She folded her hands across her chest and narrowed her eyes. "You know she doesn't live here. So what's in it for you? I get you shared a moment or a flirtation or whatever, but you're a really great guy, and she's my sister. What's really going on here?"

Thinking back to the things Gabe said, I couldn't very well tell Robin the whole truth. It wouldn't make one bit of sense that an old homeless man made it real clear that Samantha needed to be in my life and that I believed him. So I was as honest as I could be without full disclosure. "I like your sister, Robin. I like her a lot. And for whatever reason, one that I can't even fully explain myself, I'm compelled to help her make *this* the Christmas she chooses to move forward. There's something about her, and about everything that she's feeling, that just resonates with me."

"Okay, I mean I'm going to help you, because she's my sister and I think she'll love this. But it's also my job to get to the bottom of your intentions too," she said with some sternness.

"I'd be lying if I said I didn't have some feelings for her, Robin. But you know me. I'm not a bad guy."

"No, you're not a bad guy. Which is why I want to make sure you've got a clear head here too. I don't want to see you get hurt either."

I knew she was trying to be a good friend, but it mattered

little to me whether or not winning the girl happened. In that moment, I felt like I'd been given a mission. My assignment was to get Samantha's Christmas spirit back, and I chose to run with the operation full steam ahead.

"I appreciate your concern, but I'll work out the details of what might be something amazing with her when the time is right. For now, Operation Festive Flamingo is on, yes?"

I couldn't think of a better name, but Robin chuckled. "Yes, it is definitely on. I'll activate the phone tree and keep you posted."

"I'll be gathering my supplies today until the concert and working on the display tomorrow while Emily is at Mrs. Partridge's. They're building gingerbread houses or something messy that I'm glad isn't happening at my house." I would do whatever my little one wanted, but I hated some of the insane messes that would come from our projects.

"My girls will be there too." She laughed. "I don't need little bits of candy I'll be finding all summer long in my kitchen either. Mrs. Partridge is a saint for having all the kids over."

"Okay, I've got a few more calls to make, and I'm going to tell Emily the plan too."

"Sounds good . . . see you tonight, Jason."

Robin took off, and I filled Emily in on what we were doing. Christmas was her favorite holiday, too, so she sounded eager to participate.

"Is Miss Samantha your girlfriend?" she asked me.

"Not yet, Em. But maybe someday. For now, our job is to make sure this is the most special Christmas she's had in a really long time. You ready for this? It's a big job to help me, you know."

Her eyes lit up with enthusiasm. I could tell she enjoyed being a part of a secret operation, and with a heart as big as hers, I knew she'd be all about it. Plus, it had an element of shenanigans that any little girl would want in on. "Oh, I'm ready. I was made for this!"

I laughed. "Made for what?"

"I was made for secret Christmas operations. Come on, Dad. Keep up."

That kid cracked me up day and night. Sometimes I forgot how young she really was. She was mature for her age, probably from spending so much time with me. I talked to her like a grown-up from the time she was born. I got so lucky with her, and even though it had been just the two of us for most of her life, I was confident that the addition of someone special to our little family would be good for both of us. She was the perfect partner in crime.

Operation Festive Flamingo was a go.

Chapter Thirteen

Samantha

Jason had texted me a few times throughout the day, asking what I was up to and telling me he was looking forward to seeing me at the concert that evening. Our banter was fun, and I felt like a kid again. I was uplifted, almost cheerful even. I couldn't deny I was smitten. It had been so long since I'd shared a kiss that I had forgotten how wonderful it was. The butterflies, the smiles, the compliments, had shoved my aversion to Christmas under the rug.

The day was spent as Robin had promised, mostly lounging and alternating between baking and eating. Robin had to take a bunch of calls throughout the day, but I guessed it was just last-minute stuff at work. The day had been glorious, but it was almost time to get ourselves off to the holiday concert.

The children were performing a variety of songs as well as participating in the annual Nativity. It was a tradition, and one of the few holiday trappings that I always looked forward to.

I'd have to say that I loved it mostly because it was about the children, but also it took me away from my own grief. It was so easy to get caught up in the enthusiasm of the girls as they got dressed in their costumes. They were so excited to tell me all about their roles, and had offered to practice for me earlier in the day so I would know what they were going to do.

After watching Daisy and Delilah perform "Last Christmas"— the pop rock song, not the traditional carol I was expecting—I was dying to see it live and performed with music. The last two shows that I saw were great but fairly traditional. Apparently, the music teacher had retired since last Christmas, and the new, younger model was giving the holiday show an update. Their rehearsal had earned a standing ovation from Aunt Sam, that's for sure.

The five of us piled into the car—Daisy, Delilah, Robin, Michael, and myself—one big family. One thing about Friendship that I did enjoy was how close everything was. It didn't take more than ten minutes to get to the show, and we arrived quite early so that the girls could get organized and ready with the other kids. Robin left me with her husband, who I got along well with, while we milled about in the hallway before going in to find our seats. She wanted to get the girls backstage herself without dragging us all along in a parade with her.

My phone buzzed in my pocket, and it was a message from Jason.

Hey beautiful. I saved us rock star seats down front.

Sounds great. I'll let my sister know, I replied.

"So, Jason saved us seats." I glanced over to Michael, who was staring off into space.

"Jason?" he asked, looking confused. I guess Robin didn't tell him about my little dalliance.

"Oh, uh, Jason Hayes?" I didn't elaborate.

"Oh, okay. I'll let Robin know. You want to go on in and we'll find you?" he asked.

"Sure, that'll work."

Michael left to go find Robin, and my heart started to race as I opened the auditorium door. I scanned the room, and that's when I saw him. He was standing up, leaning against the seats in the row ahead of him so he could see me as soon as I walked in. I lifted my hand in a gentle wave and made my way down the long aisle toward him.

He walked out of the row to greet me with a small kiss on the cheek. "I've been thinking about you all day," he whispered, sending the butterflies I already had in my belly straight into my throat.

I didn't know what to say. I had no idea how to flirt back and felt like a speechless twit. I mustered up a, "me too," to get me by while I collected myself. Taking things up a notch, Jason grabbed my hand and led me to our seats, which were indeed front and center. We were going to be easy to spot for the girls, and we also had a perfect view of the whole stage.

"These are great seats. How early did you have to get here for these?" I asked, finally getting my face to cooperate with a smile. My sudden nerves were making me unable to act like a normal adult who could even form a normal smile.

"Not long before you. It just started to fill up. I promised Emily I'd be where she could see us, and I'm a man of my word." His grin was genuine and broad. He seemed happy, and when I met his eyes, my smile finally softened naturally. What a comforting person he was to be around.

"You sure are," I replied.

We settled in next to each other, with two more seats saved for Robin and Michael on the other side of me. After we took our coats off, Jason reached for my hand again and placed it on his knee gently. It felt like a date, even though we were there to watch all the kids, and when Robin found us, I quickly snatched my hand back, hiding it from her, although I think she saw.

"Hey guys, great seats," she said as she sat down next to me.

"You know how particular Emily is," Jason replied.

"Oh, I sure do," Robin replied with a laugh. "Mine are no different. I just went through the whole 'Mommy we want to be able to see you' discussion backstage myself. Emily looks absolutely adorable, Jason. Who did her curls?" she asked.

"I did," Jason replied, chuckling. "I'm becoming quite the Paul Mitchell these days. Or Vidal Sassoon? I dunno, I'm getting good at curling a little girl's hair."

We all laughed, but I considered what a good father he was. I didn't know much about Emily's mom, but she surely missed out on Jason. He was a keeper and would make any woman swoon.

The lights began to dim, indicating the show was starting, and we all turned our focus to the stage. As it became completely dark, Jason reached over for my hand, placing it on his knee, and gave it a little squeeze. I smiled in return and leaned into him just a bit.

My affection for this man I'd barely just met was on my mind almost the entire show. I watched him watch his daughter and was in awe by his adoration for her. I'd never thought much of having kids myself, mostly because I hadn't had a relationship that lasted long enough for it to be a consideration. Being with

him, on the receiving end of his affection while he still gave
his undivided attention to the show, was enough to make any
woman want to have his babies.

I did a lot of thinking during that show. Seeing Jason's unin-
hibited joy through the entire thing was enough to lift me right
back out of the funk that tried to seep in. All I could think of was
how soothing his presence was, however short-lived it was to be.

Chapter Fourteen

Jason

I wanted to steal a thousand kisses from her that night. But we were surrounded with friends and family, and excited kids. While I still knew she wasn't really mine, I couldn't help but think she could be, and I was going to take every opportunity that I could to make it so.

After the show, we all milled around and had hot cider and cookies with the kids, who put on a great show. The new music teacher really hit the mark with this one. Not only were the kids excited to sing and dance to new songs, but it was a refreshing change for us adults too. You could easily see how much fun the kids had, and that's what mattered the most.

I wished desperately for a few minutes alone with Samantha, but that prospect wasn't looking good. The night was winding down, and people were starting to head home. I knew that I'd see her the next night for the big surprise, but I had to find a way to sneak a kiss in somehow. So, I did what any man desperate for a woman's affection would do. I made up a reason she had to walk with me for a minute.

"Samantha, have you seen the kids' tree paintings?" It wasn't much to see, but the display was around the corner and away from the crowd.

"Tree paintings?" she asked me.

"Yes. Tree paintings. They're really quite spectacular. They're just around the corner. Let me show you?" I asked, nodding my head in that direction.

"Oh, um, sure." She turned to Robin. "Hey, we're gonna go look at the tree paintings real quick, okay?"

I took Samantha's hand and pulled her toward the corridor where artwork was hanging at a pretty good clip. As soon as we turned the corner, I pulled her into me for a kiss. She tasted like cinnamon and sugar, and when the surprise wore off, she melted into me, kissing me back.

"I thought we were going to look at some trees," she said quietly, letting a little laugh escape.

Still holding her tight, I pointed down the hallway. "There's some construction paper trees down that way. But I just wanted to get you alone for a minute."

"Well played, sir," she replied before initiating another kiss. Her lips were soft, and I could have stayed in that hallway just kissing her all night, but I knew our stolen moment had to come to an abrupt end before we got caught.

We shared a chuckle over the shenanigans we just pulled and returned to the group. I was feeling better, even though I wished she was leaving with me, not her sister.

"What did you think of the trees?" Robin asked, a slightly playful and sarcastic tone in her voice.

"Oh, the trees? They were breathtaking," Samantha replied.

"Breathtaking, eh? Pretty lofty compliment for some cut-outs," Robin replied with a laugh. "Okay, I think we have everyone. Are we ready to head home?"

Everyone was ready to go, so Emily and I walked out with the Jameson family and headed to our cars.

"We'll see you tomorrow then?" I confirmed with Robin.

"Yep, everything's all set. We'll catch up tomorrow. Have a good night you two," she said to Emily and me.

"Good night, Mrs. Jameson," Emily said, and gave Robin a hug. "Bye, Daisy . . . bye, Delilah."

"I'll see you tomorrow night. We're expecting a clear night for our flight. I'm looking forward to showing you the lights," I whispered to Samantha as I gave her a friendly hug good night.

"I can't wait," she whispered back.

Emily and I walked to my truck together hand in hand. "Really great job tonight, kiddo. I'm proud of you."

"Thanks, Dad. This was my favorite show we've ever done."

"I think it was my favorite too." I helped her get buckled in. "You ready for tomorrow?"

"Are you kidding me? I could barely keep our secret tonight. I'm so excited to see all these flamingos."

"I am, too, kid."

We headed home, and Emily was already half asleep by the time we made it there. We were about fifteen minutes away, so I couldn't blame her. What a big night. I tucked her in and checked my phone. I had a text message from Robin that said she'd secured all the hats I needed for my project. Score.

The next morning I got up bright and early and woke Emily up for breakfast. Normally, she's quite the sleepyhead, but she bounced out of bed and got dressed faster than I'd ever seen.

"Come on, Dad, we gotta get cracking," she said.

I laughed out loud. "Where did you hear that?"

"You say it all the time when you're in a hurry," she replied quite matter of factly. I didn't even realize I said it that much, but it sure was funny coming from an eight-year-old.

"You're right, kid. Let's get this show on the road."

We packed up some snacks and headed down to the hangar. When we opened the door, piled next to my plane were at least a hundred pink plastic flamingos. I needed more for what I was doing, but they were going to be delivered later that afternoon, and it was going to take all day to get them set up.

In retrospect, I probably should have recruited some help, but I didn't want to put anyone out a few days before Christmas. People were spending time with their families, and I had Emily to help as long as I could keep her attention.

"That is a lot of birds." Her little jaw was wide open. "What's the plan, Dad?"

"Well, we're gonna load them up on the trailer over there and take them out to the field next to the runway and set them all upright there."

"Won't she see them right away?" Emily asked. A very good question, but I'd thought this plan through.

"It's going to be dark out when she gets here, so she won't see them until the lights get flipped on, and we'll already be up in the air by then," I replied.

"Who's going to turn the lights on them?" she asked.

"Rob—Mrs. Jameson has offered to handle that for us. She's going to pretend that she can't go flying, and then it'll just be me and Samantha up there. Mrs. Jameson is going to turn the lights on, and the whole field will be lit up with flamingos in Santa hats. What do you think?" I asked her.

"I think this is the best Christmas surprise ever!" she squealed.

"Well, we don't have a lot of time, so let's get to it!" I held up my hand, and Emily gave me a high five.

It took us hours, but we got the first hundred flamingos set up, and I was able to run some wires for lights as well. We were just waiting on the last batch of birds and the hats to arrive. This would be the Christmas surprise to beat all Christmas surprises.

Chapter Fifteen

Samantha

Robin had to run out to do a few errands, so I was left to hang out in the house for a while. I played with Daisy and Delilah, and we discussed the very important naughty-and-nice list while I assured them that they were obviously on the nice list for being such good little girls. They showed me their dolls and told me all about their personalities and what they like to do for fun. The imagination of children would always amaze me. They were so creative, and my nieces were no exception.

Truth be told, I spent most of the rest of the day meandering through the house examining all the decorations that I knew belonged to my parents. Robin had made every effort to include our old family heirlooms and decorations throughout the house along with her own. It made me a little teary eyed, but I was determined not to be selfish or to ruin the day for anyone else just because I was feeling somewhat reminiscent and down. It came in waves really, and while I was having fun with my family, and I was looking forward to flying with Jason later that evening, I couldn't help but to revert back to my old ways when left to my thoughts too much.

When Robin returned, I asked to borrow her car so I could go for a drive. I wanted to get out of the house for a bit by myself. While it was wonderful to be with family, I was used to living alone and wanted a little time to myself away from my parents' things. The only place I could think of to go was the coffee shop. I was finished with my shopping, and it was too cold out to walk around, so a fresh cup of coffee and a book was the perfect way to spend a little time. When I arrived there, Gabe was outside.

Instead of buying him a cup of coffee to warm up outside, I decided that I'd invite him to join me inside. I felt bad that he was always outside and probably down on his luck, and it was the season of giving, after all.

"Hi, Gabe. How are you doing today?" I asked him as I approached.

"Well, Samantha, I'm doing great for an old man. How are you today? Are you all ready for Christmas?" he asked me jovially.

"I guess so," I replied. "Gabe, I'm going inside to sit and enjoy a cup of coffee. Would you like to join me?"

"I'd love to enjoy your company, young lady," he replied, a cheerful grin spreading across his round face.

"Shall we?" I motioned to the door, and he gathered his small bag and followed me in.

I quickly found us a seat in the rear of the coffee shop and then ordered coffees and cake for both of us. It's the holidays, and calories don't count. Once I'd received our order at the counter, I placed them in front of us and observed the man sitting across from me. While it was clear that he didn't have a home in Friendship, it wasn't clear to me what he was doing there at all.

"Gabe, what brought you to Friendship?" I asked.

He rested his hands in his lap and smiled softly at me. "I go where I'm needed, and the people of Friendship seemed to need me."

"What do you mean? Do you know people here? Are you from here?" I asked him, confused by his answer.

"Oh, I'm from all over, really. I know almost everyone here now," he replied without further explanation.

"I see. Are you staying through the holidays?"

"Yes, there are some things I need to do while I'm here. More people that need help."

"What kind of help?" I asked.

"My job is to help people find each other or to rediscover the Christmas magic in their hearts. Much like you, Samantha."

"Oh what? Like Santa Claus?" I laughed.

"Oh no, not like Santa." He grinned.

"So, what do you know of Christmas magic?" I asked sarcastically, thinking about my own attitude toward the holiday.

"Christmas magic never leaves us, even when we think it's faded away. You remember the way that you felt when your parents decorated your front yard with flamingos in the snow? That joy . . . it still exists within you. You just have to be willing to let it out."

"How did you know about that?" My shoulders stiffened. He's a stranger. There's no way that he could know things like that about me.

"I know all kinds of things, Samantha. I know that you've bottled up your feelings and taken your sadness out on Christmas. But that's not what your parents would have wanted. I think you know that."

I was getting upset and almost frightened by his words.

"What do you know about my parents?" How could he know any of this?

"Christmas is a feeling, not a thing. It can't be hurt the way your heart is. Taking your hurt out on Christmas won't make you feel better. But the spirit of Christmas can help you heal if you let it."

"It's just a holiday," I replied.

"Now, you and I both know that's not true." He tilted his head knowingly and raised an eyebrow, as if he were waiting for me to agree.

"Okay, so what if it is true? That still doesn't explain how you know so much about me." He was right. I knew it wasn't just a holiday, and it didn't make me feel any better or worse to hate on Christmas. It was just a different bad feeling replacing my grief temporarily.

"You're not hard to read, Samantha. I know you've suffered loss. It's never easy to get beyond that. But what if you took that loss and honored the past by starting a new future?"

"Starting a new future?" I asked.

"I understand there's a handsome pilot in this town?" he said, making me blush.

"I don't even live here, Gabe. That's absurd. It's nothing," I lied. It wasn't nothing. But I didn't live here, so how could it go anywhere anyway?

"Geography is nothing. Opportunity is everything. Don't throw away opportunities over a desire to stay stuck in the past. It doesn't serve you."

"How did you know about the flamingos?" I asked, changing the subject again.

"Your sister has told that story about the flamingos. Everyone has heard it. And I'm a very good listener." I didn't believe him, but I let it go. My thoughts shifted back to Jason and why Gabe would even mention him.

"The pilot is just a friend. I barely know him."

"That's how the best relationships in the world begin." He grinned again, and maybe it was the lights in the coffee shop, but I could've sworn they twinkled. "I need to be going, Samantha. I have some appointments."

"More Christmas magic to spread around Friendship?" I teased.

"Maybe." He winked at me.

"It was nice to talk to you today, Gabe. Please take care of yourself. It's cold out there."

"You're a kind woman, Samantha. Thank you for the coffee. And tonight, remember what I said."

With that, he bundled his coat up, grabbed his bag, and left. I watched for him out the window of the coffee shop, but I must have blinked or zoned out, because, in an instant, he was gone.

Chapter Sixteen

Jason

It was go time. Everything was in place. An all-day activity but worth every second, two hundred plastic flamingos in the middle of Massachusetts, dressed in Santa hats and lit up with floodlights, were set up in my field. Robin had brought me the hats that had filled her trunk, and Emily went through the field placing a Santa hat on every flamingo in the flock. It was incredible. The sun had just gone down, and after a check of the lights, I was ready.

The women showed up right on time, and the moment I saw Samantha, my heart raced and the excitement took over. "You ladies ready?" I asked.

"Well, actually . . ." Robin began the lie. "I can't go."

"What do you mean you can't go?" Samantha asked.

"I'm just dropping you off. Unfortunately, I'm needed down at the church. There's an angel costume situation for the Christmas service that needs my expertise to be fixed in time for Christmas," Robin replied.

"Why didn't you tell me? We could have canceled," Samantha said.

"I've gone up before. I didn't want you to miss out." Robin shrugged like it was no big deal and turned to me. "You'll bring her home later?"

"Absolutely," I replied.

Samantha looked confused and kept shifting her glance back and forth between Robin and me. "Something is going on here, isn't it?" she asked.

"Whatever do you mean?" Robin asked.

"You're up to something. I'm sure there's someone more qualified than you to fix an angel costume," Samantha replied, pursing her lips.

"Listen, I gotta go. I'm sorry about bailing on you at the last minute, but you'll have a great time. I guarantee it. I'll see you back at home." Robin pretended to head back to her car as we'd discussed and left me with Samantha.

"Well, looks like it's just the two of us. You ready?" I asked her, barely able to contain my grin.

"Uh, yeah. I am." She still seemed skeptical, but she went along with it.

Emily was hiding out waiting for us to leave, and then she was going to be with Robin to turn all the lights on when they saw our plane coming back toward the field. Robin was going to take her back to her house to have one more sleepover with the girls before Christmas. I took Samantha over to the plane, showed her a few things so she'd know what to expect, and we got buckled in. It was an exceptionally clear night, perfect for seeing holiday lights all over the area. When we got up in the air, I looked over at her to find her smiling broadly as she gazed out the windows.

"Beautiful, isn't it?" I asked into the microphone. We had on headsets so I could communicate with the local airports or other planes if need be. Our altitude was low, so I wasn't required to file a flight plan. We were able to cruise around at our leisure, which was one of my favorite things to do.

"It really is breathtaking from up here," she replied.

We flew around the county, checking out all of the holiday lights. I showed her all of the notable landmarks that you could see in the dark, and her enthusiasm was exactly what I'd hoped for. When it was time to head back and to show her the big surprise, I reached over and grabbed her hand gently.

"I have a surprise for you."

"You do?" she asked.

"Yep. I want you to look out your window, and we're going to fly by something really special." I could already see in the distance that the lights we'd set up were glowing brightly, but if you didn't know to look for it, you'd have no idea it was there.

As we approached, I lowered the plane so that she could get a clear view on her side before I flew back around. The moment she realized what was happening, I heard her gasp in my headset. "Oh my God," she said.

It was as amazing as I'd thought it would be. Two hundred flamingos in the dead of winter were dressed up for the holidays, just for her.

"Jason! Did you do this?" she asked, practically breathless.

"I had some help from some little elves, but yeah. It's for you. For your parents too." I squeezed her hand. I glanced over and saw that she was crying. "Are you okay?" I asked. I hadn't meant to make her cry, and worried that I'd upset her, I started to panic a bit.

"Oh, Jason, I don't know what to say," she replied.

"But you're okay?" She hadn't really answered my question, and the thought that my gesture had backfired was now creeping into my head.

She was silent for a moment, and then she squeezed my hand and brought it to her chest, clinging to it with both hands. "I'm more than okay." She started to laugh a little, making me nervous. Maybe I made her snap instead of winning her over. "This is the most beautiful spectacle I've seen in my entire life. My parents are laughing and smiling right now. I can feel it. It's amazing."

What a relief. "I wanted to show you that we can make new memories and still honor the old ones. I want Christmas to be special and wonderful for you again, Samantha."

"You've done just that. I'm speechless. I can't believe you made this happen."

We flew by a few more times, and she took some pictures from the sky before we landed. The girls had left, and I sent a quick text to Robin with a thumbs-up so she'd know the mission was indeed accomplished.

After we exited the airplane, I took Samantha over to my truck, where I had some hot chocolate in a thermos and poured us both a cup.

"Cheers," I said, gently tapping my paper cup to hers.

"Cheers," she replied before taking a small sip. "Why did you do all of this for me, Jason? We've practically just met."

I had an idea this talk was coming, and I'd prepared myself. "Samantha, sometimes you meet someone and just know they're meant to be with you somehow. Occasionally, it takes some nudging to get out of your box, for all of us. But the risk is worth it."

"How can this ever work?" she asked, her eyes turning toward the floor.

"Take a risk with me, Samantha." I pulled her chin back up so she'd meet my eyes.

"But I don't even live here," she said, a hint of sadness in her voice.

"I don't care where you live. I'm not letting you go. You're meant to be in my life, Samantha. That's just all there is to it. I think you know it too. Stay through the New Year, and we'll figure it out. That's the magic of Christmas, Sam. Anything is possible."

Instead of replying, she kissed me.

We stood in the hangar like teenagers, sharing a kiss that ended up becoming an annual Christmas tradition for us.

The next day, I looked for Gabe everywhere so that I could tell him everything that had happened and thank him for pushing me to go after what I wanted. But he was gone. I never saw him again. I think his work in Friendship was done. At least for me it was.

Christmas Encounter

R. J. PRESCOTT

*For Mum, who showed me that
there is always magic in everything
if only you look for it.*

Chapter One

Jensen

Paris, France

"Why don't we take the party back to my place?" the woman next to me whispered suggestively. The shade of her lipstick matched perfectly with the color of her short, clingy red dress, and her heavily made-up face was flawless. Six months ago, I would have been flattered by her offer. Now, like everything else, it just seemed fake. I wondered if I'd even recognize her without all the cosmetics. Or if she'd bother to give me the time of day if I wasn't Formula One's newest rising star. I doubted it, given that we'd been talking for twenty minutes, and the only thing she seemed interested in was my salary.

My gaze drifted across the sea of partygoers, where celebrities and movie stars mingled either with the rich and powerful, or with those who wanted to be. I sighed deeply, preparing myself to brush her off and for the inevitable argument that would follow, just as my phone started buzzing.

"Sorry. I need to take this," I replied, fishing it out of my pocket. The number was withheld, but I mentally high-fived whoever was calling for giving me an excuse to escape.

"Hello?" I said as I connected the call. A woman spoke to me, but I couldn't make out what she was saying. The conversation and sound of clinking glasses was loud, so I pushed my way through the throng of people to a set of French doors.

"Hang on a sec," I said. Closing the doors behind me, I found myself alone on a small balcony. The tiny space had barely enough room for two chairs, but the view of the Paris skyline was spectacular.

"Sorry about that. I can hear you better now," I said to the caller. After a few seconds of silence, I was beginning to wonder if we'd been disconnected.

"Is this Jensen Caldwell?" the voice asked.

"It is," I replied suspiciously.

"Jensen, it's Nancy Adler, Ronnie's wife. I'm sorry to have to be the one to tell you this, but Ronnie passed away today," she said, her voice cracking with unmasked grief.

The pain of hearing those words was physical. I sat down hard in the chair as my knees went out from under me. Hunched over, I ran my hand back and forth over my buzz cut, trying to process what she'd said.

"I don't understand. How?" I asked, my words sticking in my throat.

"It was a massive heart attack," she explained softly, her misery palpable. "He was out walking the dog when he had a cardiac arrest. The doctor said he was dead before he hit the ground."

"But he was so fit and strong," I replied. He didn't drink or smoke. He exercised regularly. I mean things like this weren't supposed to happen to people like that. It wasn't fair.

"He always had heart problems, but he kept them to himself.

His father died the same way," she explained. I felt shame hearing that. The man who'd been like a father to me had health problems, and I had had no clue. I'd been too busy hopping from race to race and party to party around Europe to care.

"I'm so sorry," I confessed. I was sorry for her loss, but my apology was for everything I'd done, everything I'd become over the last year. Now it was too late.

"Thank you," she replied. "I know you're a busy man, but the funeral will be held here next week most likely. I just thought you'd want to know, and I didn't want you to hear the news from anyone else."

"I'll be there," I said, and I would be. Nancy preferred to stay at home while Ronnie was on the circuit, so I'd only met her a handful of times, but Ronnie looked at her like she hung the moon. He worshipped her, and maybe it was too late to atone for the sins of my past, but standing next to his wife while she buried the love of her life was the least I could do.

"Thank you, Jensen. He would have liked knowing you were there," she told me.

"Is there anything I can do? Anything that you need?" I asked.

"It's kind of you to offer, but I have everything taken care of. I'm just trying to keep busy at the moment so I can get through the next few days. Perhaps . . . perhaps when you get here you'd like to stop by. I'd like to meet with you before the funeral if that would be okay with you?" she asked.

I swallowed hard, wondering if sitting down with Nancy would make this whole thing seem more real. I felt like the bottom had fallen out of my world, so I couldn't imagine what she must be going through. But she might be the only person on earth who could truly understand how I was feeling.

"I'd like that. Thank you," I answered. "I'll stop by when I get into town. I'm in Europe at the moment, so it's going to take me a while to get to you, but I'll be there as quickly as I can."

"Well, have a safe journey then," she said. "I'll text you my address when we get off the phone and the funeral details as soon as I have them."

We said our good-byes and, sure enough, my phone buzzed with a message a few seconds later as Nancy had promised. Sliding it back into my pocket, I turned my face up toward the sky. The pollution of light above the city hid a myriad of stars. I'd spent my whole life sleeping under a blanket of constellations. Knowing that they were always there meant that I had stopped looking up. What had always seemed boring and predictable, I now knew was comforting and reassuring. A shame then that my epiphany only happened when they were gone.

The piercing laugh of a party guest pulled me from my thoughts. Behind the glass doors, vintage champagne was being sipped from the finest cut crystal glasses, and beautiful dresses adorned beautiful people. The room was a showcase for wealth and power, and I'd been the focus of everyone's attention. It was everything I ever thought I wanted, and I'd never been so lonely in my entire life.

Chapter Two

Lauren

It was somewhat ironic that I now found myself perpetually trapped in a town called Friendship, yet I'd never really had what you'd call a good friend. Of course I was fully aware that I hadn't really helped myself in that department. You see, I was a liar. Not by choice of course, but I was a liar nonetheless. A grafter, a thief, a con artist. Call me what you will, but I scammed and stole and did whatever I needed to do to eat. I wasn't proud of the fact. In fact, I was bitterly ashamed. But the view from the moral high ground wasn't so attractive when you barely had the energy to walk and your stomach was seized with hunger pains.

On the rare occasions when I had a hot meal, I allowed myself to indulge in foolish, pointless fantasies. My favorite was the one where I was heavily pregnant, my husband laughing with our three children in the garden of our house by the sea and with the smell of baked goods filling the kitchen of our home as I watched my family play. I've never baked a day in my life. But one day, somehow, I was going to learn to bake a cake so big it would feed a family of six for a week. It was a stupid fantasy, and I scolded myself every time I thought of it. Happy ever afters weren't for the likes of me. Dreaming was dangerous, and I should know better.

Dumpster diving was just the dose of reality I needed to bring me back down to earth. Everything I'd saved for the last few weeks was gone. No matter how well I hid money, every place we stayed, Dad found it. You'd think a bank would keep it safe, but bank accounts were for people who earned money honestly and had identification. I'd be surprised if Dad even had a birth certificate for me. I knew my age and date of birth because I'd seen him write it on a school admissions form once, but there was a fairly good chance that he'd made it up on the spot. He promised me this time that I could look for legitimate work. But Friendship was a small town, and I had no references. With Christmas around the corner, I felt sure that someone would be hiring, but the locals looked at me with suspicion, and they were probably right about me. I wasn't honest and trustworthy.

But I wanted to be.

By the time I arrived back at the motel, I was tired, hungry, and cold. When I realized that Dad had stolen what little savings I had without leaving me anything for food, I was desperate. Desperate enough to wait for the local fast food restaurant to close before rummaging through their Dumpster in the hope of finding something edible. On the fifth Styrofoam container, I hit the jackpot. The juicy cheeseburger and fries, probably trashed as a wrong order, were still warm. Most people would have gagged at what I was about to do, but I hadn't eaten in two days. To me, it looked like nirvana.

"You gonna eat that or just stare at it droolin'?" a voice from the shadows asked me. I screamed and jumped back in shock but still managed to keep hold of my prize. Slowly, the grubby face of an old homeless guy emerged from the darkness. The way he was staring at my dinner made me squeeze it a little tighter.

"You scared me half to death. What were you doing down there?" I demanded.

"I was getting some sleep before I was rudely interrupted," he explained.

"Behind a Dumpster?" I asked suspiciously.

"What? You know of anywhere else where folks are less likely to hassle a homeless guy?" he said. He had a point.

"So, you gonna eat that or what?" he asked me. I eyed the burger and then the homeless guy and sighed deeply. Inside I was crying at the thought of losing half a meal, but this guy looked like he'd been on the streets a while. No matter what the circumstances, there was always someone worse off than you.

"How about we split it, then I'll keep searching for more?" I suggested.

"Well, you sound like an enterprising young lady, and those are my favorite kind. Please, come and partake of my humble abode, and I'll fetch the linen and silverware," he said, indicating his cardboard hovel. He bowed like a butler, making me smile. Whoever he was, he was charming. It looked as though he was stockpiling old sleeping bags and blankets, so at least we had something soft to sit on. Sitting down, I left plenty of room as he eased down with a weariness that spoke of old age and aching bones. Splitting the meal down the middle, I handed him his half, and we bit into them together, groaning simultaneously.

"This is so good," I mumbled between bites.

"The best burger I've ever had," he added. All too soon, it

was gone, but those precious calories on my empty stomach were heavenly.

"Thanks for letting me share your pallet," I said.

"Thanks for letting me share your meal," he replied.

"I'm Lauren." I introduced myself, holding out my hand. He wiped his own hand back and forth on his coat before shaking mine firmly.

"Nice to meet you, Lauren. I'm Gabriel, but you can call me Gabe," he answered.

"Do you really sleep here?" I asked him. "It's freezing out tonight. Isn't there somewhere warmer you could go?" Despite the pile of bedding, I had no doubt he'd feel the cold through to his bones. The snow that had started to fall earlier was now coming down thick and fast. Gabe had propped up a few flattened boxes to form a roof of sorts, and the fence to our back offered a little protection from the wind and snow but not much.

"Ain't no homeless shelter in a town this size. Besides, you get used to the smell pretty quick, and it's safe. Well, as safe as it can be on the streets. Speaking of which, what's a lovely young lady like yourself doing out here at this time of night?" he said.

I wrapped my coat around myself a little tighter and shivered as a cold breeze blew down the alleyway.

"My dad stole my money again, which means he's spending it at the local bar," I explained.

"If he's there, how come you ain't home?" he asked.

"Because when the money runs out, he'll head back. Sober, I can handle him. Drunk, he's not so nice. I'll take a night on the streets over dealing with that," I explained. A huge yawn came over me. Despite my promise to forage for more food, I was exhausted.

"Look, there's plenty of blankets here for both of us. Why

don't you lay your head down and sleep for a bit?" he suggested, regarding me with pity in his eyes.

"That's kind of you," I acknowledged. "If you wouldn't mind putting up with me while I have a quick nap, I'll hunt for more food afterward."

I lay down on one of the sleeping bags, and like a mother hen, he piled blanket after blanket on top of me before making himself comfortable. My eyes were heavy as I drifted off, but I caught his words as he spoke softly to me.

"Get some rest, little one. I'll watch over you tonight."

Chapter Three

Lauren

I woke to the sounds of a busy kitchen. Groggy and stiff from the cold, I looked around. A small pile of blankets was piled neatly beside me, but there was no sign of Gabe. He'd most likely gone in search of breakfast, and I figured it was probably a good idea for me to do the same. Folding and stacking everything as neatly as I could, I placed the bedding carefully into a box inside the shelter, hoping that would keep it all safe and dry. The bitter chill of winter was in the air, and I shivered as I began the walk back to the motel. Figuring that it was probably safe by now, I peered around the door to our room to find Dad passed out on the sofa. The stench of stale booze was so overpowering that I could smell him from the doorway.

A wave of despair washed over me. I wanted so much more for my life. For both of our lives. Dad had yanked me in and out of so many schools that I never really had a chance to make a friend before we'd pack up and move. Running from another one of his scams gone wrong. When I was old enough, he made me a part of them. He said no one would look at my big brown doe eyes and think I was anything but innocent. In his eyes, there was no one more or less deserving of being ripped off. Everyone was a mark. He was an equal-opportunity thief that way.

I was a penniless high school dropout with no prospects and nowhere else to go. But looking at my pitiful excuse for a father, I knew that I was done with living like this. Today, I would steal for the last time. One more job to buy a few days of food, and that was it. If I had to walk from one end of this town to the other, if I had to beg and plead or offer a free day's labor to prove myself, I was getting a job. Friendship wasn't my home, but it would be.

Snagging my only other pair of jeans, a white T-shirt, and some clean underwear from my duffel bag, I crept to the bathroom. On its highest setting, the useless shower cranked out lukewarm water at pressure barely above a trickle. I emptied a bottle of complimentary miniature shampoo onto my hair. It was cheap stuff, but smelling of apples was preferable to smelling of Dumpster. A pang of guilt hit me as I thought of Gabe. I told myself I'd go back and look for him later tonight so he could come here and shower too. Dad would pitch a fit, but it was the least he could do after the stunt he'd pulled last night. There was always a brief window of remorse when he did something like this, especially if he hit me when he'd been drinking. All too soon he'd forget, though, and it would be back to business as usual. But not for me. Not this time.

Small towns were for scams and cities for quick tricks. I could stroll through a subway car in a big city and snag four or five wallets before hopping off one train and boarding the next. But the small towns worked better for Dad when he was selling some bogus insurance policy or going door to door selling promises that would never materialize. Looking for a trick in a town like this took time. I hovered in the alley between the bank and grocery store, watching people from the safety of the shadows and mentally crossing each of them off my moral list. If they were too elderly or too young or if they looked like they were struggling themselves, I couldn't bring myself to do it.

I despaired of finding anyone until he pulled up to the sidewalk in his big, shiny truck and climbed out. Everything, from his snug-fitting designer jeans to his neatly trimmed hair, screamed money. A pair of mirrored shades covered his eyes, but he seemed distracted as he pulled his phone from his pocket to check it. Knowing that this was my moment, I slid from my hiding place and, putting my head down, walked stealthily toward him. I'd perfected the art of bumping into someone and making it look like an accident. He stumbled but righted himself quickly and grabbed me before I hit the deck, and I stared up at my own reflection in his aviators.

"I'm so sorry," I said, as I stepped back reluctantly. He smelled amazing, and I missed the warmth of his arms as soon as I left them.

"No problem," he replied with a smile. I wanted to ask him where he was from, what he was doing there, and what aftershave he wore to smell so damn good. I wanted to ask him a million things, but I didn't. Offering him a brief smile, I walked away quickly. Stuffing my hands into the pocket of my coat, I palmed the buttery soft leather of the wallet I'd just lifted.

Eight hours later, and I finally had work. By pure luck, the owner of a coffee shop had lost her temper with a sulky, teenage employee and fired her for being late again. I walked in just in time to witness the showdown and immediately volunteered myself as a replacement. The place was packed with Christmas shoppers looking for a little respite away from the cold, and sensing an opportunity, I offered to work an hour free by way of an interview.

For sixty minutes, I was polite, smiled, and made sure that nothing was too much trouble for any customer. Fortunately for me, the sullen teen had set the bar pretty low, and by the time I left, I had a part-time job starting tomorrow. Sure it was only for the holidays, but I'd take what I could get. I was being paid weekly, so I hoped that whatever I'd stolen this morning could feed me for that long.

Shame had kept me from checking, but I knew I had to. Yesterday's burger was the last thing I'd eaten, and I was starving. There was no way I'd be able to do a full day's work tomorrow without a meal. Serving delicious-looking cakes and muffins on an empty stomach had just about killed me. I wasn't too proud to eat leftovers, but I wasn't about to risk my new job by stealing them. Mournfully, I'd tossed them into the trash before stacking plates in a dishwasher.

Daydreaming about a hot meal, I crossed the road distractedly as I headed to the diner and saw the headlights before I'd even registered the screech of the brakes. The truck didn't hit me hard, but I weighed so little that I flew about six feet and landed with a jolt on the road. The driver jumped out of the cab and rushed to my side.

"Jesus, are you all right?" I shut my eyes as I savored his deep, sexy British accent.

"I feel like I've been hit by a truck," I answered sarcastically.

"Wait a minute. That's my wallet!" he said sharply, as he stared at the evidence spilled out on the road.

I was so busted.

"I found it lying on the sidewalk," I said defensively. "I haven't even opened it. I stuck it in my pocket because I was late for work, and I was just on my way to drop it off at the sheriff's office." With that, I clamped my lips together tightly. Any good thief knew how to lie well. The trick was to stick close to the truth. Give the mark enough to be believable, but don't embellish. Unfortunately, reason went out the window with this guy. There was something about him that rattled me. His face was devoid of the kind of scorn and derision I expected to see after being caught in such a precarious situation.

"Well, thank you for rescuing it for me," he replied with a smile I couldn't help but return. It was hard not to feel guilty when he was being so nice, but I reminded myself that I hadn't actually stolen from the wallet yet. I mourned the loss of a hot meal, but perhaps I'd run into this guy for a reason. The last thing I needed was to jeopardize my new employment by getting busted with a stolen wallet. He'd bought my story about finding it, so all I had to do was sweet-talk my out of the situation, and I was free and clear.

"You're welcome," I replied, my relief at his easy acceptance of my story palpable. Grabbing the wallet, I held it out for him to take. Ignoring my outstretched hand, he crouched down and lifted me effortlessly into his arms.

"What are you doing?" I shrieked. He threw me slightly into the air as he adjusted his grip, and instinctively I wrapped my arms around his neck to keep from falling.

"I'm taking you to the hospital, what do you think I'm doing?" he replied, shifting my weight so that he could open the door.

"I can't go to the hospital!" I protested.

"Did you miss the part where I hit you with my truck?" he asked humorlessly.

"Look, I don't have any insurance, and even if I did, I don't need medical attention. A hot shower and a good meal and I'll be fine, I promise," I assured him.

He smiled gently as he placed me on the seat and reached across me for my seat belt. There was something intimate and tender in the way that he strapped me in. He was taking care of me in a way I'd never been cared for. Maybe ever.

Closing my door, he jogged around to the driver's side, and I used the moment to discreetly wipe a tear from the corner of my eye, cursing myself for being so pathetic. His truck smelled new, and the leather seats were extravagant and expensive. The cab felt huge until he climbed in and I realized how big he was. The thought distracted me from my protest.

"We're going to the hospital now," he explained calmly. "We're going to wait in the emergency room until a real doctor gives you the all clear, and then I'm paying the bill and taking you for that dinner you missed out on. After that, I'll drop you anywhere you want to go. Deal?"

I was tired, hungry, and the weight of guilt was killing me, but I nodded in agreement anyway.

Chapter Four

Jensen

Four hours later, I sat in a booth at the Wallflower diner across from the most beautiful girl I'd ever seen. When she'd first bumped into me, she was so slight I'd mistaken her for a kid. Now, as I watched her devour her chicken plate special as though someone would take it away at any moment, I realized that she was just painfully thin. Malnourished even. It gutted me to think about the impact her tiny frame had taken from my truck, and I cursed myself again for not having paid more attention to the road.

Despite her constant protests that she was fine, the doctor had warned that she'd have some heavy bruising tomorrow and had prescribed some painkillers just in case. When he was done, she hobbled off the examination table, and I had to hold myself back from lifting her into my arms again. I knew she wouldn't appreciate it, but damn she'd felt good. Like she belonged there. Like a puzzle piece clicking into place, it felt right. Like nothing else had in a long time.

"Hi guys, let me get these plates for you. Now can I get you both any dessert?" our waitress asked.

"Thanks, Diana, that would be great," I answered, reading her name from the neatly printed tag on her uniform. My date looked mournfully at her empty plate, and I knew from the look on her face that she was still hungry.

"What would you like?" I asked her.

"Oh no, I'm fine," she replied, a little too quickly. She said it so often that I wondered who she was trying to convince.

"In that case," I said, grabbing the menu and scanning it quickly, "I'll have a slice of warm chocolate fudge cake, a slice of apple pie and ice cream, and a stack of pancakes with syrup, please." I replaced the menu and sat back, watching Lauren's jaw drop like a goldfish.

"No problem," Diana replied with a knowing smile. "I'll be back in a couple of minutes." With a quick wink, she disappeared into the kitchen.

"What?" I asked.

"Nothing," she said, closing her mouth, clearly too polite to question my obvious gluttony.

For the first time, we sat in awkward silence. Neither of us knowing what to say. I'd thought that a hot meal would put a smile on her face, but to my surprise, she looked as though she was going to cry.

"Hey, Lauren, we can go and find somewhere to get your prescription if the pain is starting to kick in," I offered, feeling terrible at the idea of her sitting here in silence if she was hurting.

"How do you know my name?" she asked with a small sniff as she blinked away the tears.

"Lauren Matthews . . . hospital admissions form," I reminded her, knowing she'd noted my name as well. She nodded before looking back down at her folded hands. Finally, she took a deep breath and looked me in the eyes.

"I did steal it. Your wallet, I mean. I know I told you I didn't, but I did. I'm so, so sorry, and I promise I'll never do anything like it again. It was honestly supposed to be my last one. But I took it," she said, blurting out her confession so fast that it took me a moment or two to decipher what she was saying. When she was done, her gaze returned to her hands as she twisted her fingers anxiously.

"I know," I said finally, making her head snap to attention. "I didn't feel you lift it, but when I realized it was gone, I knew exactly what had happened."

"Then why are we sitting here and not the sheriff's office?" she asked quietly.

"Because something tells me you need a break. I know by the smooth way you picked my pocket that you've done this a lot. But you're not a career criminal, or at least you don't want to be. Only someone who's really and truly starving hoovers up a meal like you just did. So, my guess is that you stole it out of desperation. I got it back safe and sound, so no harm, no foul," I said.

Rather than the look of gratitude I was expecting, she stared at me like I was an escaped mental patient.

"I feel like this is some kind of trick. Like any minute now Sherriff Haywood is going to jump out and surprise me with a pair of handcuffs," she said.

"Sounds like you know the local law pretty well," I replied, my suspicions about her lifting wallets regularly confirmed.

"It's a small town. We've only been here a couple of weeks, but Dad's already had one or two drunken run-ins with the sheriff. Makes it kind of hard to get ahead when your family name is as renowned as mine."

"But you said you'd just come from work. So you have a job now?"

"I got a job today at the coffee shop on Fourth Street. It's only for the holidays, but at least it's something. I got an honest job and a free hot meal. Today's been a good day," she said with a reluctant smile.

"You forgot about the bit where you bounced off my truck," I reminded her.

"Stop trying to rain on my parade," she replied, smiling wider.

Chapter Five

Lauren

"So what are you doing in Friendship?" I asked. "It's a long way from England. At least that's where I'm guessing you're from by the accent." It was more Jason Statham than Benedict Cumberbatch, but still, he could melt chocolate with that hot, deep voice.

"I'm not there much anymore, but I'm from East London. I'm here for the funeral of an old friend," he replied. He looked so sad and remorseful that I found myself wanting to scoot over to his side of the booth and just hug him. To offer him back a small measure of the comfort and kindness he'd given me. But I stayed where I was, not knowing how he'd feel about receiving affection from someone who'd just stolen from him.

"He must have been a really good friend for you to have come all this way."

"He was the best. A better friend to me than I was to him anyway."

"What happened?" I asked, then immediately winced as I realized how nosy and insensitive I was being.

As though he could sense my discomfort, he waved away my concerns and continued.

"I don't know if you follow motor racing, but I'm a Formula One driver. I didn't grow up in the nicest of areas, but I knew from pretty young that the only place I wanted to be was behind the wheel. I loved everything about it. The thrill, the speed, the competition. All of it. But I had no money, no real skills, and little education, so I did what half the kids on the estate were doing and started stealing cars. I didn't care what it was or who it belonged to, if it had four wheels, I took it," he admitted.

Maybe I shouldn't find it endearing that he was sharing his criminal past with me, but I did. Unless he was about to tell me that the flashy truck I'd been riding around in was stolen, he had clearly done well for himself, so maybe there was hope for me after all.

"Please tell me this story doesn't end with you hitting someone with your car," I said.

"Thankfully no. You were my first," he replied.

"I'm honored," I said sarcastically. Diana arrived at our table and proceeded to unload three dishes that would make anyone's mouth water.

"Enjoy!" she said, and gave me another wink as she headed back to the kitchen. All of it looked delicious, and I was pretty sure that I'd fall into a sugar coma just from the smell.

"Don't go hungry on my account. I'll never eat this much food by myself," he said, handing me a fork. Having eaten out of a Dumpster less than twenty-four hours ago, I couldn't bring myself to turn him down, and accepting the fork, I wasted no time in plowing into the pancakes.

"So what did happen? Were you caught? Arrested?" I asked

between mouthfuls, trying my best to retain some sense of dignity instead of shoveling in the food as fast as I could.

"In a manner of speaking. Some of my mates and I had saved up for tickets to the British Formula Renault Series. They were rubbish seats, but we didn't care. After the race was over, most people left the stadium, but the boys and I stayed till the very end. The cars had all been taken off the track, but I couldn't leave. I was a stupid kid, ramped up and full of adrenaline, so I hopped the barrier and found an unlocked safety car," he explained.

"Didn't you worry about getting caught?"

"I knew I'd get caught, but it was a once-in-a-lifetime opportunity for a little punk like me. I figured it was worth the risk. I put my foot to the floor and did one lap of the circuit before the other safety cars hit the track and barricaded me in. I don't think I breathed for the entire lap, but what a lap it was," he said wistfully.

"So what happened?" I asked, moving onto the chocolate fudge cake as he picked through the leftover pancakes. He ate a forkful before pausing to lick the maple syrup from his lips, and it struck me that there was something decidedly intimate about sharing a meal with a virtual stranger.

"One of the pit bosses tore me a new one, the police were called, and I was let off with a caution. Three days later, Ronnie came knocking at my door. Turns out he was in the stands chatting to an old friend, and he'd seen the lap. He offered me a spot then and there on a junior drivers program. The team would cover my accommodation expenses and airfare, but it meant leaving everything behind to join a boot camp for young drivers. Break the rules and you're sent packing, miss classes or training even once and you're sent packing. But toe the line and you not only get to drive some of the fastest cars in the world, you're taught how," he replied.

"So your mom and dad supported you?"

"My dad left us when I was a baby, so I don't really know him, but Mum couldn't get me out of the house fast enough. She saw an opportunity to get me out of trouble and off the estate, at least until I was old enough to start making good decisions."

"Is she still there? Your mom, I mean," I asked, smiling as he pushed the apple pie toward me.

"Nah. I used my Formula One signing bonus to buy her a lovely bungalow out in the countryside. My aunty moved in with her, and they've made a nice group of friends locally, so she's happy there," he replied.

"Are you happy?" I asked, not realizing until I said it what a personal question it was.

"Today I am," he answered, helping himself to a huge forkful of pie. We finished off our desserts in comfortable silence, and by the end, I was so full that I could barely move. Jensen paid the bill, and all too soon, we were back in his truck. I gave him directions and cringed as he pulled up to the motel.

"I know it's bad to be living out of a motel, but someday I'll have my own place," I said defensively.

"It doesn't matter where you live as long as it's home," he said.

"My home would be decorated with so many Christmas lights that you could see the house from a block away. The kitchen would smell like freshly baked gingerbread, and evergreen garlands would hang everywhere you looked," I said wistfully.

"You should see my mum's house at this time of year. By the time she's finished decorating, the place looks like Santa's grotto," he replied.

"Will you still be here for Christmas?" I asked, afraid to know the answer.

"I'll be leaving Christmas Eve," he replied, and I tried not to show how sad that made me. The last few hours had been like nothing I'd ever known. To be able to talk freely without judgment was liberating, but to know that he was leaving in less than two weeks upset me. Dragging out my good-bye would do me no good though.

"I'm only in town for a couple of weeks. Do you think we could . . . ?" Jensen asked, but I cut him off without giving him a chance to say what I knew he would.

"I'd love to. But I'm a bit of a kleptomaniac, you see. I'm good at keeping hold of nice things. Not so good at letting them go. And I have a feeling that having you around would be a very nice thing. If I get any more attached to you, there's a real risk of me kidnapping you and keeping you forever in my closet to stop you from leaving. So for your own sake, I'm going to say good-bye now," I told him.

"You're a strange girl, Lauren Matthews, but I'm glad I met you," he said.

"The strangest," I agreed with a smile. Jumping out of the truck before he had a chance to, I shut the door behind me and turned to face him.

"I'm sorry I took your wallet, but I'm glad I met you too. Thank you for dinner as well. It was the best time I've had in a long time."

"Well then, Merry Christmas," he said, looking about as happy as I was at the thought of leaving.

"Merry Christmas, Jensen. I hope Santa brings you something nice," I replied. With a wave, I walked away, back to a life where Christmas wishes were about as real as Santa Claus.

Chapter Six

Jensen

Ronnie and Nancy Adler's house was every bit as beautiful as Ronnie had described. The timber-clad home was festooned with thousands of Christmas lights that twinkled like stars, evergreen garlands were strung across the oak porch, and a huge wreath hung invitingly from the front door. Lauren would've loved the place. I wished she were there with me now.

So many times Ronnie had invited me here, but I'd always turned him down. In my downtime from racing, there were too many things to see. Too many places I wanted to go. And now I'd never get the chance to see all the things he wanted to show me. At least I'd never get the opportunity to see them through his eyes.

Talking with Lauren last night had been cathartic. Life for me had been one endless, meaningless party. I just hadn't realized how meaningless until Nancy's phone call. But one night with Lauren had offered me the magic and excitement I'd been chasing in all the wrong places, and in less than two weeks, we'd be half a world apart.

The idea was almost as depressing as the thought of having to face Nancy. Knowing that she was fully aware of just how badly I'd let Ronnie down filled me with shame. But it wasn't a shame I could hide from. Being the man he'd tried to raise me to be meant facing up to my mistakes and owning them. Still, I sat with my hands gripped to the wheel, allowing myself one more moment to get myself together, when a loud knock on the window made me jump.

"You've been sitting in this truck for twenty minutes, Jensen Caldwell. I'm kind of afraid that frostbite might set in if you don't come inside soon," Nancy said through the glass.

"Hey, Nancy," I replied as I climbed out of the truck, struggling to hide my guilty expression.

"It's good to see you, Jensen. Ronnie would be so happy that you were here," she said, and surprised the hell out of me when she threw her arms around my middle and pulled me in for warm hug.

Wrapping my arms around her shoulders, I squeezed her back. She smelt of warm cookies and cinnamon and everything I imagine all good grandmas smell like.

When she pulled away, she reached into her pocket for a handkerchief and dabbed at her eyes.

"You'll have to excuse me. I've become such a silly, sentimental old fool these last few days," she said.

"I think you're entitled to be, don't you? How're the girls holding up?" I asked, referring to Ronnie's two daughters, both of whom were happily married with children.

"About as well as can be expected. After the funeral, I'm going to stay on Megan's ranch for a little while until I decide whether or not to keep the house."

"Does she still have the same horse ranch out in Wyoming?"

I asked, remembering Ronnie telling me stories about how peaceful it was there.

"Yes, it's the same one. They take in tourists from June to September, so I'm used to staying with her in the summers to help out. I have my own little cottage on the grounds, and it's much easier to maintain than this big house. Ronnie preferred that I wasn't alone when he was on the racing circuit, and I like having Megan close by for company," she explained.

As soon as she mentioned Ronnie's name, I was flooded with guilt.

"It's okay to talk about him you know," she said with a sad smile.

"You know that it's supposed to be me comforting you, right?" I said as she threaded her arm through mine and pulled me toward the house. As soon as I walked through the door, I felt like he was there with me. Black-and-white pictures of Ronnie with racing royalty lined the hallway. His sheer joy for the sport was obvious from the happy, exuberant smile on his face. We wandered through the family room, and I noticed various racing trophies interspersed with more personal, family photographs. I stopped dead in my tracks when I caught sight of a picture of me.

"Why would he have this?" I mumbled to myself. It wasn't a staged photograph like the racing ones. It was a candid black-and-white shot, taken in an unguarded moment that blended in seamlessly with the rest of the family memories. I remembered the moment vividly. The two of us were examining a Formula One engine. It was the first Formula One engine I'd ever seen, and I'd been like a kid at Christmas, full of energy and enthusiasm and bombarding Ronnie with a million questions faster than he could answer them. In the picture, I was smiling at the camera, and he was looking at me with such a fierce expression of pride. To a stranger, we'd look like father and son.

"Why wouldn't he have it?" Nancy asked.

"Because he hated me in the end. He was so disappointed with me for partying so hard and not making the most of my opportunities," I said.

"Sit down, Jensen," she ordered, patting at the seat next to her. I obeyed without question.

"He was never disappointed in you. He was disappointed in himself," she explained.

"Why?" I asked in complete shock.

"You were twenty-three when you hit the Formula One circuit. Jensen, that's almost completely unprecedented. You went from poverty one minute to having the world at your feet the next. What young man with those same opportunities wouldn't make the same choices you made?

"If Ronnie was disappointed, it's because he felt as though he hadn't prepared you enough or shielded you enough from the hordes of people who all wanted a piece of you. People who take and take and take until there's nothing left. He didn't want that kind of life for you.

"But don't ever think he hated you, or that he was angry. He loved you, Jensen, and he was so proud of you. It was his own stupid pride kept him from calling. In fact, if you both hadn't made up by Christmas, the girls and I had planned to stage an intervention and bang both your heads together until you saw sense."

"If I'd just picked up the phone," I said, swallowing hard. "But now it's too late."

"Messing things up only means we're human. It's how we deal with these things that define who we are. You can either accept your mistakes and learn from them or you can let them consume you. If you want to make peace with your past, you have to make peace with yourself. Remember what he taught you, remember the love he had for you, and live a good life. Be happy. And I promise he'll be smiling down on you wherever he is," she said.

"How did he get lucky enough to find you, Nancy?" I asked, genuinely floored by the size of this woman's heart and her capacity to show so much compassion when she must be in so much pain.

"Oh, I said no quite a few times, believe me. My parents wanted me to marry a nice doctor, so you can imagine how they felt about the idea of Ronnie and me. It didn't matter that he went on to run a successful Formula One team. Up until the day he died, my dad thought of him as a glorified grease monkey. But Lord that man could charm the birds down from the trees. He wore me down until I said yes, and not once did I ever regret my decision. I wish the same thing for you, my boy," she said.

"With the kind of life I lead? Traveling the world, chasing race after race. It would take a miracle to find a girl who could fall in love with a guy like me," I said.

"I believe that everything that happens in the universe happens for a reason. Sometimes you need to experience the bad to recognize the good. Your miracle will come, Jensen. Just you wait and see. Christmas is a time for miracles, and if you and I haven't earned some good news, I don't know who has," she replied. "Now, let's put the kettle on shall we? I know how you Brits love a nice cup of tea in a crisis."

"What would you say if I told you I'd met someone here in town?" I said sheepishly. It worried me that she might find my interest in Lauren disrespectful to Ronnie's memory, given that the only reason I was in town was for his funeral.

"Jensen, that's wonderful news! Who is she? How did you meet?" Nancy asked.

"Her name is Lauren Matthews, and she's amazing," I said, leaning against her kitchen counter as she puttered about making tea.

"Stephen Matthew's daughter?" she asked as she stopped to turn and face me.

"Is that her father's name?" I replied.

"Jensen, be very careful. Stephen Matthews has only been here a couple of weeks, but he's already made quite a name for himself. He's trouble, and if that girl is made of the same stuff as her father, she's bad news," Nancy said sternly.

"She seems really nice, Nancy, honestly. But thanks for the warning. I'll keep it in mind," I replied.

I wanted so badly to defend Lauren's honor. To argue that she was a good person. But Nancy was the widow of the only father I'd ever had. Her opinion was important to me, and more importantly, I couldn't face disappointing her like I'd disappointed Ronnie.

"You do that, Jensen. She's exactly the sort of girl Ronnie wanted you to stay away from."

Chapter Seven

Lauren

A heaviness settled in my heart after Jensen and I parted ways, but I tried not to let it get me down for too long. One night I was sleeping on the streets and eating out of a Dumpster, and the next I was enjoying a great meal courtesy of the hottest guy I'd ever met. If that wasn't the sign I needed that things were finally beginning to go my way, I don't know what was.

"You did a great job today. Have you done any waitressing before?" Jill asked, and I felt my cheeks pink up with pride. I'd worked my fingers to the bone from the minute I'd clocked in that morning. Even when the place was empty, which wasn't often given the pretty continuous stream of Christmas shoppers, I'd busied myself wiping down tables or polishing cutlery.

"Thanks. I've done a little bit in various towns we've lived in, but we moved around a lot, so I never got to stay in the same place for long," I explained. Much to my chagrin, it was the reason why I couldn't give my new boss any references.

I truly wanted to believe that this was it though. That my

move to Friendship was permanent. That I'd finally be able to put down roots in the town where one day I might have my own family. But life rarely hands you a win without first throwing you a curve ball. And I couldn't help but feel as though my curve ball was coming.

I was fourteen the last time we'd lived in a real house. My last memory of the place was of a tirade of abuse directed at me from our angry next-door neighbor, an unwitting victim of one of Dad's scams. Of course, Dad never called them scams, referring to each and every one instead as a series of bad investments, from which he and he alone seemed to profit.

Dad tried for years to include me in his machinations, but I held out, determined to live a better life than the one he offered me. Eventually though, life and my father wore me down. Despite my best efforts to be a good girl, anyone who knew my father looked at me with suspicion and mistrust. Without my help, he would have been in prison sooner rather than later, and I would've ended up in foster care. Most people thought I was a criminal anyway, so I did what he wanted.

When Dad told me where we were moving, I thought he was crazy. The cities were big and easy to get lost in, but small towns meant that someone was always watching. Now that we were actually here, I was even more worried. He was drinking like money grew on trees, so he must be assured of getting it from somewhere, and I guessed that he had something big in the pipeline. It didn't bode well for the future I had planned here, but no matter what happened, I was done running. My life was mine and mine alone, and I was going to make the most of it, whether Dad liked it or not.

"Well, you keep working like you did today, and you'll have more shifts than you know what to do with," she said.

"Sounds good to me," I replied, sharing her smile.

"Listen, I couldn't tempt you into taking some of the leftovers home, could I? We get a fresh batch of cakes and cookies in from the bakery every morning, so we split up the leftovers at the end of the day," she said.

"As long as you're sure, that would be great, thank you. Everything smelled so delicious today. I would love to try some when I get home," I said, trying so hard not to let a note of desperation seep into my voice.

"Believe me, there's plenty to go around, honey. I'll leave a bag for you in the kitchen. Just pick it up on your way out."

"Thanks, Jill," I replied, checking over all of my tables before I clocked out.

As I left, I grabbed the paper bag marked with my name and practically skipped out of work as I glimpsed at the contents. Cupcakes, brownies, chips, sandwiches, sub rolls. It was a veritable feast, and that night Gabe definitely wasn't going hungry.

Snowflakes danced through the chilly evening air, and I wrapped my coat a little tighter around myself, more than a little worried about Gabe sleeping rough in this weather. When I finally reached the fast food joint, I hurried around to the back to the Dumpsters, finding nothing but disappointment. The boxes and blankets had all gone, and an extra Dumpster stood in the place that had been our shelter. I hoped the restaurant hadn't made him move on, because I had no idea where else to look for him.

Just then I heard my name being called. Looking up, I saw Gabe across the street. His frame was huddled against the cold, but he lifted a hand to wave at me anyway, a smile of acknowledgment spread across his face. I was so excited to see him, so keen to share my bounty, that I ran across the road without thinking. The ugly screech of brakes being slammed warned me of my stupidity, but it was too late to take any action other than to wince and brace for the hit. By the time I opened my eyes, the driver was already out of his vehicle and in front of me.

"You know we have to stop meeting like this," Jensen said, his husky British accent making my pulse race.

"I'm beginning to think you're stalking me, you know," I replied, smiling with happiness.

"Lauren, if there's anyone in this town worth stalking, I promise it's you."

"I'm not sure whether to be flattered or worried," I replied.

"Where were you going in such an all-fire hurry anyway?" he asked.

"I was trying to catch up with . . ." I turned to look for Gabe but realized as I spoke that he was gone. My gaze darted back and forth between the buildings and along the street, teeming with people walking toward the center of town.

"Who?" Jensen asked.

"His name is Gabe. He's a homeless guy I met a couple of days ago, but I think you scared him off. I was bringing him something to eat," I explained.

"Maybe he'll come back when the crowds have thinned out a little."

"Why is it so busy anyway?" I asked in confusion.

"Nancy mentioned that it was the annual Christmas lighting ceremony tonight. I was feeling restless, so I thought I'd come and check it out. Care to join me?" he asked.

I paused without knowing why. My mind was made up the minute he stepped in front of me. It felt so good to see him again that turning down the opportunity to spend an hour or two together seemed pointless. I'd miss him terribly when he was gone, but I was done trying to push him away before he had to leave.

"I'd love to," I replied.

"And if you haven't eaten, maybe we could have dinner together again afterward?" he asked somewhat sheepishly, as though he was pressing his luck and expected me to turn him down. This time I bit my lip anxiously as I thought about my reply. Of course I wanted to accept, but it didn't seem fair for him to pay two nights in a row.

"Does that look mean you want to turn me down, but you're not sure how without being rude?" he asked.

"It means that I want to buy you dinner, but I don't get paid until Saturday," I answered honestly. "It's not fair for you to pay for another meal when you paid the hospital bill and bought me dinner last night."

"I see your dilemma. The only thing that sounds fair is for you to pay for our next date on Saturday," he answered, the corner of his mouth turning up in a smile.

"Oh, we're going out Saturday as well, are we?" I answered teasingly.

"Well, if you're asking, thank you very much. I'd love to go out with you again. Now, why don't you hop in the truck while I look for a parking space, and we can see what all the fuss is about with these lights."

Chapter Eight

Lauren

In the end, we had to drive around for ages until we found somewhere to park. It seemed like the entire town had driven in just for this event. It took us ten minutes to walk back to the green, where we found ourselves at the back of a big crowd. The air was perfumed with the delicious scent of spiced apple cider, and I groaned as I smelled hot chocolate, making Jensen chuckle.

"Be right back," he said, disappearing into the throng only to emerge a few minutes later with a cup of the very thing I'd been craving.

"Here you go," he said, passing it to me.

"I think I love you." I sighed, expecting him to laugh at my reply, but he had a strange look on his face I couldn't begin to decipher.

"Ladies and gentlemen, boys and girls, thank you so much for coming this evening," the man I heard someone say was the town's mayor, began from the stage ahead.

I shivered with cold, but as I tentatively sipped at the

chocolate, I slowly began to thaw out. When Jensen slipped in behind me, steadying his hands on my waist against the jostle of the horde, I felt the warmth of his body through both of our coats. I tried to concentrate on the mayor's speech, but it was impossible. All I could think about, all I could focus on, was Jensen's thumb, lazily drawing circles on my hip.

Around us, couples, friends, and families all watched with excitement for that magical moment that signaled the start of the countdown to Christmas. It was easy to get caught up in it all. For one night, it felt like we were any other couple, enjoying the magic of Christmas with loved ones.

"Five, four, three, two, one," I heard the mob shout, and then the enchanting glow of what must have been thousands of lights illuminated the town square. Just at that moment, an icy cold snowflake landed on my nose, and I tilted my face upward so that I could watch them fall from the sky, embracing the magic of the moment. I hadn't even realized that I was leaning into Jensen's embrace. It just felt natural to be in his arms.

"It's beautiful, isn't it?" I said.

It sure is," he replied in a tone that had me looking up at him. I expected him to be as captivated by the snow as I was, but he wasn't looking at the lights. His eyes were focused on me so intently that I shivered.

"Fancy getting out of here? We can beat the crowd and head for dinner?" he said, leaning closer to whisper into my ear. His breath was warm against my face, and I nodded my head in agreement as I struggled to focus my lust-addled brain into forming actual sentences.

The crowd was marveling at Santa, who had just arrived in a rather impressive sleigh, and it was heartwarming to hear the excitement of all the children jostling for the best view.

Dumping my empty cup in a trash can, I followed behind Jensen as he negotiated a path through the crowd. When I fell behind, he reached back for my hand so that we wouldn't be split up.

Long after we'd made it through the throng, our hands remained that way, our fingers threaded tightly together, his thumb brushing against mine. I couldn't remember ever holding hands with someone. That such a simple act could feel so special and intimate, that it could make me feel so connected to someone, was quite profound. I didn't connect with people. Ever. When they looked at me, people saw what they wanted to see. In some cases, what I allowed them to see. But Jensen saw the real me, and still he wanted to hold my hand. And I wanted him to. So much that I didn't want to let him go.

We walked a fair way, and I followed blindly, not really concentrating on where we were going or even caring. I would have been happy with a sandwich as long as we ate together. That was until we walked through the doors of Grumpy's Bar and Grill. I caught sight of Dad at the bar as usual, hunched protectively over his beer and talking animatedly with a guy I didn't recognize. I was desperate to go unnoticed. If my dad saw me with Jensen, he'd immediately peg him as a mark, and it would only be a matter of time before he tried to exploit my connection with him to try and rope me into one of his scams. I wanted nothing more than to part ways with Dad, but until I could afford a place to live, that just wasn't an option. So avoiding him seemed the best tactic for the moment.

"Look, I've changed my mind about dinner. Can we just go please?" I said, pulling on Jensen's arm.

"Why? It's not even that busy yet. If we grab a table quickly, we could eat and be done before the masses roll in," he replied.

I knew that arguing with him would only draw attention to us, so, with a heavy heart, I slipped my hand from his and made my way back out into the cold. Seconds later, I could hear his heavy footsteps behind me, but I didn't slow down, ignoring his pleas for me to wait.

Eventually, he ran in front of me and grabbed me by the shoulders, forcing me to stop.

"Talk to me," he said. It was his gentle tone that undid me. He had every right to just walk away. I had been unspeakably rude in the face of his kindness, and my mood had swung, from warm and congenial to frosty and ignorant.

"My dad's in there. The same one that taught me how to lift your wallet. He's drinking away whatever money he's managed to con or swindle out of his latest victim, and I don't want him seeing you as his next one," I admitted, looking down in shame. "And if I'm honest, I don't want you looking at me differently, either, and believe me you will when you see what bad stock I come from."

"You know, my mum has a saying," he said, tucking a strand of hair behind my ear. "The worst manure grows the brightest flowers. I think it was her way of telling me that, no matter how bad my dad was, it didn't mean that I was bad too. I think the same applies for you."

"Your mom sounds like a smart woman," I said.

"She is, and I'm pleased to tell you that all the smart genes are genetic," he said with a wink that made me laugh. I felt so silly for almost crying, but I couldn't help feeling angrier at Dad that, in addition to his long list of misdemeanors, he also managed to unwittingly ruin my date.

"Listen, I don't know about you, but I'm absolutely starving. Why don't you wait in the truck and get the heater going, and

I'll go back and see if I can order something as takeout?" he suggested.

"That sounds great," I replied on a sigh, relieved that he was being so great about this. After settling me safely in the truck like the gentleman he was, he went back inside and emerged fifteen minutes later with a couple of bags.

"I don't know what that is, but it smells amazing," I said as he climbed in the cab to join me. The air was warm and permeated with the most mouth-watering scents.

"Wait until you see what I ordered. This lot's going to put us in a food coma for a week." I smiled at his enthusiasm and settled back against my seat as he pulled away. I hummed along to the radio as he drove, not really saying much until he pulled up on top of a ridge that looked down over the whole town. The flutter of snowflakes was whimsical and romantic, and the tingling echo of a Christmas carol that drifted up from the town made this the perfect setting for a festive date. Our feast was mainly bar food, but on my empty stomach, the banquet of ribs, fries, and burgers, together with the leftovers from the coffee shop, tasted like gourmet cuisine. We parked, and with the radio playing softly in the background, and smiles on our faces, we ate like kings.

Chapter Nine

Lauren

I never thought I'd be the sort of girl to waste time mooning over some guy, replaying every word of a shared conversation in my head, yet that's exactly what I found myself doing the next morning. The early breakfast rush had passed, and while I enjoyed a brief lull before the mid-morning Christmas shoppers would stop by, I cleaned down the empty tables and daydreamed of Jensen and our magical evening together.

"Lauren, isn't it?" I turned toward an older lady, who'd taken a seat at the table behind me.

"I didn't see you there. Yes, I'm Lauren. What can I get for you? I can recommend the hot chocolate, and we have a special offer on our fresh pastries this morning," I said.

"Do you think you could sit down with me for a moment?" she asked. Her request was odd, considering we'd never met before. Combined with the fact that she knew my name, I was immediately suspicious. Feeling uncomfortable, I looked toward the counter for Jill, but she must have slipped into the kitchen.

"I'm sorry, but I'm working right now. I'd be happy to get you anything you'd like, but I need to be available to wait on other customers," I replied.

"It's all right, Jill and I are old friends, and I've already asked her permission. I really won't take up more than a few minutes of your time," she said.

Taking her at her word, I sat down opposite her hesitantly.

"We've never met before, but my name is Nancy Adler," she explained.

I smiled when I realized who she was to Jensen and how she must know me.

"I'm sorry, I had no idea who you were," I replied. "Jensen has told me all about you and Ronnie. I'm so sorry for your recent loss, but Jensen speaks very highly of you both. He loved your husband very much."

"You and Jensen must be getting very close if he's talked to you about my husband. You know, Ronnie always thought of Jensen like a son. He was very protective of him, and to a degree, I feel as though that responsibility has fallen to me with his passing. My decision to come and speak with you hasn't been the easiest, but I think Ronnie would have wanted me to say something," she said.

"I don't mean to be disrespectful, Mrs. Adler, but why are you here?" I asked, cutting to the chase. My initial happiness had ebbed away with her words. The tone of her voice was gentle enough, but it was clear that her reason for being here wasn't good.

Rather than looking put out at my harsh abruptness, she looked almost sad as she considered my words. "Jill tells me that you're a nice girl and a hard worker, and she's not the sort to give praise where it isn't due. I want you to know that I'm not here because I think you're a bad person. Despite my misgivings about your father, I trust Jill, and she's had nothing but praise for you," she said.

"But despite that, you don't want me with Jensen," I said, delivering the truth she was having trouble saying.

"I want what's best for him. I want him to have the freedom to pursue his dreams. To achieve everything that he's worked so hard for. Everything that Ronnie helped him work toward. With Ronnie gone, we're all in a vulnerable place right now. All I'm asking is that you don't take advantage of that vulnerability," she explained.

"So, you're asking me not to see him anymore?" I asked.

"No, I'm not asking that. It's clear that you've become friends, and he needs a friend at the moment. All I'm asking is that, when the time comes for him to leave, you let him go. From what I hear, your father is the kind of person who might take advantage of the sort of opportunity that your association with Jensen would present. Don't let that happen. If you care about him at all, protect him from your father by letting him go. Let him achieve those big dreams of his," she replied.

I wanted to yell and scream at the unfairness of her words, but she wasn't wrong. No matter how I felt, I knew that I was a bad investment for a man like Jensen, and there was no doubt that he was better off without me. Still, the truth hurt.

"You don't need to worry about me, Mrs. Adler. I've never held out any hope of a future with a man like Jensen. When the time comes for him to go, I'll wish him well with all of my heart. Until then, I plan on making the most of the time we have together. Now if you'll excuse me, I need to get back to work," I said, and with as much dignity as I could muster, I stood and walked away from her, willing my tears not to fall.

Chapter Ten

Jensen

Dropping Lauren home after the tree lighting last night had been hell. Despite Nancy's warning, I couldn't help but miss her. She didn't have a mobile phone, which meant that keeping in touch on social media or even calling was out the window. I had talked her into letting me take a quick picture of us on my phone, though, and it was the only tangible proof I had of her existence. It was a magical moment, with the snow falling gently behind us, but what struck me was how happy we both looked. In all of the podium pictures of me accepting trophies or spraying vintage champagne, never had I come close to looking as happy as I did with Lauren. Maybe that was why I couldn't keep from staring at it. For two days, I'd left her alone with the promise that I'd pick her up again Saturday for the date she insisted on paying for. I had no intention of letting her pay for a thing, of course, but I was happy to let her believe it if it got me another date. But after gazing at her beautiful face for the last ten minutes, I knew I couldn't wait that long. Twenty minutes later, I'd showered, shaved, and was sitting in the coffee shop looking eagerly for my girl.

"What are you doing here?" she asked as she came through the kitchen and caught my eye.

"Is it okay that I'm here?" I asked, starting to second guess whether bothering her at work had been such a great idea.

"Are you kidding? It's made my day. If you don't mind hanging around for an hour, I finish at five," she said. There was no mistaking the sadness in her eyes, but still she seemed genuinely happy to see me.

"I'd wait for you all day," I replied, then winced when I realized how cheesy that sounded. Lauren didn't seem to mind though. There wasn't so much as an eye roll at my lameness.

"Well, what can I get you while you wait? My treat," she said.

"No way are you paying, but I'd like a large hot chocolate please and a slice of whatever cake you fancy," I replied.

"A grown man drinking hot chocolate has to be about the most adorable thing ever," she cooed.

"Leave me alone, woman. It's very rugged and manly."

"Let's see if you're still saying that when it arrives," she said, winking at me as she went about filling my order. I gawked as she walked away, unable to stop myself from noticing how hot she looked in that damn uniform. There wasn't anything particularly sexy about a plain black skirt and black shirt, but she could wear a burlap sack and still have grown men drooling.

On that thought, I looked around the place and realized I wasn't the only man taking an interest. At this time of year, I expected the place to be filled with Christmas shoppers and families, but there seemed to be an unusually high number of men at the coffee shop, and as I watched her work, I knew that she was the reason why. They couldn't keep their eyes off her, and as much as I wanted to act all caveman and possessive, I knew I didn't have the right. I wasn't her boyfriend, and in a little over a week, I'd be gone. Still, I sure wanted the job though. I wanted to be the one on the receiving end of her smile every night when she finished her shift.

"What did I tell you?" she said, rocking me out of my revelry. Her face was a picture of mischievous mirth as she placed a drink in front of me that wouldn't look out of place in a Disney movie. The blown glass cup was both fancy and delicate, and aside from the fact that I'd struggle to get even my index finger around the handle, the amount of marshmallows, whipped cream, and chocolate wedged into the top of it made it look more like an ice cream than a hot beverage. I wasn't sure whether to lick it or drink it.

"How am I supposed to drink this?" I asked, wondering if I should pick out the top layer of bonus edible treats and hold the thing like a soup bowl.

"I have no idea, but I can't wait to see you try," she replied.

Tentatively, I lifted the drink to my lips, ignoring the fact that she was clearly trying to suppress her laughter. It was the worst thing to have ordered in front of the girl I wanted to impress, given that there was likely as much cream on my face after one sip as there was left in the cup.

"I promise you, Jensen, your masculinity is safe. If anyone could make drinking that look hot, it's you."

I cleaned my lip with a napkin and was slightly mollified as she placed the biggest slab of chocolate fudge cake I'd ever seen down in front of me and next to it a jug of what smelled like warm fudge sauce.

"Will you marry me?" I asked after my first bite.

"Sorry. I've already promised myself to whoever makes these cakes," she replied as she walked away to wait on other tables.

As I watched Lauren work, I began to understand exactly what it was my life had been missing. But the knowledge didn't make me feel any better. I looked forward to every minute we spent together and dreaded leaving, but the reality was that I was needed back in Europe sooner rather than later. My time in Friendship was running out.

It wasn't as though I could take any of that time for granted either. Between the hours that she was working and our lack of options for communicating, every stolen moment we had together was infinitely precious. I considered asking Lauren to keep seeing me after I left, but I spent nine months a year traveling around the world and three months training.

Even if I left Friendship with the promise of returning, in the end she'd hate me for keeping her waiting. Letting her go would be the most selfless thing I could do. Until then, I'd allow myself this tiny window to savor every moment I could. Setting her free would be my gift to her. Stealing these memories would be my gift to me.

"Ready to go?" she asked, slinging a messenger bag over her shoulder as she walked toward me.

"Sure, where shall we go?" I asked, watching as she chewed on her bottom lip. We might only have known each other a matter of days, but I knew the gesture well. It meant that she was racking her brain for something to do that didn't involve money.

"How about a walk?" she suggested.

"It's too cold to walk," I replied, wincing at the idea. In the UK, it rained far more than it snowed, so I was still adjusting to the climate.

"I know!" I said, recalling something that had caught my eye on the way over. "I passed on old-fashioned cinema on Main Street, and they're showing *It's a Wonderful Life*. Why don't we go? You can't get more Christmassy than that." I silently applauded my own brilliance. Two hours in a darkened room, inches away from the girl who took my breath away, and maybe even the chance to put my arm around her. I was a genius.

She bit her lip harder, and I knew she wanted to go.

"Come on," I cajoled. "My treat."

"You can't keep paying for everything. It's not fair," she protested.

"Look, a couple of cinema tickets aren't going to break the bank, and this is an unscheduled date, so it's only right I pay. In fact, you'd actually be saving me money. If I had to try and entertain myself on my own, I'd probably end up going to some fancy restaurant and spending a fortune on a meal for one."

"Well, when you put it like that. Let's go."

She linked her arm through mine, and as we headed for the door, I felt like I'd won the lottery.

Chapter Eleven

Lauren

Jensen Caldwell was a force of nature. When he wanted something, he found a way to get it. I loved that he managed to do it without running roughshod all over me. He had money, and he wanted to shower it on me, but I didn't want to be a charity case or a sponge. I might not have much, but I had my pride, and it was hard to be on an equal footing with someone when money always seemed to tip the balance of the scales. After getting our tickets, he bought a giant soda with two straws, a huge bag of candy, and a ridiculously large bucket of popcorn.

"What's this?" he asked in confusion as we stood before the topping machine.

"Butter," I replied.

"For what?"

"For the popcorn," I explained. His answering expression was half horror, half awe.

"You don't have topping for your popcorn in England?"

"No, you either buy sweet or salted. There's none of this kind of witchcraft and wizardry."

"Buddy, you're missing out," I said, and taking the bucket from his hand, I drowned it in deliciousness.

He stole a piece and popped it into his mouth.

"Man, that is so good. I need to get one of these things for my house," he answered on a groan as he helped himself to another piece.

"I'd re-think that decision if I were you. Too many buckets of this stuff, and you can kiss those awesome abs good-bye."

"So you've been checking out my abs then. Good to know," he teased, and throwing an arm around my shoulders, he led me into the theater. I desperately wanted to make some witty comeback, but he had shocked me into silence.

The theater was empty, so I followed Jensen to the middle of the back row. He put the soda in the armrest between us and dropped the candy onto my lap next to the popcorn.

"Help yourself," he said, nodding toward the huge bounty. He draped an arm over my shoulders once again and dipped his hand back into the bucket of popcorn. As the room darkened and the screen lit up, I was still dumbstruck. I'd snuck into cinemas without paying many times, but never had I sat in the back row with a guy who bought a ticket for me. As the magic of the movie washed over me, I leaned against Jensen's shoulder, enjoying the fact that nothing had ever felt so right.

"So what did you think?" he asked, slipping his hand into mine as we walked along the sidewalk.

"It was amazing. I can't believe I haven't seen it before."

"Ah, the things that I could show you." He chuckled, dropping a kiss on the top of my head like it was the most natural thing in the world.

The snow that had been lazily drifting down around us was falling heavily when I spotted Gabriel across the road.

"Hey," I shouted over to him, and waved as I got his attention. Pulling Jensen along with me, I crossed the street to greet him.

"Well, hello. If it isn't my favorite person in the world to dine with," Gabe said, sporting a toothy grin.

"I came looking for you the other evening, but your bed was gone. I was afraid something bad had happened to you."

"Bless you, child. But don't be worrying about me. I just get itchy feet, that's all. Now who is this fine young man?" he asked, looking Jensen up and down.

"Gabe, this is my friend Jensen. Jensen, this is Gabe," I said.

"Nice to meet you, sir," Jensen said, and I fell for him a little more as he held out his hand respectfully for my homeless friend to shake.

"Nice to meet you, too, young man," Gabe replied, returning the gesture.

"Where are you staying tonight, Gabe?" I asked. There was no way I could let him sleep rough, even if I had to deal with Dad's wrath to make sure Gabe had a decent night's sleep.

"Well, little one, I think meeting you has turned my fortune around. I'll be well taken care of this evening. So you can stop worrying your pretty little head over me and start taking care of yourself," he replied.

"I think meeting you has been a good luck omen for me too!" I said, smiling. "I met Jensen, and I have a job now over at the coffee shop. So if you find yourself down on your luck, come and find me at work."

"That's very kind of you. Now, what are your plans for this evening?" he asked, and I shifted nervously. I didn't want the evening to end, but in reality I knew that there was nowhere we could go that didn't cost money, and I was unwilling to go anywhere else with him without paying my way.

"I guess I'll be heading home soon," I replied, unable to keep the slight tone of regret from my voice. "I have to work tomorrow."

"Forgive me for asking such a personal question, but would your father happen to be around five feet, ten inches with dark hair and a scar on his left cheek?"

"Yes," I replied warily. "How did you know that?"

"Perhaps then it would be better if you didn't go home so soon. Your father stumbled out of the bar about twenty minutes ago. He was somewhat inebriated and mentioned that his daughter, Lauren, was at work so he'd have the place to himself. I'm afraid that he invited the people he was with back to your home to carry on the party."

My shoulders dropped as I looked to the ground. He must have been in the bar pretty much all day to be drunk this early. I was so ashamed that I could barely look at Jensen or Gabe. Nancy had been right, and I needed to face the reality that Dad's ugliness would always bleed into my life, and if I held on to Jensen, it would eventually infect his life as well.

"Do you have anywhere else to go?" Gabe asked me gently.

"Don't worry, I'll take care of her," Jensen said.

Gabe looked at him carefully before replying. "I believe you will, young man. Well, then I hope you enjoy your evening, and I look forward to seeing you again," Gabe replied, and with a tip of his cap, he was off down the street.

"Come on," Jensen said, putting his arm around my shoulders and tucking me into his side as he started walking.

"Where are we going?"

"Somewhere safe," he replied. I didn't ask where, knowing in that moment that I'd follow him anywhere.

Chapter Twelve

Jensen

After bumping into her friend, Lauren seemed tense and withdrawn, and I sensed she was embarrassed about her father. But despite the change in her mood, I couldn't help but feel as though running into Gabriel had been a blessing. The idea of her hiding in the corner of her room or motel lobby while her father partied with a load of guys from the bar made my blood boil.

It made no sense that I'd feel so fiercely protective about a girl I hadn't so much as kissed, but I couldn't help it. Lauren was a survivor. She was fierce and strong, and despite the circumstances of our meeting, I knew she was good. Sometimes people are born into circumstances so bad that pride and principles are the currency you have no choice but to barter in order to survive. That she would spend all day on her feet to scrape together a wage that she could probably make lifting a few wallets spoke volumes about the person she was. That she was the product of bad stock didn't give me ammunition to judge her. It made be proud to stand by her side.

I could tell she was deep in thought as we walked to the pizza parlor. Knowing that, if I asked her, she'd say she wasn't hungry, I ordered a large pepperoni pie to go and a large plain cheese, just to be on the safe side. The food smelled delicious, and after paying, I steered her back onto the street. Only when we stood in front of the Snowflake Inn did she come to her senses.

"This is your stop," she said, looking up at the sign. "I guess I'll see you around then."

"Oh no, you don't. You're coming in with me," I said, giving her shoulder a little squeeze.

"Oh no. I don't think you're allowed to entertain people in your room, and I'm pretty sure they won't allow you to sit eating pizza in the lobby here," she protested.

"The owner is lovely, and I've paid good money for my room, so I can see who I please in it. And if anyone protests, I'll pay extra to cover your stay. Besides, we're only going to eat some food and watch a movie. It's not like we're throwing a wild party."

"Maybe I could stay for a little while, but I really don't want to get you in trouble," she said, though her protest was halfhearted at best. Now that the magic of our date had been somewhat dampened by her father's behavior, she looked tired, and that made me want to take care of her even more.

I opened the door for her before she changed her mind, and it turned out that her fears were unfounded. The lobby was empty but for a receptionist who was talking on the phone. We hurried past her and into the lift up to my floor.

"It's really nice here," Lauren said, walking into my room as I closed the door behind us.

"It is nice," I agreed, "and they do a great breakfast." I put the food down on the coffee table and began unloading the bag when I noticed how awkward she looked, hovering in the middle of the room as though she had no clue what to do with herself.

"Do you mind if I use the bathroom?" she asked before I had a chance to say anything.

"Of course, it's through there," I said, pointing toward the only other door in the room. As she shut the door behind her, I turned on the television and flicked through the channels until I found something worth watching. I shrugged off my coat and toed off my boots before carting all of the food to the bed and opening up the pizza boxes.

"You look very cozy there," she remarked as she walked back in.

"Hurry up and join me. You're missing the best part," I replied, nodding toward the television.

Distractedly, she dumped her shoes and jacket next to mine as she became engrossed in the film.

"I love *Home Alone*," she said, and I grinned, happy that she liked my choice. She settled precariously against the pillows, and I handed her a napkin with a huge slice of pizza, determined to put her at ease.

"Thank you," she said, and accepted the offering without protest, which was a huge win.

Half an hour later, I lifted the nearly empty pizza boxes and dumped them back on the coffee table, the two of us having nearly demolished our feast. She was still completely absorbed in the movie when I climbed back onto the bed next to her, and I knew that it was without conscious thought that she sat up slightly to make room for my arm, but I slid it under her neck anyway. She snuggled in next to me, and it felt so right. Like we'd done it a hundred times before. Like it was the most natural thing in the world. I thought back to all the amazing parties I'd attended, all the rich and famous people I'd mingled with, and all the podium wins I'd enjoyed, and yet not a moment of it compared to the pure joy of having her in my arms.

The movie ended, and another started, but by the slight rise and fall of her chest, I knew she'd fallen asleep. Warm and comfortable and with the intoxicating scent of her filling my lungs with every breath, I drifted off beside her. My last thought was to wonder what it would feel like to have this every night.

Chapter Thirteen

Lauren

Waking up warm and safe in Jensen's arms this morning had been absolute bliss. He'd even ordered a breakfast tray up to the room that we'd devoured before he walked me back to the motel so I could change for work.

I was supremely confident that nothing could sour my good mood, least of all the smelly drunkard passed out on the sofa bed in our motel room. Since the night I'd slept rough, Dad and I had successfully managed to avoid one another. As far as I was concerned, it would be the merriest holiday I'd ever had if we managed to make it all the way to Christmas without speaking. This morning when I arrived at work, my pay had been waiting. I was so paranoid about having it lost or stolen, that I'd kept it inside my bra all day. I, more than anyone else, knew how easy it was to lift a wallet or purse.

So far, Jensen's generosity, leftovers from work, and tips had allowed me to eat all week, but I needed to ration my money carefully if I was going to make it last. Especially if I wanted to try and save something out of it toward getting my own place. When I finally made it, I was going to start saving all over again for an oak bed, as beautiful as the one I'd slept in at the inn. It was the best night's sleep I'd ever had. Of course, the fact that Jensen had been my pillow all night probably had something to do with it.

There was one indulgence I'd allowed myself to make, and that was to take Jensen out on a proper date. It was the very least I could do after everything he'd done for me. Besides, one more week and he'd be gone, and I'd have the rest of my life to be careful with my money and put something aside for the future.

Before coming here, I'd been a realist. I knew what it was like to walk in the darkness behind the scenes while everyone else enjoyed the show under the spotlights. But meeting Jensen had changed my perspective. Now I saw hope where before there was only despair. Now I wanted more than just my next hot meal and somewhere safe to sleep. I wanted a future. I wasn't foolish enough to even contemplate that it would include someone as amazing as Jensen, but I did know that I wanted security. A permanent home to call my own. A job where I was liked and respected by my colleagues. And one day maybe even the chance to finish school.

I stood before the mirror and smoothed down the skirt of my red dress. The fact that Dad had bought it for me in a thrift store once as part of a con should have put a dampener on my mood, but there was nothing that could do that tonight. I said a silent prayer of thanks that I had at least one item of clothing in my wardrobe suitable for a date, and I hoped Jensen wouldn't find me too shabby. It was so easy to doubt myself when I thought about all the glamorous women he must have wined and dined on the Formula One circuit, but the fact of the matter was that he could have spent his Saturday night with any number of girls and he'd chosen to spend it with me. It was that thought that put a smile on my face and a little bit of extra color in my cheeks. I didn't have much in the way of makeup, but I swiped on a little mascara and a hint of lip gloss anyway, just as the room's doorbell rang. Dad snorted and turned over but thankfully remained asleep.

"You're beautiful," Jensen said, his mouth ajar in shock as he looked me up and down while I joined him outside.

"Thank you. You look pretty amazing yourself," I replied. He smelled so incredibly good, too, that I really was fighting the urge to just close my eyes and inhale him.

"Let me get that," he said. Taking the jacket from my hand, he held it open for me to put on before offering me his arm.

"It doesn't really go with my dress, but at least it's warm," I said, embarrassed that my coat, another thrift store bargain, was the same one I always wore. The same one I'd slept rough in only a week ago.

He stopped and turned me to face him. "Stop. It doesn't matter to me how expensive your dress is or how many clothes you have in your wardrobe. You're beautiful. Inside and out."

"Life is so unfair. To let me meet someone so kind and charming and wonderful and then have them live so far away," I whispered, brushing aside a stray tear.

He lifted his hands to cup my face and gently brushed away another tear with his thumb.

"What are you doing?" I asked as we walked along.

"It's tradition," he said, nodding his head toward the porch roof at the motel's entrance, where a bright green sprig of fresh mistletoe hung from a beautifully tied red ribbon.

"I swear that wasn't there when I got home," I said.

"Maybe life isn't so cruel after all," he replied, and stepping forward, he pressed his lips against mine. It was everything. Magic. Explosions. Fireworks. All my Christmas wishes rolled into one. It was pure and chaste but touched with a tinge of desperation. As though, through one kiss, we could imprint the memory on each other's souls. Forevermore I would remember the feel of the soft fullness of his lips, the way he held me as though he never wanted the kiss to end. And when it was over, he rested his forehead against mine, each of us as breathless as the other.

"Best. Kiss. Ever," he said.

"We can do better," I teased.

"I agree. We definitely need to get some practice in though."

"Absolutely. Practice makes perfect," I agreed.

I was dancing on clouds when he dropped me home, leaving me with another breathtaking kiss to remember him by. Every time I saw him, I swore that it was the best day of my life, but every memory we created always surpassed the last. I was falling for him, and I couldn't stop myself. I didn't even want to try.

Grumpy's Bar and Grill wasn't exactly the glamorous, high-end restaurant I'm sure Jensen was used to, but I couldn't imagine any other venue being more perfect. My skewed perspective of the place had been based on the fact that it was one of Dad's hangouts, but he was sound asleep on the sofa at home so I was assured a drama-free evening.

The only tense moment we had was when we were discussing who would pay. I insisted on picking up the tab for the evening, despite his red-faced protest that he could buy the whole bar if he wanted to and that it was ridiculous of me to waste my first paycheck when he genuinely wouldn't miss the money. I reminded him that, for the sake of my own pride, I needed this, and reluctantly, he let the subject drop after several mumbles about how a real gentleman wouldn't let a lady pay. Of course, it was probably the same reason that he ordered the cheapest thing on the menu. After we'd eaten, we danced, played pool, laughed more than I'd ever laughed in my life, and finally walked home arm in arm, leaving Jensen's truck at the bar.

"Shall we sit for a while?" I said, moving toward the rickety old porch swing in front of the motel.

"Will it hold us?" Jensen asked.

"I make no promises," I replied. Taking his chances, he sat down gingerly.

"The mistletoe is gone," I pointed out, looking up at where it had hung earlier.

"Don't worry," he said, smiling. "We don't need it anymore." We edged toward each other, and under a blanket of stars, with the bite of winter frost in the air, we kissed, and I gave Jensen Caldwell another little piece of my heart.

Chapter Fourteen

Jensen

I woke up, and I was smiling before I even opened my eyes. After our amazing date, we made out on the porch swing for half an hour before saying good night. Every day after that, I drove Lauren home when she finished her shift. Leaving her was the worst, but seeing her happy, smiling face when she saw me waiting for her was the best. Every night ended on that porch swing, and no matter how cold it might be or how tired we were, I'd never feel so much peace as I did swaying back and forth on that old hunk of rotting wood.

What I felt for Lauren was so much more than attraction. She was fast becoming my best friend. The person I wanted to talk to first about everything. The person I wanted to come home to every night. I was on cloud nine all the time, until the moment it hit me that today was the day of Ronnie's funeral. I remembered why I was here, and my euphoric glow evaporated. If Lauren and I had met a few months ago, if she had seen how I had treated the people I loved as disposable, she wouldn't have looked twice at me. I hadn't been the kind of man she deserved in the past, but I could be. Perhaps I couldn't forget my past or atone for my behavior, but I sure as hell could learn from it. I owed it to Lauren and Nancy. I owed it to Ronnie, and more importantly, I owed it to myself.

Nancy Adler's house was packed to the rafters with well-wishers. It seemed that every person I spoke to had a different story to tell about Ronnie, and I was beginning to understand that mine wasn't the only life he'd changed for the better. He'd been a truly inspirational person, and rather than sticking my head in the sand and forgetting about what had happened between us, I wanted to honor his memory. And so I spent the day chatting to his friends and family, to the people in the community who had admired him. I heard their stories of Ronnie and shared some of mine, and despite my worst fear that it would be a horribly morbid experience, it was oddly cathartic.

Through it all, Nancy had been stoic, a pillar of strength and compassion who seemed to put everyone else's grief before her own. It wasn't difficult to see why Ronnie had fallen head over heels in love with her. She'd shown me kindness and forgiveness at a time when she would have been completely justified in spouting rage and anger, and this was a testament to how wonderful she was.

The ceremony itself had been beautiful, a real celebration of life, and among the stream of photographs that were projected throughout his eulogy, I was touched to find myself in so many of them. When Ronnie and Nancy's wedding picture appeared, Nancy sobbed, and my heart broke along with hers. But after a good cry, she wiped away her tears and carried on, and I knew

I could live my whole life and never again meet someone with that kind of strength.

I was never far if she needed me, but it was long after the last guest had left and the dishes cleaned and put away that I finally had some alone time with Nancy. She was sitting on a bench in the garden when I took her a cup of tea.

"Megan showed me how you take it," I assured her. "And there isn't much in this world that can't be improved with a good cup of tea."

"Bless you, Jensen," she said as I handed over the hot drink.

"So when do you leave?" I asked. I figured she'd stay for Christmas, but her daughters were moving suitcases around when I left to find Nancy.

"As soon as I've finished my tea I imagine," she said, wistfully taking in the view.

"So soon?" I asked, surprised.

"I just can't face spending Christmas here. Truth be told, I'm not sure I'll ever be back. No matter where he was in the world, Ronnie always came home to spend the holidays with me. Everything here is just going to remind me of him and how much I missed him, so I'm going to try and make it to the ranch in time to watch my grandchildren put out their stockings for Santa. I'll steal a little of their Christmas spirit and keep it for my own. So, how about you? What are your plans?"

"I'm staying for the dance at the community center tomorrow, and then my flight home leaves Christmas Eve morning," I replied.

She said nothing but narrowed her eyes at me.

"What?" I asked, squirming under the weight of her stare.

"You're richer than Croesus, so we both know you could charter a flight to make it home tomorrow. Hell, your team would probably send a private jet if you asked them to. Taking a commercial flight on Christmas Eve means you'll probably miss Christmas Day with your mom. You're delaying leaving so that you can go to the dance with Lauren, aren't you?" she asked.

"I care about her, Nancy. Being with her is like coming home. I don't know how else to explain it. Everything just feels more real and more special when I get to share it with her," I said.

"Dammit, Jensen. Her father is poisonous. He'll drag her down, and you with them. Think of everything Ronnie wanted for you and make the sensible choice," she argued.

Her jab about Ronnie hit home, but I knew in my heart what he would do. "The last thing I ever want to do is disappoint you. But who would I be now if people judged me by the things my useless father has done? Lauren's been dealt about as bad a hand as you can get in life, and she's made the best of it. And what's more, I had Ronnie to help me get my head above water. Lauren has no one. Sometimes you just know when something is right. Ronnie knew it too. Otherwise he wouldn't have gone after you, even though your family disapproved," I reasoned.

The silence between us was awkward. It was probably the most difficult day of Nancy's life, and I regretted causing her even a moment of upset, but what I'd said needed saying. If there was now a rift between us, I had no idea how to bridge it. In the end, Nancy did it for me.

"Oh, Jensen, you must think I'm an interfering old woman. I hope you know that everything I've said and done has been with your best interests at heart. But you're right. Ronnie would've told you to go get your girl. So I'm going to mind my own business from now on and let you listen to your heart," she said, and I felt like at least one weight had been lifted from my shoulders.

"I don't think that at all. I know you're only looking out for me, and I appreciate it. But it goes both ways you know. Ronnie would want us to look out for each other. So if there's anything you need, anything I can ever do to help, all you ever have to do is call," I replied.

"Thank you, Jensen. You're a good man," she said. "I have no idea how you two are going to work things out, but if Ronnie taught me anything, it's that love will always find a way."

Chapter Fifteen

Lauren

He'd seen it all less than a week ago: my face, lightly made up with cheap cosmetics, my body in my one and only, date-suitable, thrift store dress—he'd seen it all and still Jensen looked at me as though I was a tall glass of water in the middle of a drought. I smoothed down the front of the dress nervously while he looked his fill, biting my tongue to stop myself from making excuses about why I was wearing the same outfit twice. There was no need. He knew my circumstances, and the way he looked at me gave me the confidence to believe that he didn't care. That nobody would look at me, standing next to this giant god of a man, and find me unworthy.

"You're absolutely breathtaking," he murmured, almost to himself.

I gave him a wobbly smile as I tried to keep it together. My whole plan—to handle his leaving with sophistication and dignity before crying myself to sleep the moment he'd gone—was unraveling at the seams. I didn't care that it was Christmas Eve tomorrow. Jensen was leaving, and tonight was the good-bye I'd never be ready for. "I'm not ready to lose you, Jensen. So let's make tonight the best night ever and deal with tomorrow when it gets here," I suggested.

"Lauren Matthews," he said, taking my coat and holding it out for me to put on. "I'm going to give you a night so great, you're never going to want to let me go," he replied, and taking my hand he led me into the crisp, cool night.

As we walked up to the community center, the magic of the evening began to weave its spell on me. From the Christmas songs that had me itching to dance, to the light snow on the ground and the delicious scents of mulled wine and spiced apple permeating the air, all of it painted the picture of a Christmas I'd never had but had craved so very badly.

Inside, Jensen took my coat and added to the pile by the door. "Dancing first, or a drink?" he asked.

"Most definitely dancing," I replied with a grin. If I had any excuse to have his arms around me that night, I was taking it.

"I was afraid you'd say that," he said as he took my hand and pulled me toward the dance floor. It was already full of people from over-excited children bopping enthusiastically to elderly couples waltzing their way around the room.

At the realization that half the town seemed to be there, I had a moment of self-doubt. I feared getting the cold shoulder from a community so close that everyone seemed to know everyone else. But the derision and suspicion I expected never came. As we joined in the party, people were all smiles and happiness, saying hello or nodding their approval as we shared in their joy of the moment.

The last of my self-doubt drifted away when I realized two

things. The first was that Jensen simply didn't care what other people thought of him. He lived his life the way he wanted to and didn't look for the approval of others to validate his choices. He was a good person, the very best, and being around him had made me a stronger person. The second was that he was a horrible, horrible dancer.

"What?" he asked, having caught the confused look on my face.

"What is it that you're doing there?" I said.

"Dancing," he explained, a frown marring his face as though it was completely obvious.

"Oh," I replied, my face a mask of seriousness, "I was worried for a minute you might be having some kind of seizure."

"Ha! You can talk! I've seen pensioners on this dance floor that have more moves than you. Now come on, baby, let's show 'em what we've got." He pulled me into his arms and swung me around the dance floor, much to the amusement of everyone around us. When I couldn't take any more, we escaped to a dark corner where we sipped our drinks and shared our secrets. He told me all about his friends on the team, and I shared stories of some of the places I'd been and the places I still wanted to see.

"If you could travel anywhere in the world right now, where would you go?"

"Rome," I said without having to think about it.

"It's a beautiful city, but why Rome?"

"My mom loved it there. My grandmother took her when she was little," I said. Lifting a little gold cross from where it had slipped inside my dress, I held it up to him. "She bought her this while they were there. It's the only thing I have left of hers really. Dad sold anything of value and left everything else when we were running from one of his cons."

"What happened to them both?" he asked gently, the sympathy in his gentle tone spoke of his perceptiveness.

"My grandmother died of cancer about a year after their trip. There was some money the court looked after until mom came of age, but she didn't have any other relatives, so she ended up in a foster home. I never heard the full story of how she and Dad met, but my guess is that she was looking for someone to love, and he told her what she wanted to hear so he could get his hands on her money. By the time it ran out, Dad had a wife and kid he didn't want. I think he would've walked out if Mom hadn't been hit by a car. After that he was kind of stuck with me."

I was matter of fact about my past as I spoke. I'd had many years to mourn Mom, to wonder what my life would've been like if she hadn't died. Now, when I thought of her, it was with love and happiness, not sadness.

"Anyway. Mom's best memories were of that trip she and her mom took to Rome. She told me that one day we'd go together. Eat pizza in front of the Colosseum and stand under the ceiling of the Sistine Chapel. So that's where I'd go."

"You'll make it there," he said with certainty. "Dream big, Lauren, and don't ever stop. The places you will go are only as small as your imagination." Tucking a strand of hair behind my ear, he brushed his thumb across my cheek tenderly before leaning down to kiss me, and in that moment, everything was perfect.

Chapter Sixteen

Jensen

As I packed the last of my things, my gaze kept wandering back to Lauren. When the dance ended, I drove us both back to the Snowflake Inn. It was our last night together, and I didn't have it in me to say good-bye to her at the door to her motel. Even if I convinced her to give us a chance, Mum was still expecting me to fly home for Christmas. So I'd booked Lauren a room at the inn so she'd be close to me. She protested at the cost like I knew she would, so I silenced her with kisses.

In the end, we both knew that our last few hours together were too precious to waste. She never even saw the room. We lay cuddling on my bed and talking through the night until she'd drifted off a couple of hours ago. I memorized everything I could about her as I watched her sleep. This would either be the last day I'd spend with this beautiful woman or the beginning of a new life together. All I needed now was the courage to find out which.

"Lauren, honey, I have to go," I said, waking her gently. Her eyes blinked open in confusion and then filled with tears when she realized what was happening. Launching herself into my arms, she squeezed me so tightly that I struggled not to fall off the bed.

"I'm not good at good-byes, and I don't know how to do this, so you need to go quickly, Jensen. Like ripping off a Band-Aid. Just go and don't look back, okay? You are the best person I've ever known, and I will never forget you."

I pulled back to look into her eyes, brushing away her silent tear as it fell.

"I have to get on that plane, but I don't want this to be over. I can't go back to my old life as though I'd never met you. Come with me. I'll book another ticket, and we'll figure something out when we get to England. There's nothing keeping you here," I protested.

"I don't have a passport, Jensen. And even if I did, I wouldn't go. We've only known each other a couple of weeks," she replied, her eyes full of regret.

"Then promise me you'll stay in touch. I'll buy you a phone and get it delivered. We can text and speak every day. I'll fly back as soon as I can," I pleaded.

She closed her eyes as though she was actually in pain before opening them to answer me. "No, Jensen. A clean break is for the best. You know how impossible the distance would make things between us. I'll always treasure the memories we made, but this is the right decision for us both," she replied.

"I know you're worried about the distance, but the team has a plane that will make the travel easier, and there's no reason we can't get you a passport so that you can travel with me," I argued. The thought of never seeing her again tore me apart, but seeing her give up on us without a fight gutted me.

"Please don't do this, Jensen. Don't make this harder than it needs to be," she said.

Her tone was so resolute that it broke my heart. I wanted to be with her more than I'd ever wanted anything, but I couldn't make her fight for us if she didn't feel the same.

"Then live a good life, Lauren Matthews. A big one, full of dreams and adventures, and know that I will never forget you either. Be happy. For me," I replied.

Kissing her gently on the forehead, I picked up my bag and did as she asked. I left without looking back. As I closed the door behind me, I heard the strangled sob she hadn't been able to contain, and I knew that my heart was the one thing I wouldn't be taking with me. It had belonged to Lauren from the moment we met.

About an hour away from Friendship, just outside the city of Somerhaven, I slammed on the brakes as I passed a familiar hitchhiker on the side of the road. Reversing back, I stopped when I was alongside him and lowered the window.

"Gabriel, what are you doing all the way out here?" I asked.

"Waiting for you, son," he replied, smiling. I assumed he meant that he was waiting for someone to pass by and offer him a lift.

"It's freezing. Why don't you hop in and I'll give you a ride?" I said.

"That's very kind of you," he replied, climbing into the passenger seat. "So, where's our girl then?"

"Lauren is still in Friendship. I'm flying back to England today, so we're going our separate ways," I explained, though it pained me to admit it.

"Well that's a damn shame. If ever there was a couple that belonged together, it's you two," he replied.

"It's what Lauren wanted. I asked her to come with me, or to keep in touch, but she thinks a clean break is for the best," I said.

"Of course she did. How else could she protect you from her father?" he replied.

"What do you mean?" I asked.

"Son, that girl is head over heels in love with you. She needs you. She has nothing and no one. If she's severed all ties with you, believe me, it's for your benefit not hers," he replied.

Once again, I slammed on the brakes, this time as I had an epiphany. I realized that I was a complete and utter idiot. Only hours earlier, I'd had the woman of my dreams in my arms and let her convince me to leave without putting up any real fight at all. I'd left her penniless and completely alone and as heartbroken as I was.

How could I ever have believed that this was somehow the best thing for us both? So what if the odds of a successful long-distance relationship were slim? The odds of finding her at all had been practically non-existent, but it happened. I'd been handed a miracle, and I was turning it into a tragedy.

"Gabriel, I'm sorry but I need to go back," I said.

"You do that. Now don't worry about me. I'm exactly where I need to be. You do want you need to," he said, and to my surprise, he undid his seat belt and let himself out of the truck.

"Merry Christmas, and Godspeed," he said with a smile before slamming the door shut.

Just at that moment, my phone rang. "Jensen, are you at the airport yet?" Nancy asked as soon as I connected the call.

"No. I'm actually on my way back to Friendship," I explained.

"Thank goodness. Jill's just called to tell me that Lauren's in jail. I don't know what's happened, but I think she's going to need you," Nancy said.

"I'll head straight there. Whatever it is, I'll sort it out," I replied, worried sick about what her dad had gotten her into.

"If there's anything I can do, just let me know," she said.

"Actually, I'd like to ask you a favor," I replied. We talked for a few minutes before hanging up. Turning the truck around, I looked down the barren highway for Gabriel, unwilling to leave him out in the cold … only to find that he'd completely disappeared.

Without stopping to think, I put my foot to the floor and broke more than a few speed limits as I raced back to my girl.

Chapter Seventeen

Lauren

Five hours earlier, I'd stood heart-broken at the door of the motel room, watching for the last time as my father threw his clothes into a bag. Jensen had offered me everything I'd ever wanted. And I'd rejected him. As he laid himself bare for me, I remembered every single word of Nancy's speech, and I knew that this was the moment she feared. The moment where he'd start compromising his dream or, worse still, give it up for me. So I'd pulled off the con of a lifetime and convinced him that leaving me behind was for the best.

Now I was faced with the very reality I'd protected him from. "What have you done?" I asked, knowing from the urgency of his packing that it was really bad.

"It's about time you showed up. I've not seen you for days, and then I hear today that you've been hooking up with some fancy mark. Well, I hope that boy has deep pockets, because we're going to need them if we're caught. Now pack your stuff," he demanded.

"What have you done?" I repeated, trying to remain calm.

"An acquaintance of mine sold me a copy of the database details for the community center senior citizens club. Names, addresses, contact telephone numbers, that sort of thing. So, I called a few and told them I was from the bank, calling to conduct a security check. Worried them a little with the threat that their ATM cards might be frozen and talked them into giving away their bank details to verify their account. I used that to set up an e-wallet account, and from there, I transferred a little cash into a withdrawal account." The slight note of pride in his voice sickened me. He'd deliberately targeted the weak and the vulnerable, and he was proud of himself for it.

"How much did you take?" I asked, dreading the thought of how I could possibly face anybody in this town after what he'd done.

"Don't you look at me all high and mighty. This puts food on our table. Now pack your stuff. We're going. One of the stupid pensioners freaked out and went to the sheriff."

"I'm not going with you," I said. It was the first time I'd said it, and the shock was enough to make him pause.

"What do you mean, you're not going with me? For years I've carried you, and now you're walking away? Just when we're starting to make some real money?" he replied.

"This is not a life. Running place to place, conning retirees out of their life savings. It's wrong, Dad. It's no way to live, and it ends now," I argued.

"I don't think you understand, girlie. The withdrawal account is in your name. Some stupid savings account your grandmother set up for you. I knew it would come in useful one day. So you see, it's not me that's implicated in this whole thing, it's you."

"I had nothing to do with any of this. Why would you use my name?"

"Stop acting all superior. You're no different than me. Cut from the same cloth, both of us. You don't give a crap about those people. Now I'm not asking you, I'm telling you. Pack your stuff and get moving," he shouted.

"You're wrong! I'm nothing like you. It's Christmas Eve, and you've taken from elderly people who probably couldn't afford to lose that money. I'll admit I've done things that I'll be ashamed of for the rest of my life, but I did them to eat. To survive. You do it so you can drink and gamble your life away.

"Well, I've had enough. It stops here. Run away if you want to, but I'm staying. I'll face whatever comes my way, and then I'm going straight. I just hope you can run faster than the sheriff. Because if you touch one more cent of the money in that account, then I'm doing everything I can to help him find you," I said.

I didn't see his backhand coming until I was lying on the floor.

"You're as ungrateful as your mother was. Good luck on your own," he said venomously, and grabbing his bag, he stormed out, slamming the door behind him.

I didn't allow myself to cry. I mourned the loss of Jensen in my life, but Dad's leaving felt like something that should be celebrated. Well, maybe after the swelling had gone down and I'd been arrested for a crime I hadn't committed. So, all in all, it hadn't been my best day. But despite feeling like my heart had been ripped out with Jensen gone, I knew I would never want to take back a second of the time we'd spent together. Whether he knew it or not, meeting him had changed me. He looked at the parts of me that no one else had taken the trouble to see, and he made me feel like I was worth something. He liked the person I was, and more importantly, he made me like that person too. I wasn't my father's daughter. I was me. And I was getting my butt off the floor and taking life by the balls for a change instead of running from it.

After packing up my stuff, I straightened out the room as best I could and checked out of the motel. Unsurprisingly, Dad hadn't paid the bill, so I kissed the last of my wages good-bye and handed the money over to the manager. After that, I headed to the bus station. If I was going to jail, and in all likelihood I was, I needed some place secure to store what little stuff I had. The bus station had luggage lockers, so I figured I'd stick my bag in one of those, stop off at the coffee shop to explain to Jill what was happening, and then head over to the station to turn myself in before they came looking for me. Of course, that's not what the sheriff saw when he caught me at the entrance to the bus station with a packed bag.

"This isn't what it looks like," I protested.

"Of course it's not," he replied.

Chapter Eighteen

Jensen

"I need to see Lauren Matthews," I said.

"Sir, who are you and what makes you think you can walk into my station and demand to see anybody?" the desk clerk said in a tone so bored and condescending that I had to take a deep, long breath before replying to avoid snapping back.

"My name is Jensen Caldwell. I'm a friend of Lauren's, and I heard that she'd been arrested. Whatever she's accused of, she didn't do it. I'll bet money that her father is behind this, and I need to see that she's okay," I explained.

"Well, that's very sweet, sir, and while I'm sure that a note from her boyfriend protesting her innocence would be sufficient evidence to release a suspect in England, I'm afraid we work a little different here," she retorted sarcastically.

"Wow. I see you're full of Christmas spirit today. So how about this? Either you let me see Miss Matthews now or I will have a team of the best lawyers money can buy here within the hour. The sole purpose of which will be to make your day as crappy as possible. So what's it going to be?" Was I aware that I sounded like a complete arsehole? Yes. But rationality went out the window the minute I knew Lauren was in trouble.

"Jensen?" I jerked around at the sound of Lauren's voice. The look of shock on her face matched my own. "What are you doing here?" she asked.

"I've come to save you," I replied stupidly.

"I'm fine. The sheriff asked me to come in to make a statement, but they had a case put together before they even found me. They know it was all Dad. He conned a lot of people out of their savings, but they caught him at the bank trying to withdraw the money. He's in custody now, and I'm free to go," she explained.

"Oh. That's great news. I thought ... I thought you might need me," I said, feeling like an idiot.

"How did you even know I was in trouble?" she asked.

"Gabriel told me," I explained. She looked at me and smiled. A sad, nervous smile as though she was waiting for me to turn around and leave again.

"I love you," I blurted out in the least romantic way possible. "I love you, and I realized somewhere along the highway that it doesn't matter where we found each other and how far apart we are. When you find something as precious as we have, you don't just throw it away on the possibility that things might get a bit hard down the road. I don't care how many miles I need to travel to be with you or how much work it takes for us to be together. I'm all in, and if we have even a chance at having what Ronnie and Nancy had, I'm taking it."

Every moment that she didn't reply felt like a lifetime. I'd give the world to keep her, but it didn't matter if the world wasn't enough.

"You're crazy, you know that, right?" she asked. "You and I make absolutely no sense together. But so help me, you are my fairy tale, Jensen Caldwell. I don't care where you live, and I don't care what you do for a living. As long as we're together, we'll figure everything out. I love you, and I choose us too."

I didn't give her a chance to say anything else. Instead, I closed the distance between us, lifted her up so that she wrapped her legs around my waist, and kissed her until we were both breathless. My joy was indescribable.

"Do you mind? Some of us have work to do," said the still bored-sounding desk clerk.

Resting my forehead against Lauren's, I reluctantly let her down, and with a satisfied, happy grin I didn't try to hide, I threaded my fingers through hers and pulled her toward the door.

"Merry Christmas," I said cheerfully as we passed the desk clerk.

"Bah humbug," she shouted at my back. Lauren giggled happily, and I let go of her hand to wrap my arm around her shoulder, tucking her into my side.

"Where are we?" Lauren asked, her face a picture of wonder as she stared up at the house.

"We're home," I replied. "That is, if you like it," I replied, nervous about her reaction now that we were here.

"What do you mean?" she asked, stepping out of the truck to take a closer look.

"I realized, when you were describing your dream home, that it sounded just like Nancy and Ronnie's place. It's a great place to raise a family, and it's been filled with love and laughter for a lot of years, and I figured we could use a little of that. Nancy offered it to us for Christmas, and if we like it here, she'll let us buy her out so that she can live with her daughter permanently," I explained.

Lauren didn't say a word as she stared up at the house.

"What do you think? Do you like it?" I asked finally.

"Oh, Jensen, it's unbelievable. I never dreamed of anything that was anywhere near this beautiful. But it's so far away from where you need to be," she replied.

"I can live anywhere in the world. If Ronnie and Nancy could make this work, so can we. Now, do you want to see inside?" I asked.

Her happy smile as she grabbed my hand was all the answer I needed. I slipped my fingers between hers, knowing, as I walked toward my future, that somewhere, somehow, Ronnie Adler was smiling down on me.

It's a Wonderful Holiday

HEIDI MCLAUGHLIN

For Kassidy,
You're the bravest girl I know.
Here's a little Christmas
magic for you.

Chapter One

Rory

The mid-afternoon holiday shoppers walk by the large picture window of my office. Some turn and look at the window display my coworkers put up, while others huddle into their thick winter coats to ward off the random gusts of wind. The blowing snow, which piles up on the window ledge like a quintessential painting from Norman Rockwell, gives the town of Friendship a classic New England feel.

Like most storefronts in town, the Bank & Trust building has large picture windows that look out onto the town square. Too often these days, I find myself spending time staring out, watching the world go by while I sit behind this desk not concentrating on my job.

My mind is on my family or lack thereof. My wife wants a divorce. She wants to end our marriage. Dissolve our partnership. Make us single parents to our daughter, Ruby. It doesn't matter how many ways I say it, each one hurts worse than the previous one. I'm at fault. However, accepting responsibility doesn't negate the fact that I've missed one too many dinners and important school events, forgetting to pick up Ruby when Gwen couldn't, which as a parent, is the worst feeling ever. Each time I had the same excuse—work.

I should've known something was amiss, but stress has a funny way of masking what's right in front of you. The cold shoulder, the clipped responses, the plans that didn't include me, the nights where my wife didn't wait up—were all signs I should've seen. Our quiet conversations turned into arguing, which resulted in each of us saying things we never meant to say. I told her maybe she could get a job and stop volunteering at school all the time; if she helped out I wouldn't have to cover the shopping trips to Boston or every after-school activity under the sun. I asked her what she wanted me to do, how she wanted me to fix the situation—us, our family. I demanded she tell me what to do.

She did.

It's been two months since she asked me to sleep on the couch and subsequently leave home. This was to be *our* forever home, the one where I poured my blood, sweat, and a few tears into remodeling it to her perfection, where we'd raise a handful of children and welcome our grandchildren as they chased each other on our wraparound porch. After my promotion at the bank, I hired contractors to finish the jobs I started. Doing so made sense. It meant I'd have more time with Gwen and Ruby on the weekends, except work consumed those days, too, and I let it.

A family needs to come first. To me, I thought that meant I work harder, longer hours to provide for my family. Sure, I would miss meeting Ruby's parent-teacher meeting or being a part of the school's yearly carnival, the book fair, and the end-of-year celebration, but the two most important women in my life would have the best of everything. I was wrong.

My phone rings, pulling me away from my thoughts. I glance quickly at the caller identification and groan. "Rory Sutton," I say into the receiver while keeping my eyes focused on the world outside.

"How's my investment?" My insides go cold as the rough voice of Jerry Gence barks into my ear, leaving me no choice but to return to work. Quickly, I tap a few keys on my keyboard to bring up his account. Jerry's my number one client, my meal ticket so to speak, and probably the catalyst for my divorce.

"Smooth sailing, Jerry." He calls every day with the same question and, more often than not, gets the same answer.

"Where's my money?"

"The Alibaba Group. It's the Asian version of Amazon. Their stock is doing very well, and I'm confident your portfolio will increase in no time. Of course, you're still widely invested in other stocks, bonds, and annuities." Same conversation we had yesterday and the day before, and likely the same one we'll have on Monday.

"Perfect." In my head, I imagine him sitting in a wing-backed red leather chair with a black silk robe on, rubbing his hands together as if he's the mastermind behind some elaborate plot to take over the world.

"The misses wants to know if we'll be seeing you and your wife for our annual Christmas party?"

Sighing, I turn to stare out the window, each time hoping to catch a glimpse of Gwen coming out of a store, parking her car, or even walking down the street. I haven't seen her since I moved out. This isn't my doing or anything I agree with, but Gwen thought it would be best that we use my mother as a go-between for Ruby. I hate it. I tried to fight it, but seeing Gwen cry isn't something that sits well with me so I agreed.

"Of course." This little white lie isn't going to hurt Jerry in the long run. I doubt very much that Gwen will attend with me. However, I plan to ask her. Setting myself up for rejection isn't high on my list, but neither is showing up alone. The less Jerry knows about my life, the better off I am.

Jerry prattles on about other stocks I should look at, but I'm focused on the world outside. A homeless man struggles to get across the street, tourists not paying attention to our strict town law where pedestrians have the right away. The elderly man stumbles, barely catching himself on one of the parked cars along the curb.

"I'll call you back, Jerry." I don't even bother to hang up the phone before I rush outside without my winter jacket or galoshes. The combination of slush mixed with salt lands on my pants and shoes as I hurry toward the street. "Here, let me help you." Without hesitation, my hands are on the man's forearms as I help him stand.

"My bag," he mumbles, pointing down to the ground.

"I got it," I tell him, leaving one hand on his arm while I bend to retrieve his belongings. It takes everything in my power not to gag at the stench surrounding him or comment on how lightweight his bag is. I'm wondering when was the last time he showered or when he was able to wash his clothes. Everything about him is dirty . . . from his threadbare garments, to his face, to the black stocking cap he wears over his dark hair.

I do my best to guide him to the park bench not far from my office. When we get there, I brush it off before he sits down with a heavy sigh. There's sadness in his eyes but a smile on his face.

"You gonna be okay?"

"Yes, yes. I'll be fine. These old legs don't move as fast as they used to," he tells me.

"Well, even the young ones go slow sometimes."

He smiles but quickly cuts eye contact. I don't know if I should walk him down to the police station or let him be. Is he hungry? Is he broke? Of course, he's likely both, but he's not asking me for anything. In fact, he looks content sitting here on the bench. I suppose, being on the street and homeless he knows how to survive.

A gust of wind blows through us, causing me to shiver. I reach for my wallet but realize quickly it's not in my pocket.

"You'll catch your death," he says as he pulls his coat tightly around him. The fact that he cares about me and not himself gives me pause. I nod and tell him I'll be right back before returning to the warmth of my office.

By the time I get back to my desk and my hand grabs the handle of the drawer to reach my wallet, the old man is gone. I look out the window, pressing so close that I leave oily marks from my hands and forehead, but I can't see where he went. It's almost as if he's disappeared into thin air.

The harsh tone of the disconnect signal pulls me away from the window. I pick up the phone, only to rear back from the noise and set the handle back on its cradle, shaking my head after realizing I never put the receiver back after my call with Jerry. The blotter on my desk, with its sporadic notes and dates, piques my attention. Leaning forward, I push a small pile of papers out of the way so I can read what today says. *Meet divorce lawyer.*

Instant melancholy sets in as I frown at the calendar and what my life has become. A divorce is the last thing I want, but I haven't done a very good job of showing Gwen that she and Ruby were important. *Are important.* Looking down at my watch, I have ten minutes to get across town, which in reality is only a few blocks from my office, so I can sit in an uncomfortable wooden chair while my lawyer goes over Gwen's proposal. The day the process server came into my office was worse than Gwen telling me she wanted me to move out. In the back of my mind, I figured we'd both come to our senses and figure this thing out. I was wrong and was left no choice but to hire a lawyer.

My sports coat hangs on the back of my chair. I grab it, slip my arms into it, and take my long wool winter coat off the rack. My galoshes sit on the floor mat, but one look at my shoes and I realize my shoes are already a lost cause. I search my pockets and my desk, wondering where I hid my gloves. A quick glance at the clock shows me I'm about out of time and need to leave now if I'm going to make my appointment.

It seems colder than when I was outside earlier, and I find myself pulling my coat closer and pushing my hands deep into its pockets. Despite the coat's thickness, it does nothing to take the bite out of the air or keep the wind from stinging my cheeks.

As I walk toward my lawyer's office, I'm looking down side streets and in doorways for the man I helped earlier. I don't know why, but something's pulling at me to find him, to see if he's okay. Consciously, I feel like he is, but I have a nagging desire to see him again for the reassurance.

I cross the street and head up the granite stairs leading to my attorney's office. The heat inside the building is stifling, and my frozen fingers work to undo my coat. Taking the staircase two steps at a time, the old wood creaks under my weight. The glass-paned door with its rickety handle reads Law Office, straight and to the point of the services. My office should read: Investment Banker, but we're owned by a firm out of New York City, whose name is proudly displayed on our door.

The law office is small but has an odd homey feel. I guess if you're here, you want to be comfortable. I'm not, nor do I pretend to be. I hang my wool coat and give a slight nod to the receptionist. She smiles, sort of. It's more like a half smile-half grimace. Living in a small town, everyone knows your business. When Gwen asked me to move out, I thought we'd be able to keep our issues to ourselves, maybe sort them out before drastic measures had to be taken. However, word spread like wildfire, and the gossip mill started spinning its wheel saying things like I cheated and I asked for this. It doesn't matter how many times I try to defend myself, the only people who listen are my guy friends, but even those are starting to drift away. Couples pick sides. I knew it was bound to happen.

"Mr. Sutton, please come in."

Terence Sims has been an attorney longer than I've been alive. My parents used him for a few legal transactions, and it only made sense I seek out his help as well. He sits behind his ancient oak desk in a small chair that doesn't belong with such a grand piece of furniture. "Have you given much thought to how you want to respond to Gwen's proposal?" he asks. He swivels in his chair to look at me over the rim of his glasses.

"Honestly, I haven't looked at it."

"Why not?"

"Because I don't want this divorce."

Terence leans back, and his fingers form a steeple. "It's best to settle. It's what she wants. However, her demands are out-rageous, and we need to respond with our own set." He slides about five pages of typed paper in my direction. He's taken Gwen's requests and countered them in a side-by-side argument, in a compare and contrast sort of way. Seeing the list of things Gwen wants hurts. They make my heart break. Full custody of our daughter, the house, car—mostly everything we have—she wants it all, and Terence is countering with a fifty-fifty split for Ruby, sell the home, and divide assets.

Clearing my throat, I set the papers back onto the desk and shake my head. "I don't know what to say."

"Divorce is hard, especially when one party is blindsided."

"I don't want to sell the house. Ruby ... she was born there; it's all she knows. And the thought of her having to come see me in my apartment ... " I pause in order to swallow the frog that's nestled in my airways. "I can't."

"Think this over, Rory. We have time to respond to the request." He pushes the papers toward me again, but I don't reach for them. I can't. Everything in me seems broken. The love of my life wants to clean me out, and I'm going to let her.

"What are you thinking?" he asks.

"Aside from the fact that I don't want a divorce? That I'll give Gwen whatever she asks for because of Ruby."

Terence removes his glasses and sets them on the desk. "Do me a favor. Talk to Gwen. See if you can work something out that benefits the both of you."

He has given me an idea. I'll talk to Gwen, but it won't be regarding a settlement. I'm going to do what I should've done all along, be the husband and father I'm supposed to be because the only agreement that seems amenable is the one where we're a family again.

I'm going to get my family back.

Chapter Two

Gwen

Ruby sings her made-up version of "Rudolph the Red-Nosed Reindeer" while I try to tame her naturally curly hair. Her green eyes meet mine as I stand behind her, looking at both of us in the mirror that sits atop my dresser.

"May I wear my new shoes?"

"Not today. They're for the Christmas party at church."

"Aren't we going to church?" she asks, raising her tiny eyebrow. Lately, she's been trying my patience. My therapist says it's because she's angry with me. It doesn't matter what I say or do, it's always wrong or questioned.

"Sort of. We're going with your church group to go ice-skating today."

"I've never been ice-skating with the church before."

"I know, but your cousins will be there. They'll skate with you."

"What about Daddy?"

"What about him?"

"Does he know how to ice-skate?"

"He does, but he's at work." Or so I guess. Every so often, I find myself sitting on one of the benches in the park, looking toward his office, wondering what he's doing. Is he eating right? Did he learn to iron his clothes? What does he do for dinner? Then I remember I gave up these jobs, and how he's faring has nothing to do with me.

Yet absolutely nothing has changed. Ruby and I still eat dinner by ourselves. I still take her to school, to all her appointments, and do everything I was doing when Rory was living with us. I swear, if Ruby didn't see him for visitation, she would've never realized he wasn't living here anymore.

I'm bitter. I'm also angry, sad, hurt, and confused. I thought that telling Rory I wanted a divorce would be a lightbulb moment for him, but it wasn't.

I wish I could turn off the emotions, but I can't. At night, I lie in bed and cry because I always saw myself with the perfect family. It used to feel so trivial, wishing Rory was home more, but his long work hours afforded me the luxury of staying home with Ruby. When she started school, I thought about getting a job. I mentioned it a few times, but Rory told me to stay home. Little did I know that staying home meant he wouldn't be.

I tried hard to keep my divorce secret, but the moment Rory asked for a room at the Cozy Cottage, my phone started ringing off the hook. The questions were rapid fire: *Did he cheat? Who with? Is he abusive? Do I want to get together and talk about it?* One cup of coffee and a piece of pie later, and I'm spilling my troubles to my friends. I knew better, but it felt good to talk about what I was going through with Rory. The drawback is that now everyone knows. No one can keep a secret in Friendship. The looks are there no matter where I go. Either people appear sorry for me or they refuse to make eye contact.

Is it not much to ask of Rory to be different, to put his family first, to put our marriage first? But he never has. He has to want to, and I'm not sure that he can.

"Am I done?" Ruby's voice shakes me from my thoughts. I smile softly and nod, hoping she dashes from my room before the tears start to fall. I try not to let her see me cry, because she doesn't understand. She says I shouldn't cry since I made Rory leave. Maybe she's right. I made him leave when I should've ask him to fight for us, to find solid ground where we could exist as a family.

I stare at myself in the mirror and dab a bit of blush onto my cheeks to give them a pink hue. Over the past few months, concealer has become my best friend. It hides the dark bags under my eyes and the red blotchy spots I often end up with after crying. Squaring my shoulders, I smile and tell myself that everything will be okay, that I'll be okay.

"I'm ready." Ruby stands in my doorway. She has on her peacoat along with snow boots, and nothing else, as far as I can tell.

"Thank you for getting ready, but we're going to be playing outside. Can you put on your snowsuit?"

Ruby nods. "Do you think Daddy will be there?" There's sorrow in her voice. I know she misses him. I do, too, but I can't change how I feel, even if my heart is screaming to give Rory a chance. He's had plenty.

I sigh and shake my head as I walk toward her. With my hand on her shoulder, I direct her toward the stairs. "I don't think so, Ruby."

"Why not?" Ruby jumps from the last two steps, landing flawlessly on her feet.

"It's not easy for him to get off in the middle of the day." I help Ruby continue getting ready, making sure the bib of her snowsuit is clipped together before I slip into my coat and hand Ruby her scarf.

"Maybe he'll want to see me."

"Maybe." I want to tell her not to get her hopes up, but I can't. I won't. She'll learn quickly enough that her father only puts himself first.

"It's snowing!" Ruby screams as we step out onto the porch. "Can we walk to the park?"

I nod and reach for her hand. Carefully, we navigate the stairs. I am mentally ticking off everything I'll have to do when I get home: shovel the walkway, clean the stairs, and snow-blow the driveway. Every day the list gets longer. Thinking about winter and the amount of snowfall we get, it makes me want to move to a warmer climate so I don't have to deal with any of this.

Ruby loves the snow though. It's evident by the way she's skipping through it so the fallen flakes kick up and blow in the wind. This makes her smile, and in turn, I smile too.

As soon as we hit Main Street, we feel the Christmas spirit is alive and well. There are garlands and white lights wrapped around the wrought iron light poles with red ribbons tied to them. The storefronts are decorated and festive, filling me with holiday cheer despite everything, and the carolers are out, sing-ing the songs I grew up listening to.

"Are you ready for your concert?" In a few days, the ele-mentary school will have their winter concert. Ruby has been practicing for it in her own special way. She's too young to have all the words memorized, but she tries, and does so very loudly.

"Gabe says I'm the best."

Gabe? I search through my memory bank of teachers at her school but am unable to recall someone named Gabe.

"Is Gabe new?"

Ruby shrugs. "He's my friend. I like him."

A wave of relief comes over me as I quickly realize that Gabe is likely a classmate. I think it's cute that Ruby has a crush. I remember my first crush. I was in the first or second grade, and his name was Walter. I liked him until we were in fifth grade, when he moved away. For the life of me, I can't even recall his last name, which is odd since I'm pretty sure I spent most of that year doodling his name all over my notebook and imagining the day we'd cross paths again.

Reaching for Ruby's hand, we cross the street and step into the park. The loud speakers, set in the maple trees, belt out more Christmas music, while a group of children partake in a snowball fight. Coming to the park to skate has been something everyone in town does. But it was always the afternoon with the church group that stood out the most. My mom or dad would offer to come with me, but I'd tell them to work so I could pretend I was more grown up than I really was.

From afar, my name rings out. It's faint, but there's something about a close family member yelling your name that you'll always hear. When I look around, I spot two women frantically shaking their arms in the air. Ruby and I head toward my sister Eliza and sister-in-law Amber, who have secured a coveted bench for us to sit on.

"Aunties," Ruby yells as she lets go of my hand. She rushes to them, slipping a little on the compacted snow, and giggles before finishing her sprint. Both women wrap her in hugs. Since Rory and I separated, they've been my rock, my shoulders to cry on, my voice of reason even when one of them may not agree with me. It doesn't matter what time it is, I can call either of them, and they're on my doorstep within minutes, and always with ice cream.

After I help Ruby with her ice skates and make sure her helmet is snug, I kiss her nose, much to her delight and dismay as she giggles and wobbles away from me. My niece is waiting for Ruby with her arm stretched out and her fingers wiggling. As soon as the two clasp hands, they're gliding across the ice together, heading toward a small group of kids. For the past couple of winters, Ruby has taken a six-week ice-skating course. The classes are just enough to teach her balance and how to skate forward and backward. I made the mistake of watching her first lesson, which is when they taught the group how to fall properly. I about had a heart attack that day, but Ruby thought it was the best day ever.

"You look exhausted," my sister, Eliza, says as I sit down next to her and sigh. My hand tries to find my neck, but under the bulky sweater, turtleneck, and scarf I'm wearing, it's nearly impossible, but still, I rub and twist, trying to relieve the built-up pressure.

"That's because she doesn't sleep," Amber, my sister-in-law, says, handing me a large cup of something hot. I don't care what it is. I need it, and the heat of holding the cup sends a bit of warmth through my gloved hands.

"I don't and just when I finally get a decent night's sleep, something happens, and I'm up all night. This week, Rory was served with divorce papers, and I spent half the night second-guessing myself and the rest of the night wondering why he didn't call or show up. Part of me thought he'd at least come to the house, angry, and we could talk."

My sisters scoot closer, and both give me a hug. I need it, but it's not the comfort I desire. I want Rory's arms around me. It's been so long since I've felt them that I've forgotten how they feel. The passion between us went first. The change was subtle.

We didn't have time for each other, we were too tired, too busy, or more often than not I was in bed when he finally came home from work. A good-bye kiss turned to a peck, which turned into a grumble as one of us left the room. By then, emotions were all over the place, and the stakes were high. Words said and actions taken. Both are hard to take back.

We part, giving me a chance to catch my breath. If my sisters keep at it, I'm liable to shed a few tears, and I don't want Ruby to see. And I definitely don't want pity from anyone in my church group.

"Here, maybe this will help." My sister hands me a white paper bag from the pastry shop. "It's chocolate. We all need chocolate in our lives." She sighs, but her life is perfect. I know I used to think the same about mine, but Eliza and Alex really do have a great relationship. When I look at my sister, I feel like a failure.

"Maybe he'll come around," Amber blurts out. Both Eliza and I turn to look at her, but she's staring straight ahead. I turn slightly, half expecting Rory to be standing on the other side of the rink, but he's not. He wouldn't even know to come since I never told him.

"I'm not holding my breath," I tell them both. "I thought ... Well, I'm not sure what I thought, but this wasn't it. I guess I figured we'd last a week apart, not months."

The subject needs to change. It's almost Christmas, and if I keep dwelling on my current state, I'm going to make Ruby's holiday unbearable. Just as I'm about to take a sip of what's surely lukewarm cocoa, I scan the ice rink, not once or twice but three times for my daughter. By the time I'm on my feet, my sisters are standing next to me, each clutching one of my arms.

"What's wrong?" Eliza asks.

"Ruby. Do you see her?" Without looking at them, I know they're scanning the same rink I am, maybe even beyond. "Ruby?" I yell out, but it's useless. The noise level is too high between the laughter and the holiday music playing. "Oh my God, where is she?"

"We'll find her," Amber says, pulling my arm toward her. "Let's go look."

"We should split up." It's Eliza suggestion, and while it makes sense, I don't know if my feet can move without them holding me, but they're off and running before I can get the words to form.

My hands shake, and my heart beats faster than I thought possible. Tears start to fall, turning my already cold cheek frigid. I see one of our local police officers up ahead. I try to run toward him, but the snow's knee deep where I step, making it nearly impossible to move. That's when I see her, standing away from the rink with a vagrant man.

"Ruby." I reach for her and pull her to me. She looks up and smiles. Of course, she does because she doesn't know danger, only kindness. "What have I told you about running off? You are not allowed to leave the area without permission."

"But I wanted to say . . ."

I crouch down, and my grip on her arms tightens. I'm scared. I want to tell her that talking to strangers isn't wise, but I want her to have compassion for others. "You can't disappear on me. You just can't."

"But this is Gabe. He's my friend."

Gabe? "Honey, you said Gabe was in your class."

"No, I didn't, Mommy." She looks at me, stone-faced. I know she's telling me the truth.

"Oh." I don't know what to say or think. I'm not sure how my daughter met a transient, and I'm not sure if I like it or not. I stand and pull Ruby close to me. "Ruby has told me about you," I tell him, trying to make nice. "Are you from around here?"

"No, ma'am, just passing through."

My hold on Ruby becomes tighter, even as she tries to squirm out of it. "I see. How did you meet my daughter?"

"Well, she befriended me on the playground. Decided to share her lunch with me."

I smile down at her. Her face is beaming. She did something nice, and I don't want to fault her for it. "That was a kind gesture, Ruby."

"I told you, he's my friend." I nod and start to push her back toward the rink. "It was nice to meet you, Gabe."

We're not two steps away when he speaks. "There is no love without forgiveness, and there's no forgiveness without love."

His words stop me in my tracks. I turn back around to ask him to repeat himself, but he's gone.

Chapter Three

Rory

The red circle on my calendar is a stark reminder that today, of all days, is cookie day. The day when I've promised to take Ruby to church, where we will spend hours decorating and packaging hundreds of cookies. This tradition started years ago, and as soon as Ruby was old enough, Gwen made sure our daughter participated.

When Gwen suggested I take Ruby this year, I didn't argue. Not being able to see my daughter and my wife every day has been incredibly hard. It's opened my eyes to the type of life I was living away from them, even though we were sharing the same house. Gwen and I had become nothing more than roommates who passed by with glances, forced affection, and terse words for each other. None of which were part of the vows we had taken.

The other glaring note on my desk tells me that Jerry has moved his annual party to tonight, in the middle of the week of all days, so he could indulge his wife with a European holiday. In the same breath, he reminded me that a happy wife is a happy life, and yet here I am about to make another disappointing phone call to my wife.

My hand feels heavy as I pick up the phone receiver. With the end of my pencil, I push the seven numbers that'll make the landline in our kitchen ring. Gwen and I talked about removing it when the height of the cell phone craze started, but Gwen said there's something nice about sitting down and talking to the person on the other end and giving them your undivided attention. I can easily remember Gwen, sitting on the old stool her grandmother gave us, talking to her mom while she was pregnant with Ruby. She had the worst heartburn and would often be up late at night, thinking the worst. At the time, Gwen could've easily walked across the street to talk to her mom but always chose to call.

Each ring causes my heart to stop. I'm not looking forward to the confrontation or hearing the disappointment in Gwen's voice when I tell her I have no choice but to go to Jerry's party tonight. Only a man like Jerry could do this, change the date of his gathering and expect everyone to show up, and that's exactly what I'm expected to do—show up with a smile on my face and Gwen on my arm. Neither of which I can see happening. Even if Gwen and I weren't going through a divorce, she'd never choose a party over our daughter. No, that's something only I would do, because upsetting the man who keeps a roof over my family's head weighs heavily on me. One sour word from him, and my clientele goes elsewhere. It's not just his account but the others I've gained because of his trust in me.

"Hello?" my wife's soft voice drifts through the phone.

I close my eyes briefly before I clear my throat and repeat her sentiment, and ask, "How are you?" This is the first time we've spoken since she served me with papers. That night, I drove over to the house, determined to confront my wife, but when I got there, I couldn't bring myself to get out of my truck. The lights were out, all except for the glow coming from the television. I stood and wondered what Christmas movie the two of the most important women in my life were watching. I thought about knocking, but the anger I had that night was too much, and I feared . . . well, everything.

"I'm fine, busy. Ruby will be at your mom's after school. You can pick her up there."

I sigh and run my hand over my face and hair and then back down. "About tonight."

"Rory." My name sounds harsh, as if she's gritting her teeth. "Don't do this. Not this week."

"Jerry—"

"I don't care about Jerry, and neither does Ruby. You promised, Rory. You promised our daughter that you'd take her tonight. It's all she's been talking about."

"Can you listen to me for one minute, Gwen? Please?"

"Fine," she huffs.

I sit taller in my chair, as if doing so will help me get my point across to Gwen. This is the part of my life that she doesn't understand, and it's the part that's ruined my marriage. "Jerry moved his annual holiday party to tonight; otherwise, taking Ruby wouldn't be a problem. He's expecting us to show up, together. What do you say about asking my mom to take Ruby tonight, and you and I could go to the party?"

"You're joking, right?"

"I would never joke about spending time with you."

She laughs or maybe it's a sneeze, I can't be sure. "Let me understand you correctly. You want to cancel on your daughter so you can attend a party?"

"Noooo," I say, dragging out the word. "I want us to go out, like husband and wife. It's a cookie-decorating thing at church. Surely I can make it up to her."

"You're unbelievable, Rory."

"What?" I ask dumbly. "You've always enjoyed the Gences' parties."

"Actually, I find his wife to be pretentious, their house over-decorated, and their yippy dogs extremely annoying."

"Jerry's eccentric."

"Nice excuse for someone who is rude and condescending. The answer is no." She pauses and mumbles something incoherently. "I can't believe you're doing this to Ruby."

"You know, if he wasn't such an important client, I wouldn't be calling, but he is. You know this." I can't help the defensive tone in my voice. We've had this same conversation repeatedly, and it never solves anything.

"The only thing I know is that you can't keep a promise to your own daughter, that you put this man and his money before everything."

"His money is what pays for the life you have, Gwen."

She scoffs. "There are other clients, other people who need to invest money, Rory. Jerry isn't the be all that ends all in the financial world, and right now I don't care. The only thing I care about is now I have to break it to Ruby that, once again, you're choosing this man and *his* family over your own."

"It's not like that, Gwen," I say, pinching the bridge of my nose. "I wish you could see the difference."

"Well, I can't, and I won't until you see and admit that you've allowed this man to dictate our lives. That you've allowed your job to become between us when it didn't have to. I know, Rory . . . I know you think this is how you provide for your family because it's how your father did it, but we don't live in a world like that anymore. Times have changed. I need my husband, and Ruby needs her father."

She hangs up before I can even form the words needed to tell her that I completely understand, but that my hands are tied and that canceling on Ruby is the last thing I want to do.

I don't know how long I sit there with the receiver dangling. I don't seem to care about the annoying signal coming through my phone. And I definitely don't care about the tears dripping from my eyes.

What I care about is that this is the first time I've cried since Gwen and I separated, and I want to know why. Am I so heartless that I can't shed a tear when the woman I love asks me to move out? Am I missing some emotional element that lets me feel, or am I just numb to it all?

A knock on my office door startles me into action. I place the receiver back, wipe my face, and clear my throat before telling whoever's on the other side to come in. Terence Sims steps in with his hand held up. He's holding a manila envelope, and instantly my heart drops. The divorce is the last thing I want to deal with, especially tonight.

"Just thought I'd drop these by on my way home." He sets the envelope on the corner of my desk and uses one index finger to slide it toward me.

"So kind of you," I tell him. As soon as Terence starts to sit, I stand up and reach for my sport coat. "I was just leaving."

"This will only take a minute. I highlighted the changes, and I just need your signature."

Shaking my head, I slip into my coat and step into my galoshes. "Sorry, not tonight."

"Rory, it's our counter. It'd be best if Gwen's attorney heard our argument sooner rather than later, and I'd really like to have the pages on his desk before I take vacation."

"I'll read it tonight." I won't, but I pick up the papers and give them a good shake to show Terence I'm serious. "I'll stop by tomorrow."

He rises slowly from one of the chairs that sits in front of my desk. He looks at me doubtfully but finally nods and makes his way to my office door. With his hand on the knob, he turns and looks at me. It's not a smile on his face or a frown but a look of confusion. I stand there, with my wool coat resting over my arm, waiting for him to say something, and when he decides to leave instead of confronting me, my shoulders sag in relief. Without any hesitation, I pick up the dark yellow packet and drop it into the bin destined for the shredder.

Outside, the sights, scents, and sounds of Christmas are all around me. The town recreation department spent most of the afternoon putting up the park's Christmas tree in preparation for the lighting ceremony. Carolers are on the street corner, singing their hearts out, and the coffee shop has a line out the door, likely to get hot cocoa or a warm cup of apple cider.

There were many times after I'd leave work that I'd find Gwen and Ruby waiting in line. I look now, hoping to catch them, but I know I won't. It's too early, and Ruby's still in school. That thought pulls me to a complete stop in the middle of the sidewalk. People smile, call my name, and wish me a merry Christmas as they walk by, but I'm focused on my thoughts. My daughter should be out of school right now, and I should be at work. It's rare that I ever leave early, and according to Gwen, when I do, I'm angry, resentful, and often complaining about the work I've left behind. Yet, because of Jerry, I'm on my way to my one-room apartment at the Cozy Cottage with my college-size refrigerator and portable hot plate to get ready for his party instead of being a father and following through with my promise to my daughter. The realization hits me like a ton of bricks.

Instead of heading to my apartment, I cross the road and walk toward the church, hoping to catch Gwen before she takes Ruby inside. People stop, wanting to talk, telling me how sorry they are for what I'm going through and inviting me to their home for the holidays. I hadn't even thought about where I'd spend Christmas, because I honestly thought Gwen and I would make up. But how can we, if I'm not willing to make the changes needed to keep my family together?

By the time I reach the church, the parking lot is full. I walk around back, stopping to look into one of the windows. Years ago, Reverend John asked us all to come together to create steps and install larger windows so the basement could meet the fire code and be used for functions. I've never been more thankful than I am now that I helped, because it's giving me a chance to watch my family.

My wife has her hair up in one of those buns that she rarely leaves the house wearing. I put her in that position when I told her I couldn't take Ruby. My daughter's sitting at one of the tables, by herself, slowly decorating a cookie while all the other children are laughing and happily putting the packages together that they'll deliver to all the local businesses. Their unhappiness is because of me.

I stand there until I start to shiver, but I don't leave. I sit on the bench outside, waiting for them to come out. I don't know what I'll say to them, because telling them I'm sorry doesn't seem like it'll be enough.

Gabe sits down next to me and hands me a foam cup. "You look sad."

"That obvious?"

"I know sadness," he says, taking a sip of his own cup. Undoubtedly, he has a story to tell. Maybe he's a war veteran who suffers from PTSD and left his family behind, or maybe he's like me, a workaholic who didn't spend enough time with his family. For all I know, he gave everything up and never looked back. Maybe life's easier this way.

"Are you a member of this fine establishment?" Gabe nods toward the white church.

"I used to be but haven't been in a long time."

"So you sit outside and wait for an invitation?"

"My family is in the basement. I was supposed to be there, but I let work get in the way."

"And you can't go see them?"

I shake my head. "My wife … we're separated, and I haven't done a decent enough job to show her how much she means to me."

"Am I to understand that you don't want this separation?"

I shake my head. "Not in a million years, but I've been a bad husband and my wife and daughter deserve better."

"I'm sure you don't want my advice."

I look over at the disheveled man. "I'd happily take advice from you."

He turns and smiles. "Love is patient, love is kind. It does not envy, it does not boast, it is not proud. It does not dishonor others, it is not self-seeking, it is not easily angered, it keeps no record of wrongs. Love does not delight in evil but rejoices with the truth. It always protects, always trusts, always hopes, always perseveres. Love never fails. Corinthians, chapter thirteen, verse four."

The way Gabe speaks, so eloquently and full of truth, I have no choice but to get lost in his words he speaks. I let them all sink in and repeat them in my head, over and over again until he stands. "Wait." I reach for him, grabbing his hand so he doesn't leave me. "It can't be that simple. Gwen knows I love her."

"Does she?" he asks. I open my mouth to reply, but nothing comes out. I let go of his hand and watch him walk away until I can no longer see him. The alarm on my phone goes off. It's the reminder I set for Jerry's party. I silence it and turn back toward the church to wait for my family.

Chapter Four

Gwen

The phone in the kitchen rings. In my heart, I know it's Rory. It's too early to deal with him, so I ignore it, hoping he leaves a voice mail or sends me a text message. When the ringing stops, I sigh, only to have my heart pound out of my chest at the sound of Ruby squealing in delight. I rush downstairs with my robe flowing behind me as if I'm a superhero. Only I'm not. I'm a wreck who can't be bothered to do her hair, put makeup on, or even take a shower most days.

"Ruby, who's on the phone?" I know the answer, so I'm not sure why I'd ask her. I'm tempted to take the receiver away from her, to hang it up and shoo her upstairs to get ready for her concert, but I don't. I can't even bring myself to get ready for tonight. I think, if I were to look like the old Gwen, the parents would be shocked. They're so used to this mess of a woman I've become.

"Daddy," she says, covering the bottom of the phone. I want to laugh and tell her she's cute, but I don't. "He's talking to me."

I busy myself with a cup of tea while I try to eavesdrop on

their conversation. Whatever he's saying to her, she's excited. But I hope he's not promising her anything. Another broken promise and I might come unglued. The way he brushes us aside, the way he thinks I'll always pick up the broken pieces, has taken its toll. Last night was the last time I'll do his bidding where our daughter is concerned.

"Okay, bye bye, Daddy." Ruby holds the phone out to me. "He wants to talk to you," she says with the bottom covered again. "Be nice and don't hurt his feelings." She hands me the phone and crosses her arms.

I smile, but on the inside, I'm raging and making a mental note to talk to my therapist and maybe set an appointment for my child as well. I try not to let her words sting, but they do. She has no idea about last night, how her father chose a client over her. She only knows that he couldn't make it. Ruby was upset, and I tried to make the situation better by telling her that her father would make it up to her. I don't know why I continue to protect him, to make excuses for him. I don't know why I take the brunt of her anger when it should be directed at him, but I do. I take every little jab and side remark she throws at me, because I'm her mother and I'm not about to shatter her world.

"Go get dressed for your concert," I tell her. I expect her to stomp away, but she doesn't. She starts singing one of her songs and skips out of the kitchen. I wait until I hear her thumping up the stairs before clearing my throat. "Hello?"

"Gwennie."

My eyes close, and my heart skips a beat at the nickname Rory gave me years ago. It's been years since I've heard it though. There's so much that I want to say to him right now. Mostly though, I want to know why he's called me that after so many years of forgetting to use it. "Rory."

He chuckles because this is nothing more than a game to him. I close my eyes and ask God for the will to get through this phone call. "Ruby has a concert this evening, right?"

"Yes, why?"

"Because I'm going to be there. Six thirty?"

"Did you tell her this?" I ask, needing to know if I have to mentally prepare her for when he doesn't show up. And prepare myself.

"Why wouldn't I tell her?"

I throw my free hand up in the air, even though no one is around to see how dramatic I am. It's definitely an Oscar-worthy performance right here in my kitchen. "I don't know, Rory, maybe because you didn't show up last night and I had to break it to her. I had to lie for you."

"I was there last night."

"Except you weren't," I say through gritted teeth. I try to calm down, but the anger is rolling through me. He's so clueless, but he never used to be. "In case you were wondering, I was the one with our brokenhearted daughter, trying to get her to smile."

"Look, I was there. I just couldn't bring myself to walk in after I saw you in there. You looked . . ." He pauses, and in the background I can hear paper being shuffled around. "See you at six thirty. Save me a seat."

He hangs up before I can tell him to find his own seat. It's no use, and he's leaving me no choice but to put my foot down. I dial my lawyer's number. It's late, and the call goes through to voice mail. "This is Gwen Sutton . . . "

"Mommy," Ruby's voice startles me, and I hang up. If I'm going to tell my attorney about her father and his failed promises, it's going to have to be when Ruby can't walk in on me. "Mommy," she says again from the doorway into the kitchen.

"Yes, sweetie?"

"I need your help." Standing there is my little girl with her dress on, looking flustered. Gone is the curt tone she had with me earlier. I know she doesn't mean it, but it still hurts.

"Come here, let me button your dress." She does, turning when she gets to me. "What would you like me to do with your hair?" I ask as I pat down her unruly curls only to have them spring up again.

Ruby shrugs. "A ponytail with some ribbon?"

"You got it. I'll follow you up." Together we climb the stairs and head into my bathroom where she takes a seat at my vanity. I try not to look at myself, but I can't help it. If I'm going to look somewhat presentable, a pound of makeup is going to be required.

After fixing Ruby's hair, I tell her I need to shower and get ready. "Why don't you watch television on my bed and try not to wrinkle your dress?"

"Okay."

I stand in the doorway, watching as she climbs onto the bed and settles herself in with the remote in her hand. After Rory moved out, my shower routine changed. I was a quick ten-minute person once the water came on, but now I stay in until the water turns cold and my fingers have pruned. It's peaceful and gives me time to cry, away from the prying eyes of my daughter. Tonight, though, I take a quick shower so I can get ready and look somewhat human for her concert.

When I come out, there's a dress lying on my bed for me. "What's this?" I ask Ruby.

She shrugs. "I thought you could look pretty for Daddy."

I force a smile and fight the urge to tell her he won't show up, regardless of what I'm wearing. I bite the inside of my cheek instead and take the dress back into my bathroom to get ready, rushing through my routine, angry with myself because I don't have time to dry my hair fully. "This is what divorce does to you," I say to myself in the mirror. Too bad the person staring back at me doesn't tell me to snap out of it or remind me that this is what I wanted.

By the time we get to the school, I'm a bottle of nerves. For the life of me, I can't figure out why. It's not like I haven't spoken to Rory since he left, although we haven't seen each other much, unless it's been in passing. I've been a coward and left Ruby at his mother's on the days he takes her. It's easier that way, at least for me.

After I leave Ruby with her music class, I'm standing among other parents, looking for prime seats. They're like oceanfront property, the way some parents bump and push others out of the way. And there's always *that* parent, the one who has brought their 1980s camcorder and is blocking the view of others.

I used to be that parent. The one who got here early and reserved seats, the one who skipped dinner to make sure everyone had front-row viewing. This year, I failed, and I'm sitting three rows from the back, behind a row of very tall people.

Every so often, I look toward the door, praying that Rory will walk in. I doubt I'll call him over, but seeing him would be a nice reprieve. Not for me, for Ruby. She needs to see her father, to know he still cares.

The classes file in. I crane my head to look for Ruby and smile as I see her curly ponytail bopping along. One last look toward the door yields nothing, and neither does my quick scan of the parents rushing to their seats. I try not to feel disappointed, but I am.

When the lights dim, I try not to cry. I don't know what else to do, to get it through Rory's head that he can't make promises to Ruby. Not anymore. I can't and I won't keep covering for him.

A hand touches my shoulder, and my heart soars. Crouched down next to me is Jason Hayes whose daughter Emily is a few years older than Ruby. "Is that seat taken?" he whispers.

I shake my head and tell him no as quietly as I can. He sits down next to me, thanking me. I'm not sure what to say to him, so I try to focus on the music teacher as she tells us about tonight's performance. Thankfully, Ruby's class is up first, but unfortunately, I have to stay until all the performances are finished. Normally, I wouldn't mind except the middle school band is playing again at our tree lighting ceremony, and it'll likely be the same songs as tonight.

My little Ruby stands on the risers, singing her lungs out. I can't help but feel incredibly proud of her, even when she messes up. I can tell when she does, because she covers her mouth and tries to sing even louder on the next verse.

It's an hour and half later when the concert's over. Once the lights are on, there's a mad rush to get out of the gymnasium. In the hall, there are light refreshments as we wait for our children.

"She has pipes." I jump at the sound of Rory's voice. He stands before me, his eyes sunken in with bags that match mine. His shirt is wrinkled, and it doesn't look like his slacks have been pressed. I try not to cheer, but it's a victory for me to know he never looked tousled when I was taking care of him.

"What are you doing here?" The question is ridiculous, but it's the only thing I could think to say because I wasn't expecting him to show up.

"Our daughter had a concert." As if he needed to remind me.

He steps closer, invading my personal bubble. I try to smile, but I can only look away. A few of our friends stop and chat, forcing Rory and me to make small talk with them. I'm sure it's as awkward for them as it is for us.

When Rory's hand touches the small of my back, it takes everything in me not to step away or even move nearer to him. It's been so long since I've felt the warmth of his hand that my mind is telling me one thing while my heart is saying something entirely different.

Ruby yells for her dad. I try not to let it bother me, but it does. He squats down to meet her, wrapping his arms around her before picking her up. "Mommy, did you hear me?"

"I did," I tell her as I try to put her coat on without asking Rory to put her down. "You were wonderful."

"I messed up."

"It's okay. You have a whole year to learn the songs for your next winter concert," Rory says.

"They change every year," I mumble.

He nods and carries Ruby out of the lobby, where he heads to the parking lot and stops at his car.

"I'm over there," I say, pointing toward my car.

"I thought we could go for some ice cream." Ruby screams in agreement, which makes me want to drag her father behind the school and chastise him for saying that aloud.

"Yes! Ice cream. Ice cream," Ruby starts chanting, which makes me want to drag her father behind the school and chastise him for saying that aloud.

"What do you say, Gwennie?"

"You two go ahead. I'll see you at home, Ruby." I walk toward my car and try to forget the scene that's happening behind me.

"Gwen, wait up."

"Where's Ruby?" I ask, looking at his empty hands. He points at his car.

"She's inside. She's safe."

"What do you want then?"

"You," he says, which makes my heart speed up. "I want my family back."

I shake my head. "Rory—"

"No, listen," he says as he reaches for my hands. "I'm a fool. I've made a lot of mistakes where you and Ruby are concerned, but I'm going to be better. I just need for you to give me a chance."

I pull my hands away from him and press the button on my fob to unlock my door. "I don't know, Rory. Showing up for her concert and taking her for ice cream doesn't negate everything else."

"I know it doesn't. I'm going to show you that I can be the man you fell in love with."

I half smile before disappearing behind the steering wheel of my car. I don't give Rory a chance to talk me out of it before pulling away from him. I honk at Ruby when I pass her, and she waves.

I detour through our small town of Friendship, looking at all the lights. This time of year I always love where we live, because everything's so festive. Sitting on one of the benches, with a cup in his hand, is Ruby's friend. I haven't been able to remember the words he said to me the other day at the rink. I've tried, but each time I draw a blank.

Pulling over, I park my car and rush to the diner and order two slices of pie and two cups of hot cocoa to go. "Hello."

"Hi," he says gruffly.

"Mind if I sit?"

"Not at all. I was just leaving."

"Please, stay. I bought you some pie." I set the boxes of pie and drinks down. Pulling one of the cups from the carrying case, I hand it to him. "I hope you like hot cocoa."

"Is the sky blue?"

"Normally." I laugh. I sit down next to him and open my box. Thankfully, the waitress heated everything up for us. "Do you like it?"

"I do."

"Good. I was hoping you could repeat what you said to me the other day in the park."

Gabe doesn't say much as he continues to dig into the flakey crust. We sit there, both eating and me waiting for him to tell me. I'm starting to think he doesn't remember or I imagined that he said something.

"This pie was delicious, thank you."

"You're welcome. Did you get any of the cookies the children were handing out the other night?"

He nods. "Ruby said she decorated mine special. Ruby's a extraordinary girl."

Knowing this makes me smile, but as a mother, I'm also concerned. She shouldn't take to strangers so easily. "Do you see her a lot?"

Gabe shakes his head. "Only when the children come outside. Sometimes I'll sit and read to them while they're on recess." He turns and looks at me. "Don't fret ...I asked permission first, and there's always a teacher nearby."

"I wasn't worried," I tell him, even though I was and still feel like I should check with the school.

He stands and picks up his bag of belongings. "What you're looking for, the happiness, it's with those you love."

Chapter Five

Rory

Deciding to go to church was a spur of the moment thing. I woke from a nightmare in a cold sweat, needing my family. I couldn't explain it, and I still can't, but I needed to be wherever they were.

In my dream, my wife and I weren't anything to each other. Nothing more than strangers who would pass by without making eye contact, without saying hi. When in reality, she's everything to me. Gwen represents the best of who I am and who I desire to be. Gwen's the nurturer of our family, the glue that holds us together. Waking with that feeling of dread weighing heavily on me is something I never want to experience again.

I know making it to Sunday service isn't going to change anything between Gwen and me, but it's a continuance of what I started the night of the concert. I had hoped not only for a family outing but also for the opportunity to sit next to my wife. I was late because there was traffic, which is unusual in Friendship. Add that to a packed parking lot and having to walk farther than

I planned, and by the time I reached the gym, the dimmed lights left me no choice but to stand in the back.

It worked out to be the best possible spot, aside from sitting next to my wife. From where I was, I could easily see Gwen, and as soon as Ruby's class finished, I spent the rest of the concert staring at my spouse. If the seat next to her had been empty, I would've slipped in, reached for her hand, and held it until it was time to go. However, luck was not on my side, not that night.

I know I have to do better, show her I can be the man she fell in love with, the man she married. I'm hoping to prove to her I can change. It's going to take some time, I know this, but I have to try.

Ruby spots me first. I press my finger to lips, motioning her to be quiet as I come down the aisle. She turns back around, facing forward. I imagine her legs moving back and forth in rapid succession, and any moment now, Gwen will place her hand on Ruby's knee to calm her.

The spot next to Gwen is open. I slide in, and she shifts away. I tell myself it's because she has no idea it's me, but shouldn't she know or at least sense me or has she already forgotten me and moved on? That thought makes my stomach turns queasy, and I press my hand over my gut, hoping the sensation goes away quickly.

"Hi." Gwen's voice is small, but I hear her clear as day, and that ill feeling is gone. If I ever had any doubt that Gwen is the love of my life, this small moment proved she is.

"Hi, Daddy." Ruby looks past her mom. I swear she winks, as if she had some scheme going on to get me here.

"What're you doing here?" Gwen asks.

I shrug. Honestly, if I didn't have the nightmare, I'm not

sure I would be here today, trying to prove to Gwen that I can change. That the love we shared is still there. Thoughts of love bring me back to my conversation with Gabe. I don't know what it is about that man, but he's always there when I need to talk to someone. It's like he appears out of thin air, and he always knows what to say. "I meant what I said the other night. I want my family back."

"Rory, we talked about this " she mutters and looks away. This isn't the time or place to have this conversation. I know this. I also know that time is sensitive. I want to spend Christmas with my family. I want to wake up in my bed with my wife next to me as our daughter comes running in, yelling that Santa as come. What I don't want to worry about is the counterclaim my lawyer is pushing me to sign. Truthfully, I'd love to tell him I sent it to the shredder and it can stay there. However, that all depends on Gwen, and considering the number I've done to her emotional state, I have an uphill battle this coming week.

Gwen tenses when I place my hand on hers. The jab goes right to my heart. I deserve it. I don't want to think about the last time I showed her how much I love her. It's been years. Years of excuses that have piled up and bridged a gap so wide that her only course of action is to call it quits, while mine is, well I'm not sure what mine is, but it's going to change. I'm going to change. These two women are what's most important in my life, and I need to show them.

Pastor John takes his position behind the pulpit. His hands grip the wooden stand as he looks out over his congregation. He starts the morning off by talking about the weather and how dangerously cold it could get. He reminds us to care for those who can't care for themselves and not to forgot those who have lost their way.

I scan the crowd, looking for Gabe. For all I know, he attends here. The doors have always been open to everyone, but that doesn't mean everyone comes in. For some it's hard to overlook the appearance of a homeless person or the fact that they beg for food and money. It's also hard for me to think that if I hadn't been looking out the window earlier in the week, I wouldn't have met Gabe, a man who doesn't seem to have anything except words of wisdom that have opened my eyes to the kind of man I want to be. The kind of man who puts his family first, who doesn't break promises, and is present in the lives of his wife and daughter.

The word *forgiveness* reverberates through the church. It hits home for me. It's exactly what I need to convince Gwen to do, and I know it's going to be hard. Pastor John seems to maintain eye contact in our general direction as he continues his sermon. I can't help but think he's speaking directly at me. I know it's ridiculous since the church is packed, but there's something in his words, almost as if I'm the only one here. Maybe this is his way, God's way, of telling me that I have to ask for Gwen's forgiveness. Not only for Gwen and Ruby, but for myself as well.

As soon as the service is over, I stand and exit the pew, holding my arm out for Gwen and Ruby to step in front of me. I'm milking it, I know, but I can't help it. I place my hand on Gwen's lower back and mentally prepare for her rejection. When it doesn't come, I sigh in relief.

No one stops to ask if we've reconciled, for which I'm thankful. I need a moment to say my piece to Gwen and beg for a second chance. If that means I get down on my knees, I will. I'll do anything.

I guide us to the back of the church and down the stairs where refreshments will be set up. Once we're there, Ruby runs off to sit with her Sunday school group, and I use this opportunity to pull Gwen into one of the corners.

We used to do this, she and I, long ago. Back when we first started dating and I'd come to church with her. After the service, we'd huddle in the corner, stealing kisses, away from the prying eyes of our parents and grandparents. Man, I miss those days. Back then life was simple. You woke up, did your thing, and found your girl when school was over. No stress. No bills. Just life.

"Rory—"

I hold my hand up, asking her to give me a chance to say what I need to. "Do you remember when I was supposed to take Ruby to decorate cookies?" I don't wait for her to answer before I continue. "That night, I was walking home to get ready for Jerry's party, and I don't know, something stopped me and I ended up here. I watched you and saw how unhappy I'm making you."

Gwen's hands fidget, and she looks around, likely trying to figure out if people are listening. I don't care if they are. She needs to know how I feel, and if others hear, maybe they'll be kind enough to remind her when she sees them.

"I can't do this here," she says.

She doesn't give me a chance to say anything else before she's walking away. My eyes follow her every move until she disappears behind a door. I turn back to the room and grin, although to others it probably looks like a grimace. It definitely feels like one. Pretending everything's okay is hard.

Ruby sees me and tries to smile, but her face is sad. Does she know I'm here to win her mother back? That I want to come home and be a family again?

The door Gwen disappeared behind mocks me. I finally decide I've had enough and go to it, knocking once before trying the handle. The knob turns easily, and I step inside to find my wife alone in the corner, dabbing her eyes. When she sees me, she turns to face the wall.

"Why are you here, Rory?"

"As in church or this room, Gwen? Both could be answers you may not want to hear."

Gwen doesn't turn to look at me, even as I step closer to her. "Both."

"Well, as far as church goes, I don't know. I had a nightmare ..."

"We all have nightmares, Rory. I've been living one."

"Gwen ..."

"And the other reason?"

I sigh and continue to move closer to her. "When I woke up, it took me a while to realize that what I experienced was only a dream. You and Ruby were there, but I wasn't your husband or her father. We were people living in the same town, not knowing each other, and I hated it. I felt empty and lost. Much like I feel now."

Gwen clears her throat and looks at me from over her shoulder. Makeup is smeared and running down her face, and her eyes are bloodshot. Everything in me says I need to reach for her, to pull her into my arms, to tell her I'm in love with her and will do what I can to make things right.

"I was hoping we could talk later," I say to her as my hand rests casually on her hip, but to me, there's nothing casual about touching the woman I love. I'm ready to spill my guts, to tell her how I feel.

She shakes her head.

Fine. I'll talk to her back if I have to. I have nothing to lose. "The other night, I don't know what happened, but it was like a veil was lifted and I could see clearly. Except I'm standing on the outside of this bubble, watching as my life goes by. When I see you and Ruby, you're there, but I can't touch either of you, and you can't hear me calling out your names. Then there's this moment when I think you can hear me, and you look in my direction, and you're nothing like the woman I love. Your spirit is dim, the natural glow you carry is gone, and the sparkle in your eyes doesn't exist. When I see you, I know I did that to you, that I ruined our family. I know this now, Gwen, and I hate that it's taken me years to figure this out. What I thought I was doing, working to provide the best life for you both, was nothing more than me alienating myself from the people I love."

She turns as I start to close the gap between us. Without hesitation, I pull her into my arms. She's rigid, which is understandable. With my arms wrapped around her, I breathe her in, trying to memorize the smell of her perfume because I'm going to need it to make it through the night.

"I don't know, Rory."

"I know. All I'm asking for is a chance, and if I can't prove to you that I'm worthy of your love, as your husband, we'll do things your way."

"It's not just about love. I want an equal partner. I want my husband, the father of my daughter, to make his family a priority."

"I will."

Gwen breaks eye contact and stares off. I wish I could see inside her mind to know what she's thinking. She turns back, and her eyes narrow. "You said you were here while we were decorating cookies."

I nod. "Outside, but yes."

"What about Jerry?"

Instead of loosening my grip on her, I tighten my arms and look deep into her eyes. "I didn't go to his party. The next morning, he called, and I told him that things have to change and that once five o'clock hits, I'm done for the day. I let him know that I can no longer take his calls in the middle of the night or on weekends, and from this point forward, I'll treat him like he's one of my normal clients."

"And?" She lifts her eyebrow.

"And . . . he wasn't happy." I shrug. "I don't know how things are going to be after the New Year, and frankly, I don't care. You were right, like always," I tease. "He takes up a lot of unnecessary time, which takes away from my duties at home as your husband and Ruby's father. Something had to give, and for me, it couldn't be you."

"Maybe you'd like to come with Ruby and me when we pick out our Christmas tree tomorrow?"

"I would love to." I think about kissing her on the nose but refrain. Right now, I'd really like a sprig of mistletoe to appear, because I could use all the help I could get. I look up, hoping, but nothing happens. Maybe next time.

Chapter Six

Gwen

I shoulder my bag and hold on to the strap tightly as I rush across the street toward the clothing store. The ground is slick with a combination of slush, freshly falling snow, and salt to try to melt the ice.

My first stop, though, is the coffee shop. I've had a craving for their peppermint mocha since I woke this morning, and thankfully there isn't a line. With the warm cup nestled between my hands, I bring it to my face and inhale the wintery scent, but before I can take a sip, my eyes land on the homeless man my daughter has befriended. Gabe's standing under the awning of a store a few doors down with a cup in his hand. I can't tell from here if he's asking anyone for change or if he's just holding it out, hoping someone will be kind enough to drop a few coins in there for him.

"I'd like another cup," I say to the barista. "And a small assortment of your pastries."

"Sure thing," the young girl says. Within minutes, I'm

juggling two cups and a bag of freshly made goodies, which are causing my stomach to growl.

"Hello." I stop in front of the man. He smiles and continues to shake his cup as people walk by, and much to my surprise, he's wishing them a Merry Christmas even though they're ignoring him. "How are you, Gabe?"

"I'm well, ma'am."

I smile at his politeness and hold out the extra coffee and bag of sweet treats. "These are for you." He looks at me and then to the bag. I can sense some hesitation, and it saddens me. Surely, he's hungry and would want the food. He wasn't like this the other night, and it makes me wonder if someone in town has said something to him.

"Thank you. You didn't have to do this." He opens the bag immediately and if I'm not mistaken, inhales deeply.

"I know, but my daughter thinks of you as her friend, and I'd like to ... Well I don't know what I'd like right now."

"Happiness," he says, but I'm not sure if he's talking about what I want or the fact that he's bitten into what I would call one of the best apple cider doughnuts in New England.

"I'm glad you like it." I point to the half-eaten pastry in his hand. Never mind the crumbs sticking to his face.

"You have hope," he says. "I can see it in your eyes."

My head cocks to the side as I study him. "For what?" I ask.

Gabe looks at a few passersby, making he wonder if he's ignoring me. Maybe he'd rather stand here and be by himself, or maybe he's not right in his mind or suffers from posttraumatic stress and I'm only hearing what I want, but that doesn't seem to be the case.

"Love has a funny way of making people unhappy. Yet you seem to have a spark. I can see it," he says calmly.

I want to call him crazy and tell him he has no idea what he's talking about, but he's right. This morning when I woke, I felt better, as if I had more pep in my step. Ruby noticed, too, and chatted happily with me about her last day of school before break and how she plans to sleep in on Christmas morning, which I knew was a total lie. She'll be up before the sun, jumping on my bed and begging me to get up because Santa has been to our house.

"You must follow the path laid out in front of you, not the one you think you must forge. Happiness is there, waiting for you, and as long as you have hope, you'll find it. Thank you for the coffee and doughnuts, Mrs. Sutton. It's much appreciated. I'm humbled by your kindness. It's easy to see where Ruby gets hers." He nods and bends to gather his things and walks away, leaving me speechless. On more than one occasion, this man has said exactly what I needed to hear.

I don't know how long I stand there. It's well after he's disappeared behind a building. I'm tempted to follow, to ask him again for more words of wisdom, but I'm frozen, still stunned by how eloquently he speaks. I want to know who he was before his demons took over and he ended up on the street, homeless and begging.

"What are you doing?" My sister's voice catches me off guard.

"Um ..." I look around, wondering exactly where I am. A window display catches my attention. It's a replica of *Miracle on 34th Street* with Kris Kringle holding hands with a Susan. I don't remember walking to the department store, yet here I am.

"Are you okay? Did you fall and hit your head?"

"I'm sorry, what?"

"You look confused."

"No, I'm fine, just ..."

"Just what, Gwen?"

I shake my head and smile. "Nothing. I'm good. Are we ready to shop?" I play off my confusion. I could've swore Gabe was standing near the other side of the street, closer to the park, not on the other side of town.

My sister sighs. "Yes. My list is a mile long. Do you know what you're getting Mom and Dad?"

I reach for the door. "Not a clue. They're impossible to buy for." Inside, Santa's sitting off to the side, bellowing out "ho ho ho" as we walk in. "Do you remember coming here as kids to see him?" I ask, pointing at the man dressed in red.

"I do, and I remember you pulling on the poor man's beard once because some kid told you it wasn't real."

I blanche at the memory. "Santa told me I was going to get coal in my stocking for that stunt. I was so scared on Christmas morning."

Eliza laughs hard at the memory. I was mortified. So were my parents. "Come on, let's shop," I say, dragging her down the aisle.

"Is Amber joining us?" she asks.

"No, she couldn't get the time off. Something about an end-of-the-year audit creeping up."

Eliza and I start out together but end up going our separate ways after a bit. I'm not having much luck finding anything, which is a bit bothersome. Christmas is a few days away, and I still have so much to buy.

I happen upon the men's section and hesitate before crossing the imaginary threshold. I don't need anything here since Rory's presents are tucked deeply in my closet. I haven't wrapped them, mostly because I don't know if they should come from me or Ruby. Yet I find myself thumbing through the flannel shirts that are on sale and adding a few to my pile.

"Who are these for?" Eliza picks one of the shirts up and rubs the fabric between her fingers.

"Gabe." His name pulls me up short.

"You met someone." It's not a question, but more of an accusation.

It takes me a minute to recover from my blunder. "No, I didn't, and I don't know why I said his name." I look down at the pile in my arm and realize that the last few items I've picked up are indeed for this man, who I barely know yet seem to want to help. I've volunteered before at the homeless shelter, but never have I gone out of my way to buy clothing for someone who's homeless.

"Who is he?"

"Do you remember the man Ruby was talking to at the ice rink?"

Eliza nods. "You're buying clothes for that bum?"

The word *bum* doesn't sit well with me. I grimace at her. "I see him differently. So does Ruby."

"Have you fallen and hit your head? Do I need to take you to the ER?"

"It's hard to explain, but I've spoken to him a few times and . . . I don't know, there's something about him." I pause and shake my head. "I don't expect you to understand, and maybe it's because I'm going through this thing with Rory and I'm utterly confused, but Gabe has a way of knowing what to say when I'm in doubt."

"Now I'm confused. Are you telling me that you've confided in this man?"

"No, I'm not saying that at all. Like I said, it's hard to explain."

"Well, you can explain it later over lunch."

I shouldn't be surprised when I spot Amber at the restaurant, sitting alone with two additional menus. As soon as my sister left me in the men's section, she was on her phone, and my best guess is that she called Amber and likely told her I'm having a mid-life crisis because I'm shopping for Gabe.

Eliza slides in next to Amber, leaving me no choice but to sit across from the both of them. I smile, place my stuff down next to me, pick up the menu and hide behind it, pretending everything's great. Okay, great might be stretching it, but I'm better since I last saw them at the ice rink.

The waitress stops, takes our orders and menus, leaving me vulnerable to Amber's penetrating gaze. "So, how are things at work?" I ask her.

"Oh, no you don't. We're here to talk about your mystery man."

After I roll my eyes, I stare sharply at my sister, who is conveniently looking out of the restaurant window. I'm tempted to look out as well, to see if I can spot Gabe so I can give him the things I've purchased. "First off, he's not a mystery. You saw him at the rink the other day. Second, he's not my man." I mimic her voice when I say "my man."

"Seriously, what's going on?" Amber asks as she reaches across the table to grab my hand. "You're starting to freak me out. Be straight with us, did you meet someone?"

"I think she got l-a-i—"

"Okay, now you're just being foolish, Eliza."

She shrugs.

"How else do you explain your giddiness?" Amber asks.

"What's wrong with being a little happy?" I ask them.

Amber and Eliza look at each other, and then both lean forward. "Look, I know you're technically married to my brother, but I would hope you'd still tell me ..." She looks from me to Eliza and back, "you know, if you found someone else."

"Oh my, just stop. Both of you ..." I shake my head. I imagine my happier-than-normal demeanor is likely throwing them off, but it's disheartening to think that neither of them expected or hoped that Rory and I would get back together. "Rory finally admitted that he put his job before our family and is promising to make a change."

"Do you believe him?" my sister asks. It was just days ago when I cried on their shoulders after I served divorce papers.

They both look at me, each with an eyebrow raised. Clearing my throat, I say, "I can sense that the wheels are turning in your thoughts. They're doing the same in mine. I keep questioning myself about what I should do."

"Which is?" Eliza asks.

"That's the thing, I don't know. This is unchartered territory for me."

Now it's my sister's turn to reach across the table and clasp my hand. "Why don't you start at the beginning so Amber and I can help you make the best decision?"

I nod and smile. "Rory showed up to church yesterday. He sat with Ruby and me, as if nothing had changed between us. But it's not just church. He also came to Ruby's winter concert. He was attentive to both of us, acting like a doting father and being a husband who affectionately touches his wife. I wanted to scream and dance for joy over the attention, because this is exactly what I've wanted for so long."

"And then what happened?" Eliza shifts her position.

"Did he spend the night?" Amber leans forward.

"No. He kept Ruby at his apartment and took her to school the next morning." I pause as the waitress stops by with our lunches. "Anyway, I'm sitting in church, and the next thing I know, Rory sits down next to me, and he held my hand through the service."

"How'd that feel?" My sister wants to know.

"Good. My palms sweated like they used to when we started dating. After the service, we spoke ... well, he did. I stood there, staring at the wall because I couldn't face him. He knows his job's an issue and says he's going to change, that it'll be family first."

Amber looks at me questioningly. "So what's the problem?"

I smile weakly. "I don't know if I believe him." I turn my attention toward my turkey club, taking a few bites before wiping my mouth and meeting their gazes again.

My sister speaks first. "Before I start babbling, know that I love you and support whatever you do. So playing devil's advocate, Rory moves home, things are good, like he's coming home by five and all that jazz," she says in between bites, "does that fix things between the two of you?"

"Maybe?" I shrug. "It's been awhile since we actually acted like husband and wife behind closed doors."

"Do you want that with him?" This time it's Amber asking.

I swallow the giant knot forming in my throat. "I miss him. He's all I've ever really known, and these past months have been torture. I don't sleep and hardly eat. Last night was the first night I went to sleep without crying. And I woke up happy. I'm ridiculously happy that he's joining Ruby and me tonight."

"What's tonight?" Amber wants to know.

"We're getting our Christmas tree."

"And you're going to reconnect in the bedroom." Eliza waggles her eyebrows only to have Amber elbow her in her side. Sometimes I think Eliza has a one-track mind when it comes to some things.

Thankfully, she decides her lunch is more important and focuses her attention there. We continue to talk, but mostly about the kids starting vacation soon and how it's never enough time and who is hosting what for the holidays. I'm off the hook for being a hostess this year, though, which I'm relieved about. If things were to work out for Rory and me, it'd probably be best if we're given some time away from family. The last thing either of us needs is our parents' meddling.

I'm trying not to get ahead of myself when it comes to Rory. I want to believe him and trust he's making the changes needed, but something deep inside gives me pause when it shouldn't. I don't like being alone, so it's not that I've enjoyed my so-called freedom, so what is it? It's Jerry and the hold he has on my husband. I fear our marriage won't be strong enough to resist that man and his financial needs.

Rory deserves a second chance. That's the conclusion I come to as I'm strolling through the park after lunch. Much to my surprise, I run into Gabe again, but this time he's sitting on the bench reading a book. "Hello."

"Oh, Mrs. Sutton. It's such a pleasure seeing you again." He folds the corner of the page down and sets his novel next to him before I can catch the title.

"I have something for you." I hand him the bag of clothes. "I don't know if they'll fit, so you'll have to let me know the next time I see you if I need to make any exchanges."

He rifles through the bag, pulls one of the shirts out, and rubs it against his cheek. "Soft."

"And hopefully warm."

"Thank you."

"Have a good night, Gabe."

"You too, Mrs. Sutton."

Chapter Seven

Rory

Like clockwork, I'm on time and standing at the entrance to the tree farm. Ruby screams my name, and I look over the heads of the other people until I spot Gwen weaving through the people. When I do, my heart beats a bit faster. I've missed her.

I hurry through the crowd until I'm face-to-face with her. I desperately want to kiss her, but the fear of rejection is too much to handle. Baby steps. That's what I have to take with Gwen.

I crouch down and pick Ruby up. With her in my arms, I pull Gwen to my side and kiss her stocking cap–covered forehead. While my lips may not touch her skin, the intent is there. She must know this. I'm surprised when she takes my hand in hers, but work hard to keep my emotions in check.

"Shall we go get our tree?" I ask the two of them. If Gwen's shocked that I said *our*, she doesn't show it. I have hope that I'll be there on Christmas morning, whether it means waking up in the house or just arriving before Ruby rolls out of bed. Either way, I'm going to do what I can in the next few days to show my wife how serious I am.

"I want the hugest tree there is."

"We don't have space for the hugest tree," Gwen tells Ruby.

"Well, can we get a really big tree? One that's taller than Daddy?"

"We'll see what we find," I tell her. It's been our tradition to pick up our tree about one week before Christmas. Both of us grew up having artificial trees in our homes, and when we had our first place, we said we wanted something real. Our first Christmas together, we got our tree the day after Thanksgiving, and it dried out two weeks after. You couldn't walk by it without needles falling off, leaving us no choice but to take it down. The next one faired a bit better, until we finally decided that a week before Christmas was the perfect time. Of course, that left us with fewer options, but we didn't mind the Charlie Brown versions at all.

As soon as we step onto the compacted snow, Ruby is squirming to get out of my arms. I set her down, and she's off running. I let my arm dangle at my side, waiting and hoping that Gwen will reach for my hand again, but she doesn't, so I do what any man who's trying to win his wife back would do and take hers.

We stroll through the aisles, kept dry by the overhead covering. Glass lightbulbs are wound around the posts, lighting the pathway, and Christmas music plays through the speakers hung in the corners. From the time Gwen and I bought our first tree, we've been coming to this place. I don't know if it's the ambience or the fact that the trees are cut locally that keeps us coming back.

"I found it," Ruby yells from a row or two away from us. Gwen and I make our way there, to find Ruby standing with one of the helpers, who is dressed like an elf. Shockingly, the tree they are standing by is not massively tall or round but seemingly perfect for our living room. The branches are full, and it stands a little above six feet, which means lifting Ruby to put the topper on will be easy.

"What do you think, Gwen?"

Ruby continues to stand next to the tree with one hand on her hip and a big ole smile on her face.

"I think it's—"

"The best tree ever," Ruby interrupts. She jumps up and down before she starts doing a little dance.

"We'll take it," I tell the elf.

"Santa will love this one. I'll get it bagged and loaded into your truck."

As much as I don't want to let go of Gwen's hand, I do so I can pick Ruby up. It's been hard being away from them.

The realization that I've let my duties slip has weighed heavily on me since the night I sat outside the church, waiting for the two loves of my life to come out. So leaving work today at five was like breathing for the first time. The tellers all stood there with their mouths open when I told them I wouldn't be back for the rest of the day. I'm serious about what I said to Gwen . . . no more late nights.

I don't know what else do to. Do I take her on a vacation? Give her jewelry? Get on my hands and knees and beg for forgiveness? The latter is easy. All she has to do is say the word.

"Are you coming?"

I look at the woman who makes my heart beat faster. Our arms reach toward each other. She's just one small step away from me. Gwen smiles and gives my hand a little tug, pulling me forward. I fall in step next to her, our arms brushing against each other's as we walk toward the counter to pay for the tree.

My wallet's out before she can dig into her purse. I hand the cashier a wad of twenties and tell her to keep the change. "Rory, you didn't have to pay for the tree."

"I'll let you pick up the treats for tonight." I say this as a way to compromise. She's been on her own for a few months, and I don't want her to think I'm trying to take away any of her freedom. I plan to be her equal partner moving forward.

"Does that mean you're staying to help decorate?"

My heart soars. This woman I love and have hurt so deeply has found a way to open her heart again and let me in. I don't care if it's an inch, I'm taking it for all it's worth and turning it into something great, something meaningful, and I'm never letting her go again. "Is that an invite?"

"Of course. Ruby wants you there."

Ruby, but not my wife. It seems like I have an uphill journey to win back the love of my life. "I'd love to be there." I always have and can't imagine spending this night away from my girls.

Once the tree is loaded into my truck, I follow Gwen back to our house, hoping she didn't forget about the treats. Knowing Gwen, she has the ingredients for her grandma's homemade hot cocoa out and ready to go, along with some fresh gingerbread and a tray of cookies. All things I didn't think I'd miss until this moment. Our house always smells like cinnamon during the holidays, and I honestly can't wait to step into our home once again.

As soon as Gwen parks, Ruby's out of the car and racing toward my truck. She's trying to climb into the back by the time I reach her. "Slow down, Ruby bean."

"I can't. Santa will be here soon, and we have to get this baby up," she says, clapping her hands.

"Santa comes with or without a tree."

Ruby stops and sets her hands on her hips. If it weren't so dark out, I'd be able to see her face. I bet her nose is scrunched up and her eyes are almost closed because she hasn't mastered the art of squinting yet. "Santa needs a tree to put all my presents under."

"Oh yeah, how many do you think you're getting?" I ask, as I open the lift gate of the truck. I grab hold of the netting on the tree and pull it forward.

"A hundred," Ruby says, excitedly.

"A hundred presents. Wow, that seems like a lot. What about the other children, are they getting a hundred too?"

"I dunno."

"Do you need that many gifts?"

"Sure."

Once I have the tree propped against my truck, I pick Ruby up and set her on the tailgate. I stay there, eye level with her. "I think you'll get one present from Santa, just like last year."

"Well, some kids in my class get hundreds from him."

"Well, I don't know what goes on in your friends' houses, but at the Suttons', we appreciate the one gift Santa brings us. Do you know why?"

She shakes her head.

"Because that means children who are less fortunate can receive presents too. If you and your classmates were to receive a hundred presents each, how many would that be?"

"A lot."

"Do you think you need a lot of presents or would it be nice to share with other kids who may not get as much from their mommy and daddy?"

Ruby thinks about this for a moment. "I think I'd like to share."

"That's my girl." I help her down from the truck, pick up the tree, and toss it over my shoulder, hoping that I'm not breaking any of the branches. Ruby leads the way, chatting about how she's going to tell Santa that she only needs one present.

As soon as I step into the entryway, I feel instantly at home. It seems silly to say, but being gone for the past month and a half has really made me forget how wonderful it is to be here. I inhale deeply, trying to burn the sweet scent of this place into my memory so, when I'm back at my apartment and staring at the ceiling tonight, I can remember this moment and the other happy ones that are sure to come this evening.

"Rory?"

"Huh, what?"

Gwen is standing in the archway that separates the living room from the rest of the house. "I asked if you planned to come in with the tree or if you were going to stand there all night holding it."

"Oh, sorry." I don't tell her I was caught up in the moment. I don't want to add any pressure or make her feel guilty. The last thing I want is for her to shut down and go back into her shell. I finally made a breakthrough with her the other day and want to keep the progress going.

Gwen already has the tree stand set up, making it easy for me to plop the tree into the stand. "Can you hold it steady for me?" She does as I ask, while I drop down and tighten the screws on the base. "Is it straight?"

"Yes, it's perfect."

"Not yet, Mommy. It needs decorations!" Ruby yells from somewhere behind me.

I stand and brush some pine needles off my pants before making my way toward Gwen. "Yeah, Mommy. No tree is complete without lights, bulbs, daycare and school ornaments, and the Santa topper."

I place my hands on her hips and her sharp intake of breath tells me that she likes what I'm doing. She steps closer, so close that I'd only have to lean forward slightly in order to kiss her, but I hold my ground. Part of me is scared. I'm not foolish enough to think, because I'm here, she's ready to forget just yet.

"Everything's in the totes. I brought them up from the basement already." Her voice is quiet, her tell when she's nervous. I'm going to tone down the affection and maybe wait for her to approach me.

"I'll string the lights and you . . . "

" . . . I'll get the treats," she says, finishing my sentence.

I watch her walk away before I turn back toward the living room and tree. Ruby is standing here with a wide grin on her face. I just shake my head, dig into the tote, and pull out the string of white lights that I wrapped up tightly last year.

Gwen returns with a tray of hot chocolate, cookies, and of course, the gingerbread that I've been craving. Once I have the lights strung, I stand back and watch the ladies get to work. They dance around each other, putting ornaments all over the tree. It doesn't matter if our daughter clusters everything in one spot. Once she's in bed, Gwen will make a few adjustments to even everything out.

"Ladies, this looks wonderful," I tell them in between bites.

"Don't eat all the cookies, Daddy."

"Sorry, I can't help it. I love Mommy's cooking."

Gwen tries to hide it, but I see her blushing. This is yet another mark against me in the husband department. I've forgotten how to compliment my wife. Telling her she's beautiful, that the meal she's cooked tastes good, or thanking her for ironing my clothes, should be automatic. I took her for granted, and that has to change, especially if I'm going to prove that I'm worthy of her love.

When the last ornament is placed on the tree, Ruby brings the Santa topper over to me. I lift her high into the air and get as close to the tree as I can. She slips him over the topmost branch with Gwen there to plug him in.

"We'll get the lights," I tell Gwen before carrying Ruby over to the wall. She presses the switch, shutting off the overhead light and the lamps that sit on the end tables. The room darkens, but there's a little glow from the outside where the moon hits the snow.

"Now, Mommy." On Ruby's command, Gwen flips on the tree lights, magically lighting up our living room. Ruby starts clapping and wiggles so I'll let her down. She dances around, singing about Santa coming to town. Gwen and I let her go on for a few minutes before we call for bedtime. The loud grumbles mix with the saddest face ever.

"Come on, Ruby. I'll take you to bed," I say.

"I'm not tired."

"Give Mommy a kiss good night," I tell her, not playing her game.

"Good night, Ruby. I love you."

"I love you too." Ruby pouts her way to her room, mumbling something about how life isn't fair. If she thinks this now, she's in for a rude awakening when she becomes an adult. After she's changed and has been to the bathroom, I'm tucking her in. She pulls a book off her bedside table and hands it to me. "Mommy's reading this to me."

I flip to where Gwen left off and start reading the Nativity story about baby Jesus. When I say the name *Gabriel*, it gives me pause, and makes me think about the transient man that I've run into a few times. I haven't seen him the last couple of days, and thinking about him now makes me wonder where he's been.

It's not long until Ruby's grown quiet. I close her book and place it back on her nightstand before slipping out of her room. I stand in the doorway, unable to move. If things don't work out with her mother, nights like these will be few. I suppose it's something I should be used to since I was hardly home in time to tuck her in. This is where I want to be every night.

Downstairs, Gwen is finishing up in the kitchen. She's wiping down the counter with her hair pulled into a bun, the sleeves of her shirt rolled to her elbows, and her feet bare. She hums along with the song on the radio while I stand there watching her.

She turns, jumps, and places her hand over her heart. "You scared me, Rory."

"Sorry." Pushing myself away from the doorjamb, I walk to the island and pull out one of the bar stools. "I didn't mean to startle you."

"It's fine. Did she go down okay?"

"Yeah, I read to her. When did you buy her that book?"

"I didn't. Her friend Gabe gave it to her."

"Gabe?"

Gwen nods. "He's a homeless man that she's befriended. At first, I was wary, but I've spoken to the school and there's always a teacher there when he goes in and reads to the kids. For some reason, she's taken to him."

"So have I," I tell her. "I can't explain it, but every time I see him, I want to help him, but he's the one helping me."

"Same here. He's helping me too."

I stand and go to Gwen. As much as I want to stay, I can't. She's not ready, and I'm not going to push her. "I had an amazing evening, Gwen. Thank you." I pull her into my arms and kiss the top of her head. I try to step away, but she won't let go.

"Not yet," she mumbles into my shirt. "I just need one more minute."

So do I, but I don't tell her. I give her what she asks for before leaving her in the kitchen. I'm determined to make her fall in love with me again.

Chapter Eight

Gwen

Since Rory showed up at Ruby's concert, we've seen him every night and sometimes during the day. Just yesterday, he surprised us during lunch. Ruby and I were watching a movie, snuggled on the couch, when the doorbell rang. Rory was standing there with carryout bags in his hand from our favorite burger place two towns over.

It didn't take a genius to do the math. He left work early to do this for us, unless, of course, he had someone go pick it up for him. Either way, it was the thought that counted, and Ruby was happy to spend a little bit of the afternoon with her father.

You can't pretend happiness. I was delighted he was there. The coy touches he used in church graduated to not so subtle when he pulled me into his arms and kissed my neck. His soft, gentle lips pressed against my skin reminded me of when we were younger and life was simpler. After he left, I cried for an hour, unsure of what I should do. The logical answer is to give him another chance, but there's something inside of me that fears he'll revert to his old self, and that's not something I can handle.

I stare at myself in my bedroom mirror. My hair is in a French twist, and a red pendant my grandmother gave me years ago accents my black dress. Tonight is the Christmas party for Rory's company. I hadn't planned to go, but I don't have a valid excuse why I shouldn't. He's trying to be a better husband and father, and if I hold him back, I have no one to blame but myself. Still, I'm nervous. I don't know what to say when people ask if we're back together. Mostly because I'm not sure. Yes, I love him and want to be his wife, but he's only reformed his workaholic tendencies a week ago. Does that make him a changed man?

"Mommy, you look beautiful." Ruby's voice startles me. I jump, and my hand swats my perfume bottle. Luckily, I'm able to catch it before it crashes to the ground. After setting it back on my dresser, I hold it tightly while taking a deep breath to calm down. I don't know why I'm so nervous. It's not like Rory and I haven't been on a date before.

"Because this one is different," I mutter to myself. Tonight is a turning point for us.

"Mommy, are you are okay?"

I nod and finally look at my little girl, who's dressed in elf pajamas, complete with a hat. She makes me laugh on a daily basis, even when she's frustrated with the situation Rory and I have put her in. I don't pretend to understand what she's going through, because my parents and grandparents are still married. "I'm fine, sweetie. You just caught me by surprise."

"You look pretty."

"Thank you. Are you ready for your fun night with your cousins?"

"Yes, but are you coming home?"

I go to her and crouch down, which isn't easy in a dress. "Of course I am. Why wouldn't I come home?"

She shrugs. "Because when Daddy tucks me in at night, he's not here for breakfast." Her voice cracks at the end. I hadn't thought about how she'd feel when he's here as opposed to when he's not. Rory's made it a point to tuck her in every night, but I hadn't thought about what she'd think or expect in the morning. I was just happy he was here for her. I need to make a decision and stick to it, because the back and forth isn't good on Ruby. It's not good on me, and I imagine Rory feels the same way.

I scoop her up, bring her over to my bed, and sit her on my lap. "Do you remember when we talked about Mommy and Daddy needing some time apart?" Ruby nods. "Well, what I didn't tell you is that Mommy and Daddy have been trying to spend some time together, to work on the things keeping us apart."

"Frankie says her mommy hates her daddy. Do you hate Daddy?"

Why would any parent say that about their spouse or ex? I shake my head and fight back a wave of tears. "I love your daddy very much, and he loves me."

"I think he loves me more," she says without missing a beat.

"You're probably right. You're his favorite."

"That's because I don't make him pick up his socks or wash his coffee cup and you do."

Oh, how I want to tell her that these little things go a long, long way in a relationship. That romance isn't just giving your wife a kiss good-bye in the morning or thanking her for keeping your house tidy and making your dinner; it's taking an extra step to help out, to be there unexpectedly. It's putting your wife and family first; it's pulling your wife into an embrace because she's standing there and you can't resist her. All things Rory was good at in the beginning. All things I was good at too. He's not the only one to blame for these problems we're going through.

"Well, have you smelled his socks?" I ask her. "P.U." I wave my hand back and forth in front of my nose, which makes her laugh. "No one should have to touch those stinky things."

"Daddy doesn't smell."

"How do you know? Have you been sniffing his toes?"

She laughs. "No, but when I hug him, he smells good." Yes, yes he does. Since the time we started dating, Rory has always worn some musky scent of cologne. It didn't matter what the scent was, I was putty in his hands.

"Why don't you—" My words are cut off by the sound of the doorbell ringing. Ruby is off my lap and running toward the stairs, yelling that she'll get it before I can even move a muscle. I follow her down the stairs as quickly as possible. She swings the door open, and Rory is standing there dressed in a black tuxedo with a bouquet of flowers in his hand.

"Daddy!" she squeals, and jumps into his arms. I stand there with my heart beating out of my chest, my mouth parched, and my palms sweating. He bends down to give her a kiss but keeps eye contact with me. Butterflies flutter in my tummy, and my knees go weak. There isn't a doubt in my mind that I'm in love with this man, but I have to be one hundred percent sure that he's in love with me.

Rory moves away from Ruby and stalks toward me. I hold on to the railing for support. Not because I'm going to fall, but out of fear I may throw myself at him.

"You look ..." He takes a step back, pulls his lower lip between his teeth, and shakes his head slightly. "I'm not sure you should be out in public like this."

It takes me a moment to find my voice. "What, why?" I ask,

feeling for a hair that might be out of place, automatically assuming something is wrong.

"Because every man at the party is going to be looking at you, and I'm not sure I have the energy to keep them away." He steps closer, cupping my cheek with his free hand. "I'm having a hard time here, Gwen."

"Me too," I whisper. Rory leans forward and brushes his lips against mine. Like the first time we kissed, my body explodes with its own personal set of sparklers, never dulling. He pulls away all too soon. It could be from the cheering our daughter is doing or the fact that someone is clearing their throat behind him.

I look over his shoulder to find my sister standing in our entryway. Her beaming smile says it all, and yet my thundering heart is screaming something else. Something I don't want to hear or even think. I don't want to think Rory's here because of the holidays. Deep in my heart, I know he's changing, and for the better. It's not some game or some ploy to get back into my good graces. I have to believe Rory and not the nagging, unhelpful voice that seems to linger.

"Oh good, you're here. Rory and I can go now," I say, using Rory's assistance to step down the last two stairs.

Rory picks up my shawl and drapes it over my shoulders. "It's good to see you, Eliza," he says before ushering me out the door. There's a strain between them. It's expected. My hope is that they can overcome this obstacle and be friends again, regardless of how Rory and I end up.

We reach the old McMullan mansion in only a few minutes. The drawback and bonus to living in a small town is that everything's close but never far enough away that your car can get warm in the middle of winter. Not that I need it, because

Rory's hand is on my leg, and that's enough to keep the fire simmering within me.

At the mansion, the valet is there to open our doors. When the valet reaches for my hand, Rory is there instead, pushing him out of the way. "I've got her," he tells the young kid who backs away quickly.

"Was that necessary?"

"Probably not, but the last thing I want is for someone else to touch you. It's a bit possessive, but I'm afraid I'd be rather jealous if another man held your hand tonight."

His words take me by surprise. This is a side of Rory that I haven't seen in well over a year. While I like it, it makes me question everything. I pull him over to the side, away from the entrance. I need answers. "Where is all of this coming from?"

"What do you mean?"

"The romantic gestures, the flowers, which I forgot to thank you for by the way, the sweet tender touches and compliments?"

Rory sighs and runs his hand through his hair, messing it up. He tries to smooth it down, but it's no use. "When you asked me to move out, I was so angry. I couldn't understand because I was giving you and Ruby everything. Night after night, I would lie in bed, wondering why. Then it hit me. Somewhere along the way, we lost us. I started working more, and you started needing less from me. It took you kicking me to the curb to realize that we can have the best life, together. That my job can end on time, and I can be the father and husband you need me to be.

"I tried to imagine my life without you. I tried to picture the future, you with another man. And ..." He pauses and shakes his head. "That's when I knew I *had* to change. I had to fix what I broke because when I look at us as a family, you've been there, guiding and encouraging me, and I'm the one who shut everyone out.

"Gwen, I love you more than I can put into words, and I will do anything to make our marriage work. All I'm asking for is one chance. I just need one because I promise I'll never mess up this badly again."

Before I can answer, before I can give him my heartfelt reply, someone yells our names. Friends of ours are standing on the steps, waving us down frantically. I don't know about Rory, but I haven't seen them since before Thanksgiving and am unaware whether or not they know about Rory and I separating.

"Do they know?" I ask. He shakes his head. "Well good." I link my arm with his and all but drag him toward the stairs. It's a coward move, but I need time to think and process his words. He's telling me everything I want to hear, and while this should make me happy, I'm skeptical, and I don't want to be. "Diane and Larry, it's so great to see you. How's Boston treating you?"

"It's beautiful, especially this time of the year," Diane says as we embrace each other. "When are you going to come visit?"

I look at Rory. He shrugs, leaving the answer up to me. "Probably once the snow has melted. Maybe for spring break, we'll drive over."

"That would be wonderful."

The four of us make our way into the mansion and into the grand ballroom. Rory and I have spent many evenings here, from proms to our wedding reception. When I was younger, I fell in love with the arched entryways, the marble columns, and domed rooms. This is where Cinderella comes to meet her Prince, even if it's only for one magical night.

After dinner, Rory takes me out onto the dance floor. The jazz band plays a light selection of music, making it easy for us to sway together. He holds me close, gazing into my eyes. I wonder what he's seeking. Is it a response to his statement earlier or something else?

"At Last" by Etta James starts, and he pulls me closer. This was our wedding song, and I can't help but get lost in the memory of the evening we became husband and wife. My hand moves to the back of his head, and my fingers tangle with his hair. I lean forward and kiss him, keeping it chaste. "Will you come home tonight?"

"Just for tonight?" His voice is a bit raspy.

"No, forever. Please come home, Rory."

Chapter Nine

Rory

I don't care how well my wife plans, she always forgets something on Christmas Eve. This year, it's the rolls, and finding rolls the night before a major holiday, in a small town grocery store, is nearly impossible, so I have no other options but to buy the ingredients to make them homemade. Is this what Gwen wants? Nope, but going home empty-handed is out of the question. I could drive out of town, going store to store, but I have a feeling the outcome is going to be the same. Besides, I plan to help her.

It's nice to see I'm not the only husband here. In fact, everyone in line in front of me is male, and most are grumbling to each other about being out right now. For me, this is happiness. When she asked me to come home, I could barely contain myself. We left the party instantly, forgetting to say good-bye to the people I work with, and went straight home, where I showed her how much I love her. The next morning, I packed up my tiny apartment and turned in my keys, hoping to never see the likes of that place again.

Now that I'm home and we're a family again, I feel like a new man. For a time, I thought I was going to lose everything, and I still may on the financial end of things, but I'll have my girls, and they're most important part of my life. They're all I need.

After wishing the cashier a Merry Christmas, I'm back in my truck to head home. According to the instructions I read on the web, the dough has to rise for about an hour and a half or so, which gives Gwen and I some time to work on other things. I spent most of yesterday occupying Ruby while Gwen wrapped presents, so I'm looking forward to some quality time with my wife.

Before returning home, I decide to drive through town one last time to look at the decorations and the town's Christmas tree. By the end of the week, everything will change as we celebrate the New Year and then Valentine's Day.

The years are starting to go by too fast. Just yesterday, it was April, and my clients were frantically filing their taxes before the deadline, and now it's the end of the year and I'm left wondering if I accomplished everything I needed.

I've never been a man who makes resolutions, but this year I am: to work on my marriage. It's taken a hard lesson to make me realize that marriage is a job. Both of us have to constantly work to make it the best it can be. We're both to blame for what happened earlier. However, I shoulder most of it. We've both vowed to never put ourselves in that situation again. Communication is key.

On my drive through town, I spot Gabe, sitting on the park bench. He's alone, of course, and from my car, it looks like he's asleep. I pull up along the curb and get out, pulling my coat closer to fight the chill in the air.

"Hello, Gabe?"

He startles. "Mr. Sutton, it's far too cold for you to be out. You should head home to your family."

"I was just on my way, but I saw you sitting here so I thought I'd join you for a few minutes." I sit down next to him and shiver. I don't want to say he was instrumental in my reconciliation with Gwen, but he definitely guided me with his words of wisdom. "I haven't seen you the past couple of days."

"No, I guess my time here is almost done."

"What do you mean?"

Gabe chuckles but doesn't say anything. I don't know whether I should press him for more or just let it go. "How's Ruby?" he asks.

"She's doing well."

He nods. "A sweet little girl who loves her mommy and daddy. She also likes to read, ice-skate, and play tag."

"Yes, she gives us a run for our money. How would you like to see her tonight?"

Gabe looks at me with surprise in his eyes. "It's Christmas Eve. You should be with your family, Mr. Sutton."

He's right. I stand and extend my hand to him. "Something tells me my family would be delighted if you joined us for dinner tonight."

He looks from me to my hand and back again. When he starts to shake his head, I put my hand up. "If it weren't for you, I don't know if I'd be able to spend Christmas with my family. You helped me see the error of my ways." Gabe smiles. "Spend the evening with my family, let us properly thank you."

"If you insist."

"It'd be our pleasure to have you sit at our table, Gabe." He follows me to my truck and gets in without any assistance. I don't bother to text Gwen to tell her I'm bringing him home. Something tells me she's going to be okay with this.

"Your home is beautiful," he says as soon as pull into the driveway.

"Thank you," I reply, staring at the front of the house. I wish I could take credit for the outside, but I can't. Gwen did this. She made sure our home still felt like Christmas even though I wasn't around. The garland with its white lights is a welcoming feature as we climb the steps onto the porch, and the wreath that hangs on our door is decorated with red and white ribbons, but it's the angel that dangles in the middle that catches me off guard. I've never seen it before.

"Haven't you ever seen an angel before?" Gabe asks, clearly recognizing my hesitation at the door.

"It's not that. We've always used a snowman or Santa. The angel is new." I look back at Gabe and have to do a double take. It seems as if he's cleaned himself up, even though it's impossible. Without taking my eyes off him, I open the door and announce that I'm home.

"Gabe!" Ruby screams as soon as we step in. "Daddy, this is my friend Gabe. He's the one who gave me the book you've been reading to me at night."

In this moment, everything becomes clear to me. This man is more than who he says, but that's his secret to tell. To me, he's the man who gave me the words I needed to figure out my life.

"Gabe, what a surprise." As soon as I see Gwen, I go to her, giving her a kiss.

"This is okay, right?" I whisper into her ear.

"Of course it is." She kisses me on the cheek and sidesteps me. "Gabe, would you like me to take your jacket?"

"No, I'm afraid I should leave it on. But a washroom would be splendid."

"I'll show him," Ruby says. She grabs his hand and pulls the old man down the hallway.

Gwen and I head into the kitchen, where I have to break the news about dinner rolls. Looking at the clock and the timer on the oven, it dawns on me that we don't have enough time to make our own.

"I'm sorry I took so long. Gabe was sitting on the bench, so I stopped to talk to him. And also the store was out of rolls, and I thought we could make them homemade." I shrug and point to the clock.

"It's fine, Rory. We can make do without rolls tonight."

"Hey, babe. Do you believe in angels?"

My question gives her pause. She turns to face me. "This year, I believe in miracles, and if an angel is the one making those happen for us, then yes, I do."

"Smells delicious," Gabe interrupts us as he and Ruby enter the kitchen. Much to my surprise, he's taken off his coat and seems to have on a nice new flannel.

"Oh, Gabe, that shirt looks wonderful on you," Gwen says happily. "It fits well, I see."

"Yes, Mrs. Sutton. I can't thank you enough."

"Call me Gwen. We're happy to help. Ruby, why don't you take our guest into the dining room? Your father and I will bring dinner out."

As soon as Ruby and Gabe are in the other room, I ask Gwen, "Did you buy him clothes?"

"I did. I don't know why. I was shopping for you, and the next thing I knew I had a pile for him."

I pull her into my arms. "You're the best, Gwen Sutton. I love you, and I'm sorry for letting work cloud my priorities."

Gwen presses her lips to mine. "I love you, Rory."

Together we carry our Christmas Eve meal into the dining room, each taking turns dishing up plates for everyone. After I sit down, I reach for Gwen's and Ruby's hands.

"Ruby, would like to lead us in giving thanks this evening?" I ask her.

She nods and grabs Gabe's hand, holding it proudly. "I give thanks for my family and my new best friend Gabe, and thank him for bringing my mommy and daddy back together."

Just as Ruby finishes, a bell from atop the Christmas tree rings. Gwen and I both look up. Ruby is smiling, almost giddy.

"You know, I've heard that every time a bell rings, an angel gets his wings," I say.

And Gabe . . . well, he just tilts his head toward us and winks.